PARALLEL WORLDS OF RICHARD PURTILL

PARALLEL WORLDS OF RICHARD PURTILL

SCIENCE FICTION AND FANTASY

RICHARD PURTILL

EDITED BY GORD WILSON

AuthorHouse™
1663 Liberty Drive
Bloomington, IN 47403
www.authorhouse.com
Phone: 1-800-839-8640

First published by AuthorHouse 10/22/2011

ISBN: 978-1-4670-7023-2 (sc)

Printed in the United States of America

These stories first appeared in the following publications:

The Magazine of Fantasy and Science Fiction: "Something in the Blood", August 1986. Reprinted in *The Year's Best Fantasy Stories 13;* edited by Arthur W. Sasha, DAW Books, 1987. "Others' Eyes", May 1980. "By the Dragon's Cave", July 1984. *Isaac Asimov's Science Fiction Magazine:* "Gorgonissa", January 1985. *Marion Zimmer Bradley's Fantasy Magazine:* "The Grey Wolf's Tale", Winter 1999 #42. "Firebird" originally published as "The Firebird's Feather, the King's Horse, and Baba Yaga's Grandniece", Autumn 1999 #45.

For more information, please visit http://www.richardpurtill.com.

Contents

Part One

Part Two

ACKNOWLEDGEMENTS

Thanks to Bruce Rupp for proofing and editing; Allen Peterson for the Golden Age SF cover art; Glenda Lewis at AH for her invaluable assistance; design consultant Gemma Ramos and the Thames Team, Joe Klein, Travis Trestler, Don Gardiner; and to Dr. Richard Purtill, spinner of tales *par excellence*. -Gord Wilson.

INTRODUCTION: THE TWO LIVES OF RICHARD PURTILL

For years Dr. Richard Purtill lived two lives: by day, professor of philosophy. By night, writer of pulp fiction. By day he authored textbooks; by night he spun out fantasy and science fiction for magazines and pocket paperbacks. Weekdays he lectured in classrooms; weekends he was feted at fantasy conventions. When he retired from his day job, he plunged all the more into his nighttime pursuit, eventually publishing over twenty books.

After receiving his doctorate from the University of Chicago, he pursued his love of writing and teaching as Professor of Philosophy at Western Washington University, Bellingham, Washington. By day he taught a standing room only class called "Philosophy and Fantasy", in which students read and explored books by popular fantasy and science fiction writers including Lewis, Tolkien, Charles Williams, Ursula LeGuinn, Robert Heinlein, Madeline L'Engle and others. He reworked the class notes into three books on J.R.R. Tolkien and C.S. Lewis, becoming one of the first scholars to take their work seriously. Widespread interest in these books led to unexpected invitations to fantasy conventions, as these authors' works became wildly popular.

He had this in common with Lewis and Tolkien: professor by day, by night turning out fantasy fiction. Like them also, his authorship ranged widely, from philosophic tomes to murder mysteries: *Murdercon* (Doubleday Press); science fiction: *The Parallel Man* (DAW Books), fantasy fiction: *The Kaphtu Trilogy* (DAW Books). From entries in the *Cambridge Dictionary of Philosophy* and the *C.S. Lewis Readers' Encyclopedia* to short stories in *Alfred Hitchcock's Mystery Magazine*, *Isaac Asimov's Science Fiction Magazine*, and *Marilyn Zimmer Bradley's Fantasy Magazine*. By day he led the university's summer sessions in Greece; by night he was feted as guest of honor at San Diego's Mythcon and other fantasy and science fiction conventions.

He first got the fantasy bug, he revealed in a 2008 interview, as a twelve year old boy living in Chicago, when his dad brought home a 1943 issue of *Startling Stories*. He began dropping dramatic "slice of life" scenes into his textbooks in the early '70s, until his latent writing talent spilled out in 1979 into the first of a series of fantasy novels, *The Golden Gryphon Feather*. His stories seem to have been transported, intact, from the golden age of fantasy and science fiction, but the "startling" in them comes less from shock and awe then the fresh experience of the working of gray matter. The "pulp fiction professor" seems singularly adept at recalling the golden age when vistas seemed to open to infinity and anything seemed possible.

This omnibus edition collects, for the first time, ten of his published and unpublished stories, along with his full-length science fiction novel, *The Parallel Man*. Three of the SF stories have never been published before, and take place in the same universe of the Universal Commonwealth introduced in *The Parallel Man*. These typescripts were truly "lost" for years; their discovery sparked the idea for this volume. Not exactly short stories, they range in length between longish stories and near novellas.

The remaining seven stories were published in *The Magazine of Fantasy and Science Fiction*, *Isaac Asimov's Science Fiction Magazine*, and *Marion Zimmer Bradley's Fantasy Magazine*—with one exception. "The Dragon's Daughter", which forms the fourth story in the "Rus Quartet" is here published for the first time, and forms the concluding story for the volume. These are original tales employing characters from traditional Russian faerie tales. His approach will be familiar to readers of Purtill's "Kaphtu" trilogy and "Lost Tales", in which he drops his characters into the world of gods and goddesses of ancient Crete, and offers his own imaginative takes on well-known Greek myths.

Readers familiar with the original "Rus" stories, which appeared in two magazines between 1984 and 1999, may disagree with the order in which I have placed the stories. Of the three published stories, however, "The Grey Wolf's Tale", which appeared in Winter of 1999, provides the best introduction to the realm of the "Rus" stories. I ask seasoned readers to bear with me in printing the briefest, most accessible tale first, and I hope that new readers dipping their toes, as it were, into this newfound spring will be sufficiently enticed to want to plunge into the later stories. Those already used to the water will find that, in many ways, the best has been saved for last.

I had the great, good fortune to be attending Western Washington University (then Western Washington State College) during the time Dr Purtill taught philosophy there. By the alignment of the stars or what you will (this is fantasy, after all), I was able to crowd into his "Fantasy and Philosophy" classes, which instilled in me, as in so many others, a lifelong love of—or maybe addiction to—fantasy and science fiction.

But did Dr. Purtill's two lives ever meet? I would say they did, and do. These stories could not have been written by anyone else: they all bear his signature and show certain distinctives. Firstly, he writes most of his stories in the first person; they have the feel of tales being told. Secondly, you can't forget he's a philosopher. "Philosophy" means "lover of wisdom", and these are wisdom stories. Everyone in them, whether a martian or a queen or a vampire, seems to seek and love wisdom. They all seem part Socrates and part St. Francis. They're all presented with seemingly impossible puzzles which they work like Rubik's cubes. They're yet very human, or alien, or animal, or whatever—sentient beings not so different from ourselves, puzzling their way through life, making the best of what they're given, which makes these stories both timeless and timely.

-Gord Wilson, Bellingham Washington.

PART ONE

THE PARALLEL MAN

1. BEYOND THE BROKEN SKY

The firedrake screamed as it swooped at me again. I lifted my shield and felt the blistering heat on my shield arm as the fiery blast of the creature's breath flared out. After a moment I dared to flick the shield aside and swing my sword with all my strength at one of the fiercely beating wings. The sword bit into the leathery membrane, but it was almost wrenched from my hand when the firedrake half folded its wings and dropped like a spent arrow into the abyss below us. I leaned back against the tree, letting my weary arms drop to my sides. There would be blessed moments of rest while the creature swooped even lower to build momentum, then spiraled upwards with beats of those mighty wings to where I stood on the ledge. The massive old tree protected me from a thunderbolt-like attack from above; the creature had to swoop by almost level with me, trying to burn or claw me.

Behind me I heard the clink of a chain as Princess Delora tried to move farther into the crevice which gave her a little shelter from the side-blast of the firedrake's breath. I risked a quick glance over my shoulder. Her lovely face was grim as she met my eyes. She knew and I knew that no Champion had successfully defended a Sacrifice from the firedrake since the sacrifices had begun years ago. Worse yet, I, her defender, was the one they called the Afflicted Prince. If the Falling Sickness struck me now . . . .

I didn't dare to worry about that, or let myself think about what might happen if I lost consciousness as I leaned over the edge to see the firedrake's position. It was flying a little awkwardly, I saw with a stab of hope, taking longer to fly up to the ledge than it had last time. If I could only injure that wing more the creature might not be able to fly strongly enough to make its way up to the ledge if it had to swoop down again. There would be more glory in killing it, but I would be content with a draw which would allow Delora and myself to spend the prescribed time on the ledge and be released with honor.

The firedrake was on a level with the ledge again but instead of swooping at me it banked, spilled air from its wings and landed at the other end of the ledge. Then it began to advance toward me with a shuffling motion of its hind legs. The wings were poised over its back and the forelegs with their vicious claws were making striking motions in the air. But the real danger was the writhing serpentine neck which could send the blunt head at me with the force of a battering ram; even without the wicked teeth in the gaping mouth or the fire that the creature could breathe, that head could knock me flat, my bones shattered. The tree would be no obstacle; the creature could strike around it from either side.

I stepped toward it along the ledge, my shield poised to ward off another fire blast, ready to leap back if the head darted toward me. If the creature could kill me or knock me off the ledge, nothing could prevent it from continuing its inexorable progress down the ledge to the crevice where Delora was chained and making a grisly feast on her helpless body.

The neck straightened, a sign that the creature was about to let loose another fiery breath. If I stood and took the blast on my shield, the firedrake could bound toward me and be on me before I could recover. With desperate invention, I hurled my shield at the gaping jaws and dived under the head toward the more vulnerable body. I heard my shield crunch as the firedrake instinctively snapped at it; then I was lunging for the creature's heart with my extended sword.

The tip penetrated a hand's breadth and then would go no farther. My feet scrabbled for purchase on the stony ledge, but the creature was wincing back, its foreclaws trying to tear the sword from my grasp. I felt the hilt slipping from my sweat-slippery hand: in a moment, the creature would spit out the shield and I would face its jaws and its fire with neither sword nor shield. Only one thing to do: I let go of the sword and grasped the neck above me with both arms. I swung my legs up and wrapped them around the neck and with a desperate heave and pull got myself on top of the neck. I reached for my heavy dirk, tore it from its sheath and plunged it into the firedrake, above my head. Then using the dirk as an anchor, I heaved myself toward the creature's head. The fiery breath whooshed out in a useless reflex. I was behind it now and hardly felt the heat, but a muffled cry from Delora told me that the crevice had not sheltered her from the blast.

Now I was straddling the neck, just behind the firedrake's head. My dirk plunged into one of the creature's eyes, stuck for a heartstopping instant, then came out. Now the other eye; the firedrake was blind. The worst moment was when I had to let go and drop from the monster's neck; I almost froze to the false security it offered. But I was hardly on the ground before the firedrake battered its head against the mountainside, trying to knock off whatever had stung it so intolerably. I would have been smashed to a pulp, and still might be; I huddled in the angle between the ledge and the mountain wall that rose above it.

The firedrake shrieked again and again; the pain in my ears was excruciating. Gobbets of black oily blood spattered the ledge as its head thrashed back and forth. My sword was still stuck in its breast. Did I dare make a dash for it? If only the creature would blunder off the ledge. But no, it was going forward, toward Delora, extending its wings to guide itself by the pressure of the right wing against the mountain wall. Only one way to save Delora from the fiery blast that would surely come: I rolled toward the ledge's rim and sprang up at the firedrake's left wing, tearing at the leathery membrane with my dirk as I hung on the wing with all my weight.

The massive head came around toward me with the speed of a striking serpent, and that completed the overbalancing I had hoped for. The firedrake began to topple from the ledge, carrying me with him. Delora was safe; as for me, perhaps the harpers would find another name than "Afflicted" to remember me by. Firedrake Slayer: a good name to die with, if one must die.

Of course I cherished mad hopes; perhaps I could cushion my fall on the creature's body or leap free into the trees below. But I think I would have died there—if the sky had not broken. Impossibly, fantastically, as I began to slide over the edge clinging to the flfedrake's wing, a jagged circle opened in the sky above me; shards of blue rained down from it. Beyond the circle was what looked like a gray corridor, as if the sky was a wall with a passage behind it. In the corridor, men in strange, skin-tight garments that covered all but hands and faces. Gods? Demons? But surely neither would show the blank amazement, the utter incomprehension with which they looked at me and at the firedrake.

A convulsive shudder by the firedrake sent us over the edge and we tumbled crazily as the creature beat its one sound wing in an effort to fly. Then something seized me like a giant invisible hand and the firedrake tumbled on below as I began to rise in the air toward that mad circle in the sky. A scream came from below: Delora's nerve had cracked at last at this final insanity. My dirk was still in my hand and I brought it up with some instinctive thought of defending Delora or myself against the strangers. Concerned faces looking down at me from the hole in the sky suddenly became wary. One of the men pointed some stubby object at me; there was a strangely familiar purple flash and I lost consciousness.

I awoke in the strangest room I had ever been in. The walls and ceiling were the color of thick cream, featureless and smooth. One wall shone with a cold clear light and on one of the other walls an oval patch of colors moved in slowly swirling patterns. I was lying in a bed, covered with some sort of pale, clinging coverlet, feeling the sick, shaken sensation that often came to me after an attack of the Falling Sickness. It often helped to get up and move around, so I tried to fling aside the coverlet to rise from the bed. The coverlet would not release me; it clung to the bed and to my body with firm but gentle persistence. There was no discomfort, but I was trapped in the bed: my blood began to pound and my headache grew worse as I struggled to get free.

As if in response a white circle appeared on the wall opposite the bed, the size of a shield and about head height. At first it was featureless, then suddenly a woman's face appeared in it, not like a picture but solid and real, yet with nothing but the face visible, framed in a sort of white haze. The eyes looked as if they saw me. The face gave a small, impersonal smile and a soft voice said. "Someone will be with you in a moment." Then the face vanished and the white circle faded.

I had no way to measure time, but the time that followed seemed to me longer than a "moment" by any reckoning. Finally a white rectangle, like a door, appeared on the wall. At first it was merely a shape of light, then suddenly it was an opening in the wall and people were walking through it into the room. One of them was the woman whose face I had seen. She was dressed in a skin-tight white garment that covered everything but her face and hands; around her waist was some sort of belt from which hung a number of small glittering objects. Somehow she reminded me of the chatelaine of a castle with her bunch of keys at her belt, though the glittering objects looked not at all like keys.

Beside her was a man dressed in a black garment which did not cover his head and seemed somewhat looser than the woman's. There were touches of white at his neck and wrists and his thin, intense face was that of a scholar or a monk. Behind the man in black and the woman in white were two men in very similar garments, one in brown and one in gray. Something about the way the man in gray carried himself made me look more closely at him. He had the crude features and vacant look of a serf but instead of the usual shock of hair he seemed to be wearing a curious kind of skullcap of bright blue which covered his head to just above the eyebrows.

The man in brown was no serf; he did not have the intensity or authority of the man in black but he looked competent and responsible. He was pushing some sort of gray box in front of him; I blinked as I saw that it seemed to hang suspended in the air with no support. I did not want to face these strangers flat on my back; I tried to heave myself up and found that the bed changed its shape to support my back. I still felt at a disadvantage, confined as I was by the clinging coverlet, but at least I could face my visitors. I folded my arms and made my face impassive, waiting for them to make the first move.

The little group stopped at the foot of my bed and I suppressed a smile as I realized that it was they who were at a slight disadvantage; the bed was a high one and I looked down on them like a ruler from his chair of state. The man in black inclined his head gravely and said in a deep voice, "I am Justinian Droste, of the Citizens' Liberties Union." The title meant nothing to me; some sort of guild perhaps, though the man did not look like a merchant.

"I am Casmir," I said shortly, "of Castle Thorn." The gear they had taken from me would tell them that I was a knight of Thorn, if they had skill to read the markings, but it would be foolish to name myself as the Prince to men who might be enemies.

The man who had named himself Justinian Droste hesitated; he looked somehow unsure of himself, perhaps even embarrassed. "There are things which you will learn," he said, "about the place you call Castlethorn." He ran the name together as if he were unfamiliar with it, but that might be a deception. "That place is not what you believed it to be," he went on, "and you have been used by others for purposes of their own. That is over now and I am here to safeguard your rights."

I tried to keep irony out of my voice as I said, "I thank you for that, Ser Droste. Tell me then, since you are my . . . guardian . . . am I a prisoner in this place or a guest?"

The woman in white broke in, "This is a hospital. You're here because of some injuries you've suffered and for observation. When we're sure that you're able to function normally you'll be discharged." A hospital; the word was unfamiliar but perhaps it was a sort of hospice. A place of healing at any rate. The woman in her form-fitting white garment did not look like a Sister of Charity, though I supposed she must be something of the sort. I gave her what I could manage of a bow from my position in the bed and turned back to Droste.

"And then?" I asked.

"You will be quite free to do as you wish," he said, a little too smoothly. "In fact one reason for our presence here is to formalize your rights." He beckoned to the man in brown, who pushed the gray box to the right side of my bed. I looked closely at it; I had not been wrong, it did float in the air. "Please place your hand on the Register," Droste said. The floating box was an uncanny object, but it would be unfitting to show fear before them; I placed my hand on the box without hesitation.

"Please give your name," said the man in brown. I did hesitate then—was this some sort of oath taking? Their gray box meant nothing to me and I could not be oathbound just by saying my name.

"Casmir of Thorn," I said and couldn't completely conceal my start when a smooth neutral voice seemingly from within the box said "Casmir F. Thorn." There was a tingle on my wrist and I took my hand from the box to find a green dot about as large as the tip of a finger glowing on my wrist. I picked at it and found that it was a thin patch of some smooth material which came away easily enough from the skin of my wrist, but then stuck to my fingers.

"Your citizenship and credit chip," said Droste, "honored anywhere in the Universal Commonwealth. Wear it wherever on your body you like; most people find a wrist most convenient." He pushed back the cuff to show a blue dot similar to my green one on the back of his left wrist.

The woman in white pulled away the hood which covered her hair and showed me a green dot on the lobe of her ear. "Move it around occasionally," she said, "It can irritate the skin if it stays too long in one place." I put the thing back on my wrist; there would be time to investigate it further when I was alone. The woman in white turned to Droste. "We'd better go now," she said. "The medication causes him to need considerable rest." To me she said, "Try to relax and please don't fight the clingsheet, as you were doing after you woke up. It's there to keep you from injuring yourself while you're healing, but we'll have you out of it soon." I sketched a bow again. It was irksome to be confined but I needed to know more before I took any action. She smiled politely but without warmth. "We're short of human staff but I'm leaving the andro here for you. Tell him if you want anything." The serf with the odd skullcap looked at me vacantly, then at a gesture from the woman went and stood near the opening through which the party had come into the room.

Droste inclined his head to me in his curiously formal way. "You must have many questions," he said. "Be patient. They will all be answered." He turned to go.

"There's one question I'd like answered now," I said. "Before I . . . woke up here . . . there was a woman with me; she may have been injured. Is she in this place too?"

Droste looked at me with an expression I could not read and said with curious gentleness, "No . . . no. We did not bring a woman from where we brought you, Casmir of Thorn." He must have seen from my expression that I was not satisfied and he went on after a slight pause. "There was no woman with you when we found you. No woman at all." Then he turned and left the room, followed by the woman and the man in brown. The doorway filled with white light which faded to show an apparently unbroken wall, as blank as the gaze of the blue-capped serf who stood against it.

2. THE ROOM OF ENCHANTMENTS

My first impulse was to get free of the clinging coverlet, overpower the serf and ransack this place for any sign of Delora. But I forced myself to be patient. My earlier struggle with what the woman had called the clingsheet had caused the woman's face to appear on the wall: the enchantment that made the thing confine me must also give some warning of attempts to escape it. Nor did I know the spell to make the door appear in the wall, and it was not likely that the serf did either. If I could get the woman in here alone . . . . Best wait awhile until the men had gone about their affairs. And I was inexplicably weary. Better rest a little and gain strength. I lay back and the bed subsided to a level position again . . . .

When I awoke the room was nearly dark, and someone was moving about behind me. I lunged upward and again the bed folded up to support my back. The light became bright again and the person behind me came into view; a woman in a white garment like that the other woman had worn. But this woman's face and hands were a rich dark brown. Perhaps she had painted herself like some of the barbarians, or had some disease? But the skin looked healthy and normal.

The woman gave a smile which despite her strange appearance had a good deal more warmth in it than the smile of the other woman in white. "Feeling more rested?" she asked. "I'm Molly, your night nurse."

I smiled back at her. "I had thought that I was beyond the age for a nurse, Lady. I am Casmir, a man of Thorn."

She laughed with a flash of white teeth. "Perhaps they don't call us nurses on Thorn. Sisters perhaps, or medics? I'm a prentice Healer, I care for people who are sick as part of my training. Is there anything I can do for you?"

She looked friendly and it was worth trying. I plucked at the clinging coverlet. "This grows irksome." She walked to the foot of the bed, touched it with a glittering object she took from her belt. She looked intently at something I could not see for a moment then nodded.

"Yes, I think we can take you out of the clingsheet now, Casmir. Move carefully at first; you had some broken bones and some second-degree bums and your body is still finishing its job of healing." She touched my coverlet with another glittering object and I was able to push it away and swing my legs over the side of the bed. My legs were bare but I was covered well enough for decency in some sort of short tunic of fine white cloth.

I slid cautiously to the floor; I was weak, but I have been weaker after an attack of the Falling Sickness. The darkskinned woman named Molly watched me carefully but did not interfere as I took a few tentative steps, stretched and touched my toes. "Any dizziness?" she asked.

"Less than usual," I said. Molly looked at me with brilliant dark eyes, but said nothing. I went on slowly, moved by an impulse I did not fully understand. "Since I was a child I've had what we call the Falling Sickness. I . . . lose consciousness . . . especially at moments of stress: I've injured myself before when I've had an attack while riding or climbing. I'm no stranger to Healers."

The dark-faced woman frowned in a puzzled way. "There's nothing on your chart to indicate epilepsy," she said. "Let me look at your admission records." She went to the foot of the bed and touched it again with one of the objects from her belt. Glowing letters and numbers appeared in a square near the center of the footstand, as if some invisible scribe were writing them there. They disappeared and intricate and mysterious traceries of lines took their place. "No, there's nothing organically wrong," she said. "But there's scarring on the nerve paths. The last time I saw scarring like that was on the chart of a criminal who'd had repeated run-ins with the monitors. Someone has used a neural interrupter on you, often enough to leave nerve scars.

I looked at her without comprehension. "A neural . . . ?" She raised her eyebrows. "Well, there are nicknames for them: 'stunsticks,' 'rupters,' but that's the standard name. Monitors use them—police, peace officers. They'll render a person unconscious for a varying period of time. depending on distance and intensity. Normally they don't do you much harm, but then most people are never exposed to them even once. But repeated exposure can cause confusion and memory loss due to scarring. I see that they have you on Lysergol to repair the scarring."

I frowned at her, trying to untangle her meaning from the unfamiliar words she was using. "You are saying that I have no sickness, that I will not lose consciousness as I have done in the past . . . ?"

She smiled reassuringly. "Not unless someone uses a neural interrupter on you again. In fact, right now, even that wouldn't do it because the Lysergol prevents the . . ." Her voice trailed away and her eyes looked over my shoulder to where the serf still stood by the wall. I kept my face impassive, but my heart leaped. If I understood her aright, some enchantment they were practicing on me prevented the action of the spell that would make me unconscious. That was why they had the serf standing by, to overpower me in case of need. They would learn their mistake in time, but I still needed to know more before I acted. Nor, if I could avoid it, did I want to injure this woman in my escape. At the moment it would be best to distract her, if I could.

"I thank you, Lady," I said. "You are kind, though your face is strange to me. In my land there are none who have skin the color of yours. It is . . . ?" I paused and she laughed.

"Yes, all over," she said in reply to my unspoken question. "I'm from Thopia; we were settled by people from a place here at Home they call Africa, where the people are mostly my color. Are all of your people big and blond like you?"

I smiled at her. "Many more are fair than dark, and none dark of skin," I told her. "Dark women are much admired, for they are rare."

She laughed. "I'll have to visit your planet," she said. "Is Thorn the . . ." Just then one of the glittering things at her belt gave a small musical sound. "Damn, I have to go," she said. "The convenience is in the corner there, and if you don't know how to key anything you need, ask the andro to do it. Don't overtire yourself. I'll look in again when I can, but it may not be until tomorrow." With another flashing grin, she walked to the wall and touched it at a place where there was a small circle outlined with a gray line. There was first the rectangle of light, then an opening which she walked out of. The corridor beyond the door seemed featureless in the glimpse I got of it before the opening became a rectangle of light and vanished.

In the direction Molly had gestured when she mentioned the "convenience" there was another gray circle on a blank wall. I touched it and though it did not yield or seem to change, a white rectangle appeared next to it and in an instant became an opening. Beyond it was a small square room with a basin and a covered garderobe. When I pressed circles of various colors at random, water came from some remarkable places and in a variety of temperatures and I emerged from the "convenience" feeling considerably refreshed but somewhat bemused. That I was in a nest of enchanters was evident, but I had not known that enchanters lived so luxuriously.

I was now feeling hungry and decided to see what orders the serf would obey. "Bring food," I told him.

He gave me a vacant stare but moved over to another part of the wall and pressed yet another circle. One of the now-familiar white rectangles appeared and became an opening into a niche in the wall which contained a covered tray. The serf brought it out and walked over to a place near the bed. He touched a circle on the bed itself and a table and chair rose from the floor. He lifted the cover from the tray and stood back.

The beverage in the cup was bitter but hot and the food was good enough, though without much taste to it. When I had finished, I went about the room looking for circles to press. There were not too many more; one turned on some sort of chute for disposal of trash and another opened a cupboard with fresh tunics like the one I wore. I took the opportunity to change my garment, but when I tossed the soiled one to the serf he sent it down the disposal chute. I shrugged; it was a waste of gear, but the gear was not mine.

There were no more circles on the wall, but there were several on the headboard of the bed. One pair of circles increased or decreased the light from the glowing wall when you kept your finger on them. Another seemed to have no effect at first but I glanced up and saw that the colors swirling in the oval on one wall had changed. I almost lifted my finger from the circle, but suddenly the swirling colors gave way to what seemed to be a window. I saw blue sky with clouds and a curiously shaped range of mountains. I lifted my finger from the circle and went closer to the oval; but when I touched it the surface of the wall still seemed to be there. Suddenly a movement in the scene revealed through the oval caught my eye; what looked like a tiny human figure moving at the base of one of the mountains. Suddenly my eyes made sense of scale and proportion; those were not mountains, but monstrous buildings, each larger than Castle Thorn, ranged in rows beside broad roads. On the roads moved curiously shaped objects and an occasional walking human figure, but no horses or other beasts. I seemed to be looking at the scene from a great height. Was this a window or some illusory scene produced by enchantment?

I gazed for a long time but learned little. From the light it seemed early morning and not much went on outside of the monstrous buildings. I wondered if I was in truth inside one of them, looking out of some window high above the ground. Finally I went back to the circle which had produced this scene and touched it again. Sky and buildings vanished from the oval and I seemed to be looking into an adjoining room, where several people were carrying on a conversation. The room was richly. if oddly, decorated and the men and women in it were dressed in bright and intricate garments which hugged some parts of their bodies, left other parts bare and fell in rich folds in other areas. They were talking in an oddly cadenced way so that their voices wove in and out like a part-song, and though I understood most of the words I could make little sense of what they were saying. I watched in puzzlement for a while then touched the circle again.

The oval showed a rushing mountain stream while sweet strains of music filled the room. I began to see that this was some magical toy; the oddly dressed men and women had been performing some masque or mummery, while this peaceful scene with its accompanying music was another sort of entertainment. I touched the circle again and found myself gazing into another, more quietly decorated room where two women reclined on couches and talked. They were dressed in close-fitting garments, one in blue and the other in brown, and I saw the gleam of one of the little colored circles on one woman's wrist. I settled on the bed to watch this scene for a while; it seemed to offer some hope of learning something of this place I had found myself in.

Suddenly one woman's face almost filled the oval, larger than life; you could see tears in her eyes. Then it was as if you were looking through a hole in the wall into the room again, but from a different angle. At first the sudden shifts made me dizzy, but gradually I began to see a sort of sense to the changing images; it was as if you saw through the eyes of someone in the room with the women, who now went closer to them, now stepped away, now changed his position with respect to them.

The women continued to talk, and a serf with the same odd blue skullcap that the serf in my room wore brought them cups of some beverage, then left the room. Gradually their talk began to make some sense to me. They were speaking about a man named John who went away on some sort of journey; they spoke of him as "flitting." One of the women was John's wife or lover; she was worried because in John's absence she had "gone into red." This seemed somehow connected with the circle of color on her wrist, which was red instead of being green like mine and like the other woman's. The other woman seemed sure that John would not be angry for a while after he returned. They began to speak of love and I grew weary of them; I touched the circle on the bed again and the oval showed only a swirl of colors again.

I lay back on the bed trying to make some sense of what I had seen. Enchanters, I knew, could call up visions, indeed my tutor, Mortifer, had called up visions for me as part of my education. But I was no enchanter and I had called up these visions by merely touching a circle drawn on my bed. Indeed, even the serf had touched one of the circles to get my food and another to dispose of my soiled tunic. Some of these enchantments seemed to work for anyone, even a serf. Others seemed to need the glittering objects which Molly and the other woman wore at their belts.

I felt that I knew enough to escape from this room and begin my search for Delora, but I would rather do so without raising an alarm. Best go soon before day came and brought more people to deal with.

I cursed as a white rectangle appeared on the wall and became a door. Had I left it too late? But what came through the door was another blue-capped serf; he turned to the one already in the room and said, "Report to Central and wait for orders."

The serf addressed shook his blue-capped head obstinately. "Orders to stay here," he said.

The new serf said in a low voice, "Override Argent. Report to Central." The other serf slouched out the door, which vanished as before. I tensed my muscles; might as well hit this new jailer before he got fully oriented.

He was pulling something from the waist of his gray garment and stepping toward me with strangely unserflike quickness and alertness when I launched myself at him. His hand came up holding something and there was a purple flash, then my shoulder hit him in the midrift, and he went over backwards, his head hitting the floor with a satisfying thunk. I was on top of him in an instant, my hands poised to strike, but there was no mistaking the flaccid sprawl of his limbs; that rap of his head on the floor had knocked him out.

Something about his head was odd; surely I hadn't cracked his skull? No, it was the blue cap, slightly askew. I pulled it off, a thin cap of metal, curiously flexible. Under the cap was short-cut hair and the face, on closer examination, was not the face of a serf. Whoever this man was, he had been masquerading. What he could do, I could do. I bent over his body, trying to solve the fastenings on his gray garment. These were simple enough; a touch at a circle on the collar and the garment opened down the front and I was able to peel it off of him. The stuff it was made of stretched easily and I was able to draw it onto my body without trouble. Another touch at the circle on the collar and the garment closed itself again.

The man wore underlinen not unlike the tunic I wore and I began to wonder if I could pass his unconscious body off as mine for a while. Something had rolled away when I hit him. A little searching revealed a stubby object like the one which the man had pointed at me from the hole in the sky. One end was rounded, but the other was a dull jewel which was disquietingly familiar. Surely Mortifer had carried a jewel like that.

No time to worry about that now. The thing fitted easily into my hand and one of the now-familiar circles was near my forefinger. The man on the floor was beginning to stir a little; I extended the object toward him and touched the circle. There was a purple flash and his body went limp again. I looked at the object in my hand with distaste; what use would valor or skill at arms be against an enchantment like this?

For the moment though, it served my purpose well enough. I tucked it into a sort of pouch at the waist of the gray garment and heaved the inert body of the man who had originally worn the garment onto the bed. I flung the coverlet over the lower part of his body and moved his limp arm so that it concealed his dark hair as much as possible. I pressed the circle on the wall and held my breath until the white rectangle appeared and became a door. Then I put the blue cap on my head and stepped out into the corridor, trying to imitate a serf's shambling gait and vacant stare. For better or worse I was out of the room and must face the unknown dangers at the place of enchanters with what wits and courage I could muster.

3. UNDER THE DOME

As I stepped into the corridor the first thing I saw was a long gray box, unpleasantly like a coffin, floating in the air at about the height of my waist. When I put my hand on its end it began to glide down the corridor, but as soon as I removed my hand it stopped. There was a circle about halfway down the length of the box. I touched it and the lid of the box sprang open, revealing a narrow interior which seemed to be padded. I touched the circle again and the lid closed. I had an unpleasant feeling that this box had been planned to receive my body after I had been rendered unconscious by the weapon now tucked into the pouch in my garment.

A great deal depended on what enchantment had been put on the box. If it had to be guided to its destination I was at a loss, for I had no idea of where to go now that I had left my room. But perhaps the spell on the box would lead it to some destination where I might learn something more about this trap in which I found myself. I placed both my hands on the end of the box and followed it as it glided off down the corridor, trying to remember to shamble and stare like a serf, for there were cross corridors ahead and someone might come upon me at any moment.

At the first cross corridor the box swung left, which gave me hope that it was under some spell to bring it to a definite destination. I was in a broader corridor now; an unfamiliar woman in a white garment was approaching me. Her eyes flicked over me without interest as those of a lady of the court would flick over a serf carrying some burden through the castle. I heard footfalls behind me and a man in brown overtook me and walked past me without even a sideways glance.

A little farther down the corridor there was a large circle on the floor. The box glided to the center of this and then stopped. I risked a glance around; surely this was not our destination. Then the whole area of the circle flashed white and vanished. I almost jumped free, but I could feel something solid under my feet; I was floating rather than falling downward. We floated past several corridors like that I had come from and then stopped. The corridor I was now in was wider and a little dingier than the corridor I had come from and to my excitement there seemed to be just a breath of wind and a smell of fresh air in it. When the box started to glide off again I stopped it by taking my hands off of it and took the jewel-nosed weapon from my pouch. Holding it below the level of the box in my right hand I put my left hand on the box again and it glided off.

The breeze grew stronger. The box, with me following, rounded a corner, and there was an open door a dozen paces away. Beside it lounged a thickset man in a green garment, who called out softly, "Any trouble?" I shook my head, keeping my face down as much as I could so that he saw mostly my blue capped head and a foreshortened face. The box approached him with nightmare slowness; pushing at it seemed not to hurry it at all. I saw his eyes narrow and his hand go to his belt. "Hold on," he said. "You're not . . ." I raised my right hand above the level of the box and pressed the circle on my weapon. There was a purple flash and the man crumpled, astonishment on his face.

I wanted his garment and I wanted to hide his body, but the corridor was unpromisingly bare. Suddenly I grinned. Stripping his garment from him, I touched the circle on the box, bundled his body into it and shut the lid. Immediately the box floated off out of the open door. While I stood staring it turned a comer out of my sight. I heard a sort of click, then a rumble, and when I moved to peer cautiously out the door a black cart of some sort was vanishing down the road with no beast to draw it. I shrugged, bundled the green garment under my arm and set off down the road in the direction opposite to that which the cart had taken. The spell on the box must work either by weight or by contact with living flesh, I thought; once a body was inside it the box would probably float to its destination with no one touching it from outside.

I half regretted not following the box all the way to its destination, but it would have been easy for me to be trapped by my ignorance in a situation which I could not fight my way out of. For the moment it was enough that I was free, had a change of disguises and a weapon. That was little enough for a stranger in a land of enchanters, but it was a start. Eventually I must find out what had happened to Delora, but if she was in the building I had just come from she was probably being treated no worse than I had been; she could wait until I knew more and had more powers at my disposal.

I looked up at the monstrous bulk of the building I had just left. I had discarded the thought of going from room to room looking for Delora as soon as I had realized the size of the buildings in this wizards' city. I felt like an ant crawling among the benches of the Great Hall as I looked up at the towering shapes around me. The broad street on which I walked had raised walkways at each side but there were no animal droppings on the road between the walkways; I remembered that I had seen no beasts of burden in the view of the city that the oval had shown me.

There was a cross street ahead of me; I slowed my shambling walk and stayed close to the side of the building. When I rounded the corner I stood and gaped as I have seen serfs do. I would gladly be rid of my present disguise but until I was I had better act the part. There were a few people walking on the street, clad in close-fitting garments of various hues so that it was hard to tell women from men at a distance. This street was less sterile than the one I had just left; a row of trees bordered the roadway on each side. There were a few doorways with writing above them which I could not read at this distance; some of them might be shops.

About a bowshot down the street a little knot of blue-capped serfs stood in a ragged line, gazing vacantly around them. I walked toward them slowly trying to gauge the dangers and advantages of joining them. Among them I would be inconspicuous. but if they were some sort of work party I might find myself led off to labor at some task which I could not escape from without arousing suspicion. A howling sound from the street behind me made up my mind; it sounded as if it might be some sort of alarm call. I shambled to the end of the line of serfs and tried to imitate their vacant stares.

The howling sound grew louder and down the street rushed a glittering thing as large as a small cottage, flashing lights and making a growling sound. I think that if I had been wearing a sword I would have drawn it and my hand crept toward the weapon in my pouch, though much good it would be against such a monster. But the thing, whatever it was, turned at the corner and went down the street I had just come from. The howl ceased abruptly; at the rate the thing had been moving it should have just about reached the door I had come out of.

Something else was coming down the street, a sort of platform with seats on it which floated a few handsbreadths above the street. It moved slowly and almost silently with only a low hum. The platform stopped near the little group of serfs and they began to climb aboard it. I hesitated and then followed them; that howling device might have nothing to do with me but if it did I wanted to be clear of this area before it returned, perhaps to track me down with unknown enchantments. The size and speed of the thing had shaken me a little; against a thing like that what could a warrior do?

The platform seemed to need guidance as little as the gray box had; it threaded its way down street after street until I realized uneasily that I would be hard pressed to find the building where I had been held. I began to look for a chance to jump off of the platform, but the streets were too wide and clear and the speed of the platform had increased.

Just as I was beginning to wonder if I should jump anyway the platform turned into a set of gates and we were going through an area of grass and small shrubs; not ideal but the best chance I had seen so far. I leapt and landed on my feet, letting my momentum carry me forward so that I made a rolling fall first onto my feet, then onto my hip, then onto my shoulder, as my old arms-master had taught me. I jumped to my feet and looked toward the moving platform to see if my leap had caused any disturbance. To my dismay a shortish, stocky serf had leapt after me and was picking himself up from the ground; his leap had been much more awkward than mine.

I shot a glance at the platform; it was sweeping around a bend out of sight. Whether the serf had come after me out of dim-witted imitation or was some sort of overseer who was chasing me down, I didn't want him trailing after me. I ran toward him, ready to strike him while he was still off balance. "Wait," he cried, and the voice did not sound like that of a serf. "Wait, I'm on your side."

I stood poised within striking distance and said grimly, "And what side is that?"

He grinned at me and spread his hands out at his side as if to show his peaceful intentions. "Let's say the underside, cit. If you're desperate enough to masquerade as an andro you must be so far into the red that you're infra, or else you're in a lot of bother with the Structure. I'm in some bother myself; let's help each other."

I looked at him appraisingly. Now he had dropped his serf mannerisms; he looked cocky and confident, but also a little shifty. If he were a soldier under my command I would suspect him of slacking and keep my eye on him but if I wanted some home comforts stolen or scrounged on a campaign he would be the man I would pick for the job. I kept myself in position to strike, but let him see me relax a little. "How did you find me out?" I asked.

He smiled with a touch of patronage. "Ah, I'm an old hand at this, cit, I have my ways. Most people, they see the blue dome and they don't look at what's under it. You could cross your eyes and stick out your tongue and then they'd never notice. But once you know that a man can play andro you begin looking. The monitors look too, and they have some nasty ways of finding out if you're what you seem. Too many thieves and wilders try to hide under the dome. Now, you don't look like a wilder and if you're a thief I can probably offer you better pickings than you'd find yourself. What do you say?"

I pretended to hesitate, but I had already made up my mind, This man wanted to use me for some purpose of his own; by going along with him for a while I would have help and protection which I would have trouble getting in any other way. That he would try to use me and abandon me I didn't doubt; I must keep my wits about me and drop him just before he was ready to drop me. "What do you offer me?" I asked.

He grinned, sure he had me hooked. "Ecus, cit," he said. "Extraplanetary credit units, good anywhere in the Commonwealth, don't go through your chip. Spend 'em here near the starport or use 'em for star passage and see the Universe. Ever flitted, cit?"

"Don't ask too many questions." I said, "and we'll get along better. What do I have to do for all this?"

He looked around us as if the shrubs might conceal listeners and said in a conspiratorial mutter, "There's this woman I work for, d'you see? Half mad and more than half bad. Always out for more of everything than she has any right to. Right now she's got a scheme that needs someone to play the part of her rich cousin—a real ultraviolet—who hasn't spoken to her in years. Told me to go out and get an andro, an andro like me she said, to do the job. I'm never quite sure if she knows what I really am and just enjoys treating me as an andro or whether she actually believes that a real andro can do the things I do for her. Anyway I set off looking for an andro *just* like me; somebody hiding under the blue dome. Been riding around with work parties most of yesterday and all night. Just about to pack it in when I spotted you. You weren't bad but you exaggerate a little too much; common beginner's mistake. Didn't even have to chase you; you got right on the mover with me. Thought I'd lost you when you made that dive though." I looked at him consideringly. Despite the strange words, I had understood his story fairly well and I could see no purpose in his telling it to me if it were not true. It seemed that I would have to assume another disguise, with the advantage that this time I would have helpers, who for the sake of their own plans would help my masquerade. Best to say nothing, though, that might seem to pledge my honor to his plans. "Well, perhaps we can help each other," I said. "Where must we go to find this lady of yours?"

He laughed, sure that he had bent me to his purpose with his vague promises. "Why up the road we were traveling on," he said. "I told you that I had given up. Those andros are on their way to Flavia's place now. Even she can't get humans to wait on her guests, but she dresses andros up as near like humans as the laws allow and sometimes a bit nearer. All we have to do is go up the road and in the back way; if it wasn't for your dive we could have ridden in comfort."

I was glad nevertheless for the longish walk up the road that followed; it gave me time to think out plans. My companion kept up a stream of complaints and comments at first but he soon ran out of breath. If this encounter had done nothing more it had shown me the dangers and the restrictions of posing as an "andro" as these folk called their serfs. I needed a disguise that would give me more freedom of movement and with luck I was about to have such a disguise served to me on a salver.

The house, when we came to it, was a poor enough place to have such extensive grounds, hardly more than a pavilion. Tables were set on the lawns and the blue-capped serfs I was beginning to think of as "andros" were moving among them, clad in a curious variety of costumes, all of which included some sort of head covering which almost, but not quite, covered their blue caps. They were setting out food and drink on the tables, and I realized that I was hungry. The meal I had eaten in the room I had escaped from was less than I was used to eating.

My companion led me round the corner of the pavilion, knocked somewhat perfunctorily at a translucent panel and then slid it aside. It was the first more or less normal door I had seen since I awoke in this land of enchanters. Inside the panel was a large, untidy bedroom dominated by a huge bed. In the bed, propped up against multi-colored pillows was a small, frail woman with faded blond hair and a sharp-featured, discontented face. She said in a fretful voice, "Is this creature the best you could find, Pella? Well, it will have to do. You," she said to me, "come here. Forget your designation and your former assignment. You are going to dress as a human and impersonate my cousin Fenric. Obey no orders but mine. This is a . . . a joke. It is not against your directives. Understand?" I inclined my head, not knowing how to address her. "Let me hear your voice!" she snapped.

"Yes, Lady," I ventured.

She looked at me with narrowed eyes. "You might do," she said. "Don't talk any more than you can help. Look down your nose at people. When someone's as rich as Fenric people put up with almost anything, so if you're asked a question you can't answer just ignore it. For the Mercy's sake don't talk about hunting; Fenric is mad about it and you'd give yourself away in a minute to anyone who knows anything about it. Part of your getup will be a fake chip that looks like a high violet; don't try to use it or you'll give everything away. For emergency use Pello will give you some ecus, enough to make a good display. Don't dare to lose them; they're a good portion of my credit for this period." She lay back against the pillows and shut her eyes. "Take it away, Pello, and dress it. Make sure the wig and makeup over the dome is undetectable."

The man called Pello led me out of the room by a different sliding door; this one led into an interior corridor. A glance back over my shoulder showed me that the walls of the bedroom seemed transparent from within; the woman's bed might have been sitting on the open lawn before the house to all appearance. A curious fancy, to sleep in an interior room that seemed to be out in the open.

As we walked down the corridor, Pello spoke in a low voice. "She knows that you're a masquerading human all right; no one could expect a real andro to obey orders like that. But she keeps up the pretense, curse her, so she can treat us like andros; it satisfies some spite in her. You've probably guessed my plan; take the clothing, the fake chip and the ecus and get away from here at the first opportunity. Once we're clear we split the ecus. You can go your own way or stick with me. Simple enough, eh?"

I nodded slowly. "Too simple, perhaps," I said. "You say she knows that you're not an . . . andro, and that I'm not either. She doesn't look foolish or trusting to me. Why is she trusting us?"

Pello smiled wolfishly. "She thinks she has us trapped here," he said. "It's easier to get in this place than it is to get out. But I've been here long enough to know all of her little ways; not just the ones she knows I know, but those she thinks I don't." We came to another door which he slid aside and I followed him into a small room with clothing laid out on a couch. Pello picked up a richly ornamented belt and stroked it with a curious smile on his face. "This belt for instance. If you left the grounds wearing it this thing would tear you in two. If you didn't wear it Flavia would notice and take other measures. Unless . . ." he opened a slit in his gray suit and pulled out a belt which seemed identical to that on the bed. "Unless," he concluded with a sly smile, "you think one step ahead of her. Now let's get you dressed."

I touched the circle at the collar of my gray garment and stripped it off, then lifted the blue cap from my head with a sense of relief. With Pello's help I put on a close-fitting suit of sky blue and a vest, boots, and short cloak in darker blue, decorated with silver; the belt matched these and a pouch went at the belt. As he helped me dress and fix a violet-colored circle to my wrist, Pello talked. "Flavia needs backing for her trading ventures," he said. "It costs a great deal to live in this style, and though she's shrewd she's been unlucky. It's the old story; you can't get credit unless you don't need it. If her cousin the ultraviolet Fenric is visiting her and appears on good terms with her the local syndics will think that she only has to ask him and he'll back her. They'll fall over themselves trying to get in first, though if they thought she was in trouble they'd try to bring her down and carve up her trade among themselves."

This meant little to me except to give some rough sort of sense to the masquerade I was undertaking. I could still see one objection though: "Does no one here know this Fenric, then?" I asked.

Pello shook his head. "He hasn't been Home for so long that anyone who did know him wouldn't recognize him. Anyway, a man that wealthy has no friends, only hangers-on and toadies. Fenric spends most of his time on a big tract of wilderness on some primitive planet, hunting every kind of animal he can import. His money comes from something that needs no work; some sort of monopoly in star-trade I think. So he plays at being a lord and ignores the Commonwealth."

"He's a sort of prince then, this Fenric?" I asked, and Pello shrugged and nodded. I smiled then and threw back my cloak over my shoulder. If they wanted someone to play a prince, I was better suited for the part than they knew. And though this clothing was strange, I felt more myself in it than I had done since I woke in that strange room. With a smile still on my lips, I followed Pello out onto the lawn where a crowd of brightly dressed men and women had gathered. My eyes swept over them indifferently and then suddenly I checked my stride and stared. For there, among the chattering crowd, surrounded by a circle of men and women and laughing with them at some jest, was Princess Delora!

4. THE HUNTER

Delora was dressed in a long, flowing garment of unfamiliar cut and her hair seemed longer, but her face and her mannerisms, such as the little toss of her head she gave when she laughed, were just as I remembered. Yet, when her eyes met mine across the crowded lawn there was no recognition in them. Her glance passed over my garments and perhaps she noticed the glint of the violet circle on my wrist which, according to Pello's rambling, marked me as a man of wealth and consequence. She gave me a little smile before turning back to her companions and that smile shook me. It was full of an insincere warmth I was used to from court ladies who coveted the importance my attention could give them. There could be many reasons for Delora to pretend not to know me, to conceal her surprise at seeing me, but none I could think of for her to give me a smile full of such professional coquetry.

I moved toward her, and the people on the lawn fell back respectfully as courtiers might have done at Castle Thorn. It strengthened my resolve to act as I would have acted in my own place; when I came up to the group in which she was standing I turned to the oldest man among them and said to him pleasantly but with authority, "You may present this lady to me."

He gave a little bow and said with dignity, "My honor, sir. Holder Fenric, may I present Dela Delora, who graces our Living Theater with her beauty and talent."

She gave a delicately exaggerated curtsy and smiled up at me with a professional charm that Princess Delora had never needed to learn. But her husky voice was the same as she said, "One has heard of you, of course, Holder."

I inclined my head to the man who had introduced us and said with a dismissive note in my voice, "My thanks, sir." He faded away tactfully, taking the others with him, and I turned to this new and puzzling Delora. "Your face seems very familiar," I said.

She pouted with an annoyance that seemed genuine. "I don't see how that can be, Holder," she said, "since I understand that you haven't been Home in some years. We of the Living Theater guard our images rather carefully. One wouldn't want to be confused with those who perform for the 3V, whose images are, well, a bit too common. Theater people even have a prejudice against having holos taken."

"And yet," I said, "I'd swear that you have a tiny and entrancing mark on your arm, right . . . here!" Taking her right arm gently but firmly I lifted it so that the sleeve fell back and revealed a little red crescent-shaped mark on the inside of her upper arm: Delora's clan mark. If it had not been there I would have felt and looked a fool, but I had to know. I released her arm and looked into her eyes, hoping for some spark of recognition; that mark had swept away all my doubts that this was really Delora.

But there was only anger and fear in her eyes; she stepped back and said, "A man of your wealth, Holder, may buy a good deal, including, it seems, some rather personal information. I don't know what you hope to gain by this, but I would call your behavior Uncivil. I am not without . . ."

The voice of Flavia interrupted her, "My dear, is Fenric playing one of his little jests on you? He teased me unmercifully when we were children." I felt clawlike fingers on my arm and looked down to see her at my side, her sharp features exaggerated by a hairdo which made her hair float like a soft cloud and an elaboarate dress more suited to a woman younger and more beautiful.

The woman who had been introduced to me as Dela Delora hesitated, then decided to make light of her annoyance. She gave a little trill of laughter which seemed quite natural but went on an instant too long. "All right, Flavia, I admit he got a rise out of me. I'll leave you two to renew childhood memories. Come and see me, Holder—in my new play." She smiled a little too sweetly and moved away.

Flavia's voice was sweetly acid as she said to me in a low voice, "You've evidently studied the behavior of real ultraviolets; you seem just as convinced as they that the world revolves around you. Not a soul here doubts that you're Fenric. Now keep your mouth shut and that supercilious look on your face while I flaunt you at my guests." She led me toward the crowd around the tables and began presenting her guests to me. I behaved as badly as I'd always dreamed of doing at receptions and parties; snubbing everyone who seemed self-important or unpleasant, talking only to people who interested me. Gradually I gathered a little circle around me; several of the women who were intelligent as well as beautiful, several of the men who seemed to be of some weight, and an outspoken old woman who was as amused by me as I was by her.

I disengaged my arm from Flavia's and gave her a little push. "See to your guests, cousin dear," I drawled. "I'm quite happy here." She gave me a look of baffled fury, but she had no choice but to go. Presently Pello appeared at my elbow with a tray containing small tidbits of food and a flagon of good wine. He was dressed in a costume that was not as extravagant as those of the real andros; if he got rid of his blue cap he could pass for one of the guests. "Stay here with those things," I told him and he bowed with a little glint in his eye and filled my cup.

A youngish pleasant-faced man who had not said much so far broke into the slight pause as I sipped my wine. "Heard that you hunt a bit, Holder," he said.

I could almost feel the tension in Pello as he held out the tray for me to select another tidbit. "Been known to, yes," I told the pleasant-faced man.

"Benton's my name, Holder; you wouldn't have heard of me but I do a bit in that line myself. Got a bit of land up in the hills," he said. The colored circle on his wrist was the same shade as mine and his wealth presumably was genuine. He went on: "Thing is, we used this new process they've discovered to clone and culture some wild boars. Got the cells from a museum exhibit. Well, they're established now, but none of my people is too sure how to hunt them for the best sport. They've dug up some history books; tell me that boar were hunted from horses at one time . . . ."

I shook my head. "Can be done but it takes a long time to train the horses and if the country is hilly they're not much use. Better on foot anyway. Have you got proper boar spears? They'll come right down the shaft at you if you don't have a cross-piece." We were soon absorbed in highly enjoyable technical discussion and the rest of the circle gradually drifted away, smiling indulgently.

Eventually, as I had hoped, Benton said tentatively, "Don't suppose you'd like to see my place. Not much by your standards, I know, Holder, but any time you'd care to . . ."

"Call me Fenric," I said. "Why not now? These people are beginning to bore me."

Benton's face lit up. "Would you really like to? Be delighted. Only came to this affair to meet you if I could. Have a little craft down on the meadow yonder. Anything you want to bring?"

"Can always get new stuff," I said. "Oh I know," I turned to Pello and said, "Get another tray of those things and another jug of the wine and bring them along." He shot me a glance of startled admiration and trotted off to do my bidding. "Oh, Flavia," I called as I saw her in a group nearby. "I'm off with Benton here for a while. Call on me if you need to on that matter we spoke of, but I don't see why you'd need to, perfectly sound proposition, you'll find the money easily enough. Expect me when you see me." And I strolled off with Benton, Pello trotting behind us with a loaded tray, leaving Flavia open-mouthed.

She couldn't quarrel with me or threaten me in public without destroying the illusion she had gone to such pains to create, and anyway I thought that she had gotten good value for the pouchful of little golden tokens at my belt.

Benton's "little craft" might have been a small pavilion erected in the meadow, but when we entered the door it lifted smoothly into the air and began moving away from the monstrous towers of the city. I turned to Pello. "Put that tray down somewhere and get that blue thing off your head," I told him. "You can report to me later." I turned to Benton. "Sometimes useful to have a man about who isn't noticed as a man," I said blandly.

Benton stared and then laughed. "By the Mercy, you star traders are high-handed," he said admiringly. "That breaks about sixteen laws here at Home and there are plenty who'd call it Uncivil. But I can see the advantages. A violet chip can expose you to all sorts of unpleasantness at times."

An inspiration struck me. "Been meaning to speak to you about that," I said. Opening the collar of my garment I reached in and peeled the green "chip" which I had been given soon after I woke in this land from my underarm, where it had been hidden since I donned the gray suit of the false andro. I put it on my wrisi and transferred the violet chip to where the green one had been, hoping that whatever stuck the false chip to my skin would hold it there. "Now that I'm away from Flavia's I prefer not to be known as Fenric. The name that goes with this one is Casmir Thorn. So far as anyone is concerned I'm here to advise you on hunting boar.

Benton seemed genuinely shaken. "I didn't know if was even possible for a private citizen to have a second chip," he said. "Of course you hear stories about Commonwealth agents being given false identities but . . . you don't do a little work for the UC on the side, do you, Casmir?"

I smiled at him. "I don't like lying and I don't like refusing to answer questions from a friend," I said. "The less you ask me the less I'll have to do either." Benton laughed and shrugged, but there was admiration in his eyes; whatever explanation he was imagining for my mysterious activities was evidently creditable to me. I was quite pleased with myself; at one stroke I had cut away the immense complication of pretending to be a wealthy man of whose real life I knew nothing. I might still betray myself by my ignorance in conversation with these folk, but I did not have to keep up the character of Fenric.

As it turned out, I need not have worried. Young Benton was an enthusiast of hunting and was glad to talk of nothing else. For a knight of Thorn, hunting is part of the yearly round; one of the things that is done in season, for food and to exercise the skills of hand and eye that a knight needs. As the prince, I had been expected to take the lead in hunting as well as in war, and older and more experienced men had quietly made sure that I knew my business. I had heard plenty of hunting stories, for that was one of their ways of teaching, and I had myself taken most of the kinds of birds and beasts that are counted worth hunting; deer and wild pigs for the table, of course, but also beasts of the warren: wolves, foxes and wildcats, badgers, martens and otter, even squirrels and hares. And, of course, I had hawked for hares and for game birds.

There is a skill to taking each of these beasts, and my teachers would not have counted me a hunter if I had not known each of these skills. Benton seemed to know little of such skills, except for the most elementary sort of tracking; his talk was all of hunts in which he had put his life at risk against large and dangerous beasts, including many whose nature I could only guess at from details he let drop in the telling. Of course a hunter must have courage; a stag may tum at bay and boars are notoriously dangerous and unpredictable. But battle, not the chase, is the place to demonstrate bravery; skill is what counts in the hunt.

In fact, I was growing a little weary of Benton's stories, for an armed and skillful man is in little real danger from a brute beast. But then he said something which changed my mind. Looking around the richly furnished room where we sat on cushioned chairs while our magical craft flew high in the air, Benton said hesitantly, "Most of my friends think I'm a bit of a fool to spend so much time and credit on hunting, you know. But it seems more . . . more real than most things a man can do these days. Just your own skill and a few primitive weapons against, well, against Nature. No machines to do it for you, to get between you and the thing you're doing."

Remembering the giant towers, the broad sterile streets with their few trees for show, thinking of weapons which made a man unconscious with the pressure of a finger, I began to realize that the hunt would have a value for these enchanters which a man of Thorn could scarcely understand. If they went to war it would probably be with strange wizardries which would leave little room for strength or bravery. I smiled at Benton and said, "You'll be glad enough of a spear between you and the boar; a full-grown tusker can rip a man from knee to breast and lay him stark dead with one stroke. Have these beasts been hunted at all yet?"

Benton shook his head. "Not these; they're just out of the tanks not long ago. But we managed to salvage some memory chains from the beast in the museum exhibit. Don't know if you've followed the techniques they're using these days for memory recovery from dead cells. They reckon that by what they call mix and blend techniques they can create quite a good facsimile of the original memory, with some artificial memories mixed in. Of course they'd only really know if they tried it on humans, and the Citizens' Liberties Union would be after them if they tried that. Not to say it hasn't been done in secret, of course."

"Ran across a man named Droste," I said as casually as I could manage. "Justinian Droste, I think, who had some sort of connection with that group."

Benton grinned. "'Oh yes, Droste is quite a big noise here at Home, though you may not have heard of him. Always on the 3V or in the latest fax, complaining about someone being deprived of their rights." He laughed. "Been looking a bit silly today, though. Had a big case built up against some scientist for experimentation on humans. Then his star witness or chief exhibit, the man who was the victim of the experiments, disappeared. Without him Droste has no case. Joke is Droste's own principles are getting in the way of looking for the man. Since he's a citizen he has a right to privacy. They can't even broadcast a holo of him, only appeal for him to come forward. Droste claims the man's been kidnapped, but his evidence isn't too strong. For all anyone knows, he just got tired of the food at Central Receiving and decided to check himself out informally."

Most of this was meaningless to me, but at least it assured me that Droste was a man of some note, who could be found if I wanted to find him. Since Droste seemed to know something about how I had come to this city of the enchanters, I might have to seek him out eventually.

I was tired enough of his hunting tales to pretend more interest than I really felt. I made some noncommittal noise, which encouraged Benton to go on. "Story just broke," he said, "but it should be in the fax by now. Let's see." He touched something on the arm of his chair and from a slit in a low table by his side came a thin sheet of some flimsy parchment-like material, covered with writing. "Ah yes, here it is on the first sheet," said Benton, "with a backup on another sheet, which I'll key if you're interested." He handed me the sheet, which was covered with writing in small square characters which it took me a moment to master, though I am a fair scribe. In large letters at the top of the sheet were the words, "CLU Head Accuses Academician," then my hand clenched on the sheet, crumpling it in involuntary betrayal of my emotions. For under those words were two pictures, more vivid and lifelike than any painting I had ever seen in church or castle. One showed the face of Justinian Droste looking much as I had seen him from my bed soon after I awoke. The other face, staring out at me from the picture with a familiar saturnine glower was that of my tutor and guardian, Mortifer the Enchanter!

5. BENTON HALL

After the first shock, it almost seemed inevitable. Mortifer was an enchanter, I was in a land of enchanters, so surely he must have played some part in bringing me here. I had never entirely trusted Mortifer, despite my respect for my father, who had trusted the enchanter so well that he set him over me as my tutor and guardian. Despite his outward suavity and respectful air, Mortifer had always struck me as a cold man who regarded other people only as pieces in some elaborate game. Perhaps he had brought me to this land to play some part in some game of his; well, he would find me an unwieldy tool. I remembered that as a youth I had sometimes outwitted better players at board games by moving my pieces about almost at random and letting them wrack their brains to discover the elaborate stratagems they thought lay behind my moves. I was doing much the same in this deadlier game, keeping on the move and in disguise, hoping that one of my random moves would lead to some advantage for me.

Benton had not noticed my agitation, for he was intent on another sheet of the same kind as the one he had handed me. "Doesn't really say much," he complained. "The backup is all details on the careers of the two men and the original story didn't say all that much either, just hints that Mortifer had been caught more or less red-handed experimenting on humans and that Droste had the alleged subject of the experiments. Then there was a late break saying that the man had disappeared, with Droste all but accusing Mortifer of kidnapping or worse."

"This Mortifer," I said as casually as I could manage, "from where does he come, of what Academy is he a member?"

Benton chuckled. "By the Mercy, you're right. If a man's an academician there must be an academy about somewhere. Well, let's see, must be on the fax here somewhere. Ah yes; Royal Academy of Life Sciences of Carpathia."

I nearly blurted out that if there were any "Royal Academy" in the land of Carpathia, I, the Prince Royal of Carpathia, should know of it; but I restrained my tongue. Whatever lies Mortifer had told he had at least used the name of my homeland in those lies and this gave me a reason to put the question I was burning to ask: "And where is this place Carpathia?" I said, keeping my voice as steady as I could.

But Benton's answer made little sense. "One of those little star systems out on the Tail, I think," he said with a shrug. "One terranorm planet which went pretty well back to nature during the Wars of Unity. Fairly flourishing place, now, I believe—reasonable amount of trade. Would have thought that you'd know more about it than I, since you're a startrader. Shouldn't be more than a few days flit from Home in a modern starship."

He was looking very slightly puzzled, a puzzlement that might turn to suspicion, and much as I longed to press my questions I shrugged and turned the conversation to his obsession, knowing that it would distract him.

"Ah well," I said, "can't remember everything. I've forgotten already how many boars you told me you had." He was off at once on questions and stories about hunting which lasted until his flying pavilion came to earth with a very slight jarring sensation. Out of politeness, I had not even been able to read further on the lettered sheet he had given me, but I folded it and shoved it in my pouch for future reading.

The flying pavilion was grounded beside a sort of lodge, a rustic enough place but with some dignity. There were blue-capped serfs to meet us at the door and, to my joy, a blazing fire on the hearth in the great hall. Benton smiled at the pleasure I did not try to hide. "Try to keep up the old ways here," he said. "'I'd like you to try some of my venison, if you're hungry, and some Napa I have laid down here." I agreed heartily since only the edge had been taken from my appetite by the snacks served at Flavia's gathering. A table was set for us before the fire, but we had hardly begun to eat when a slim green-clad figure appeared at the entrance hall, obviously feminine, despite red hair cut like a boy's. She had a bow in her hand and a dagger at her belt. Benton rose to his feet with a smile. "Mirianne," he said. "Nice to see you up here. Mirianne, this is, er, Casmir Thorn. Casmir, my sister, Mirianne, who laughs at my hobby but drops in on me when she needs a change from her usual pursuits."

"Pursuits is right," said the girl. "Nice to be the hunter instead of the hunted for a change. At least the men you bring up here are interested in hunting animals rather than heiresses—usually. But welcome to Benton Hall anyway, Casmir Thorn." Her eyes met mine as her fingers rubbed the violet-colored circle on her earlobe in a gesture that seemed unconscious, but may have been meant to give point to her words.

I grinned at her; there was something rather engaging about this forthright young heiress. "Why lady," I told her, "I am not here to hunt for an heiress, only for a little sport with your brother's boars. But I can see the attractions of—nobler quarry."

She laughed at that, and fell into easy conversation with her brother and myself. I asked what sport she had found with her bow, and from that the talk turned to archery. Before long we were shooting her hunting arrows at targets here and there in the hall, as men will do sometimes in a hunting lodge after the evening meal when no ladies are present. Here the lady was the worst of us, and crowed with laughter when we lodged an arrow in the mouth of a deer head hung high on the wall or shot a shaft into the opening of a wine flagon held presented toward us by a serf. There is a knack to this kind of indoor shooting, usually done with the bows at half-pull and I can usually put an arrow where I want it every time in such games, though at real shooting out of doors I do not rank with the best. By the end of the evening Benton and his sister were well pleased with me for slight enough reasons, and I went to my bed well pleased with the evening and with their company.

In the morning we broke our fast with bread and sweet preserves, along with a hot bitter liquid that was refreshing once you got used to its wry taste. Benton showed me his arms room and I belted on a short sword and dagger, feeling foolishly relieved to be armed again, though I knew that edged weapons would be of little use against the enchanter's weapons I had seen. Benton had spears of various patterns and I showed him the right length for a boar spear and where to place a cross-bar. Benton summoned a man in brown, who carried off the spear and returned surprisingly quickly with several made to the same pattern but with cross-bars.

Carrying the spears, we set off down the hill upon which the lodge was built to look at the thickets where the wild pigs had established themselves. Benton had whistled up a dog, which seemed more a pet than a hunter and Mirianne had her bow and a quiver of hunting arrows, but it was more an amble and an exploration than a hunt. As we reached some broken ground, small hillocks overgrown with underbrush, Benton hesitated. "There's a sonic fence along here," he said, "and the beasties we're after are inside it. We're not really prepared . . . ." Just then the dog by his side began to bark noisily. Then, his excitement growing, the beast sprang from Benton's side to chase something that scuttled away in the underbrush. "Oh damn," said Benton, "he's got a neutralizer in his collar; he's right through the fence. Ranger! Come back here, you idiot!" He ran forward, shouting and whistling, with Mirianne and me at his side. For a second I had a feeling of panic, then felt a sort of vibration deep in my bones, but in a stride I felt normal again.

"If you hadn't spoiled him . . ." Mirianne had begun when there was a sharp yipping sound and the dog ran back toward us, his tail between his legs, followed by a long lithe form that was chillingly familiar.

"Young tusket," I told my companions. "Most dangerous kind. Keep your spear pointed at him." I fell into a guard stance, tracking the boar with my spear-head, my hands in position on the shaft to thrust or take the shock of an impact. An old boar will stand his ground and threaten, a sow is usually dangerous only when she is defending her young, but a young boar is as dangerous as he is unpredictable.

This one slashed at the dog, and then, as I had feared, swerved toward us. "Spread out," I called to the others. Mirianne was carrying a spear and I had to treat her as a hunter, not as a lady to be protected. With the three of us to choose from, no longer in a clump but spread out in a line, the young boar hesitated. If he wanted to run between us and escape, I for one would let him; I had no need for meat or trophies and here among strangers I had no reputation to maintain. A prince must be first in the chase, as in all things, but a private person may choose not to compete.

The best thing would be for the boar to attack me; I could dispatch him with the skill of long practice. The worst would be for the boar to go for Mirianne; she had spirit but even if she had the skill she did not have the weight to stop the beast. Neither the best nor the worst happened; the boar went for Benton. "Shoulder," I shouted and he shifted the aim of his spear-head from the head, an almost impossible target, to the shoulder. The spearpoint skidded over the rough skin of the boar, then caught, and pierced through the ribs just behind the left foreleg. If the boar had the cunning to swerve away from Benton it could simply run off the point and be free to attack again. But with the insensate fury of its kind it tried frantically to reach the target it had picked.

As it scrabbled its way toward Benton the spear pierced its internal organs, but it must have missed the heart, for the creature's strength seemed unabated. When it reached the cross-bar its full weight bore on Benton for the first time; he staggered backwards a few paces. "Down," I cried, "ground the spearbutt if you can." It would have been best if he had thrown his weight at the boar, almost as if he were as eager get at the boar as the boar was to get at him, but that was not something I could explain in a few shouted words. He did almost as well, though, by bearing down with his weight on the spearbutt until he had got it lower than the point which was deep in the boar's guts. Helped by a small hillock behind him he grounded the butt and let the boar pump out its blood and life against the unyielding toughness of the spear.

I had been ready to run full tilt into the boar's side with my spear if Benton had not held him, but now I relaxed a little, shifted my spear to my left hand and drew my shortsword. So long as Benton was holding him all was well. If Benton weakened I could hamstring the boar and end it. Mirianne moved up beside me, pale but in control of herself. She looked at the thrashing boar with horrified fascination, but she neither shrank back from it nor gloated at its overthrow. My liking for her increased and I gave her a quick smile. "Almost over now," I told her and then called to Benton, "Shall I finish it for you?" He gave a jerky nod, as his muscles still strained against the boar's struggles, and I darted in, grabbed a foreleg and flipped the boar on its back. A quick hard slash and the throat was cut. Blood flowed; the limbs thrashed more slowly and stopped. There was a stink of death as muscles relaxed. I grinned at the exhausted Benton. "Now you know how to kill a boar," I said.

He stood up, working his cramped fingers. "By the Mercy," he said, and it was half a prayer and half an oath. He smiled at me and said with fair pretense of jauntiness, "Thanks for letting me have this one. But if we meet another one today, I think I may let you kill it."

I shook my head. "The boar chose you. And you did very well for your first. Next time bear forward with your weight and try to use the leverage of the spear to get the beast off its feet . . ." I went on with my advice until he had recovered his breath and his composure. Then I tactfully urged him toward the lodge, on the pretext of sending serfs back for the meat. If I judged him correctly, Benton's courage was of the sort that rises to meet a challenge, but leaves the man shaken afterward. I remembered young knights with that temperament vomiting after a battle, their bodies taking revenge for the strain that had been put on them.

When we arrived back at the lodge, Benton left Mirianne and me with a murmured apology. Mirianne turned to me and said in a low voice, "Thank you for what you did; and for what you didn't do. He's too hard on himself in many ways, but I think that for once he feels he's done well. I don't know what you are, Casmir Thorn, aside from being a very cool and professional huntsman, but if we can do anything for you . . ."

I smiled at her and said lightly, "At the moment I could do with a change of clothing and to have my man, Pello, found and sent to me."

"Of course," she said. She looked at me searchingly, then touched my arm lightly and went on into the lodge. I found my own room and stripped off my garments and relaxed in a stream of water in the "convenience". It was a pleasure; it would be easy to get used to and I wondered if something of the sort could be devised at Castle Thorn if I ever got back there.

When I had dried myself on towels that looked rough but were marvelously smooth, Pello appeared at the doorway, carrying an armload of clothing. He looked at me with an enigmatic expression and laid his burden on the bed. "From the lady of the house," he said. "You're in high favor it seems. I've been evading questions about you; my ignorance was taken for great discretion. Apparently you really do know about hunting. If I hadn't seen holos of him, I'd begin to think that you were really Fenric."

I smiled grimly. "Hunting is probably the only thing that Fenric and I have in common," I said.

Pello looked at me speculatively. "Here at Home and on most planets I know of hunting as an amusement for the very wealthy," he said, "and yet the C and C chip of yours looks plain, ordinary green to me. Or is that a fake too? And if it isn't, what in the Mercy's name were you doing under that fake blue dome?"

I looked into his eyes which were a dark gray. "Suppose you tell me your story first," I said. It would be a lie of course, but the sort of lie it was might tell me something about the man.

He looked down at his hands, then looked into my eyes again with a good imitation of candor. "My name is Joseph Pellow," he said. "Pellow with a 'w'. I was a starflitter once, but I got into trouble on a Szilar planet and the lizards got me Banned. Took my free ride Home and squandered the ecus I'd been paid off in trying to forget my Banning. Tried to get more and only got into trouble. Finally, the only thing for it was to go under the dome. What I want now is to get out to one of the newer human colonies. Things are too rigid here at Home; no scope for an enterprising man. With my share of the ecus in that pouch . . ." His eyes flicked over to where I had left my soiled clothing.

I hid a smile and picked up the belt with the pouch. Opening the pouch I spilled out the small gold-colored discs it contained and told Pellow, "Divide them into two piles; I'll choose one and leave you the other." He gave me an admiring grin and did as I had told him. I watched his hands to see that none of the discs disappeared.

"Benton can't stay here much longer," he told me, "he has business to attend to in the City. He'd leave you here to hunt if you wanted, but I wouldn't advise it; you're too isolated here if the Fenric thing blows up, as it might. You have quick wits and good luck, cit; I'll be happy to stay with you if you want me. What are your plans?"

I looked at him and said slowly, "Stay with me if you wish, Joseph Pellow. I plan to make a journey, if I am not prevented. A journey to a place called Carpathia."

6. THE VOYAGE OF *ARGO*

Pellow darted a sharp glance at me. "And where may that be?" he asked.

I tried to remember the exact words that Benton had used. "One of those little star systems out on the Tail," I said.

Pellow's hands closed protectively over his little pile of golden discs. "Star passage is expensive," he said. "Still . . . wait, though. Benton is a trader. Surely he can arrange passage for us if you ask him. From the questions his sister asked me, they have the idea that you do some sort of secret work. If you told him that you wanted to get to Carpathia unobtrusively, he'd probably be able to arrange passage for us on a cargo ship. It's done often enough; I know from my days as a flitter."

I hesitated. Some obscure sense that I was somehow being pursued or sought told me to leave no trail that could be followed. But surely if Benton thought that I was on some secret errand he would tum away anyone trying to trace me. I had done little enough for him but he felt himself obliged to me. In fact, I felt the obligation went in the other direction, but I liked young Benton and did not mind being obliged to him. "All right," I said reluctantly, "I'll speak to him."

Benton was engagingly eager to do something for me and to prove himself a man of importance. He unlocked a small room full of gleaming machines and flashing lights, spoke to several disembodied voices and imaged faces, then turned to me and said with a smile, "We're in luck. A startrader who owes our

House a favor actually has a cargo going to Carpathia. You and Pellow will travel as special supercargoes responsible for that shipment. The ship is a little Independent carrying a variety of small shipments. But the captain is experienced and the ship is fairly new. She'll lift day after tomorrow if that suits you, and you can go aboard tomorrow night." He waved my thanks aside and plunged into plans for a boar hunt and feast the next day.

Between the hunt and the feast I was in little condition to take much note of my surroundings when Benton's flying pavilion carried me back to the city the following evening. The pavilion landed on a broad sweep of what looked like lawn, brightly lit by glowing globes on tall poles. When Pellow and I emerged from the pavilion, though, the stuff underfoot was not grass, but some slightly resilient stuff the color of grass. A tough, competent-looking man in dark, close-fitting garments met us and led us past immense mysterious structures to a great circular thing like a giant's shield flung carelessly on the false greensward. A square opening in the edge of the thing was evidently an entryway; a light warmer than that of the globes spilled from it.

I could see as we entered that the outer walls of this thing were immensely thick, made of some smooth dark stuff. Inside there was a sort of high desk occupied by a slender man with the look of a clerk. On the wall behind the desk the word "Argo" was written in golden letters and beneath it a stylized picture of a small sailing galley that might have sailed the Inner Sea. Standing beside the desk talking to the clerk-like man was a tall dark-haired woman of remarkable beauty, who had an air of absolute authority. She might have been a reigning queen. I was not surprised when my guide saluted her and said, "These are the two men from Degnan Freres, Captain."

She nodded and gave us a brief smile which lit up her dark eyes. "I'm Elena Petros," she said. "Welcome aboard *Argo*. Your cargo is already sealed in Gamma hold. I'm not sure what point there is to sending you with it, but you're welcome enough to the spare cabin." Her eyes flicked over Pellow, then measured me with an approving look I might have resented from a woman less magnificent than this one.

"You have the look of a Carpathian," she told me. "I presume that you're homeward bound."

A sudden feeling of uncertainty swept over me. "I hope so, Lady," I said. Could it really be so easy as this, stepping onto this strange vessel and voyaging back to the place I had come from? Could Castle Thorn and the court of Carpathia exist in the same world as this place of enchantments? Young Benton had spoken as if a cargo to Carpathia was a commonplace enough affair, but surely nothing like this great dark disc had ever been seen in the skies of my homeland.

Captain Elena Petros looked into my eyes. Her own magnificent dark eyes seemed to pierce my soul. "Will home be home when you get back?" she said softly. "Yes, it's a feeling that starflitters know well." She gave another of her brilliant smiles and turned to the clerkly man. "There shouldn't be anything else coming aboard tonight, Tamma," she told him. "You might as well seal the sally port and show these cits to their cabin." The man saluted and slid down from his high stool. He touched a circle on the desk, and with a deep hum the ramp by which we had climbed up to this entryway lifted from the ground, pivoting on the threshold. It covered the doorway by which we had entered, fitting flush with the inner wall with a slight click. Those thick walls and the door made by the ramp made a formidable barrier. Against what? I wondered.

I learned the next morning, as I sat on my bed in a room that except for its smaller size might have been the room I had awakened in in the place they had called a "hospital." As in that other room, there was an oval of swirling colors on the wall, which Pellow called a "View." Touching one of the now-familiar circles made the colors vanish, to be replaced by what seemed to be a window looking out on the area we had walked through the night before. Dawn was still streaking the sky with colors when three red flashes chased each other across the scene and a woman's voice spoke from the air. "Lift off in thirty seconds," said the voice, "Off-duty crew and passengers secure for liftoff."

There was a deep rumble and the fabric of the room shook very slightly. In the oval view the ground suddenly dropped away, and I saw again, as I had seen from Benton's flying pavilion, the towers of the enchanters' city. It was set among rolling hills: I looked for Benton's estate and lodge but we were soon too high to see any building of ordinary size. Higher and higher we went: I saw snow-capped mountains off to one side and a blue infinity that could only be the sea a long way off on the other side. The panorama was already vaster than any I had seen from the highest peak in Carpathia, but we rose yet higher; what sky I could see tumed strangely dark, and the land beneath me seemed to take on a curve. As I watched in fascination the arc of the sky grew in proportion to the land and stars began to appear. After I don't know how long I saw the starry sky engulf the land and sea, until the place we had come from was only a circle of misty blue set in a night sky full of stars.

Pellow's voice brought me out of my trance. "Spectacular, isn't it?" he said softly. "We take off on gravity-effect engines and it's most economical to head straight for the sun, so you see the whole dayside." Then he said more briskly, "There's time for breakfast before we go Q. Not that you'll feel the lack of it when you're Q-time, but your body needs it and you might as well eat while you can still enjoy it." From a niche in the wall very much like that in the "hospital" room he produced a tray of food and drink far tastier than the food in the "hospital" had been. Pellow grinned. "Trust a Greek captain to see that the Departure Day breakfast is a good one," he said.

The three flashes came again and the voice said, "Prepare to go Q." Pellow shrugged and carried our dishes back to the niche where they were whisked away as if by invisible fingers. A whooshing sound as of a great wind sighed through the room for a moment and Pellow cocked his head to listen. "Letting air out of the cargo holds," he said. "The captain leaves it till the last moment for some reason. Wonder what the cargo is that we're supposed to be in charge of." He went to his bunk and stretched himself out, turning his face to the wall. Three flashes again and the disembodied voice said, "Entering Q space."

In the View the starry sky blinked out, to be replaced by a curious gray blankness through which amorphous gray shapes moved slowly. After a moment I tore my eyes away and turned my face to the wall as Pellow had done. Waves of hot and cold seemed to move through my body and I had the unpleasant feeling that those gray shapes were moving unseen through the room and through my body. My heart pounded, then seemed to stop and start again. A weight seemed to rest on my chest and I struggled for breath, then the weight vanished and I was panting in shallow breaths. My sight blurred, then cleared again. Gradually I settled into a sort of dull apathy, as if my body and my emotions had been worn out by the rapid oscillations of sensation, and had retreated to a dumb quiescence.

Pellow lifted his head and spoke in a dull monotone. "The first few minutes are the worst, after that your body overloads. You won't feel like doing anything, but it's important for you to move around, and take some nourishment when it's provided, otherwise it's worse when you come out of it. You can let yourself go during what would be the sleep period so long as you're able to rouse yourself at the change of watches. It will seem like three or four days until we come out of Q and you'll feel about as you do now for five or ten days afterward, unless you take some steps. I can help you there; starflitters get to know a few tricks . . ." His voice trailed off and he stared dully ahead of him.

"What is this . . . this . . . state?" I asked him. Pellow gave the ghost of a shrug.

"I'm not sure anyone knows, really," he said. "We go outside of normal space and time, into—this. We call it quasi-space and quasi-time, Q space and Q time for short. We come back into realspace an immense distance away from where we started. Carpathia is twelve zir from Home; light takes about fifty odd years to make the journey. So far as anyone can tell the ship has taken no realtime at all to make the journey. If you could go Q near a planetary mass starflits would be a great deal easier. As it is, you have to get about fifty diameters out from your departure planet before you can flit and your point of arrival has to be a long way out from any planetary mass. We may take as much as a day or two realtime from POA to planetside. But we'll still be in emotional freeze—we won't care."

Indeed, I cared for little in the time that followed, or seemed to follow. But I forced myself to activity, mindful of Pellow's warning. I did endless exercises, which never seemed to raise a sweat or leave me tired, forced myself to rise from the bed promptly at the bell which marked the change of watch, and made myself swallow the tasteless food which appeared in the niche in our cabin. On a long campaign I have been so tired that I fought and marched and choked down food like a man asleep yet walking; this was like those times except that I felt no weariness, only a dull apathy that made it easy to lie unmoving in my bunk during the time of "sleep".

The second "day" I went out of the door of my room, not because I had any desire to, but because some small part of my mind which still judged and willed told me that I should learn what I could of this vessel in which I rode. I wandered long gray corridors and saw sights which might almost have overturned my reason had my emotions not been frozen. Not all of the crewmen on that ship were human. Some were like giant lizards without tails, who walked on two feet. Their glittering black eyes had double lids and their face was covered with fine scales which grew larger on what you could see of their bodies. They were clothed, but more lightly clad than the human crewmen, as if they found the rooms too hot. There was a furred creature with three pale blue eyes and a feathered being with a head like an owl's. Some of the crewmen who seemed otherwise human had grayish skin or strange vari-colored eyes.

No one hindered me as I wandered through the corridors and I saw strange sights in some of the rooms that I ventured into. A large room held row after row of crystal boxes, each holding a human infant, dead or frozen in some strange sleep. Another room was like an antechamber to a larger room which was separated from it by a large transparent wall. Beyond the wall seemed to be pale green water in which floated something like a giant flower. But as I stood and gazed eyes opened in the flower and surveyed me with what seemed to be intelligence.

Once I came to a door that seemed to be guarded by a crewman who stood beside it. I looked at him and made a gesture of inquiry. He spoke into a small disc on his wrist, seemed to listen, then touched a circle which opened the door. Inside was a great circular room filled with glittering shapes and lights which marched in slow patterns across panels. Before the panels sat crewmen, some human and some not. Several glanced my way; the feathered creature seeming to turn his head completely around to do so. At one end of the room was a chair like a throne, and behind it a semicircular sweep of carpeted floor. Pacing along this floor in what seemed to be a well-worn path, her hands clasped loosely behind her back, was the captain, Elena Petros. She came to the end of her carpeted area, turned and saw me. She gestured me to come to her and I walked over and stood at the edge of the carpet, somehow reluctant to step onto what seemed a private preserve.

Her face and voice seemed almost normal as she greeted me. but it was all will power and magnificent control; her fine eyes had no sparkle and her body was slack when she did not make it move to her will. "You're very active for a passenger, Citizen Thorn," she said. "Some of them do nothing but stare at the walls. You'll be glad of it when you get planetside; you should be out of freeze in the minimum time. Right now we're busy trying to chart a possible anomaly. But come back to the bridge after we come out of Q; you'll get a better view of planetfall from here. It won't mean much at the time, but it will be something to remember."

I saluted and left her then, casting an incurious eye on crewmen who stared intently at lighted panels or manipulated curious instruments. Again I exercised, ate and prowled the corridors. Eventually, lights flashed again and a starry sky glowed again on the View in my room. A faint vibration began in the fabric of the ship and after a while one star began to shine more and more brightly. Soon it became a tiny disc, too bright to look at until Pellow touched a circle at the side of the screen and the brilliance faded to a bearable level. "This is a crew cabin," he said. "Cut-off would be automatic on the View in a passenger cabin. Otherwise some passengers would stare at the primary till they damaged their sight."

He stood back from the View, then walked toward it, scanning the stars, Eventually he pointed to a star fainter than many of the others. "That's a planet," he said. "Probably Carpathia, because we seem to be heading for it." He pressed another circle beside the View and the stars altered their pattern. The faint star was now a tiny disc and the star which had shone so bright was a white circle near the edge of the View. "Long way out yet," he said. "We won't land until tomorrow. I'd try to sleep if I were you; it will be real sleep now that we're out of Q." I lay down on my bed and after a while began to feel drowsy. For the first time since I had boarded this strange craft I lost consciousness.

I awoke feeling heavy and unrefreshed, cleaned myself up and made my way back to the circular room Elena Petros had called the "bridge." Several panels in the room now showed starry sky with a blue disc in the center. The captain was seated in her throne-like chair and beckoned me to her side. On a great screen which faced her chair I saw starry sky and a blue disc the size of a man's head at the center. It all looked very much as things had looked at the beginning of our voyage and I coldly realized a truth that had, for now, no emotional impact. We had journeyed the heavens, from star to star.

"Let's have extreme magnification on the port city," said Elena Petros, and suddenly the screen before us showed a view from a great height of a sprawling city, even larger than the city I had left to begin this voyage, but on a more human scale with buildings large and small, old and new, jumbled together.

"This is Thorn," said Captain Petros. For a moment I didn't comprehend. Thorn was a little village, huddled below the Castle. Then a familiar outline caught my eye, and my eyes traced the craggy shape of the Hill of Thorn up to the towers and balllements above. There were a few changes, but very few. Standing above the vast alien sprawl of the unfamiliar city was Castle Thorn, the home of my fathers, which I had left, surely, no more than a week ago!

7. CASTLE THORN

Elena Petros turned to me and asked with that same controlled appearance of normality, "Are you familiar with the city, Casmir?"

"My ancestors lived there," I said, gesturing at the castle. She nodded. "Of course, Casmir Thorn; you're named for the city. Your family must have left soon after Rediscovery, though; Carpathia hasn't been in the Commonwealth all that long, if I remember the data fax we got on the planet. Do you have relatives here?"

I shook my head. "I don't know," I said. I wondered in a remote fashion what my emotions would have been if they had not been frozen by the enchanted voyage I had taken. For Thorn to have grown from the village I remembered to this sprawling city must have taken generation upon generation. Had our magical voyage taken centuries? But no, Pellow had said that these star voyages took no real time at all, despite the days that seemed to pass. And Pellow had no reason to lie—or had he? Whom could I trust, whom could I believe in this land of enchanters which seemed to have reached out and engulfed my homeland? The problem was agonizing, but I felt no agony, locked as I was in the frozen emotions which were the price of star voyaging.

We landed in the city as routinely as we had left the city where I had boarded *Argo*; there was another great stretch of the false lawn with the same glowing globes on high poles. There were fewer of the enigmatic structures, and only two of the great discs which must be "starships" like *Argo*. Of course, we felt nothing as the ship landed, but I felt a certain detached admiration for the evident competence and efficiency of Captain Petros and her crew as *Argo* settled her immense bulk on the false greensward as lightly as a leaf falling from a tree.

"Finished with the engines," said Elena Petros. "Open the sally port and prepare to receive planetary officials." She turned to me. "We generally get rid of passengers fairly quickly, Casmir Thorn, but you and your companion are quasi-crew. If you'd like, use your cabin for a while until you get oriented here on Carpathia. The duty officer at the sally port will give you a ship's badge which will get you in and out of the starport and let you use the crew shuttles into the city."

"I thank you, Lady," I said. Was Elena Petros merely being kind, or did she have some hidden motive, I wondered coldly. Perhaps she saw some advantage to be gained from learning more about my reasons for coming to Carpathia. Pellow had told me that the captain of an independent starship like *Argo* had to be a shrewd trader, quick to seize opportunity. Perhaps. too, Elena Petros had some interest in me as a man; there had been a certain spark between us before our emotions had been frozen.

I turned to go, but she stopped me with a gesture. "I don't know what your business is on Carpathia, Casmir Thorn," she said, "but if you're ready to leave before *Argo* lifts, come and see me about a real crew berth. The technical things can be learned—many of them can be autolearned. But the ability to function as well as you did in Q condition is something that's very rare. This flit was just a delivery run. After it, we're outward bound for some trading on our own. There's wealth as well as adventure in the star trade. If that appeals to you, I can always use a good man."

I tried to put some feeling into my voice as I said, "I will remember your words, Captain, and I thank you again." As I left the bridge I considered her offer. I was a man ripped out of his own place and flung into a world which was often incomprehensible. If I could find no way back to my own place, I could certainly do a great deal worse than to join the small, disciplined world of *Argo*. But before I abandoned the world I remembered to try to see what I could make of this new one, I wanted to know how and why I had lost my old world. I had a feeling that Mortifer might know, and Mortifer, according to the "fax" which Benton had given me, was in this city of Thorn.

If it were not for my frozen emotions, I might have stormed my way into Mortifer's presence and demanded an explanation. But in the cold light of reason, without emotion to influence me, I saw that the better course was to learn everything I could before trying to confront Mortifer. Most of the city was strange to me, but the castle which loomed above the city on its rocky crag was at least outwardly familiar. I decided to make it my first goal.

Benton had given gifts of clothing to me when I left his lodge. During the voyage I had simply pulled on whatever garments came to hand, but now I looked through Benton's gifts and did my best to find garments that would not have looked wildly out of place at my father's court. At the sally port I was given a little circular patch of black which seemed to have a star gleaming in its center. "Most of us wear them over our C and C chip," said the duty officer. "Marks us as starcrew and it's no business of the planetaries how much credit we have, since we pay in ecus anyway. Captain said to treat you as crew, so I'll give you the same advice as I'd give a new crewman. Stay in the port area until you come out of freeze; planetaries are often scared of starcrew or hostile to them. They don't understand freeze and they have strange ideas about it. If you're anxious to get out of freeze as quickly as possible, don't fool around with the so-called emotional therapists; go to a blackout."

At my look of incomprehension, he explained, "They're plays, short and pretty melodramatic. But somehow all that stage emotion seems to unfreeze your own emotions. See a good blackout and get a good night's sleep and by tomorrow morning you may begin to feel human. If not, repeat the treatment. We were two days on GE drive that's two days out of Q. Cutting it a little fine, but you kept active in Q and that helps."

I hesitated, then decided to take his advice. Much as I grudged the time, I realized that a man in emotional freeze was conspicuous and I did not want to be conspicuous when I set out to find what I could about Mortifer and about what had happened to me.

There was certainly nothing recognizable and almost nothing Carpathian about the area around the starport. The men and women who filled the taverns and wandered the streets in various stages of emotional freeze were the same strange mixture of faces as I had encountered aboard *Argo*, along with others even stranger; lithe, brown creatures who seemed to slither rather than walk, and exotically plumed beings who almost seemed to float along.

It was easy enough to find a blackout; there were several theaters near the starport gates. The first surprise was that the play featured both humans and the scaled lizard-like creatures I had learned to call Szilara. There were four players: a male and female Szilar, and a human man and woman.

The plot, looking, back on it, was thin enough stuff; a tale of danger and hairsbreadth escapes with the Szilara as villains, the woman as victim and the man as rescuing hero. But it was well written and well acted. At first it seemed merely interesting, then it became absorbing. At a tense moment in the plot I found myself gripping the arms of my seat and realized that my emotions were returning. By the end of the play I was joining in the catcalls which greeted the appearance of the villains and shouting myself hoarse to cheer on the hero.

The play ended abruptly with the lights turned out at a high point of tension; the "blackout" from which the plays took their name. As the lights went on again and the audience filed out, I exchanged sheepish smiles with other men and women whose badges proclaimed them as starcrew. We felt foolish, but we felt human again.

It was late and I headed for the starport gates, planning to get some proper rest and head for the castle in the morning. A small man in brown caught my attention with a courteous gesture as I strolled away from the theater and I paused to see what he wanted of me. On closer inspection there was something rather unpleasant about his smooth manner and foppish appearance, and I regretted not having ignored him. He came to my side and spoke in a low rapid voice, not looking at my face; "The honorable startrader may wish to complete his emotional recovery by sampling our wares," he said, "the finest gynas, perfect simulacra of the most beautiful women in the Commonwealth, programmed for your pleasure . . . ."

I did not completely understand what he was offering, but I understood well enough to be disgusted. "Be off with you!" I said and raised my hand as if to cuff him. He cringed and slid off into the shadows.

"Good for you, flitter," said a woman's voice. behind me. I turned to see a richly dressed woman of considerable beauty, with a hardness to her voice and features that let me guess her profession. "Too many flitters are spending their credit on those mechanical dolls. Afraid of a real woman, most of them. If you're not, I'll give you a special rate for sending that puppet pimp about his business."

I gave her a grin. "Not tonight, my pretty one. But good hunting," I said. She gave a little trill of laughter, raised a hand in salute and strolled languidly off, her eyes searching the faces of the men who were emerging from the theater.

Back aboard *Argo* I found Pellow lying on his bunk and told him of my adventures. He nodded dully, still wrapped in emotional freeze. "Yes, blackouts will do the job all right, but I don't want out of freeze until I leave this ship," he said. "It will be bad enough knowing I can't flit again except as a passenger without living in crew quarters and seeing starflitters about me every day. I'll look for lodgings in the city tomorrow, I think. What about you?"

I hesitated. "I may know more after tomorrow. Don't leave *Argo* for good without leaving me word of where I can find you." He nodded listlessly and was stretching out again as I asked, "These gynas the man spoke of, what are they? The bawdy called them dolls, and puppets."

Pellow shrugged. "That's what they are, mechanicals just like andros. Technically I suppose they'd have to expose the blue dome under their wigs if they ever went out of doors. But you'll never find them outside a bawdy house. Physically they're a perfect replica of a woman but their programming is pretty limited; they're made for only one thing. The ones that are replicas of famous actresses and other well-known women are kept in pretty tight seclusion; their owners would be in big trouble if the duplication could be proved. You hear stories of women who've been copied without their permission hiring wilders to break up a bawdy house and destroy the gynas. On the other hand, you hear stories of 3V stars who let themselves be duplicated for a share of the profits."

I groped. for a way to put the question I wanted to ask without exposing my ignorance. "The andros—I've seen none of them here so far."

Pellow shook his head. "No, I wouldn't expect to see any here. They can't flit, the effects of Q on them are too unpredictable. A general-purpose andro like we were pretending to be costs a small fortune to build; more than most cits make in five years. It's not worthwhile making them on a backwater planet like this; there are humans to do even the most menial jobs. Gynas are another matter; you can always peddle exotic sex, especially near a starport."

I fell into my bunk, my head whirling. The "andros," then, were some sort of doll or puppet, moved by enchanters' arts. No wonder they gaped and stared in poor imitation of humanity. But what about the serfs I remembered, surely they were natural men, born and not built by magical arts. But except for their shocks of unkempt hair . . . . Suddenly I had a sort of double image: serfs as I had remembered them up to now and then a different set of images; serfs grinning, laughing, drinking; buxom serf women smiling at me and shock-headed children tumbling on the cottage floors. My heart pounded and I broke out in a sweat. Up to now I had not doubted my memories. I had reckoned myself a sane man in a mad world of enchantment. What if it were I who was mad . . . ?

I made myself breathe deeply and relax. Whatever had been done to me, some things I could hold to. I knew enough of hunting to win Benton's respect. I could handle myself well enough in this strange world to make Elena Petros offer me a berth on *Argo*. Whatever I learned about myself I was my own man and could hold my own in this or any other world. And surely my memories of Castle Thorn and my life there could not all be false. I knew that castle as well as I knew my own hands—or did I? Tomorrow would tell. I made myself sleep.

The next day it took an effort to keep my voice steady as I asked the guard at the starport gate about transportation to the castle. He shrugged. "Oh yes, you can get there all right, they run tours. But not many flitters care to go. Tell you what, go over to the passenger gate round the fence there; cut across the field. There are probably regular tours leaving from there for visitors with time to kill here. Some of the tours are free; the city merchants run them to attract business. I'd take off your crew badge and hope they take you for a wealthy cit."

I thanked the man and cut across the false grass to the gate he had indicated. A more grandly dressed gatekeeper looked at me oddly, then told me to wait. Presently he returned with another man. "The regular tour is gone, citizen, but Jelleck here will give you a lift to the castle gate and find a tour you can join." I thanked him and accompanied the other man to a moving platform smaller and faster than the one I had ridden with the andros the day I first met Pellow. I settled in a seat beside the man named Jelleck and was whisked through crowded streets toward the castle. Nothing I saw looked familiar until we came to the castle gates. Where I remembered a moat there was a broad paved area, but the gates themselves and the walls above were heart-stoppingly familiar.

The man named Jelleck looked around him. "If you'll wait here, citizen, I'll find a guide for you," he said, and entered the castle through a small postern gate that I did not remember. I climbed off the platform and stretched. Another unfamiliar object near the gates was a statue standing immediately before the gates, a man in armor with an unfurled flag in one hand and a bared sword in the other. I strolled casually over to look at it and was suddenly standing there staring, unable to move. Dimly I heard a child's voice behind me, "Mama, look! The man standing there looks just like the statute of King Casmir the Protector!"

8. THE HALL OF KINGS

I heard a chuckle at my side and turned to see a young man with a studious look about him, clothed in a shabby robe that looked somewhat like a monk's habit. "The child's right, ser," he said. "You're the spitting image of the Blessed King. You must have Jagellon blood all right, though by your clothing you're from off-planet. Would you like a guide, ser? I'm a poor student and promise you that your fee will all be spent on students' necessaries—books and wine."

I laughed, liking the look of the young man, and flipped him one of the golden discs from my pouch; since one had bought me admittance to the blackout I reckoned it a fair fee for a guide. His face grew grave and with an obvious struggle he made as if to hand it back to me. "This is far too much for a guide, ser," he said. "And I can't give you exchange."

I pushed his hand away. "Keep it for your studies then, ser scholar," I said, "and enough wine not to interfere with the studying."

He laughed at that, but his eyes were bright as he carefully stowed the disc in his clothing. "This will buy me things from off-planet that will save me much time in my studies," he said awkwardly. "I thank you, ser, and I'm at your disposal for as long as you like. Come round to the Little Gate, going through the gift shop yonder spoils the castle for anyone with taste. Do you know any Carpathian history, ser, or should I start at the beginning?"

"Treat me like a child at his first lessons," I said.

He chuckled again and fell into a lecturing tone as we walked along the paved area with the castle walls soaring above us. "Well, ser, Carpathia was colonized just before the Wars of Unity when, of course, the remoter colonies were soon cut off. A Szilar raider torched the techno complex, which they hadn't had time to decentralize, and the planet slid right back to the feudal age in a few generations. The colonists had to go back to the most primitive subsistence farming and the starcrew who were stranded here when their ship was torched became a feudal aristocracy. The captain of the ship was a man named Casmir Jagellon who had a hobby of reading ancient history from Home. He formed his crew into an order of knighthood and got about the long task of building up civilization again."

"To restore the Golden Days . . ." I said softly. It was a phrase from my knightly oath.

The young scholar shot me a startled glance. "But if you know the oath of the Knights of Thorn . . ." he began.

I shook my head, "Never mind, go on as you began," I said. "A child at his first lessons."

He shrugged and went on. "Well, ser, Casmir Jagellon became King Casmir the First and built the first castle here on Castle Crag. Some colonists revolted and went off to found their own societies. But most of those reverted to barbarism. Actually we know more about this early history than we do about the later history of Carpathia because for a while some sophisticated. recording devices survived which could make record chips. When those broke down or wore out records were kept only with pen and ink on reed paper, and not all of these records survived. There was a Dark Age, a period from which more legends and myth than real history survive. For instance, if you look at the shield of King Casmir the Protector on the statue outside you'll see a winged fire-breathing lizard, a firedrake. Most scholars now say they're only legends, influenced by old stories from Home like the Bilbo-saga. Some scholars think they really existed, but they're in the minority."

"Why does . . . King Casmir . . . have one on his shield?" I asked.

He chuckled. "Oh, the usual thing, he killed a firedrake and rescued a princess."

"Was her name Delora?" I asked, trying to keep my voice calm.

The young scholar shook his head. "Oh no, one of the Hedwigas, I think. Delora isn't a Carpathian name, even, and I'm sure it doesn't come into any of the legends."

A day or so ago I would have backed my own memory against a scholar's knowledge of legends but with my new uncertainty his words gave me a sharp stab of uneasiness. "How about Mortifer?" I said.

He laughed. "Oh yes, he comes into that legend as a cross between the wicked enchanter and the usurping regent. King Casmir eventually banished him, I think. But there are a lot of Mortifers in Carpathian history, some heroes, and some villains. Mortifer is one of the old Carpathian family names, probably descended from one of the original starcrew, though that name doesn't appear on the log as we have it. Ah, here's the Little Gate."

We entered a small but richly decorated gate; again its position but not its style matched my memories. As I expected, we stood within the courtyard of the castle with the Great Tower soaring above us. Built into the wall near us was a small church; the scholar led me into its nave and left me to look at the great altar and the carved and gilded statues while he crossed himself and knelt briefly to pray. I stood looking about me, while more suppressed memories flitted through my mind; Mass at the high altar with the flash of swords and sound of trumpets at the Elevation, catechism lessons from an old priest who had been my tutor before Mortifer. How could I have forgotten?

The scholar did not speak until we were out of the church; then he said quietly, "That chapel is still the Cathedral of Thorn and for the Carpathians who keep the Old Faith, the holiest place on Carpathia. The First

Chaplain is buried there and Holy Queen Hedwig. Not the kings, though, they're all buried in the Hall of Kings on the other side of the castle. There was quite a furor a few years ago when some scientists from the Royal Academy got permission to examine some of the bodies for archeological purposes. Carpathia isn't a monarchy anymore, of course, but the Old Carpathia Party talked about desecration of our history."

"The king who stands before the castle . . ." I said slowly. He nodded. "Your look-alike? He was Casmir the Tenth. He united all the little kingdoms and really started Carpathia on the road to civilization. You couldn't be descended from him; he was quite a devout man by all accounts and faithful to the princess he rescued. Some of his descendants were a bit more—er—prolific and no doubt your family . . . . Well, the direct line died out before Rediscovery and if there had been a legitimate cadet branch . . . ."

He was growing more embarrassed as he tangled himself in explanations. "I take your point," I said. "How is Carpathia ruled now?"

The scholar looked troubled. "Theoretically it's a Direct Democracy," he said, "but the old families interfere a lot. The present Mortifer doesn't hold political office; he's an Academician, but according to the Old Carpathian Party he has a lot more influence than he should have on government decisions. Right now he's in some sort of trouble at Home and the government is resisting attempts to extradite or even question him. Well, you're not interested in Carpathian politics. Would you like to see the Great Tower or . . ."

"The Hall of Kings, I think," I told him. "What sort of thing does this Mortifer do? Does he live here in Thorn?"

"Oh yes," said the young man. "He has a suite of rooms at the Royal Academy which a lot of scholars think should be put to use as research space; another example of his influence. They must be some of the best rooms in the city way up at the top of the building like that. Here, let's go up the guards' stair and along the battlements. You can see the Academy over on Hedwiga's Hill across the valley." As I followed the young scholar up the well-worn familiar steps I reflected that my golden circle had been well spent. The young man was so eager to please me that I had only to express interest in a subject to be flooded with all of the information the young man knew.

"There's Hedwiga's Hill, with the Institute on top," said my companion as we reached the battlements. As I had half expected, "Hedwiga's Hill" was the Mount of Sacrifice. There looked to be a small chapel of some sort on the ledge where I remembered fighting the firedrake, and the top of the hill had been carved and quarried so that the whole top of the hill was a great building. It was built of the gray local stone, but had no battlements or towers; it looked more like a monastery than a castle, but somehow it echoed the look of the castle whose walls we stood on. Some master builder had taken care to see that the two buildings which dominated the town below should not jar with each other.

The town itself was a fairer sight, looked at from this more human height, than it had been from *Argo*. I could see the glint of fountains in the squares and the green of parks scattered here and there among the streets. Around the castle were the old winding streets that I remembered, but farther away the streets went in broader curves that followed lines of the country. The rigid geometry of the city of enchanters where I had boarded *Argo* was happily absent. I began to feel a sense of belonging here, a sense of possession, and with it a sense of responsibility. "A beautiful city," I said to the scholar.

He nodded, slowly looking out over the city. "Yes," he said quietly. "I want to travel through the Commonwealth; there's so much to see, to learn. But always I'll want to come back to Thorn, to meditate on what I've learned. I don't know whether I'll ever be elected to the Academy over there, but there are humbler places where perhaps more real scholarship goes on."

Just then I heard footsteps on the stairs we had come up, and turned to see the man Jelleck, who had brought me to the castle from the starport. He was followed by a burly man who eyed me with a curiously appraising look. "I've found you a guide, ser," said Jelleck, gesturing to the man beside him.

"Thanks for that," I told him, "but I have found my own guide." If there had been some small coins in my pouch, I might have tossed him one; but if a golden ecu was too much for a guide, it was too much for the smaller service he had rendered, and my supply of the little circlets was limited.

My young scholar-guide cut in. "You're not one of the regular guides," he told the burly man. "Where's your medallion? The Castle guides barely tolerate us scholars guiding people here; you can get into serious trouble doing guide's work without authorization."

Jelleck opened his mouth but the other man took his arm in what looked like no gentle grip. "We had a guide waiting for you below," said the burly man glibly. "But if the citizen here has no need of him, we'll dismiss him. Come on, Jelleck." He hustled Jelleck back down the stairs.

The scholar grinned at me. "The tough had better sense than the tout," he said. "Some unauthorized guiding does go on, of course, because you can't be sure that one person showing another the castle isn't just a citizen showing a country cousin the sights of Thorn. But if anyone is caught taking a fee, the official guides will take it to court. That muscleman looked the type who might try to bully an extra fee out of a timid tourist; he'll get nailed for Uncivil behavior someday, if that's his game. Not that he'd get far with you, ser."

I smiled at that, but I realized now what the burly man's look of appraisal had been; the look of one fighting man sizing up another. A faint chill of uneasiness came over me. Even if Jelleck was a rogue and had some dishonest ploy in mind, was he not risking a great deal, since I knew his name and he was known to the gateman at the starport? The sense of being pursued, which had faded with my other emotions on *Argo*, came back in full force. I looked around me as the scholar talked of kings and battles, trying to think of what I could do if I were attacked here. How many memories of this castle could I trust, how much would this strangely altered Castle Thorn fight on my side?

The Hall of Kings was new to me; a strongly-built place half hall and half chapel perched on a crag at one side of the castle and connected to the battlements by a high-flung bridge of wood. I hesitated before setting foot on the bridge; the place was a cul de sac. Still, not many could come at me at once over that bridge; the passage could be defended fairly easily by a determined man.

As if echoing my thought the young scholar said, "Casmir the Fourteenth made a stand here when his enemies seized the Castle by treachery. He burned the bridge behind him and held out until loyal troops relieved him. Later renovaters have wanted to rebuild the bridge in stone but the traditionalists have always objected, and so the bridge is wooden just as in the days it was burned. Of course, the timbers have been renewed, but it still makes some visitors from high-tech worlds nervous; they don't really trust natural materials like wood."

The bridge was sturdy enough, and the interior of the hall which we entered through massive wooden doors had a dignified simplicity. There was a central aisle lit by clerstory windows above, and off of this aisle was a series of alcoves like small side chapels in a great church. Some of these contained obvious mausoleums, others held statuary groups or plaques. A shield hung above the entrance to each alcove and a flagstaff projected above each shield. The flags on the staffs were tattered and faded, but you could see the Crown and Sword design on each; they had been the personal standards of the dead kings.

I walked softly down the aisle until I came to an alcove below a familiar shield. The alcove contained nothing but a massive rectangular slab of dark stone. Plunged into the stone slab as if driven there by a mighty force was a sword I recognized. I stood there gazing somberly at it, wondering if I were a ghost or a living man, whether I stood before this dark slab or lay beneath it.

A sharp gasp from the young scholar aroused me from my reverie. Following his gaze I saw the burly man who had accosted us along with Jelleck, striding across the bridge. He was followed by three men even bigger and brawnier and all of them looked grim and purposeful. Suddenly the gatekeeper's odd looks at me and his delays, Jelleck's odd eagerness to help me into the city and the burly man's appraising glance came together into a sinister pattern. I had been sniffed out by the faceless enemies who pursued me and skillfully herded into this trap, a trap that was about to close on me!

9. FACE TO FACE

My next move was half instinctive, half desperation. I reached for the hilt of the sword on the tomb and pulled. It came as easily into my hand as if it had been in a greased sheath. Above my head a great bell tolled once; perhaps an alarm set off by my impulsive action. But I had no time to think of that; I ran sword in hand for the door, to meet my attackers on the bridge where they could surround me. I took a grim delight in their faces as I burst out of the door, sword at the ready. The first man fumbled at his belt, but before he could draw any weapon I had dealt him a stunning blow on the side of his head with the flat of my sword. He crumpled to the floor of the bridge and I leaped over his body to dash the pommel of the sword into the face of the next man following. He staggered back into the arms of the next man and two quick swipes with the flat of the sword stunned them both. The last man was a little out of reach but I feinted a thrust at him to keep him off balance. His nerve broke and he turned and ran.

I wheeled to see if any of the others were recovering, but the young scholar was standing over them with what looked like a heavy candlestick, snatched perhaps from some altar in the Hall of Kings. We exchanged grins and he started to speak, but suddenly there was a curious sound, half howl, half whistle, from the air above us. I looked up to see a circular platform swooping down upon us. On it stood a woman in dark blue garments with a stylized shield covering her chest and a close-fitting helmet on her head. "Oh lord, a monitor," said the scholar. "If these men deny that they meant to attack us . . ."

I stepped close to him and with an odd reluctance pressed the sword hilt into his hand. "Keep this under your robe and walk slowly into the Hall," I said in a low voice. "Restore the sword to where it came from while I parley with this . . . monitor." If the woman approaching us was a keeper of the law I had no wish to use a sword on her, and if I had no weapon in my hand I could play the injured innocent better. The scholar grinned again and slipped unobtrusively back to the door of the Hall as the woman maneuvered her flying platform to land on the wide space on the battlements where the bridge to the Hall of Kings began.

As soon as her platform touched ground the monitor leaped lightly off of it and came toward me, a stubby instrument of familiar aspect held in one hand, the dark lens pointing at my chest.

"What's going on?" she asked in a voice that was musical yet filled with authority.

I had decided on a story that kept fairly close to the truth. "This man offered himself as a guide; when I refused he grew angry. When he came at me with three companions I thought it best to strike first."

She lifted an elegantly arched eyebrow, stepped past me without taking her eyes from me or ceasing to train her weapon on me and turned over one of my assailants with a booted foot. "Their faces make good witnesses to your story," she drawled. "This one's a known tough and Wilder. If you'd come to my prowler, citizen, I'd like a statement from you."

At her gesture I preceded her to the platform, which was surmounted by a stubby, waist-high column which held blinking lights and cryptic levers. "Step on the black area, please," she said and I did so. She stepped on the platform opposite me and put a hand on the column. Suddenly we were in the air and I clutched frantically for a hand-hold which protruded from the column. "I'll return you to Castle Thorn after your statement," she said calmly. I risked a glance below to see houses spread below us like a pampered child's model city. When a bird flew under us I turned my gaze to the sky. The woman smiled slightly. "You can't fall off," she said. "The gravity effect keeps you on." I tried to look a great deal calmer than I felt, but I probably did not deceive her.

My stomach protested as we swooped down again to land. I looked around; we were on the roof of a building which towered high over the city; I could see Castle Thorn on its crag across the valley filled with houses. Suddenly an alarm bell tolled in my mind. This must be the building on "Hedwiga's Hill," the Academy as they called it. Below me, perhaps just under my feet were the apartments of Mortifer!

I must have stiffened because the woman took a step back and trained her weapon on me. "I see you've guessed something," she said. "You have two choices now, walk or be carried. It will be easier for both of us if you walk." I shrugged and followed her directions to stand on a marked area on the roof. She spoke into a small disc she took from her belt and the whole area flashed white and vanished; we sank slowly into the room below, a featureless antechamber. A door flashed into being on one wall and I was ushered into a richly furnished room. Seated on a thronelike chair was the man I had come so far to see, Mortifer the Enchanter. I was meeting him on his own terms, but at least we were face to face at last.

There was no other chair. in the room but there was a massive table not far from him; I strolled over to it and sat on its edge. Crossing my legs I waited for Mortifer to break the silence. He had to tum his head a little to see me and his lips tightened with an annoyance he could not quite hide from me.

The woman's voice came from behind me. "He laid out three of the toughs and the other took to his heels. Lucky I was there in reserve, Councillor."

Mortifer's voice was dry as he said, "You did your job, they did not. It is noted." He was always a bad leader, grudging of his praise and cruel in his reprimands.

I turned my head to look at the woman and gave her a smile. "You were quick and clever," I said. "Well played." She was so startled that she returned my smile for a moment until Mortifer's growl took the smile and the color from her face and sent her scurrying out of the room.

I turned to Mortifer. "You're better served than you deserve," I said, "as always."

He glowered, but did not rise to the bait. "You would have stood where you are standing long before this," he said, "if you had not been a stubborn maker of trouble."

"As always?" I asked blandly and his control snapped.

"Always!" he sneered in icy rage. "You are a creature of a moment; I grew you in my tanks not two years ago. What you think you remember I put into your head, except for those two years. During that time you were a puppet in a toy theater of my devising. For a while it looked as if I might learn a little from you, but interfering fools spoiled that. You're a bit of apparatus for a botched experiment; it's time to throw you on the trash pile before you do more damage."

It was something I had half feared, ever since I had heard the story of Justinian Droste's case against Mortifer and then soon after the story of young Benton's boars. Yet there was some comfort in that, if I understood it rightly. "Grown, perhaps," I said, "but from what? Did you desecrate a dead king's body for the flesh from which you grew me, Mortifer of the

Royal Academy? And if you did, can I not say that I am Casmir's flesh and Casmir's bone? Can't I say, even that I am Casmir?"

His eyes lit up with a dark glee as he replied. "Your prototype was always enamored with hair-splitting and useless metaphysics. It seems that I didn't manage to suppress that in you. Well, riddle me this, metaphysician. If growing you from Casmir's tissue samples makes you Casmir, then what about the other one I grew from those samples? If you are identical with Casmir, so is he. But things equal to the same thing are equal to each other, aren't they? So you two must be the same. But you're not; for one thing you're here and the other one is—elsewhere. So neither of you can be Casmir."

It was a shock, but it was also a triumph, for I felt sure that it had been no part of his plan to tell me of this other Casmir. Trying to keep an appearance of calm and keep pressure on Mortifer, I shrugged and drew myself up to sit tailor fashion on the table. "It doesn't follow, Mortifer; you were always weak at logic," I said mockingly. "All you've proved is that both of us can't be the original Casmir, not that one of us can't."

Weak at logic or not Mortifer had a passion for argument; I had often lured him into disputes when his lessons bored me. He leaned forward, clutching the arms of his chair, his face dark with anger. "Nonsense," he said venomously. "There's nothing to choose between you; cultured from the same sample, put in identical artificial environments, subjected to the same stimuli. That was the point of the whole thing: to show, to prove that you'd act identically, that humans are as much machines as andros are, that free will is a philosopher's dream!"

"And did you prove it?" I said mockingly, probing at the weakness I sensed behind his bluster.

His refusal to answer was itself an answer. He rose to his feet, his eyes blazing. "The experiment was botched, spoiled," he cried, "and now it's time to throw away the mess that's left."

I tensed, but my feet were not quite set—if I could only buy a moment's time . . . . Then a faint musical note sounded from the back of Mortifer's chair and a woman's voice said, "Councillor, there's a mob coming up the Hill toward the institute."

Mortifer half turned toward the chair back and said impatiently, "A mob? What has that to do with me? How dare you interrupt . . ."

The voice, which I was sure was that of the woman who had brought me here said, "Ser, they're led by a man in a scholar's robe; I think the same fellow I saw just before I landed at the Castle, talking to the man who is in there with you. And they're shouting something . . . something very odd. Something about 'Casmir's come again'."

There was a moment's silence and I could hear Mortifer grinding his teeth, a nasty habit of his when in a rage. "Prepare the disposal chamber," he said after a moment. "They'll find no Casmir here."

"But ser," the voice came, "this man is . . . you said he was little more than an andro, but . . ." I blessed the impulse that had made me praise the woman and make some sort of human contact with her. It was a good moment to improve on, that contact.

"I am a citizen of the Commonwealth," I said, baring my wrist with its green circle, hoping that the woman could see into the chamber by some spyhole. "Have you no laws against killing a citizen? Is there no punishment for that, even for Mortifer's servants? For the killer at least, even if he escapes?" My feet were nearly set now; it was hellishly uncomfortable but they were side by side under my buttocks, with enough contact with the table to give me some leverage. I slouched to give my arms as much flex as possible; my hands were flat on the table.

"I'll torch you myself!" screamed Mortifer, beginning to draw something from his garments, "and that insubordinate wench." I launched myself straight into his face, with every ounce of my strength, bringing my arms up after I leaped so that my clenched fists on either side of my head made my head and arms the head of a human battering ram.

My leap was not quite as strong as I had hoped; I struck him in the chest and not in the face. He was protected in some way. it was like hitting an image of stone but my weight and momentum could not completely be nullified by his defenses; I heard his breath whoosh out and his chair went over with a resounding crash, sending us both to the floor. I grabbed him by the arms and rolled toward the heavy table I had been sitting on. He would hardly have received me alone without guardsmen to hand but if I could get that table between me and the door and keep hold of Mortifer perhaps I could make him my hostage.

Now we were under the table. I lay with all my weight on Mortifer and kicked the table top from underneath. It toppled, and I had my barricade. Suddenly I felt Mortifer's arms move in my hands and something hard thrust into my belly. "Let go," Mortifer grated, "or I'll torch your guts out." If he could have done it without risk to himself, my racing brain told me, he would have done it, not threatened; I made as if to obey, relaxing my hold on his arms, then as he thrust me away from him, I dropped my hands to capture his and jerked suddenly upwards. Over his head, his weapon would be useless; and I could pin him again.

Suddenly there was a blinding flash; my eyes were dazzled and my face burned. I could smell my own burned hair and for a moment all I could do was hold on frantically. But then there was no strength to Mortifer's limbs, no resistance, and I raised myself to hands and knees, peering down at the ruined body below me. There was an acrid smell, but it was not the smell of burned flesh. Liquid flowed sluggishly, but it was dark, not red. I looked down, and as the dazzle cleared from my vision I saw below me the wreck of Mortifer's form. The false flesh curled back like burned parchment and beneath it was the glint of half molten metal, uncounted tiny threads of varied colors, enigmatic crystals. Mortifer, the enchanter, was a magical puppet, not human flesh and blood! Then my dazzled senses failed, my overstrained muscles relaxed and I fell to the floor, half conscous of a rending sound behind me, as the floor seemed to shake, then strike me in the face with a mighty blow.

10. UNDER THE HILLS

Firedrake Slayer: a good name to die with if one must die. As the mighty monster slipped off the edge I thrust my left hand into a rent in the wing I had made with my dirk, and plunged the dirk itself into the base of the wing, using it again as an anchor. My feet scrabbled, but could find no purchase; I hung by my hands alone as we left the ledge, and the frantic beating of the blinded beast's other wing tossed us in mad spirals. Down, down, down, nearer to death on the crags below. I was hanging below the beast; it would land on me and crush me.

A branch whipped my cheek and I suddenly smelled evergreen sap. With the greatest effort of will of my life I made my hands release their hold and I fell through the air. Branches cracked, my fall slowed, and for a second I dared to hope. Then my leg hit something solid and snapped as the branches had snapped. There was a terrible pain and I lost consciousness.

There were fevered dreams afterward that seemed to last for centuries. But one day I awoke to brightness in my eyes and the smell of bread baking somewhere. A serf's dull eyes were regarding me from a face that seemed to float above me. Then as I tried to move the face vanished and I nearly lost consciousness again in the pain from my leg and ribs and head. The room swam around me, then came into focus again; my own room at Castle Thorn. The sword of my fathers was back in its rack on the wall, a newly painted shield beside it. The arms were my own, the Sword and Crown, but without the "file", the "difference" which marked me as the oldest son of the king. That shield should be borne by my father, not by me. I was staring dully at the shield, my mind refusing to work, when Stanislaus, the court physician, bustled into the room, his face beaming.

"Hail, firedrake slayer!" he said. "Hail, Casmir, protector of the kingdom! Rest now and heal. All is well." I must have made some feeble gesture toward the shield, because his face became grave. "Your father's heart could not hold the sorrow of your peril and the joy of your victory without bursting," he said solemnly. "Casmir the Ninth is dead. Long live King Casmir, Tenth of the Line!" That was too much and I lapsed into unconsciousness again.

After that were long lazy days and nights with less pain and fewer nightmares. Delora came to me once or twice, suitably chaperoned, and laid a cool hand on my brow. Her skin was reddened and her eyebrows and lashes scorched away, but she was lovely as ever. Her thanks were flowery, but had little real warmth behind them and a dull irritation stirred under my lethargy. She was lovely but was there a real woman behind that beautiful facade? I remembered . . . what did I remember? Laughing faces, tender looks . . . . Were they real memories, or fantasies? I slept again.

Little triumphs marked my days; cutting my own meat, being supported, none too gently, by two serfs as I got out of bed to use the garderobe. There was a day when I knew that I had my life back, if not all my strength; I was a man who had been broken and was weak, no longer a broken man. It was on that day my old life ended.

I was lying in my bed in a sort of restful doze, postponing the moment that I would have to take up the reins of power. Mortifer was away and that gave me time to drift and heal. As soon as he returned there would be a test of wills, one I meant to win. My father's age and weakness—yes weakness, I could call it by its name now—no longer put me in Mortifer's power. I was no longer his pupil and would never be his puppet. I was determined to show him that. If only the Falling Sickness did not betray me, as it had done before in confrontations with Mortifer.

Suddenly I realized that the small noises of the everyday functioning of the castle had ceased. I looked over at the serf who stood by the door ready to summon help or run errands. He was unnaturally still and as I gazed at him I realized that he was not breathing, not even blinking. The hair rose on the back of my neck and my skin tingled. Enchantment! Mortifer must be back, and this must be his way of attack, sudden, swift and silent. Was I, too, paralyzed? No, I felt as fit and able as ever. As blood coursed in my body in response to the challenge I felt fitter than I had since my fight with the firedrake. I leaped to my feet, and ripped my sword and shield from the wall. I thrust my feet into the soft boots beside the bed and tiptoed to the door.

It opened silently; the hinges had been well-oiled, not to disturb a wounded man's sleep. In the corridor a serf and a mirror courtier stood frozen like statues. I crept softly past them, my ears straining for any sound. There! That could only be the gates of the Great Hall being opened; I would know that creak and groan anywhere. A small stair not far along this corridor would bring me out onto the dais; it was a way for the royal family to slip away from a feast that went on too long. Should I take a more indirect way? No! The King of Carpathia should face his enemies boldly, not creep like a rat in his own hold!

They were standing in the center of the Great Hall, a little knot of men in strange garments. Their leader was not Mortifer, but a man I had never seen before in strange close-fitting garments of green so dark it was almost black in some lights. Behind him was a man in brown with a strange object, which, gleamed and sparkled . . . in his hands? No, floating in the air before him! Enchantments!

They had not seen me yet; they were gaping around the Hall. I stepped suddenly out onto the dais, letting my sword touch my shield to make a small ringing sound. Every eye turned to me, but no one made a hostile move. The green-clad leader looked at me impassively, but the man in brown gasped, "The same man—the same in every detail!"

The leader said in a steady voice, "That was what we might have expected, given what else we know.'" He turned his gray eyes to me and said, "I am Justinian Droste. You are . . . Casmir?"

I nodded, trying to keep my face impassive. "Casmir, King of Carpathia, Tenth of the Line. And you, I suppose, are creatures of Mortifer's?"

The man named Justinian Droste gave a short laugh and said with apparent sincerity, "We're no friends to Mortifer, King Casmir. In fact, we're here to help you against Mortifer, if you'll let us. Help you in ways you can hardly guess at yet."

I lifted a skeptical eyebrow at them. "And what do you want in return for your—help?" All the same my blood was pounding in excitement. Mortifer was powerful and wily; despite all my royal power and authority I had half-feared the issue of any struggle between us. But with a rival gang of enchanters on my side, perhaps I could break Mortifer, break him and banish him as I had longed to do ever since he had wormed his way into my father's confidence.

Droste looked into my eyes and said softly, "We want to bring Mortifer down. Just that. Will you help us?"

I held his eyes for a long moment and then nodded slowly.

"If I can do it without prejudice to my people and my kingdom, I will."

Justinian Droste sighed. "Your people and your kingdom, yes. I'm afraid that's the first shock I have for you. But after the mistakes we made last time I'm determined to tell you everything. Perhaps it's easier to show you than to tell you, though." He walked over to the side of the hall; one of the castle serfs was frozen there where he had been wiping a table. Droste took a small globe from a pouch at his waist and pressed it, making a fine mist issue from a small orifice at one side of the globe. Droste directed the spray at his own hand and rubbed it lightly into the wrist. "This stuff is harmless," he said; "just a solvent for a common adhesive. Notice that it does nothing to the hair on the back of my hand."

He stepped over to the serf, lifted the fellow's shock of hair and sprayed under it. Then he pulled gently and the whole shock of hair came off in his hand. Under it was a dome of gleaming metallic blue, like a skullcap, coming almost to the serf's eyebrows. Justinian Droste stepped back and nodded to the man in brown who touched the blue dome with a small glittering object, then put both of his hands on the dome and gave it a sharp twist. The whole top of the serf's head came off in his hands and he laid it on the table the serf had been wiping. The thing was like a mushroom; the "stem" had been inside the lower part of the serf's head.

"A control unit," said Droste. "This is a fairly standard low-level general purpose android, generally called an 'andro.' All of the servitors in this place are of the same type; they haven't even bothered to give them false foreheads under that mop of hair. I take it that you've been conditioned not to pay much attention to servitors, so they didn't take much trouble with them." He turned to the man in brown. "Andres, give me the stat of the plot of the other place." He studied a sheet of what looked like parchment or stiff cloth for a moment then said formally, "Follow me, please, King Casmir."

"Wait," I said. "This—thing—is not flesh and blood? It is a . . . puppet, moved by magical arts?" Droste nodded, his face grave. I laid my shield on the table and gripped my sword. Trying to think of what remained of the serf as no more than a lay figure for practice, I swung the sword over my head and dealt the thing a mighty blow. What was left of the head and one shoulder and arm bounced to the floor. There was no blood and no bone, only the gleam of metal, the glitter of some sort of crystal, and a tangle of multicolored threads and tubes. "Yes," I said, dully, "yes, the thing is what you said."

"By the Mercy," said the man in brown, whom Droste had called Andres. "If you went on 3V with that act, you'd make a fortune." Droste gave him a sharp look and he fell silent, following Droste and myself as we headed for the main staircase out of the Hall. I stole a glance at the glittering object he pushed along with him; without a doubt it did float in the air.

Droste led me to an ornamental door and turned. "What is behind this door, King Casmir?" he asked. "Have you ever been inside it?"

I shook my head. "It is the Ladies' Suite," I said, "the Solar, the bedchambers of the unmarried court ladies, sewing rooms and the like. As a bachelor knight it is all forbidden territory to me."

Droste nodded soberly, "Much of the castle is, is it not, on one pretext or another? Let's look inside the door." It resisted and Andres applied another of his glittering instruments to it. The door swung open, revealing a large gray chamber with no windows and no other doors. The walls were perfectly smooth and the room was without any furniture. Around the walls stood a dozen or so women, some in the dress of court ladies, others garbed as upper servants. All the faces were familiar; women I was used to seeing about the castle. Droste stepped over to the nearest, sprayed at the hairline and lifted the hair to reveal a blue dome. A flap of skinlike stuff peeled away from the forehead, revealing the blue.

"These are what are called 'gynas'," said Droste quietly. "They're replicas of real women, and a great deal more detailed physically than a GP andro like the servitors. Ordinarily they're only used for, well, rather discreditable purposes. Some of the male courtiers are probably from similar sources, but women generally have more sense than to . . . well it does happen though. But probably some of them are custom-made, both male and female. The resources of a good-sized planet were open to the people who constructed this place. If you'll come out onto the battlements with me I'll show you more." As I followed him out into the hallway he said, "There are no children here, are there?"

I shook my head. "We sent them away when the firedrakes came. They don't seem to fly across the river. That's why the Castle is so empty, my father didn't want to separate families more than could be helped . . ." My voice died away.

Justinian Droste said dryly, "There's very little call for child-size andros, and no tapes for childlike behavior. Their resources weren't unlimited. Speaking of the, ah, firedrakes, how many have you seen close up at one time? More than one?" I shook my head and Droste nodded. "We only found one," he said, "That must have been custom-made. Someone had done it quite a bit of damage, though. Ah, here's the way out onto the battlements. Do you notice anything odd?"

I looked around me at the familiar scene. Around the horizon were the circling mountains; below us at the foot of the Castle Crag were the huts and cottages of Thorn village. Across the valley was what was now being called the Mount of Sacrifice, a name of ill-omen. But that was . . . . Suddenly something about the clouds struck me. There was almost always a wind at Castle Thorn, especially at this time of year. I had hardly ever seen the clouds completely still at Thorn, even in midsummer. But now the clouds were utterly motionless, as if on a blazing midsummer day.

"We're underground here, King Casmir," said Droste's voice in my ear. "The sky and clouds are holographic projections; so is most of the more distant scenery. Normally the cloud movement would be following a taped program but the little gadget that Andres is taking care of so assiduously stops all motion which depends on—well, certain electronic processes which are rather basic. I take it that you've been able to leave the castle very little and on those occasions you'll have gone north or roughly east."

At my stupefied look he shrugged lightly. "Those are side caverns," he said, "some of the scenery there is real. Any other direction you'd soon run into rock."

"But when I was a boy I ranged all over the countryside," I burst out. "!t's only the last two years that we've been hemmed in like this."

Droste's tone was less somber as he said, "Two years, yes. That seems to be the time that this has been going on. Before that your memories are probably genuine, though they've been tampered with."

The state of shocked lethargy gave way to a surge of hope.

"Then all this is just some sort of spell cast over me for the last two years?" I asked. "Of course, that's when Mortifer came with his warning of the firedrakes. When they came as he predicted my father would hear nothing against him. But I never trusted him. What did he do—kidnap me and imprison me here? The kingdom . . . my father . . . are they . . . ?" Hope died as I saw the look on Droste's face. I swallowed a lump in my throat and faltered. "In some of the old tales they say that men taken under the hills by the elvish folk have returned to find their friends grown old or dead; that a year with them under the hills is many years in the world of mortals. Is it . . . something like that?"

"Not quite, perhaps," said Droste gently. "But as nearly that as you're ready to hear now, I think."

"How long?" I asked, making my voice as strong as I could.

Droste's eyes met mine as he said quietly, "As nearly as we can tell, from the time of your last genuine memory until now is about five hundred years."

11. A DOUBLE TALE

After that I was too dazed to put up much resistance to what they asked of me. I followed the man named Justinian Droste to a part of the battlements which, because it overlooked the Ladies Court, was normally forbidden to bachelor knights. A sort of bridge made of some gray metallic substance extended from the battlements to . . . I rubbed my eyes and looked again. A long arrow's flight away there was a jagged hole in the sky itself, and the metal bridge disappeared into it! Beyond the hole there was a gray-walled corridor which reminded me of the room in which the immobile "court ladies" had stood.

"Block out the bridge and the gap with your hand, then take it away," said Droste quietly. "Then you'll get some idea of the tricks of perspective which they used in building this place." I did as he said. When my hand covered the bridge and the hole I seemed to be looking out into a broad vista of mountains beyond the valley in which Castle Crag stood. But when I took my hand away I could see that the sky and mountains were some sort of picture, marvelously done, and that a strongly shot arrow could easily have struck that "sky."

The bridge was narrow but steady as a rock as I put my foot on it. "You wish me to go this way?" I asked Droste, and he nodded. Half expecting to fall through the bridge or find myself in some unimaginable heaven or hell when I had crossed it, I walked over the bridge, with only a glance at what seemed to be the abyss below me. I have always had a good head for heights, but the feeling that I was in a waking dream helped take away any apprehension I might have felt at the strange bridge and its impossible terminus.

The "sky" seemed to be made of some translucent stuff, some of which lay in shards on the floor of the gray corridor. I picked up a shard and looked at it, feeling as if I were a child in a nursery-story dream. The corridor itself was drably utilitarian, with smooth gray walls and a slightly resilient floor of somewhat darker gray. Droste came over the bridge behind me and walked along by my side. After a long stretch of corridor we came to a great circular space larger than the inside of the castle keep. Above us there was no roof; we stood as if at the bottom of a great well. The circle of blue high above was no larger than a shield. "That's the real sky," said Droste.

In the middle of the circular space were two great metal discs on which stood glittering machines and chairs which looked luxuriously soft. Seated in a chair near the center of the disc was a woman in close-fitting garments like Droste's; she faced a glittering array of lights and switches on a sort of table before her. As we walked toward the disc she turned toward us, and her whole chair swiveled to match her movement; a minor marvel, but one which startled me more than some of the greater marvels I had seen. "Citizen Droste?" she said sharply, seeing my sword; her hands moved sharply toward one part of the array of lights and switches before her.

"It's all right," said Droste reassuringly and I felt a small spurt of amusement as I realized that the woman must have thought that I had taken Droste captive. In fact, I was captive, not to his weapons, for he had shown none, but to my own ignorance. Until I knew more—much more—I did not dare to take action. But time and observation are great healers of ignorance; I could wait.

Droste waved me courteously to a seat on the platform and said to the woman, "Take us on in to the city; General Hospital. Andres will take the rest of the party back on the cargo disc." The woman looked a little dubiously at my sword, which I had laid across my knees for lack of a better place to put it, but gave a sort of salute and busied herself at her table, Suddenly I realized that the ground had dropped away and that we were rising in the shaft like a bucket in the well I had likened it to.

As we cleared the rim of the shaft I saw about me low arid hills and scrubby vegetation. We continued to rise until we were high above the hills, with the mouth of the shaft we had come out of only a small dark circle. Then the platform began to move smoothly and silently above the ground. We were moving away from the sun, which if this new world was anything like the one I was used to, meant that we were going east or west. But the dry desert landscape and clear sky gave me no hint whether it was morning or evening.

Presently I could see ahead of us what I thought at first was a curious group of mountain peaks. Then a certain regularity of shape and arrangement told me that these were monstrous buildings, each not only bigger than Castle Thorn but bigger than Castle Crag, Castle Thorn and all. There seemed to be parks and gardens at the foot of the towers, and one great stretch of what seemed to be greensward, looking oddly out of place in the desert setting. The woman spoke into the air as we approached the towers and was answered by a disembodied voice. Her hands played among the levers on her table and she said to Droste, "We'll have to loop around the starport; a starship is lifting and their GE fields can interfere even at this distance; it's a big cargo ship."

Droste nodded and leaned forward to look at the stretch of greensward, which we were now swerving to pass on our right. From the green area a gigantic black disc began to rise into the air. As it rose I thought that I could feel a faint tremor in our own flight, but that was soon gone as the black disc rose higher and higher until it dwindled into a dot in the sky. "Ever want to flit?" Droste asked the woman.

She shook her head with a smile. "Home is good enough for me," she said. "The operational height of this little buggy is as far as I want to get from Mother Earth."

Droste smiled back at her and turned to me. "You're coming out into a wider world in more senses than one, King Casmir," he said. "'Wider than you can know now."

I laughed shortly. "So it would seem, ser," I said. "No need to call me King, though; it is clear enough that my kingdom down under the hills was only a mummery, and my true throne gone to others these many years. The family name of the lords of Thorn is Jagellon; that, I suppose, is still mine."

"Indeed," said Droste with a curious note in his voice. Could it be pity? But he went on in a serious tone. "You know better than I what you have lost," he said. "But there is plenty for you to thank the Mercy for. I've seen other people from pre-tech societies meet our modern gadgetry for the first time and show everything from panic, to fear to religious awe, to retreat into insanity. And it's worse for you because of the way you've been deceived for the past two years and the sudden way you learned of it. But you've hardly turned a hair."

It was an odd phrase but I could see that he meant that I had shown no sign of fear or amazement. What else, I wondered, did he expect from a knight of Thorn? But perhaps he knew as little of the knights of Thorn as I of what he termed "gadgetry".

I tried to keep that impassivity he had praised as our flying disc rushed toward one of the great towers, lifting at the last possible moment to come to rest on a broad flat roof at the top of the tower. As the woman dropped her hands from her table of lights she cast me a glance; I thought that in her own way she had been testing my courage. I grinned at her and she was startled into an answering smile. I heard and felt a brisk breeze blowing at the top of the tower and realized that a sort of barely perceivable thickening of the air which had surrounded our disc in flight had now vanished.

"This is a hospital, a place of healing," said Droste. "With your permission our Healers will give you a quick going over and see what sort of shape you're in. You show the signs of freshly healed hurts." I nodded without showing any emotion, but a sudden stab of hope shot through me. Whatever these people were, enchanters or something else, they seemed to have powers that would have been called magical in Carpathia. Their healing arts must be well advanced beyond anything known in my homeland. Perhaps, perhaps they could heal me of the Falling Sickness and make me a whole man again. I had often thought that I would trade my kingdom for freedom from the Falling Sickness; perhaps my wish had been strangely granted.

I followed Droste over to a part of the roof that seemed no different from the rest except that it had a large circle painted on it. We came to a halt and I looked at Droste in puzzlement, but suddenly the part of the roof within the circle flashed white and then began to sink slowly. I could not quite check an instinctive movement and Droste said quietly, "Just another means of transportation. It will take us down to the examining room." I nodded and rested my hands on the hilt of my sword, noting as I did so that the sword point went a little way into the material below my feet. Perhaps at need I could hack my way out of any place I wanted free of.

But when the sinking circle stopped in a room filled with more gleaming objects across which lights flashed I was faced with a small woman with an untidy mop of gray hair, clothed in a close-fitting white garment. "Please put the sword and your outer garments on the table there and come over to the examination area," she said crisply, and I obeyed meekly. She reminded me strongly of my old nurse and I could imagine her reaction if I demanded to keep my sword.

The "examining area" was another circle on the floor, but this one did not move. I stood within it and my skin tingled, then turned hot and cold as the gray-haired woman moved from one to another of the small tables and chests which ringed the circle on which I stood. Another woman dressed in white came from somewhere else in the room and looked at me in surprise. I concealed my own surprise, for her skin was darker than that of an old herdsman burned by the suns of many summers, and her hair was a mass of tightly coiled black ringlets. After the first surprise of her appearance I found her beautiful in her own way and I gave her a smile. She smiled back and said, "Hello, Casmir."

"Perhaps you'd better tell him how you happen to know his name," said Justinian Droste, who had been standing in the background.

The dark woman said, "We met about a month ago when I was on night duty at Central Receiving Hospital in Alba Cirque. He hadn't seen a dark-skinned person before and we talked a little about that. He was a bit worried about a history of what sounded like epileptic seizures. but from the nervepath scarring it looked as if someone had used a neural interrupter on him repeatedly over a period of a couple of years. They were treating him with Lysergol and the scarring should be . . . Oh!"

She was looking at the surface of one of the tables and her face was troubled. "The scarring is back, as bad as ever!" she said. "I don't see how that's possible, in fact I'd say it was medically impossible. Unless . . ." She looked at me with a question in her eyes.

"No, my Lady," I said. "I have not seen you before—to my loss," I turned to Droste, "It seems that I have a double," I told him.

He nodded, his face grim. "Not only you but the whole setup in which we found you." Some things which he and the man called Andres had said flashed through my mind: "The same man," Andres had said, and Droste had spoken of a map of "the other place" as a guide to Castle Thorn.

There was an indrawn breath from the dark woman and she said softly, "The Mortifer case!"

I caught her eyes and spoke gently, but with authority. "You have guessed something, Lady. Can you riddle me this riddle?"

She looked gravely into my eyes and said, "You and the man I met must be clones, duplicates grown from the cells of a prototype. There are new techniques for retrieving memories from the cellular record of the prototype; that was what Academician Mortifer was experimenting with, from the reports I've heard. Experiments have been done on animals but experimentation on humans is strictly forbidden by Commonwealth law, and clones have the same rights as naturalborns." Her eyes went to Droste.

"You're Justinian Droste, aren't you?" she asked, "of the Citizen's Liberties Union? Your group tracked down Mortifer's experiments and denounced him to the authorities."

Droste nodded and turned to me. "You had to know sooner or later," he said, "and perhaps this is as good a way as any. Our group, as Nurse Nerere says, is opposed to experimentation on human beings—or sapient beings of any species for that matter. Most attempts at such experimentation need rather elaborate technological support; we have ways of getting to know about such things. Not long ago we got on the track of Mortifer's experiments. First we found the first cavern, with your double and an identical setup to the one we took you from. We arrived at a rather dramatic moment, in fact."

He hesitated, then went on. "I'll tell you about that another time. Anyway, we investigated the setup and found some rather curious relay equipment. Eventually we traced the relays and found your cavern. There don't seem to be any more. So far as I can tell, Mortifer had set up two identical men in identical surroundings and was subjecting them to identical stimuli. What he hoped to prove I'm not sure."

I looked at my hands, at what I could see of my body. "Then I am . . . a . . . a homunculus?" I asked. "Made by Mortifer in the image of some real man?" My voice I think I kept steady, but only with a tremendous effort.

"No," said the dark woman fiercely, "you're as human as any of us; you've just been birthed by a more elaborate process. Ordinary conception uses cells from both parents; your cells are taken only from your prototype. But his cells contain genetic coding from two parents. Probably the most sensible way to look at it is that you, your double and your prototype are identical triplets, except that the prototype was born first and by more traditional means."

"Your humanity is recognized by the Commonwealth," said Droste, "and I'll soon give you evidence of that. For that matter it's recognized by the church your prototype belonged to, if that matters to you. It would have to him; he was a devout man by all accounts. But Mortifer might have interfered with those memories; it would fit what I know of the man."

I was calmer now, not only because of their words but because I was realizing that no matter what my birth I was alive and in possession of my powers. Then another dismaying thought struck me. "My . . . prototype . . . he must be . . ."

Droste nodded and said calmly, "Dead these five hundred years. But before he died he unified Carpathia; he's remembered as the greatest of their kings. And your double gave signs of some rather unusual talents before he disappeared."

I gazed at him in consternation, suddenly realizing how much I had been looking forward to seeing my other self. "Disappeared?" I said.

Droste nodded. "He left Central Receiving soon after Nurse Nerere talked to him. At first we thought he'd been kidnapped, but it seems he foiled a kidnap attempt on his own and went . . . exploring . . . . We've traced him as far as Carpathia, the real Carpathia. But the trail ends there; he seems to have vanished completely after the destruction of Mortifer's laboratory."

12. THE JAGELLON GIFT

I glanced sharply at Droste. "Mortifer is a man of these times then?" I asked.

Droste shrugged. "Perhaps of these times and the times of Casmir the Tenth," he said. "There's a Mortifer in many of the old tales and legends of Carpathia. It may just be a family name, but there seems to be no record of a young Mortifer or a father and son Mortifer alive at the same time. We have techniques for extending life; what's popularly called Lifestretch. The ordinary limit is about three hundred years, but Mortifer knows a lot about the life sciences. Perhaps he's found a way to extend his own life even longer; perhaps he's even cloned himself and transferred memories. We just don't know."

"So the Mortifer I remember . . ." I said slowly.

"May be a mixture of memories of the 'original' Mortifer and the one alive today, if they aren't the same man," said Droste. "But there's one further complication. As far as we can guess as to what he was up to Mortifer's plan must have involved giving you and your double the same experiences at the same times. When you and your double both saw Mortifer at least one of them must have been an android. There's something called a repeating android, which is a duplicate of a human keyed to exactly duplicate the actions taken by that human. A ruler who feared assassination might have a duplicate throne room built, hidden away somewhere. In the hidden room he might interact with holovision pictures of the people in the real room; they would see the android do just the actions the ruler was performing. But if an assassin torched the android the ruler would be unharmed."

"So Mortifer, too, has a double," I said slowly, as my mind raced over the possible implications of this.

"Perhaps not any longer," said Droste. "We found the remains of a repeating android in the ruins of Mortifer's laboratory. Perhaps he has another up his sleeve though; he certainly has enough accumulated wealth and expertise to build a dozen of them. His duplicates, however, can only do what the real Mortifer is doing. Your double is another human being, very much like you but free and independent. Even if it's true, as some claim, that clones given identical stimuli would act the same, he's had thirty days of experiences you haven't had. But I'm inclined myself to believe that clones are individual persons who could react differently even given the same history and environment."

"Be that as it may," I said. "I have a good idea of what my double is doing now. He pursued Mortifer to—what did you call it?—his laboratory. When he found only this duplicating thing you told me of I think that he must have continued to pursue the real Mortifer. Find Mortifer and you'll find the other Casmir not far behind him, I suspect."

Justinian Droste gave me a wry smile. "We've been hunting Mortifer ever since we first had evidence of his experiments," he said. "Your double had better luck than we did. My best plan now is to give you every assistance I can and let you see if you can duplicate the success of the other Casmir. And may the Mercy help Mortifer if either of you catch him! First things first though." He turned to the gray-haired woman. "Does he need any treatment?" he asked.

The woman surveyed me with a disgruntled air. "Oh, he's healthy enough," she said. "I've seldom seen a better physical specimen. I'd like to give him an injection of Lysergol for that nerve-path scarring. Normally it's not policy to let anyone with that in their blood out of custody since the Lysergol will inhibit the action of a neural interrupter. In this case I presume that's something of an advantage."

I looked to the dark woman for an explanation and she did not fail me. "A neural interrupter is a device which can render you unconscious; our peace officers use it for social control. Both you and your double have had one used on you repeatedly. I suspect that Mortifer simply rendered you unconscious when something started to go wrong in his experiments. That would account for the 'falling sickness' that the other Casmir described. As I told him, there's no organic reason for you to suffer fainting spells."

My heart leaped; this made up for much. "My thanks, Lady," I said. "When my quest is done I would like to thank you more adequately." I turned to Droste. "This land is strange to me," I told him. "I'll find Mortifer but it will be quicker if you help."

He nodded. "You'll have all the help that the Citizen's Liberty Union can give you," he said, "and to begin with, I'd like to register you as a citizen of the Commonwealth. It obliges you to keep our laws. But I think you'll find those simple and reasonable enough. In return you'll have the privileges of a citizen, which include a basic allowance of credit for food and other necessities. Anything beyond that you'll have to earn by your own efforts. But I have the authority to put you on staff as a temporary investigator for the CLU; we can cover your expenses and even pay you a modest wage. By the time you find Mortifer I suspect you will have found a place in our society that you want to occupy."

I hesitated but then agreed. I knew nothing of the laws of this land and perhaps it was rash to agree to obey them, but from what I had seen of Droste and the others they seemed decent folk; I thought that I could live by the laws they lived by. I was asked to put my hand on a gray box and repeat my name. "Casmir the King . . ." I began, then stopped, remembering what my kingdom consisted of. "Casmir T. King", said a voice from the box. Then a light flashed and the voice said, "Duplicate file, Casmir F. Thorn".

"I could have told you that," said the gray-haired woman. "The C and C chip keys on the genotype; when I worked in Maternity we always had trouble recording identical twins. The simplest thing to do immediately is to key it as a lost chip replacement until you can get it straightened out with Central." Droste nodded and she did something to the box that caused the light to go out. I felt a faint tingle on my wrist and when I raised my hand from the box I found a circular patch of blue on my wrist.

The dark woman came to my aid again. "It's just a patch of stuff that sticks to your skin," she said. "Move it around to avoid skin irritation. If you want to buy anything you'll put your patch in contact with a terminal and credit will be transferred from your personal account. Any credit you earn will probably be transferred directly to your account. The color of the patch indicates your credit balance. Green is normal; yellow and orange indicate increasing depletion of the account and red means that you're broke. Blue, indigo and violet indicate increasing credit surplus. Since yours is blue I presume that the CLU has already credited you for the job they want you to do."

"No," broke in Droste, "we haven't." He gave a short laugh. "Since this is a duplicate chip that must mean that the other Casmir has earned a credit surplus somehow. Furthermore that credit surplus either originated here at Home or else a surcharge was paid to post it in Central Credit. I think we can stop worrying about your double, Casmir King; he seems to be doing very well in our society."

Before they let me go free from the "hospital" they held a thing to my arm which they said would put a healing liquid in my blood and subjected me to a few more of their glittering boxes. I used the opportunity to find that the dark woman' s name was Molly Nerere and that she could always be reached through Central Receiving Hospital in Alba Cirque. At last I was allowed to leave with Droste; we ascended again to the roof and took our flying disc again to another monstrous building. Another sinking disc took us to a corridor with several doors. At Droste's instruction I pressed my wrist with its colored patch on a shining metallic plaque near one door. The door flashed white and vanished and we walked into a room with a bed, table and chairs, decorated in muted colors.

"This is a fairly standard transient hostel room," said Droste. "You can pay more for something more luxurious if you like but that's on your personal credit; the CLU will credit your account to cover this." He moved about the room, showing me how to get food from a niche in the wall and cleanse myself in what he called the "convenience." "If I were you I'd rest for a while," Droste told me. "The oval patch on the wall is called a View; if you press the contact on the bed frame there it will show you pictures that you may find interesting. It's for entertainment more than for education but you can learn quite a bit from watching it. I'll be back in the morning with what information I can get on Mortifer and on 'Casmir Thorn.' You're certainly free to leave the room and wander around the city but I think you may have had enough culture shock for one day."

I was suddenly conscious of a great weariness. As soon as Droste left me I flung myself on the bed and fell asleep almost immediately, though my dreams were troubled. When I awoke I broke my fast to the accompaniment of music and a picture of a rushing mountain stream; the result of my first experiment with the "View." It made me long for the woods of my boyhood, or rather, I realized, the boyhood of King Casmir the Tenth of Carpathia.

I thought of leaving the room then but the thought of the mistakes I might make in finding my way about discouraged me. Instead I began to see what I could learn from the "View." The solid-looking, marvelously realistic pictures it showed soon fascinated me and when Droste returned he found me propped up on the bed watching the pictures.

He laughed when he saw what I was watching. "They call those 'soaps' for some reason," he said.

"They're dramas of domestic life; a very good choice for learning some everyday things about our society. I can't get over how quickly both you and the other Casmir have adapted yourself to our way of life. Ability to adapt is one component of intelligence of course, but it's more than that. Most people are strongly conditioned by their culture; they expect things to go a certain way and react with confusion or hostility if things aren't as they expect."

I shrugged. "The change from my old life was so drastic and so sudden that there was no choice except to learn quickly and to seize every opportunity," I said.

Droste laughed again. "Well, your double certainly seized every opportunity. So far as we can reconstruct his adventures this is what happened; an attempt was made to kidnap him from the hospital in Alba Cirque by a man disguised as an android by wearing a blue cap that simulated the blue dome of an android control unit. The other Casmir overpowered the kidnapper and left him in his own hospital bed, then made his way out of the hospital. Then somehow he hooked up with a rather criminal type named Joseph Pellow who was also disguised as an android. Apparently Pellow was attempting to spy on or steal from a rich merchant, Flavia Lorne, by using the android disguise. However, Lorne is none too honest herself; she involved your double in a scheme to impersonate her cousin. She was on the brink of financial ruin and the idea was to convince her creditors that her wealthy cousin was on good terms with her and would back her financially. The other Casmir used his impersonation to make friends with a wealthy trader named Benton who is an enthusiast for hunting wild animals. The other Casmir so impressed Benton and his sister Mirianne that they used their business connections to get him starpassage to Carpathia. Have you realized, Casmir, that the real Carpathia is a world circling another star?"

I nodded somberly. "Putting together some half-legendary lore preserved by the Knights of Thorn with what I've seen on the View, I've realized that this is not the world I remember. In fact, it can only be Earth, the place where the human race originated."

Justinian Droste looked at me in amazement. "No wonder your prototype was able to unify a planet; your ability to make use of scraps of information is truly extraordinary. Most people call this planet simply 'Home' now; a fashion that started in the colonies but spread back to Earth. Carpathia is what we call a 'terranorm' planet, very much like Earth, which is why it was colonized."

"What happened to the other Casmir on Carpathia?" I asked.

Droste shook his head, his face somber. "We know very little," he said. "He appeared one day at Castle Thorn and created considerable furor by taking a sword out of a lock field on the tomb of Casmir the Tenth. The lock field was keyed to Casmir the Tenth, so of course either you or your double could retrieve objects from it. Apparently your double used the sword to fight off some sort of attack prompted by Mortifer. Then an agent of Mortifer's, pretending to be a monitor—a peace officer—got him to go to Mortifer's laboratory, probably by trickery. A young scholar your double had befriended used the incident with the sword to raise a mob to try to rescue him from Mortifer. But when they broke into the laboratory the place looked as if it had been destroyed by a series of explosions and there was no sign of any human being; only the destroyed repeater android."

I looked at Droste. "And that's the end of the story?" I asked. The story had told me one thing that Justinian Droste seemed to have missed. The other Casmir evidently had, and was putting to good use, the Jagellon gift for inspiring personal loyalty in people after a very brief contact. Each of the people the other Casmir had come into contact with had done everything in their power to help him. Some of them, no doubt, had convinced themselves that they were using the other Casmir for their own purposes, but all of them had served his purpose. Droste himself, if he but knew it, was serving me as well as if he had been my sworn man. The responsibility that goes with the Jagellon gift is to see that no one suffers by serving us.

Droste was speaking in reply to my last question. "The only person we haven't managed to contact is the captain of *Argo*, the starship that took your double to Carpathia. She's taken her ship on a trading tour of the more primitive worlds and there's no way to contact her without a tremendous expenditure of credit. The trail of both Mortifer and the other Casmir seems to end on Carpathia."

"So be it," I said. "To Carpathia I will go."

"Well, I suppose we can arrange that," said Droste with a show of reluctance. "You seem to be our only hope of catching up with Mortifer."

"Oh, I'll catch up with him," I said absently, remembering that Mortifer was one of the few men I had met who was able to resist the Jagellon gift. "But what happens then is less certain. When the boar turns to bay then he is most dangerous."

13. THE BRIDGE

Star traveling is no great matter if you travel, as I traveled to Carpathia, as a passenger on a gigantic passenger and cargo ship. The physical and emotional effects of "flitting" had been carefully explained to me by Justinian Droste and I exercised my body strenuously in the place provided on the starship. It was little used, and most of my fellow passengers seemed to spend their time inactive in their cabins. There was a View in my cabin with a variety of stories in pictures; by watching those intended for children I increased considerably my knowledge of the age I found myself in.

Droste had warned me what to expect, and when we were landing and the View showed me the sprawling city which surrounds Castle Crag and the unchanged Castle Thorn, I was in emotional freeze. I had been instructed by Droste that most "emotional therapists" who visited starships on landing were worse than useless, but if by any chance there was a Caphellan among them it could probably free me from the emotional freeze immediately, especially if I had been physically active on the voyage. It turned out that one did come aboard and I secured its services.

The very sight of the creature was almost enough to release my emotions though I had seen nonhuman sapients on the View. It was like a skeleton loosely draped in motheaten fur. From its round head three pale blue eyes looked at me with what seemed to me to be insolence and I growled at the creature, "Well, do what you're paid for—if you can!" Suddenly I realized that I was *feeling*. Boredom and impatience flooded through me; the first emotion I had felt since we had entered quasi-space.

The creature blinked. I felt surprised and then realized I was feeling its surprise. Then waves of tranquil happiness engulfed me. "I beg your pardon," said the Caphellan. "You are extremely sensitive to emotion, for a human. I did not realize that you would pick up my impatience with a task I perform only to earn credit to support my studies at the Academy of Life Sciences here. Are you by any chance a human from Chrysenomia?"

"No," I replied with a smile. "I am of Carpathian stock. Tell me a little about the Academy."

The creature blinked and was silent for a moment, then it began to scuttle backwards out of the cabin. "You are sending out a very strong emotional binding," it said. "I do not choose to be subjected to it. Seek your information elsewhere." It was gone before I could say a word, and it had not collected its very substantial fee. I would gladly have paid twice the fee for the very valuable information it had given me; the Jagellon Gift could affect nonhumans too. Justinian Droste had told me that the Caphellans were what he called "empaths": they could sense the emotions of others and make others share their own emotions. It was not surprising that such a creature sensed the operation of the Jagellon Gift but the most significant thing was that it seemed to have no defense against it but retreat. Mortifer, though, seemed immune to the Gift, so others might well be; I had better not be overconfident.

Helped considerably by having watched a View sequence for children on "Your First Starflit," I got my gear from the purser and carried it to the starport transient hostel where I secured a room. Here the procedure was somewhat different than when Droste had helped me secure a room at the transient hostel on the planet I was beginning to think of as Home. Comparatively few people were able to travel from star to star, and the colored patches worked only on the planet on which you were registered. For a stiff fee you could transfer registration but most starflitters carried small golden circlets called ecus which were an interstellar medium of exchange. When I pressed one of these ecus to the plate beside the door of the hostel room its gold color faded and it became worthless. For the three days I had paid for I was the master of the room; it would open only to the touch of my thumb on the plate. Food and drink came with the room at no extra fee, but if I did not choose to use them I would receive no credit. The View sequence for children had explained all this at somewhat tedious length, but in emotional freeze I had felt no boredom, and I was glad for the information now.

Mortifer's quarters and "laboratory" had been at the Academy of Life Sciences, not an easy place for a layman to enter, from what Droste had told me. For that reason I had jumped at the chance that the Caphellan seemed to offer for an entree. But that scheme had failed. My only other point of reference was Castle Thorn itself; I might as well start there. It was easy enough to get there; free tours ran from the hostel to the castle, using discs which skimmed the ground rather than flying through the air. Whether they could fly at need was one of the many things I needed to know more of.

Hats were little worn in these days, for most garments had hoods which could be unfolded from their collars at need. But some men and women wore hats for show if not for necessity, and when Justinian Droste had helped me to buy clothing I had selected a wide-brimmed affair which shaded my face and hid my hair. Anyone who looked closely at my face would identify me with the other Casmir, but I was safe from a casual glance. I had a healthy respect for Mortifer; whether or not he was himself lurking somewhere on Carpathia he would have spies on the lookout for me, I was sure. If I had been in Mortifer's position I would have given serious thought to ordering my spies to kill on sight anyone who looked like Casmir the Tenth. The hat was some slender protection against being cut down from a distance before I could recognize the danger.

Nevertheless, my nerves were on the stretch as I stepped off of the transport disc beneath the walls of Castle Thorn. Mortifer knew that I existed and must have guessed that his enemies would find me and that I would be on his trail. It would be natural for him to set traps wherever I was likely to appear, and this place was one of the likeliest. Personal weapons were banned by law in this society; that would not stop Mortifer or his minions but it made it hard for me to defend myself. Fortunately knives and clubs were too primitive to be thought of as weapons by these people; I had a hunter's knife at my belt and carried a stout walking stick.

I caught a motion out of the corner of my eye and whirled, shifting my grip on the stick as a man ran toward me. But the face above the shabby robe was beaming with friendship. I relaxed; this could only be the young scholar whom the other Casmir had bound to him with the Gift. "Good ser," he panted, trying to catch his breath. "I knew that you'd return! They made me put the sword back eventually, but all Carpathia knows that you drew it from the stone. Everyone is singing the old songs and the membership of the Old Carpathian Society has tripled!"

I grinned at his enthusiasm and gave his shoulder a friendly squeeze; it felt thin and bony under the worn robe. "I hear that you raised a hue and cry to rescue me from Mortifer, ser scholar," I said.

He smiled bashfully. "Perhaps there was no need, ser, but when I saw the monitor's platform fly you straight across the valley to Mortifer's quarters I was sure that he meant you some harm. When we broke down the doors and found the destruction I thought sure that you'd been killed, but the scanners found no organic material at all, so I dared to hope. How in the name of the Mercy did you escape, ser?"

"It's a long tale," I said, wishing that I knew it myself.

"What would happen if I drew that sword out again?"

The young scholar's face was bright with eagerness. "If only you would, ser," he cried. "The Old Carpathians have been making plans; they have the petition all ready to call a special election for Tribune of the People. If you carried that sword around the Old Town news would spread like a mountain fire and you'd be elected Tribune by acclamation. As Tribune you could call for a vote of the people on any matter before the Council, and people would respond, not ignore the elections as they've been doing when Mortifer's gang was manipulating things."

It was a mad proposal; what had I to do with the affairs of this strange new Carpathia? Still the thought of spoiling some schemes of Mortifer's was tempting; that might bring the fox out of his lair. And a position of power might help me to deal with Mortifer when I found him. But what responsibilities would this office of Tribune involve? What would I do if I had to pursue Mortifer somewhere away from Carpathia? In the end, it was the unquestioning devotion in the young scholar's face which decided me. "You're a mad folk to choose a man for office because of an old face and an old sword," I said, "but it suits me well to spoil Mortifer's schemes. Mad as it is, I'll do it."

"Come then, before anyone can interfere," said the scholar. "My name, ser, which I never had a chance to tell you, is Paul Sobeski. The Castle guides are on our side and I'll get one to send word to Society headquarters as soon as we have the sword."

"If the Castle guides are on our side, who might interfere?" I asked him.

Paul Sobeski gave me a sidelong look. "Well, ser, we found some strange things in Mortifer's quarters but we didn't find his body. What we did find was a repeating android, or the remains of one and they can't be controlled from too far away. So Mortifer must have been on Carpathia and probably even in Thorn when you were taken to his quarters. He's lain low since, because the people were howling for his blood after that incident. But even if he's not in Thorn some of his agents are. Some of them are in official positions; the woman who took you to him was a real monitor. I don't know how far Mortifer's party will go but they'll certainly try to put legal difficulties in your way about the sword. In theory I suppose that it's government property and if the Castle guards weren't a law unto themselves the government people would have insisted on locking it away or putting a guard over it."

He was leading me past a statue by the main gate and as I glanced up at it I saw that it had a face that might have been my father's face as he was when I was a boy. A moment later I realized that it was also the face that I saw in the mirror, my own face.

"By the Mercy, it gave me a turn when I first saw you standing and looking at that statue," said Sobeski. "I thought then that you were a Jagellon descendant through some illegitimate line. But when you pulled the sword from the stone . . ."

"I am a clone, taken from the cells of Casmir the Tenth," I told him. "I have many of his memories and perhaps a few of his gifts."

"By the Mercy!" said Paul Sobeski eagerly. "Then Casmir really has come again! A few of the Old Carpathians are so traditional that they won't like the clone part, but for most of us it will make it even better. It's good to have a leader who's the descendant of a great king, but to have a man identical with that king is glorious!"

I thought to myself that though young Paul thought of me as "leader" probably the other Old Carpathian leaders were thinking "figurehead"—let them think so until it suited me to change their minds; it is always easier to use folk when they think they are using you.

We entered a small gate, passed through a little shop that sold models of the Castle and figurines intended to be Knights of Thorn, and came out into a familiar courtyard. "We'd best go straight to the Hall of Kings, ser," said Sobeski, leading me up to the batttlements and along them to where a graceful wooden bridge spanned a dizzying gap over to a rocky crag crowned with a little chapel. That crag had always worried me: too close to the castle walls—a determined enemy could climb it and shoot arrows over the battlements. The chapel they had built on it made it worse, if anything; it could be seized and used to shelter the enemy. Then I reminded myself that my prototype had united Carpathia; no need since then to worry about Carpathian enemies attacking Castle Thorn, and the flying platforms of these days made a joke of walls and battlements.

We crossed the bridge and entered the chapel they called the Hall of Kings. It was, I saw, a mausoleum, with tombs of many kings and memorials to those whose bodies could not be brought here for burial. From the quarterings on the shields we passed I saw that the descendants of Casmir the Tenth had cannily intermarried with all of the old royal families of the former independent kingdoms. It was wise policy, but I wondered if the later kings had been very pleased with those wives as wives. Perhaps there was some reason for Paul Sobeski thinking that the later kings might have left illegitimate descendants.

We came to the tomb of my prototype, Casmir the Tenth. The sword stuck in the stone on its surface was not the workaday sword whose duplicate was with my gear at the transient hostel, but a magnificent ceremonial thing, the Coronation Sword. I recognized too the slab in which it was set. When my father had shown me its trick I had thought it a piece of sorcery; now I knew it for a device familiar in these days, a lock field. It looked like a block of dark stone, but to the person "keyed" to it the stone became as permeable as water. Any non-living object could be placed in the field and seem to sink into the "stone" and be sealed there. I wondered what had made my prototype leave the Coronation Sword half in and half out of the field, and why it had not been re-keyed to his son and his son's sons.

I touched the "stone" with one hand, as the other Casmir must instinctively have done, and then pulled the sword out of it. A great bell tolled twice somewhere above us. Paul Sobeski's face was puzzled. "It tolled once when you pulled it out before," he said, "and no one could discover what bell had rung or how it was operated."

I shrugged; some device of my prototype perhaps. Looking around me I saw a little knot of spectators at the bridge, mainly dignified-looking men in garments that looked like the ceremonial dress of the Knights of Thorn. Each wore a medallion round his neck. "The Castle Guides, ser," said Paul. "They keep the tradition of the Knights of Thorn and they'll follow you unquestioningly once they learn who you are."

I gave them the Knight's Salute with the great sword and walked toward them. They respectfully stepped back, leaving the bridge clear for me. As well they did, for as I came to the center of the bridge a purple light flashed from the back of the crowd. Paul Sobeski crumpled unconscious at my side and would have gone over the edge if I had not caught him. Before I could do anything more there was an even brighter flash and the roar of flames. The wooden bridge was on fire beneath me and a wall of flames flared between me and the safety of the battlements!

14. THE BALCONY

I snatched young Paul up into my arms and whirled toward the Hall of Kings, but whatever had set the bridge on fire had struck behind me too; I was trapped between two walls of flame. The bridge gave an ominous crack and seemed to sink slightly beneath us. Throwing Paul over my shoulder, I crouched, trying to visualize exactly the distance between me and the battlements as I had seen it before the flames sprung up. I yanked at the scholar's robe which the young Sobeski wore, pulling it away from the front of his body, which was protected by being against my shoulder. Using the material as a sort of shield over my face I plunged into the flames with a bound which carried me almost to the battlements. My feet crunched on wood already half charred and the stench of the burning cloth was in my nostrils. But with another leap I got close enough to the battlements to sprawl across them. Strong hands grasped Paul and myself and drew us over the battlements to safety.

The Castle Guards were crouching behind the battlements; evidently some danger still hovered in the air between the Castle proper and the Hall of Kings. One gray-haired guide was crouched at the entrance of the stairway, fumbling with something which I recognized as a crossbow. As soon as I had made sure that the other guides had beaten out the flames on my hair and clothing and were tending Paul Sobeski, I got across the intervening space with a rush and a tumbling roll and took the crossbow from his hands. He had it almost cranked up; I gave a few more turns and slipped the crank off and thrust it into my belt.

I tested the quarrell with my fingers; it was firmly seated. I brought the stock to my shoulder, made sure that I had a proper grip and stood up, my eyes searching the sky. On a small platform hovering in the air was a man with a long tube in his hands; there was a small flame at the tip of the tube that grew longer as he swivelled it toward me. With one practiced movement I aimed and pulled the trigger, then dropped down again: Flame seared over my head, but before I had dropped I had seen the crossbow quarrell blossoming from the throat of the man on the platform. I raised my head cautiously and saw that the man was huddled on the floor of his flying platform; his fire weapon spouting aimlessly into the air as the platform revolved slowly. As I watched, the flame died and the platform hung in the air, rocking slightly. There were no other enemies in sight, and I handed the crossbow back to the guide with a smile.

He gave me the hand salute of the Knights of Thorn and said hoarsely, "Thank the Mercy that I remembered that this thing hung on the wall in the room below. I ran for it as soon as I saw that bastard start torching the bridge; but I could never have shot it as you did, and there was only the one arrow in it."

"Thanks to you for your quick wits," I said. "Perhaps it is a good omen that a weapon from the old times has conquered those of these times."

That raised a ragged laugh among the guides. One of them called, "One for Old Carpathia," and another cried, "Casmir's come again," at which they all gave a cheer. I saluted them and went to see to Paul Sobeski, who was sitting up, dazed and groaning. His hair, like mine, was singed, but the only severe burns were on the back of his legs, where his gown had not protected him. I realized that the back of my left hand which had held him over my shoulder, was smarting. A guide bearing a white box with a red cross on it applied a soothing salve to our burns and we were both soon much more comfortable. Another guide respectfully handed me the Coronation Sword which I had dropped when I handed Paul over to the guides.

One of the guides, a well-fleshed man of middle years, said respectfully, "My lord, the Old Carpathian Party headquarters have been notified, but by your leave it's not safe to parade through the Old Town as the scholar suggested. There's a balcony on the North Wall which some of the last kings used to address the people and it has some modern safeguards against attack. The fire will draw a crowd to the Castle anyhow; if we close the gates and hang a Jagellon banner from the balcony, there should be a good crowd assembled there in no time."

"Well thought of," I told him. "See it done." He saluted and left and I turned to the remaining guides. "Is there clothing here from the time of my ancestors that could be worn without disrespect to the dead?" I asked them. "No crowns or emblems of royalty, mark you, but the court dress of a Knight of Thorn, bearing the Jagellon arms." Two guides looked at each other and nodded, then saluted and trotted off.

A young man, not in guide's dress, pushed through to me, gave an awkward bow and said, "Ser, the Committee has filed the proper notice for the special election of a Tribune. There are 3V crews on their way to record your statement to the electors and the vote will be taken after the evening news. Probably your only competition will be some of the perennial candidates who always file for everything going, but you have to get sixty percent of those who voted on the last issue. Luckily that's not very many; citizen participation has been low lately. Now there's the problem of citizenship; I presume you're not registered on Carpathia and unless your current registration is at Home."

"My citizenship was registered at Home and has not been changed," I said.

The young man looked relieved. "Oh, that's all right then; anyone who is registered at Home can acquire Carpathian citizenship by a simple declaration of intention to reside on Carpathia and obey local laws. It's an old privilege from colonial days. Umm there's a fax here, ser, with some suggested remarks since you're, er, not familiar with local conditions."

I looked at the sheet full of rhetorical phrases and references to names about which I knew nothing, smiled politely at the young man, folded the sheet and put it into my pouch. "I thank you," I said, "but I think that I will make my own speech. You may tell the men who wish to record my 'statement' that I will be speaking to the people from the balcony on the North Wall. If that will not serve their turn I will speak to them afterwards. All of you have my leave to withdraw except the scholar Paul Sobeski." The young man from the Old Carpathians was reluctant to go, but he was tactfully surrounded and led away by the guides. I smiled to myself; it was good to have trusty men about me again.

I turned to Sobeski; "Paul," I said, "you have until the crowd gathers to tell me all that I must know of the Tribune's duties and what will give the people reason to put me in that office. I find it hard to believe that many of them care that much for the Jagellon line in these days. What grievances have they that a Tribune can relieve; what hope can I give them that I can in conscience pledge my honor to?"

Paul grinned. "You underestimate the power of the Jagellon legend," he said, "but there is plenty that a Tribune can do and many wrongs that you can truthfully promise to right. In theory we have a Direct Democracy; the people vote by keying their Views with their C and C chips. Supposedly all matters at general policy go to the people and only technical matters are decided by the elected Council. But if there's no Tribune the Council decides what is a policy matter and what is merely administrative. The present Council has been using that power to keep the real decisions out of the hands of the people."

"What particular evils have they done?" I asked.

Paul Sobeski frowned thoughtfully. "We don't have time to go into specifics, but basically it's the same old story that you find throughout human history. Szilar history too, for that matter, or the history of any aggressive species, though empathic species like the Caphellans have other sorts of problems. Anyway, those in power build up their own little empires, using the machinery of government to get wealth and power for themselves and their toadies, while the ordinary citizen can't get justice against them. Actually, those in government who only want the luxuries of life are relatively harmless; the ones who do real harm are those who enjoy bullying others for the sense of power it gives them or those who have big plans for interfering with other people's lives. One thing that's caused a lot of resentment is the new Eugenics Code, regulating marriage and childbearing. It's said that Mortifer is behind that and that what he's really trying to do is to use the entire planet as an experimental laboratory to test out some theories of his about selective breeding."

Two Castle guides approached us with garments across their arms and waited deferentially just out of earshot. "That must be enough for the moment," I told Paul, "but we must speak more of this; stay near me and we will use the first opportunity." I signalled the two guides to approach and put on the garments which they had brought me; a surcoat with the Jagellon eagle embroidered on the breast, ornamental boots, a sword-belt and scabbard for the Coronation sword, and a great cloak of imperial red. One of them had had the presence of mind to find a basin of water and a towel, and I cleansed myself a little before I dressed.

The same man offered to find scissors and trim my singed hair, but I shook my head. "For now, let us show our battle scars," I told him with a smile.

"There's already a large crowd assembled, my lord," said the other guide, "and the 3V men have set up to record your speech from the balcony. I'd say that the crowd was getting a little impatient."

"I come," I said, and let myself be led through familiar corridors to a room that had once been a solar for the court ladies. The windows had been enlarged and a large stone balcony built out, looking over a stretch of lawn below the castle. The grass was crowded with a great mass of people looking expectantly up at the balcony, over the edge of which a great banner with the Jagellon eagle was hanging.

"There are built-in pickups for the 3V and also a great many hidden defences for this area," said one of the guides. "Some of the last Jagellons had a great many enemies to contend with."

I nodded, but as I walked out onto the balcony I felt very exposed. No arrow could reach me here from the crowd, and I was still immune to the flashing purple light that rendered a man unconscious, but no doubt there were many weapons I had not dreamed of in this time and place. Then I forgot fear as I heard a great shout go up from the crowd as I appeared on the balcony. I stood in silence for a moment, trying to reach out for contact with them. There were a great many people there, but in many ways a crowd is but one man, as any leader knows.

"People of Carpathia," I said, and some device magnified my voice so that it could be heard by all of those below. "Men and women of Thorn. We have a common heritage and a common enemy, Mortifer the Academician." At his name there was a sort of growl from the crowd that lifted my hopes. "This man, who is trying to meddle with your lives for his 'experiments' also meddled with mine. He took flesh from the dead king, Casmir the Tenth, and from it he grew another man, myself, with Casmir's form and Casmir's memories. I will not say that I am Casmir, the tenth king of Carpathia: that great man lies buried in the Hall of Kings. But some of his knowledge and some of his gifts I do have, and I have his heart too, full of love for Carpathia." There was a great cheer at that; I had them in my hands.

"Mortifer intended to use me, to play with me for his sport and his instruction," I told them, "just as he has tried to use this whole world of Carpathia. Good friends have helped me get free of Mortifer; I and my friends would like to make you free of him too. You have an ancient and honorable office, that of Tribune of the People. Some who love Carpathia and its history have proposed me for that office . . . ." There were so many cheers at this that I had to wait to make myself heard.

"I am told by those I trust," I went on, "that although in form the people rule Carpathia, in truth you are at the mercy of many petty tyrants. If you make me your choice for Tribune, I will free you from these tyrants and put the rule truly back into your hands." There were more cheers at this, and I thought of ending my speech, but there were a few moves that Mortifer might make which it would be wise to guard against.

"There will be those who say that I am no true man, since I was not born as most men are," I said, "but I have just come from Home, the birthplace of the human race, and those in authority there have given me the mark of citizenship." I held up my wrist so that they could see the blue dot. "But Carpathia is my place; I will always return here and always make my home here, whether or not you trust me with this responsibility." Again I was stopped by cheers.

"Subtle men may suggest that I am only a tool of Mortifer, a new trick to deceive you," I said. "As if he had need of any such trick, so firmly does he have you in his hands. But I tell you, and trusty men well known to you will bear me out, that Mortifer has not ceased to try to kill me since I set foot on this world. The ashes of the bridge to the Hall of Kings are still smoking where Mortifer's man tried to burn me down as I came from reclaiming the sword put in the stone by Casmir the Tenth." I drew the sword and held it up and the cheer seemed to shake the Castle.

"This sword and the garments I now wear are treasures of Carpathia, legacies to you from an earlier and perhaps a braver time," I said. "Think of me too, as a legacy from that old Carpathia. Use me, as I would use this sword, to defend justice and freedom!" The cheers went on and on, and I decided to leave it at that, but I had to return to the balcony three times to respond to the cheers before I thought it wise to go.

The portly middle-aged guide who seemed to be their chief leader came to me then and saluted. "My lord," he said, "I've taken the responsibility of clearing the Castle of everyone except the Guides and a few people from the Old Carpathian Party who would like to consult with you. We are the remnants of the old Knights of Thorn, ser, and we have some ancient rights in this place which have been little used for centuries. The guides, ser, the Knights, would like to give you the old Oath as our Commander, and offer you the Commander's quarters in the Castle for as long as you wish to make use of them. Once you're elected Tribune you'll have plenty of safeguards, but it's my advice that you stay here at least until you're elected. Mortifer can't get at you here without destroying the Castle, and even he would have trouble doing that."

I gave my assent and in the chapel of the Castle took their oaths and renewed my own. Then over a scratch meal I consulted with the Old Carpathians about what wrongs should be righted and how it could be done. An elderly woman who was the titular head of the party because of her Jagellon blood was the most helpful to me; the others still hoped, I think, to use me to advance their own schemes. "In theory the Tribune can't advance any legislation on his own," the woman told me, "but myself and a few other Old Carpathians are still Council members; you've only to tell us what you want proposed and we'll do it, then you can use your powers to take it to the people."

"*If* he's elected . . ." said one of the others, but just then one of the guides appeared at the door. I nodded permission for him to speak and he said resonantly, "My Lord Tribune, you have been elected with the greatest number of votes ever cast in Carpathia!"

15. THE ISLAND

Good rulers are long remembered, but there are few songs and stories about them, for the business of bringing peace and justice to a land is mostly hard work, which makes a poor story. With the aid of Wanda Jagellon, the woman who was titular head of the Old Carpathian Society and Ladislas Mankowitz, the Chief Guide of Castle Thorn, I managed to use the power of the Tribune to root out the worst of the abuses which had grown up. Time after time Wanda or one of the other Old Carpathians would rise in the Council to propose some needed change, and time after time I would judge, "Let go to the People," before the Council could vote it down. The streets of Thorn and other cities were empty after the time of the evening meal as the citizens watched the debates on their Views and keyed their voting contacts. Then there came the time for Council elections; the Old Carpathians swept the elections and the fight became more subtle. I had to keep the Old Carpathian Party from re-establishing Mortifer's tyranny with their folk instead of his. But at last we won that fight too.

Everywhere we had encountered tentacles of Mortifer's power; in the Council, in the Civil Service, in the academies. Some of his followers I won over, some I had to cast out of office or destroy politically, financially or even physically. My own life was constantly under threat; the Castle Guides became again the Knights of Thorn and the Tribune's bodyguard, recruiting younger men to do part of the job. The Guild of Scholars took over guide's duties in those parts of the Castle that the Knights and I were not using. Time and again we encountered Mortifer's agents or followers, but of Mortifer himself there was no sign. I was beginning to wonder if I should pass on the Tribune's office to Wanda or Ladislas and seek Mortifer off-world.

Then late one night, as I worked alone in my quarters a personal call came in on my View. We had established a special code for those who wished to speak to me privately; much information had reached me in that way from those who feared reprisal if they approached the Tribune in any other way. Because of that, the code was such that there was no way of discovering from what place the call originated. I was not completely surprised, then, when on this night the View showed me the saturnine countenance of Mortifer himself. I ignored his face and searched the background of the picture for any clue to his location. He was too clever for that; it was a gray-walled room that could have been any general utility room in any modern structure on Carpathia. The one thing that the call did tell me was that Mortifer was probably still on Thorn; there was no sign of the subtle clues which technicians had told me would mark a feed-in from off-planet.

"You have already spoiled many lifetimes of work, Casmir King,"said Mortifer in a sneering tone. "I see that it is time that I dealt with you myself."

I looked back at him with as little expression as I could manage; this man knew me even better than I knew him, having spied on me in moments which I had thought were private; I wanted to give him no clues to my thoughts. I lifted an eyebrow and said as casually as I could, "Your agents have had no great success in dealing with me, Mortifer. What more do you think that you can do?"

Mortifer gave a sardonic smile. "I know how your mind works, Casmir King,'" he said. "You want to get your hands on me and you will take risks to do it. For my own purposes it suits me to meet you face to face. I think that your vanity will make it hard for you to refuse that offer. Name a time and place where you think that neither of us can betray the other. I will meet you there and show my superiority to you by outwitting your precautions. Then you will be in my hands again, though you may believe that I will be in yours."

My mind raced, rejecting possibility after possibility, then I said slowly, "In the river at the foot of this crag there is a little island which has been left wild because of a tragedy which happened there many years ago. I will set guards on the banks who will permit nothing to come to that island from this time until midnight tomorrow night. At that time I will swim over from the shore to the island and wait for you. The guards will let one man, either swimming or, in deference to your age, in a wooden boat, land on that island after me. Screens will be set to prevent either of us taking any metal or any energy device onto the island. We will be face to face with only our bodies and our wits. The first of us to leave the island may pass freely where he wills; you have my word on that. Thus, you may come and parley and leave freely. Or you may come and try to kill me and leave in safety after you have done it. But the screens will keep you from sending an android in your place, since there are both metal and energy devices in an android. Does it content you?"

Mortifer's face was impassive, but I could tell from the way his eyes slitted that he was thinking. Then a little quirk at the comer of his mouth betrayed the fact that he was pleased. "Agreed," he said. "After midnight tomorrow." Then the image was gone.

I gave orders to have the island searched by men and machines and to have guards and screens set up on the banks. "Don't neglect any possibility," I told my men. "Look out for any openings under water, such as old sewers. If anything comes up or down that river except one lone human in a wooden boat or swimming take whatever measures are necessary to destroy or capture it. Let anyone who can think of a way to outwit these precautions discuss it with my bodyguard. If a way can be thought of countering the danger, do it without consulting me; only if you see some peril which cannot be countered should you tell me of it."

Mortifer undoubtedly had at least one scheme which pleased him enough to make him agree to my terms; before the time of our meeting he would undoubtedly have others in reserve. I was wagering that my strength and wit would be equal to anything which Mortifer could do alone and without arms. Some form of poison would perhaps be his safest trick, and I took thought about how he might try to infect me with it and how I could counter him. I would not put it past him to give himself some disease to pass on to me but if he could cure himself of it, surely I could be cured myself. Would he send an agent, or a clone from his own flesh infected with something incurable? That had to be thought of; I consulted with physicians as to what poison or disease he might use. They pumped me full of their potions and assured me that for a day or two I was proof against any poison or disease which could be spread by simple contact. Something in the bloodstream was another matter; if it came to a fight I would have to beware scratches or bites.

For my part I put great hope in one simple and secret weapon; the Jagellon Gift. There was a good chance that I had never met the real Mortifer in the flesh; that he had used two repeating androids, one at each replica of Castle Thorn. For surely to meet either myself or the other Casmir in the flesh while sending an android to the other would have meant a difference in his treatment of us which would have threatened his scheme of "everything the same," for the two of us. If he had met me only through the medium of an android then perhaps he was not an exception to the success of the Jagellon Gift, and I might be able to confuse him if not actually bend him to my will. But even apart from the Jagellon Gift I had ensured that the surroundings of our meeting were more in the world I remembered than in this world of machines and energy devices that I lived in now. A primitive island offered many possibilities.

I swam over a little before midnight, so as to reach the island exactly at the stroke of twelve as it sounded from one of the churches in the city. Then I set to work to use every second until Mortifer arrived. Mortifer might know this island, might have studied maps and pictures of it with care, but I had played on this island as a boy and he would never know it as I knew it.

I had swum over in shirt and breeches with supple leather shoes tied round my neck with their own laces. I soon found the rocks that broke into sharp shards when properly tapped. On the third try I had a workable knife with which I cut myself a staff and a bow, stringing it with a bootlace. The other lace I used to tie sharp stone points onto the sturdy reeds I made into arrows. It was a stroke of luck that I found a shore bird's nest with some feathers in it and three eggs. With a grin I took the eggs and put them in a sack I improvised from my shirt-tail; they might make distracting missiles. I withdrew to a hollow in the rocky hill at the center of the island and watched the shore while I split the feathers and stuck them to my crude arrows with a glue improvised from birdlime and the white of an egg. The island was too high to climb on three sides; a swimmer or a man in a boat could only land on the shore within my field of view. So long as the sliver of moon was not obscured by clouds I had perfect observation of anything approaching that shore. When I had fletched the arrows I made a sling from my other shirt-tail and a few remaining bits of shoelace, then folded the tops of my boots down to hold them on comfortably without their laces.

I was now armed as well as I could arm myself quickly to keep Mortifer at a distance if it came to a combat. He would only fight me, I reckoned, if he had poison or some other device up his sleeve; even if he had been my equal at combat he would chance nothing on a fair fight. I had reckoned correctly that he would not come immediately, hoping to play on my nerves by the delay, When I had been younger and more impatient he had sometimes got under my guard by playing a waiting game and I had thought that he would try that trick again. I let myself relax, keeping only my senses on the stretch.

I was aware of the smells of the island and the small, normal sounds of birds and little animals going about their nocturnal affairs. Suddenly there was the squawk of a sea bird and a splash. I grinned; there was one point on the cliffs where it looked as if they could be climbed, but many a skinned knee and knuckle had taught me that the appearance was illusory. Still, five hundred years might have worn down even that hard rock; I did not relax again until the grumpy muttering of the sea bird assured me that the climber had given up that route. Without ignoring other possibilities I looked most often to the end of the beach nearest the cliff that my opponent had tried to climb. There were broken rocks there and a man swimming along the cliffs might use them as shelter to make a stealthy approach to the beach.

At last I caught a glimpse of a shadowy form among the rocks. As long as it stayed there I could see little of it, but eventually my opponent would have to land. After a long pause, during which he must have been surveying the island as best he could, I saw an oblong shadow drift into shore and heard the scrunch of gravel. Against the paler color of the beach I could see that it was an inflatable boat. By great good fortune one of my men had suggested that I use such a craft to save myself a swim and I had been curious enough to examine one. A thought struck me and I picked up an arrow and fitted it on the bow I had made. Such boats were normally inflated with air, but what was to prevent Mortifer from filling it with a noxious gas and releasing it against me unexpectedly? As soon as I saw the figure of a man slip away from the boat for the shelter of a rock I drew back the arrow and fired it at the inflatable boat.

At that distance with so large a target even my crude weapon could hardly miss. There was a loud hiss and the boat shriveled and dwindled. The dark figure on the beach ran frantically away from it and I thought that my guess had been a good one; if he merely feared another arrow he would have done better to stay behind his rock. "I said a wooden boat," I called softly and then quietly slid over the edge of my hollow into a little ravine beside it.

As well I did, for the figure on the beach raised his hand and there was a snapping sound and a missile of some sort hummed over my head into the hollow. A good try for a snap shot at a voice from the dark. I thought that what he had must be something like a small crossbow; the missile had buzzed like a crossbow quarrell. If that was so, he would need to reset it before he could fire again. I rose to my feet, swung my sling around my head once and let fly an egg at his position. There was a squelching sound as it hit and the dark figure plunged back into the sea. I grinned as I slid into another prepared position, a little closer to the beach. I had reckoned that my opponent's imagination would magnify a simple bird's egg into some noxious substance which he would try to wash off as quickly as possible.

He was indeed scrubbing at his skin where the egg had hit, then he plunged into the water again and swam a few strokes. But in a moment he rose to his feet, tossed something away from him and waded back into shore. A voice which could have been Mortifer's but which sounded different enough to put me on guard called out. "All right! First round to you, Casmir King! I am counting on the fact that you want to question me, not just kill me. I have no other weapons; come down to the beach and talk. If you do, I may answer some of your questions."

I trusted him not at all, but that was a powerful bait, as he knew it would be. "Walk over to the large rock to your right," I called, "and sit on it with your hands at your sides. I'll come down to you."

As I remembered, the rock was just a bit too high for even a tall man to sit on with his feet on the ground; my opponent had to perch on it with his feet dangling. From that position he could not come at me without a betraying movement to warn me. When he was sitting down I came softly down the hill and stepped out on the beach a short spearcast away from him. My bow and arrows I had dropped just short of the beach, my staff I held in my hand and my sling with a stone in it was tucked into my breeches in the back. "This will do for now," I said. "Now tell me, Mortifer, if Mortifer you be, what was the reason for your treatment of me; why the false Carpathia in the cavern, why the androids that looked like the folk of old?"

The figure on the beach shrugged. His face looked like Mortifer's from this distance but something about the body didn't fit. The voice, though, sounded more like Mortifer's when he spoke: "It was a controlled environment; I hoped to learn a good deal about the behavior of a born leader like yourself; perhaps things I could apply to my own purposes. But there was another reason too. Casmir the Tenth defeated my plans for him and then escaped me by dying. It amused me to make a reborn Casmir my experimental subject and eventually my tool."

"Your tool for what?" I asked as calmly as I could.

"Why, to rule Carpathia first and after that a wider realm," said the other man mockingly. "With the proper opportunities Casmir could have built an interstellar kingdom, not just united a planet. You've made a good start here, Casmir King; any day your puppets in the Council could propose a restoration of the monarchy with you as king and the people would pass the measure. Perhaps that's what I'll have Casmir King do when he leaves this island."

"And how do you propose to make me do that?" I asked as mockingly as I could.

"Oh, not you," said the man on the rock, and put his hands to his head. He pulled something from his head and face and looked up at me with a smile. The smile was the crooked smile of Mortifer, but the face revealed in the moonlight was my own face!

16. THE GHOST HOUND

"'Another clone, of course," said the man on the rock, "but with my memories instead of those of Casmir the Tenth. That proved—unfortunate—in your case. Besides that I've come to the conclusion that the factor I'm looking for is genetic; I can ignore Casmir's background and training."

"And the original Mortifer?" I asked softly.

The other man shrugged. "He still exists, so even if you killed this body, Casmir King, you wouldn't have defeated me. But I'll kill you, of course, and then go back to your followers and take over what you've built up. I suppose that I'd better smash your face in or else someone might raise uncomfortable questions. A pity; I'd like to get you in the laboratory and take you apart carefully."

"You haven't got me yet, either to smash or to take apart," I said mockingly.

The other man gave a nasty laugh, all the more disconcerting because it was in my own voice. I realized that when he spoke it was the speech patterns and intonations that made him sound like Mortifer; the voice had always been mine.

"I can take you when I wish," he said. "Do you think that I'd set up an experiment without an emergency cutoff in case things went wrong? All I have to do is speak one word that will key a reflex I put into you in the tanks. Your breath, your heart, your whole involuntary nervous system will stop. Brain damage in a few moments, death in a few more; I won't even have to touch you. You can't possibly reach me in time to keep me from saying that one fatal word. So keep your distance my barbarian warrior; you don't have long to live in any case and I'd like to know a little more before I finish you."

I felt as if an icy hand were squeezing my guts, but I forced my wits to work. "And what happens to your body when that word is spoken?" I said softly. "Or even if that word won't kill you, isn't there another which will? Do you think that the original Mortifer will leave you alive after you've served his purposes?

Let me help you get rid of *him* and let me live to help you. I'm in your hands if what you say is true; I could never be a threat to you. I'll do whatever you want, put on the mask of Mortifer you wore here and pretend to be your prisoner . . ." My hand groped frantically in the pouch behind me; if that nest was old enough the yolk of the eggs should be thick and glutinous. Would they do? They had to, there was nothing else I could get in time.

"No," said the other man, "I don't dare trust you . . ." I crunched the eggs in my hand and clapped my hands to my ears, filling my ear holes with a mess of yolk, white and shell. Yelling like a maniac I ran at the other man with my stick. His mouth was working but I could hear nothing but an undifferentiated sound. I thrust at his throat with the sharpened end of my stick but he was as quick as I; he struck the stick aside and grabbed for me.

We grappled and rolled on the beach, bodies equally matched and skills of combat seemingly equal too. Several times he almost held me down, while he tried to shout in my ear. Every blow I could land went to his mouth, his throat, his diaphragm. He kneed me and I doubled over in pain, the flaked stone knife digging into my gut as I bent. We were too equally matched; I had to use that knife. I plucked it from my waistband and aimed up for his stomach, but a sudden wriggle of his body deflected my aim and I felt it slip between his ribs. Blood gushed and an expression of astonishment came over the face so like my face; the limbs relaxed. I thought it was a mortal blow, but I dared not trust him; my hand groped for a rock on the beach and I smashed his skull with it. Before my blood could cool I hit again and again, obliterating his face as he had planned to obliterate mine.

I stumbled to the edge of the water and washed myself, compulsively retching but unable to bring up anything. A fragment of an old verse ran through my mind:

I fought a dead man on the shore
And I think the man was me . . .

Presently my shuddering ceased and I walked back to look at the body, its head now a bloody mess. "Forgive me, brother," I said uselessly. From the moment I had known what he was I had known he had to die. He might have had the Jagellon Gift, and the combination of that gift and Mortifer's mind was too dangerous to let loose in the world. But the necessity was bitter; another score against Mortifer. Had I committed suicide, fratricide or simple murder? I wondered. At any rate there was another death I must accomplish; it was too dangerous to parley with Mortifer any longer, or try to question him; I must kill him on sight.

I examined the body minutely, but it told me nothing. Was this yet a third clone or had Mortifer captured Casmir Thorn, stolen his memories and replaced his mind with Mortifer's? There was no way that I could see of telling. What would have happened to this man eventually? Would the Jagellon heritage have overcome the Mortifer memories given time enough? I wanted to think so, and that made this death yet more bitter. Wearily I made a rough cairn of beach rocks over the body, entered the water again and swam with slow strokes back to the place where I had gone into the river to swim to the island. Once ashore, I dispatched technical crews to the island, took a transport disc to the Castle and summoned my closest advisors.

"I met a duplicate of myself on the island," I told them bluntly. "Mortifer's plan was that the duplicate would come back and take my place. Before we go any farther I want you each to question me about things that have happened since we met until you are absolutely sure that I am the man you elected Tribune."

Once the inquisition was over I told them the whole story of my encounter on the island and told them for the first time about "Casmir Thorn." Then I drew some morals. "I am vulnerable," I told them. "If the man on the island told the truth—and his behavior tells me he did—Mortifer can kill me any time that he can have one word spoken in my ear. I see no way of guarding against that; one of you might tell me tomorrow that a man named Rumplestiltskin had been trying to reach me and I might fall over dead before your eyes."

"Not necessarily," said Wanda Jagellon. "I was a nurse for a while before I got involved in politics and I'll wager that once the reflex is triggered you can be kept alive in a heartlung field until a psychoneurologist can find the reflex and override it. I'll give orders to have a medical team with the right equipment standing by in the Castle."

"My thanks to you, Lady Wanda," I said with a lighter heart. "That makes the case less desperate, but still it restricts me to places where I can get such medical help quickly. Furthermore, Mortifer could strike me down at a moment of crisis and leave all in confusion. It is past time that we had another Tribune; will you take on the task, my Lady?"

She nodded with a little smile. "The people will accept a Jagellon woman I think, but only as your deputy. I'll be the junior Tribune and take over if you are incapacitated."

"My thanks," I said. "It is no light burden that you take on, as well you know. The other problem, though, is what to do if Mortifer introduces another duplicate at some crucial moment. Mortifer has secret supporters still, and many resources. What if a duplicate appeared on the View with some lying tale? At best it would confuse the people and destroy confidence in us; at worst it might enable Mortifer to take over somehow."

Wanda frowned. "Your strictly legal powers depend on the Council being in session. Things are slow; we can keep the Council in recess for a while."

Paul Sobeski tapped his fingers on the table around which we sat. "'What we need is some means of identifying you as yourself which a duplicate can't easily reproduce—or steal. The trouble is that all the means of identification in our society depend on genotypes and a clone would have the same genotype and key the same identity tests. And it has to be a publicly visible sign of identity. You could have a firedrake tattooed on your chest and we would know that a duplicate without the tattoo wasn't you, but as soon as you publicize anything of that kind Mortifer could reproduce it on his clone."

"There are unique gems in the Treasury here at the Castle . . ." began Ladislas Mankowitz.

I shook my head. "I wouldn't put it past Mortifer to duplicate any material object. He duplicated Castle Thorn itself—twice! Anyway, if we put our trust in something like that Mortifer has only to steal it somehow and it becomes a weapon against us."

Ladislas knit his brows. "Something alive?" he suggested tentatively. "A dog perhaps."

"Not a dog," I said. "Any duplicate would smell just as I do and I don't think a dog could tell us apart. The difference between me and a duplicate made by Mortifer would be in the mind and a dog can't smell your mind."

"No," said Wanda softly, but with excitement, "not an ordinary dog. But a Caphellan ghost-hound can!" She turned to Ladislas. "Get on to the exotic importers, Ladislas. I doubt if there's a ghost-hound on Carpathia, so put in a special order. I'll use my personal credit to give Mortifer a little less chance of getting to us." She turned to me. "The Caphellans are extreme empaths . . ."

"Yes," I said. "I've met one."

"Good, then I don't need to explain the Caphellans," she said. "As you might guess they find it extremely painful to go among other species who have uncontrolled emotions by Caphellan standards. To a Caphellan you or I are constantly 'shouting' our emotions and are completely 'deaf' to the emotions of others. Imagine living among deaf people who constantly bawled at the top of their voices. So Caphellans living in other societies are extremely reclusive. At home Caphellans have little use for pets;

they get constant emotional support from other Caphellans. An isolated Caphellan feels the lack of that support so they've bred a sub-sapient Caphellan life-form into a sort of a super-pet for Caphellans who have to live away from other Caphellans. They form a unique emotional bond with their master or mistress."

I frowned. "I don't see why if I got such a creature Mortifer couldn't acquire one too and bond it to his duplicate."

Wanda smiled, "Ah, but you don't know the unique characteristics of a ghost hound. They sniff out hatred and fear; that should make it harder for a traitor to get near you. But most important they can detect when a person is lying. In particular, if its master lies a ghost-hound 'blushes'—turns a deep rich red all over." She added dryly, "They aren't popular pets among non-empaths."

"It may just work," I said slowly. "There's a Caphellan at the Academy, or was when I landed here on Carpathia. See if it has a ghost-hound and will cooperate in making some sort of presentation of it to me on the View. Don't cancel the order to the importers, Ladislas; even if the Caphellan parts with his beast I presume that it will want a replacement."

The Caphellan was located and agreed to trade us the ghost-hound for a round trip starpassage to Caphella. "In the emotional freeze of a starflit I won't miss my pet," the creature said, "and after restoring my soul by communion with my people I can bring back a young Lar, a "ghosthound" as you call them. My own beast is getting rather old. Ordinarily it would not transfer its loyalties to a new owner, but in your case I think there will be no trouble." The Caphellan gave me an enigmatic glance from its three eyes and I remembered that it had been able to detect operation of the Jagellon Gift.

We had a rather impressive little ceremony broadcast on the View. The Caphellan presented me with his ghost-hound.

"I am returning to Caphella for a while and can find another," it said. "Your planet has been kind to me; I think that this will be for the good of your planet and your Tribune."

I thanked him and turned to face the receptors which sent out my image to the Views in homes and public buildings all over Carpathia. "I have never lied to you, so far as I remember," I said. "If I try to do so from now on, you will easily catch me out, for Trinka, my ghost-hound, will always be with me. If I do tell you a lie, see what happens." I thought for a moment and then said earnestly. "I am completely happy about never being able to tell a lie without Trinka giving me away." I grinned as a flood of red color flowed over Trinka's body from the tip of her nose to her feathery tail. It was a remarkable sight, for Trinka looked not unlike a white Afghan hound, but her fur was not hair but a sort of soft quills filled with liquid, which is what in fact changed color.

I looked into the receptors again. "Even an honest man does not like to have to tell the truth," I said. "The reason that I have accepted Trinka, and will keep her with me constantly is that Mortifer, my enemy and yours, is still plotting against us. He has tried to kill me and will try again, and for that reason I am going to have to restrict my activities for a while. I ask you to give your votes to Wanda Jagellon as Second Tribune, so that she can help me with my duties and take over if Mortifer succeeds in putting me out of action. Mortifer may also try to substitute someone for me; someone who looks like me in every way, but is a creature of his own. So long as you see Trinka with me you will know that you can trust what I say if I warn you of a danger or ask you to take action. If you see me without my ghost-hound, beware! Even if it looks like me it may not be me." That should take care of the most obvious moves that Mortifer could make, having a duplicate commit some atrocity for instance to destroy my popularity. Better tell Ladislas not to cancel the order for another ghost-hound though; poor Trinka was probably a prime target for assassination now.

"I tell you most sincerely that Mortifer is a danger to Carpathia and even to the Commonwealth as well as to me. Any citizen who has information that might help us find him is urged to contact us at the Tribune's special code; for the time being that View will be manned by a team of operators who will record your information."

I looked into the receptors then and said softly, "Mortifer, kill me if you can, for if you do not I will put an end to you and your plans."

17. THE LAKE OF THE CRATER

In the end it was a child and a clerk who led us to Mortifer. Paul Sobeski, who was acting as my secretary, had supervised the first sorting out of the flood of messages which followed my appeal for information about Mortifer. After over a week of work he came to me one day and said, "I'd like you to hear two record chips taken from the calls we got about Mortifer. Put together, I think that they might give us a valuable clue."

When the first chip was inserted in the playback it showed on the View an elderly woman with a precise, fussy air. "'I am the chief dispatcher for the Central Chemical Concern," she said. "We used to supply the laboratory of Academician Mortifer at the Academy in Thorn. In dispatching one gets used to a certain pattern of supplies for a given customer; in many cases one could fill the order almost automatically. But there is enough judgment involved that the job can't be computerized. After the election of Our Tribune orders from the Mortifer laboratory ceased and I rather expected to have an overstock on some rare items. However, I've noticed that all of these items continue to be ordered. The orders are spread out between a dozen different customers, many of them new customers. Those who aren't new haven't ordered these particular items in the past. Put together the orders from those dozen firms almost exactly duplicate the typical order from the Mortifer laboratory. Most of the firms are east of the mountains, but when occasionally I get a rush order for an item it almost always goes west. Two special rush orders have gone to a rather odd location; a little town on the edge of Lake of the Crater Crown Preserve. My husband and I have vacationed in that Preserve; I can't think of any enterprise in that little town which could possibly use such chemicals."

She paused and blushed very slightly. "When I was a girl I used to be very fond of stories about King Casmir the Protector. When Our Tribune came to us . . . Well, I just wouldn't want anything to happen to Our Tribune. I used to respect Academician Mortifer, but if he is trying to kill Our Tribune he must be a very wicked man and he should be caught as soon as possible."

The playback ceased and I turned to Paul. "As soon as we have time I'd like to thank that woman in person, Paul," I said. "Wanda has offered me various family heirlooms from the time of Casmir the Tenth; see if you can find something among them that this woman might like and ask Wanda if she will give it to me to pass on to our informant as a token of appreciation."

Paul made a note with his pen on a pad of paper—a scholar's affectation in this day of recording chips—and said, "I'm sure she will. The next message is from a child; a boy who lives on a farm near that Crown Preserve."

The boy might have been a farm lad of my old times: sturdy, freckled, clad in a faded shirt. "Well, I don't know if this will be any help," his recorded image said, "but it's sure funny. We live just on the edge of Lake of the Crater Preserve. Us kids around here always used to swim in the lake, and the rangers never said anything. But a couple of years ago the Preserve was pretty well closed down; they said the scientists from the Academy in Thorn were using the lake for experiments. When Dad tried to protest he didn't get anywhere; eventually he found out that Councillor Mortifer was behind these experiments and in those days, before Tribune Casmir came, you just couldn't buck old Mortifer."

He paused and spoke a little more awkwardly. "Well, us kids were mad, and we've been sneaking over at night and in the early mornings to swim. I'm sorry if we've been breaking the law but we didn't think it was fair. So anyway my friend Jimmy and I have seen some awfully funny stuff going on in that lake. They take boats out at night and drop big cases of stuff right into the water in the middle of the lake. And we've seen transport discs going down into the water too, and one time we almost got caught when we were swimming and a transport disc came right out of the water. So since old Mortifer was behind getting the lake closed I figure that maybe it was something Tribune Casmir oughta know. And . . . if this is some help to you, could you maybe see . . . about getting the lake open again for swimming, Tribune?"

Paul and I both chuckled as the playback finished. "Once we had those two leads we did some further checking and found some other leads pointing to that location," said Paul. "We're pretty sure that it's a secret stronghold of Mortifer's; perhaps his main base now you've driven him underground. There's a good chance that he himself might be there. I'd like your permission to send in an assault team of monitors; the charges pending against Mortifer are serious enough to get us a search and seize warrant from the High Court of Justice."

I frowned. "If I know Mortifer he won't be taken easily; he probably has half a dozen escape routes. I think that our best chance is to intercept the next big shipment and get ourselves dropped into Mortifer's stronghold in some of these big crates the boy spoke of."

Paul sighed. "You say 'ourselves.' You *are* going to insist on going then?"

I grinned at him. "Did you doubt it?"

He smiled wryly back. "Not really. All right; the Tribune has certain powers of investigation which we can probably stretch to cover this. You're certainly as much an expert at hand-to-hand combat as most monitors, and they'll certainly follow you with enthusiasm. But take every precaution, Casmir. Carpathia is recovering nicely from Mortifer, but we'll need you around, at least as a symbol, for some time yet. Besides that, your friends would miss you."

"And I you," I said. "Don't worry, Paul. This new life is much too interesting to throw away recklessly. I'll wear earplugs against that 'magic word' of Mortifer's and take some other precautions, too. Ask the Healers if it's safe for the whole assault group to have Lysergol injections so we can't be knocked out by neural interruption. We'll carry those Fire Service shields against torching and wear regular monitor's body shields against projectiles. If we can get inside the defenses by being delivered like packages, I have hopes that those things will be enough."

Paul nodded. "Yes and you'd better wear Support Suits and carry a reasonable air supply too. That way if Mortifer floods the place or tries some sort of gas attack you'll be all right. In fact, with Support Suits you can be neatly sealed inside those cases and not have to be worried about air holes or what happens when they drop you in the lake."

For all that, we were uncomfortable enough in our packing cases as the boat carried us over the surface of the Lake of the Crater. Some of us had been in those cases longer than others; we had tried to insert ourselves into Mortifer's supply chain as unobtrusively as possible, burglaring warehouses in the dead of night to substitute monitors for supplies. An "accident" involving a cargo disc had enabled us to substitute the last few cases in the confusion. Luckily Mortifer tended to use standard sized chests large enough, though barely, to hold a man. A few boxes too small to hold a monitor were packed with equipment we hoped would prove useful.

The sound of the engine that drove the boat ceased, and I heard clanking sounds through my packing case. Very careful observation from the shore by our agents had told us the routine that was followed; the boat was moored to a buoy tethered just below the surface and the cases were tipped overboard from the side of the boat, which then returned to a boathouse on the shore of the lake.

Presently, the case I was in was lifted and dropped into the water. I was head-down for a moment, then the case was righted by the weights which had been placed at my feet to make the case weigh the same amount as the one we had substituted it for. Presently, there was a bump and silence for a while. Then the case was pushed sideways for a ways and there was another pause. A loud humming began and I felt myself descending again. Then there was a gurgle of water running away.

I moved aside a little hatch which had been built into my case and peered out through the piece of dark translucent material which, I hoped, concealed my spyhole. The cases were standing in a large circular chamber from which water was gradually draining; harsh white lights behind protective transparent panels lit the scene. When the water was gone a heavy round door opened in one wall and blue-domed androids with cargo handling equipment came into the room. I let them take a case or two to the door so that there was one case inside the door and another blocking it. Then I simultaneously keyed a machine I held and kicked the release that made my case fall away in two halves.

The androids froze, as they had at the false Castle Thorn when Droste and his men invaded it. I blew a blast on a whistle which I had carried on a chain round my neck and all of the cases carrying monitors split and spilled out their contents. Each man or woman ran to perform assigned tasks; making sure the door was well blocked so that it could not be closed on us, retrieving pieces of equipment from the smaller cases.

We formed up in skirmishing order and went down the corridor upon which the door opened. No effort had been made to close the door, though it was remotely, not manually, operated. Either our invasion had been unobserved or else the enemy was playing a waiting game. Reluctantly I keyed the contact that would turn off my sound receptors; from now on I must travel deaf and let others be my ears. We were all anonymous in dark-colored Support Suits, but Mortifer knew me well enough to realize that I would want to be in the assault group myself. If he spoke the word that would stop my heart and breath there might be no time for my companions to aid me, even though one of them was a Healer and carried emergency medical equipment.

The monitors carried equipment to override any ordinary door lock and we left no room unexplored as we passed along the corridor. This was a storage and service area; one room held neat stacks of supplies, another a transport disc in the process of repair. There were stored foods in some rooms and one was a wine cellar. Mortifer, I remembered, prided himself on his discriminating palate for wine, and since he was not a man to indulge his servants it was an encouraging sign that Mortifer himself lived here at least some of the time.

Now we passed small utilitarian bedrooms, all empty. Some human staff must live here then, at least part of the time. Presently a few more pretentious bedrooms showed that Mortifer sometimes housed guests or had human servants to whom he allowed some luxuries.

We now reached a more elaborate door closing off the passage; our lock-opening machine took several minutes to solve the problem of opening it. Eventually the door flashed open and we entered a long, richly decorated corridor; there were soft carpets underfoot and paintings on the wall. As we went down the corridor a man in dark clothing emerged from a side room carrying a tray with dishes on it. A neural interrupter flashed and he dropped to the floor, but not before he had time to utter a warning cry into a disc on his wrist. I couldn't hear what he had yelled, of course, but it was probably enough to warn Mortifer.

I reached over my shoulder and pulled my sword from its sheath strapped to my back, and all of our party unslung fire-shields and held them at the ready. We went down the corridor at a trot, dashing past doors, as members of our party peeled off to deal with whatever the side rooms might contain.

The corridor ended in a circular anteroom from which three elaborate doors opened; solid doors hung on hinges—not the usual doors which flashed white and vanished to allow entrance. As we came to the anteroom some instinct made me halt my group. We waited, pressed against the corridor wall until the men who had fallen behind to deal with the side rooms joined us, signalling "All clear." The Healer touched me on the shoulder and handed me a little message square. In glowing letters on its surface I read, "Hidden speakers giving alarm. Have several times repeated sequence of nonsense syllables; may be your 'deathword.'"

I nodded and signaled for a very special member of our group; an andro with a highly unusual power source and very simple programming. It dashed out into the anteroom, headed for the center door. Flame flared from the ceiling and when the andro protected itself with an upflung shield, the floor under it flashed white and the andro dropped from sight into some pit or abyss below.

I grinned mirthlessly and waved some of our special equipment forward. A device which vibrated so intensely that I could feel it through the soles of my feet immobilized the floor, while heavy-duty torchers flared out to destroy the painted ceiling of the anteroom and the weapons hidden above it.

My voice sounding strange in my deadened ears, I said, "Squad Three, left door. Squad Four, right door. Squads One and Two through the center door with me. Go!"

We crossed the antechamber in a few bounds and fell on the doors. On each side of me I could hear the other squads battering on locked or barricaded doors, but the central door burst open as we threw our weight on it and we burst into a room very much like the pictures I had seen of Mortifer' s laboratory at the Academy in Thorn.

Mortifer himself was seated on a throne-like chair with a console of contacts and flashing lights before him. Behind him a display screen showed us ourselves bursting into the room as if in a mirror. Mortifer's mouth moved but of course I could hear nothing. Then with his crooked smile on his face he touched a contact before him. The room shuddered and the floor pressed on my feet. The screen behind Mortifer showed the surface of the lake now, and a strange object breaking its surface. Suddenly I realized that this room in which we stood was part of some flying vehicle, in which Mortifer was trying to escape.

I stepped forward, sword at the ready and Mortifer smiled again. He pressed another contact and on the screen behind him, written in letters of fire appeared the words:

AVAUNT FRANKENSTEIN!

My vision blurred, my knees buckled as I dropped to the floor dimly conscious that both heart and breath had ceased.

18. THE STARSHIP

I regained consciousness to find the Healer from my assault team bending over me. My head ached and my breathing was heavy and unnatural. I realized that my breathing was not under my control. "Relax a minute more," whispered the Healer, and I realized that he had turned on my sound receptors. "We had a program all set to defuse that reflex once it was triggered," murmured the Healer. "Give it a moment to operate and I can shut off the heart-lung field."

I realized that I was lying on a carpeted floor with a forest of legs around me; my two squads had surrounded me, sheltering me with their bodies. The floor under me vibrated as I remembered the transport disc vibrating on my first ride in one, when we had passed near the starship taking off. I heard Mortifer's voice over the heads of my men. "You may arrest me as much as you wish, monitor, but in a few minutes we will be on my starship and I think my defenses will hold you off until then. You had better lay down your weapons or my men will cut you down as soon as we are inside the cargo bay."

The leader of Squad One knelt by my side and whispered, "Any instructions, ser?"

Fighting the heavy involuntary breathing I whispered back, "Keep him talking . . . give up weapons if you must . . . drop a flamer near my hand . . . ."

A great shadow darkened the sky above us and I could see that the giant transport disc which formed the "floor" of Mortifer's secret laboratory was floating up into an open cargo bay on the great black disc of a starship. I heard my squadleader talking as calmly as if he had been standing on the streets of Thorn. "Academician Mortifer, this will get you nowhere. Kidnapping aboard a starship is a Commonwealth offense. Our support team undoubtedly had you under observation and a U.C. ship will be dispatched after you from Thorn starport. You will be stopped before you can go Q and come back to face increased charges."

"Nothing on Carpathia can stop this ship or keep my ship from slipping away into quasi-space," snapped Mortifer. "Drop your weapons or my men will cut you down." The squadleader gave a quiet order and weapons rained down about me, one flamer dropping neatly into my open hand.

Under cover of this the Healer whispered, "We've killed the reflex; I'm turning off the field." My breathing became normal again, but I practiced breathing as shallowly as I could; I might have to play dead in hopes of seizing some opportunity later. I heard the ominous clang of the closing doors of the cargo bay and the hiss of air equalizing pressure.

I was still sheltered by my monitors when I heard a woman's voice from a direction that could only be on the floor of the cargo bay. "Everything all right, Councillor Mortifer?" the voice asked. I turned my head slowly and stealthily so that when my squads moved away my "dead" open eyes could see as much as possible.

"On my part, yes," said Mortifer's voice, "but what about yours? This starship isn't *Sceptre*!"

"The Tribune had *Sceptre* impounded," said the woman's voice. "We had to seize this trading ship to carry out your instructions to meet you here." The fascinating thing about that was that it was a lie; we had not been able to trace the ownership of any starship to Mortifer or his friends; I had never even heard of the starship *Sceptre*, much less given orders to impound her. Someone was playing Mortifer false; had some of his own folk revolted?

"Fool," snapped Mortifer, showing his usual stupidity about handling his subordinates. If that tale had been true the woman deserved commendation, not insults. "Fool," he repeated. "Nothing could have caught *Sceptre*, but you've trapped us on some lumbering trader which will be run down before we can slip into quasi-space."

"I assure you, Councillor, not a single starship will lift to pursue us," said the woman. "What do you want done with these monitors?"

"Over against that wall for the moment," said Mortifer and the squads of monitors filed off of the disc which held the laboratory, showing me a group of humans in Support Suits not unlike ours with heavy weapons trained on my monitors. The woman who had been speaking to Mortifer was evidently the pale, red-haired woman who stood not far from me. I saw that she too wore a monitor's uniform and remembered the woman monitor who had tricked Casmir Thorn into Mortifer's hands. "Freeze this body until I can get around to dissecting it," said Mortifer matter of factly. That gave me little time; whatever move I made would have to be made before I went into the freezer. They would hardly be foolish enough to put me in it in my Support Suit; even turned off it would impede the quick-freeze action.

"Shall I intern the monitors in some of the crew rooms?" asked the red-haired woman.

"No," said Mortifer almost casually. "They are of no use to me. Cut them down."

The woman looked at him and became even paler. "Ser, I can't do that," she said.

"Can't!" exclaimed Mortifer. I half saw from the comer of my eye that he had risen from his console and was coming toward me. "You've disobeyed me for the last time, wench. I'll torch you first and then cut the others down myself." He reached down for a flamer dropped by one of my monitors. With a roll and a bound I had him from behind; one of my arms around his throat and my sword point touching his neck just under his ear.

"Drop your weapons," I called to the red-haired woman and her followers. To my surprise they broke into broad grins and lowered their weapons immediately. A door flashed open behind them and a tall man accompanied by a dog came out of it. The dog was a ghost-hound, not Trinka but a younger dog, and I thought a male. The man had a face tanned by some fiercer sun than that of Carpathia, a scar on his forehead and a flamboyant blond mustache. But the eyes were my eyes and the grin my grin as he laid his hand on the ghost-hound's head and said, "Peace, my brother. I'm Casmir Thorn, and this piratical-looking bunch are my crew-mates on Starship *Argo*, in which you stand." The ghost-hound remained placidly white as he went on. "The lady with the fiery locks is our friend, Nadia Ivanovna, who had the courage to pretend to still be Mortifer's creature after she had changed her allegiance to me."

Our eyes met across the room; he knew as well as I the strength of the Jagellon Gift. "Our apologies for the mummery, but we had to lure Mortifer away from the controls of that thing you rode up here on; he could have done considerable damage to *Argo* from that console and he was shielded besides. The sword is probably not necessary, brother, but keep a good hold on Mortifer's throat; he may have a few other death-words for you or me and I'd prefer not to find out the hard way. Nadia, my dear, if you would use a neural interrupter on Mortifer I doubt if you would do my brother any harm; I'm sure he is as full of Lysergol as I would be in his place."

Looking rather stunned, Nadia Ivanovna looked to me for permission and when I grinned at her and nodded, she pointed a familiar stubby weapon at Mortifer, who struggled frantically in my arms. There was a purple flash and he slumped, but I did not release him.

"Quite right, brother," said Casmir Thorn. "He might be faking. Nadia, a stasis suit for the distinguished Academician." The red-haired woman slipped a sort of gray shroud over Mortifer and two of my monitors took charge of him.

"We seem to have done it, brother," I said to Casmir Thorn.

He grinned. "With both of us against him, poor Mortifer had very little chance," he said. "Not to mention our allies. Gorda, go see if Mortifer is really fast asleep." The young ghost-hound padded over to where the shrouded Mortifer was held by the monitors, sniffed at him, yawned and sat down and scratched.

I laughed. "Mortifer seems to be no threat," I said. "I suppose Gorda is the replacement ghost-hound we ordered."

Casmir Thorn nodded. "I hope that you don't mind paying a rather high freight rate for him," he said. "My captain is a good friend but also a shrewd business woman. Gorda comes direct from Chrysonomia, the only planet where humans and Caphellans live together. I recommend that we each spend some time there."

I nodded thoughtfully; the ghost-hounds had renewed the interest in Caphellans which had been stirred by my first meeting with one. "They may have much to teach us," I agreed. I walked over to stand near Casmir Thorn, and both crew members and monitors withdrew respectfully, leaving us alone at one side of the cargo bay. "You've been on *Argo* since you destroyed Mortifer's laboratory in Thorn?" I asked.

"Oh, he did that himself to keep his secrets from falling into the hands of the mob that came to rescue me. I never learned that young scholar's name," said Casmir Thorn.

"Paul Sobeski," I said. "He's my secretary now. If you had contacted him again, you might be Tribune now instead of me."

He shrugged. "Nadia got me out of the exploding laboratory and warned me about the death-word. Since I didn't know when Mortifer might spring that on me, it seemed safer to take up Captain Petros on an offer of a berth on *Argo*, leaving Nadia to work from within. But when I heard of an order for a Caphellan ghost-hound by Casmir King, Tribune of Carpathia, clone of King Casmir the Tenth . . ."

I laughed. "You didn't want to miss out on the end," I told him.

He laughed in his turn. "Of course not," he said. "And just as well for you that I got here in time, contacted Nadia, and arranged to disable *Sceptre* and have *Argo* make the rendezvous. Of course, either of us alone might have done it, but as it was what you didn't do, I did."

"And what you didn't do, I did," I finished. "Yes, that's something to be thought of for the future. Not that we always want to work together."

"But we ought to duplicate experiences where possible." said Casmir Thorn. "I think I can persuade Captain Petros to train another green recruit when you can get away."

"And you should have no trouble getting elected Tribune; the Jagellon legend is still very strong on Carpathia," I replied.

"Paul Sobeski and some others know about us, but we'll have to break the news of your existence to the people eventually."

"You'll need to meet a nurse named Molly and an ultraviolet named Benton, and his sister," said the other Casmir."

"And we both need to consult with Justinian Droste."

"I've met Molly," I said, "and that reminds me our credit accounts are the same, unless Droste has taken steps to get that straightened out, and I don't think he has."

Casmir Thorn shrugged. "Leave it as it is, if they'll let us," he said. "Half of my pay as a starship crewman goes to Central Credit at Home, the other half I get in ecus. So we have credit at Home."

"And plenty on Carpathia," I told him. "The Tribune's stipend is fairly modest, but I haven't had a chance to spend much of it."

"'Good," said Casmir Thorn. "I've spent most of my ecus on artifacts from off-world."

Just then a crewman approached us and said a little uncertainly, "Casmir?"

The other Casmir grinned and said, "We're both Casmir, Jogo, but he's only the Tribune of Carpathia and I'm the second "supercargo of *Argo*."

"Aw well, we can't all be lucky," said the crewman with perfect seriousness. "He looks just like you did when you came aboard. Anyway, Captain wants you both on the bridge. Says if you don't want to go right back to Thorn she wants to know who's paying for all this time on GE. In fact I guess she wants to know that anyway."

"I think I can answer that one," I said. "And I'd like to communicate with my backup crew, too. Will someone find my monitors somewhere to rest up?"

"Sure," said Jogo. "I'll take 'em to the crew lounge and give 'em a drink if they'll take it; we're not going Q anytime soon."

"Tell them from me that they're off duty except for the ones in charge of Mortifer," I said, "and they'll get their chance to celebrate later."

"Yesser," said Jogo and strode off with the catlike tread that seemed to be characteristic of starcrew.

The other Casmir chuckled. "You must have impressed him to get a 'ser'," he said. "We starflitters rather look down on you planetaries."

Once back in Thorn Mortifer was handed over to Universal Commonwealth authorities; safer than trying to keep him on Carpathia where some of his secret sympathizers might work to free him. I requested the Council to reimburse Captain Elena Petros for all expenses incurred by *Argo* and to open the Lake of the Crater for swimming by local children as soon as possible. Such "requests" were increasingly mere formalities which worried me more than a little. I didn't mind being watchdog of Carpathia's liberties, but I had no desire to be her king.

It was late that night when all of the formalities were over and Casmir Thorn and I paced the battlements of Castle Thorn in the moonlight. Soberly I told Casmir Thorn of the last time I had seen a face like mine by moonlight.

"Needless to say, 'I would have done the same," he told me. "Our talents and Mortifer's mind was a combination just too dangerous to take any chances with."

"What are the limits of our talent?" I asked him. "Would a man like Justinian Droste or a woman like Wanda Jagellon do something against their conscience because of the loyalty we inspire?"

He shook his head slowly. "I hope not," he said. "Otherwise the burden becomes almost too great to bear. Perhaps the Caphellans can help us find our limits—and our strengths. Will you flit when *Argo* lifts or shall I?"

"I'd better go this time," I said. "Otherwise you'll be too far ahead of me in the crew hierarchy. You can stand for Tribune or not as you please; things are quiet now. You can live here in the castle in any case; the Knights are regarding us as co-Commanders, and the rooms go with that office, not with the Tribune's office."

He nodded. "Perhaps I'll wait and see," he said. "We don't want to slip into being *de facto* kings and a rest from a Casmir as Tribune might help there. Besides, I want to explore some of the back country, see how much it has changed. No need for us to parallel exactly, so long as each keeps in touch with the other's experience."

"Will we always parallel?" I mused. "Could we ever come into conflict?"

The other Casmir frowned thoughtfully. "We're different men, that I know. I think, for one thing, that you're more reflective than I and I'm more inclined to act before I think. I wish we had Mortifer's records; I suspect that our differences started even back in those identical environments. But of course we're far more like than unlike: closer than brothers, closer than twins. For better or worse we'll grow more unlike our prototype; he never had a parallel Casmir. As for whether you and I will ever come into conflict, I find it hard to imagine but I don't know . . . ."

"If we do," I said, looking up at the stars, "we can arrange that our paths don't cross at the same place at the same time. It's a big universe, big enough for . . . what can you call us? . . . a parallel man."

BLACKOUT

The ad had been honest enough:

Experienced Actor With UEC
To act in, direct and write blackouts
Long established startouring company
Contact G. Dark, Location Alpha 512

It didn't call the blackouts "short dramatic productions" or use any other euphemisms. And any blackout company that could afford the price of startouring must be making a lot of money. Hard money too: extraplanetary credit units, which was all that they'd take at the boxoffice unit in most blackouts. Planet money fluctuates but ecus are backed by the Universal Commonwealth itself and they always buy the same amount of the goods that really matter to a starflitter: starpassage and UC standard equipment.

Location Alpha was one of those interchangeable office blocks you find on any planet that has startrade: brightwalls in pastel colors, abstract Views in the darkwalls moving to innocuous music, UC standard secretary units. But when I thumbed the doorplate on room 512, I was told to enter by a real voice, not one of those perfectly neutral machine voices. The interview room was unusual too. They all contain a secretary unit and a few moderately comfortable chairs. The brightwall is always behind the secretary unit and one of the cheaper tricks that interviewers use is to make it glare in your eyes.

This brightwall was keyed in a strange way, in strips of color. The top strip was a clear light blue green shot through with streaks of pink, the next strip was deep blue with flickers of lighter blue running through it and the bottom strip was a not very luminous yellow brown. The total effect was that of a scene just before dawn on an ocean beach: it could have been the view from my grandma's shack on the beach back home in Fiji. I looked at it in fascination: I hadn't known that a brightwall could be keyed like that.

I was so interested in the brightwall that for a moment I didn't see the man behind the secretary unit: maybe that was the idea of keying it that way. But once seen the man was worth looking at: he had dark hair and one of those ageless mobile faces that are so common among actors. He had excellent presence and his voice when he spoke was very evidently a trained one, but he had that indefinable "withered" look that comes from too many lifestretches. I wondered how many stretches he'd had: this man must be old, I thought, impressed despite myself.

He recognized me, which is always flattering, especially from a fellow professional. The richly modulated voice was just enthusiastic enough. "Mr. Edward Black, is it not? I am Gedeon Dark. I've had the pleasure of seeing you on several occasions, both in Shakespeare and in modern things. The Equity Card is a formality in your case, sir, but I'll enjoy the privilege of reviewing your credits."

I bowed and handed my UEC to him, and he waved me to a chair as he fitted it into the desk unit. He lifted the lightshield to get the best contrast on the holos, but I could hear some of the dialogue from the projection, though the sound was directional, aimed toward his chair.

There's room for about eight minutes of recording on a standard UE card: some actors carry a supplementary card with additional credits, but I figure that if you can't show that you can act in eight minutes you might as well forget it. Dark watched all eight minutes, his head slightly bent toward the projection, his face intent. I finish my credits with one of the lesser known soliloquys from *Hamlet* : "How all occasions do inform against me . . . ." I could hear my recorded voice rising on the last lines, but Dark was silent for a moment after the projection ended. Then he turned his eyes on me, caught my eyes and paused before he spoke: stretched near the limits as he was he still had wonderful technique.

"You know, of course, Mr. Black, that it is the psi component in live theatre that keeps us treading the boards instead of being replaced by these little shadow plays," he began, gesturing at the place where the projections had appeared on his desk.

I nodded. "Yes sir; nowadays they give courses on parapsychology as part of the required curriculum at the Royal Academy of Dramatic Arts," I said with a smile that I hoped hid my puzzlement at this lecture on basics. He caught it nevertheless: he had magnificent rapport. In his heyday he must have been a great actor.

"Bear with me a moment, Mr. Black," he said quietly. "Since you've studied psionics perhaps you remember the first corollary to Stugiatski's Law?"

I tried to cast my mind back to that parapsych class years ago. "It states that psi phenomena can't be produced mechanically, does it not?"

He shook his head with a smile. "That is the law itself, sir. The first corollary states that psi phenomena cannot be *re*produced mechanically. Thus in your magnificent rendering of Hamlet's speech on your credits I got your words, your gestures, your inflections, but not your rapport with your audience, not the outpouring of emotion you transmitted psionically as you gave that speech. Not everyone knows that this is the basic difference between even the best projected theatre and live theatre, but enough people are aware of a difference to keep living theatre precariously in existence."

He paused again and raised a hand in a curiously compelling gesture. "So for ordinary living theatre, the psionic component is vital. But for my kind of theatre it is more than that: it is its whole reason for being. The emotion conveyed psionically by a gifted actor is the only thing that can unloose the frozen emotions of those who have traveled across space locked in that strange phenomenon we call Q-time. Even with gifted actors the emotion must be simple, it must be strong. It must, if you like, be raw and primitive. But that is not enough: the actors must be gifted, quite literally; endowed with the talent for psionic communication that makes a great actor. Blackouts, sir, are the most difficult form of theatre. I do not ask you to believe that entirely now: the prejudices you have learned in the 'legitimate' theatre are probably too strong. But I ask you to entertain it as a hypothesis, a conjecture."

He smiled again and deliberately misquoted: "To entertain conjecture for a time."

It was impossible not to play back to him, not to imitate his seriousness and his formal matter. "I can only say, sir, that I will do my best to do so." I was rewarded with one of his flashing smiles.

"Then, sir, let me welcome you as a member of Dark's Blackout Company." His manner at once shifted to the businesslike. "The company has four members, as is traditional. My powers have faded with age: I no longer act. You will play opposite my daughter, Jocylon; the other two members of the company are the Honorable S'han and her partner S'vry. You have, I take it, no objection to acting with Szilara?"

I was surprised, but my assurances were sincere as I said, "My only misgiving is that the saurians will undoubtedly know Shakespeare much better than I do. But surely a mixed human—Szilara company is unusual?"

His face was somber as he shook his head. "No my young friend, it is rather common in blackout companies, for a rather discreditable reason. Many of the companies make considerable use of . . . tensions between the species."

I was really shocked this time and did not conceal it. Planetaries have species prejudices of course: I've heard Szilara called "lizards" on Earth itself and once on a Szilara planet off the major star lanes I had the opportunity to collect some choice Szilara names for humans: "rnuckworm" is a translatable equivalent of one of the politer epithets. But the Saurians who had called me that did not know I spoke Szilar: to your face even planetary Szilara are painfully polite. Flitters like to think of themselves as totally unprejudiced: I had never seen any sign of species prejudice among starflitters.

I looked Dark in the eyes and said, "I hope that you don't expect me to . . . ."

He interrupted me with a gesture. "By no means. Dark's Blackouts have never relied on cheap sensationalism. At any rate, what is done on the stage is your business: part of your job is to adapt material in the public domain or write original material. No playwright of any note, unfortunately writes directly for the blackouts. And I fear I must ask you to have something ready for our next engagement: in about a week realtime after we flit to the next planet."

I shrugged. "No one can do creative work in Q-time," I said. "So it will have to be an adaption. Will your audiences sit still for Shakespeare, suitably updated?"

He nodded with a smile. "They will indeed," he returned, "so long as the action elements are emphasized, and the ending is in the blackout tradition, on a high point of emotion and ideally with a certain ambiguity. It might be tactful to consult the Honorable S'han, but my daughter and S'vry will simply learn whatever lines you give them and accept your direction. Let me introduce you to the rest of the company and to our grips." He rose and led me through a door in one wall of the room, which he had keyed from the secretary unit. I was impressed: the company evidently had a suite in this Location, and such accomodations do not come cheap.

Jocylon Dark was dark and lovely, with a thoroughly professional manner. I prefer to find my sexual adventures outside the company I act in and Jocylon evidently had the same view: there was no sexual challenge or appraisal in her attitude toward me. S'vry, like most male Szilara, was completely self-effacing in the presence of a dominant female, but seemed to be competent. I treated S'han with elaborate politeness, hissing her initial "s" for three full beats which was one more than she was really entitled to. After a little initial skirmishing she decided to treat me as a female, that is as an equal. Her attitude toward Jocylon was pretty much like her attitude to S'vry: she was "reversing' the sexes" as the Szilara say, which would make it a good deal easier for me to direct her and only seemed to amuse Jocylon.

As I expected, both Szilara knew the works of Shakespeare verbatim. Some Szilara practically worship the Bard and would object to cutting or adapting his plays, but S'han had the right attitude; old Will was a man of the theatre and would be pleased to see his works reaching a new audience, even if they had to be adapted to do so. We agreed to do an updated version of *Othello*, a play with which I have a love-hate relationship since in the Dark Ages it is one of the few roles an actor of my complexion could have played.

I would play Othello, Jocylon Desdemona, S'han Iago and S'vry a role that combined most of the other essential parts. The court of Venice became a Commonwealth planet during the Wars of Unity, with Othello an out-Commonwealth barbarian general. We concentrated on the main story line: Iago's attempts to destroy Othello's marriage to Desdemona by creating jealousy. I decided to end the play with

Othello's killing of Desdemona. Desdemona you may remember wakes up as Othello starts to smother her and attempts to save herself by pleading with him, even trying to seduce him. We agreed to curtain with the issue in doubt: sound blackout strategy. The last spoken lines in my revision were "Put out the light . . . and then put out the light", one of the hardest lines in Shakespeare to give the right reading to, but one of the most effective if done well.

For scenery and minor "actors" the company had what stage people call, heaven knows why, a "Spelvin", which is essentially a programmable holographic projector. This unit would even do costumes for the living actors which, when you consider the coordination involved, is rather impressive in itself. But of course Equity doesn't allow stock tapes for minor parts: the four of us had to set to work immediately recording the small roles and we had to be very careful that the taped fill-ins amounted to no more than ten percent of our live roles as Equity rules require.

Dark himself was unobtrusively helpful in dozens of ways but did no acting at all: I wondered if he had given up his UE card as some old actors do, to make room for younger people.

We flitted from that planet almost immediately of course and did our rehearsals and taping on the world where our next engagement was scheduled. Actors are not immune to the numbing effects of Q-time and we needed to release our own emotions before we could release those of others. No one who has not startoured can realize how odd the first rehearsals after you come out of Q-time can be: you have to go on pure technique with no feel for the role at all. A friend of mine compared it once to making love in a spacesuit, except that he was a little more graphic.

Once you get used to it, however, doing your early rehearsals under emotional anesthesia can be rather useful: you get all the mechanics taped about the time your emotions start coming back and the acting itself seems to bring them back more quickly. Dark's Blackouts worked on a four-week cycle: a week's rehearsal, three weeks of performance and then flit to the next engagement. The shortest week on any DC planet is five days and the longest ten, with Earth's seven day week being surprisingly common. Short weeks tend to go with long days, so even on a planet with a five-day week it's usually possible to be "up" for your first performance, though just barely. Our first planet after I joined Dark had a ten day week. Fortunately, because I needed every second of it.

Earth English is one of the UC Standard Languages, of course, and any spaceman has to autolearn all twelve Standards. So we played in English and any planetaries that didn't understand it had to pay double ticket price, in ecus, for standardized translator units, English to local language only.

We rented that kind of thing locally and part of Dark's job was to make sure that such arrangements went smoothly. He was, in effect, our stage manager, and was in charge of our crew of grips, three men and three women. They were all human and all vaguely Malay or Phillipino in appearance. But their strangely luminescent silvery eyes showed that they were from some planet far from Earth and all of them had the same withered appearance as Dark: I wondered how many centuries they had toured wrth hlm.

If you wonder what grips do in a production with no solid scenery or costumes, so did I sometimes, but as least part of the answer was that they did everything from renting the theatre to selling tickets to getting us all aboard the starship for our next engagement. Some of them were marvelous techs: little things like keying standard brightwalls to make striking works of abstract art they did just for amusement, their own or Dark's. They communicated among themselves occasionally in some language of their own, but all of them spoke all twelve Standards without any trace of accent.

By the end of the first week of our first engagement I was delighted with my new job and wondering why I had ever bothered touring in conventional plays. Every audience started dead cold, of course; that was what took me a week to get used to. But by the end of the play you were lifting them out of their seats: I'd never had better rapport with audiences.

S'han was overbearing, spiteful and quarrelsome offstage and a magnificent actor onstage: for the sake of her Iago performance I would have put up with far worse behavior. Neither Jocylon or S'vry could carry a scene by themselves or in combination with each other, but they played up magnificently to S'han or myself. That made for some awkward staging at times: run through *Othello* and see how many scenes feature neither Iago nor the Moor. But I realized the difficulty soon enough to write around it: using the necessary minimum of scenes without either S'han or myself as "rests" between emotional heights.

With the enthusiasm of one who had been reluctantly but completely converted I became a staunch advocate of the blackout as an important form of theatre: I was now proud rather than ashamed of what I was doing and welcomed the few opportunities I had to argue the merits of the blackout with "legitimate" actors. But I didn't want to spend the rest of my life doing blackouts: I needed holos of what I was doing to impress "legitimate'" producers when I got ready to make a move. Gedeon Dark would never consent to my recording the show or any part of it, I knew: he had a positive phobia about recording live theatre. And normal holorecording equipment is about as unobtrusive as an elephant zork. What I needed was a high quality miniature holorecorder. They existed all right but most of them are in the hands of UC officers and none that I knew of were available for frivolous purposes like recording a blackout.

Still, it was worth trying, so I went to the nearest thing to a UC officer that I had any personal pull with: a starship captain who had taken me out for dinner several times after performances. The captain was Greek and female: there are plenty of Greeks flitting as starcrew and a fair number of women, but not many Greek women. Elena Petros was very Greek and very female: as shrewd and adventurous as Odysseus and as strikingly beautiful as her namesake, Helen of Troy. She had seduced me with no resistance at all on my part and we had both enjoyed the experience. The next time she showed up at the stagedoor I took her to dinner, and told her what I needed.

She looked at me thoughtfully over the remains of our dolmades and moussaka. (wherever Greek starcrew land some other Greek will start a restaurant). "You are very lucky *mavros mou*," she said, using the Greek term of endearment. "One of my other lovers is a holotech and I think through him I can get what you require."

Elena didn't name her contact and I firmly repressed my curiosity: it was none of my business. But she got hold of him quickly and the holorecorder was in her hands within a few days. It was a spy outfit of some kind with the works in a belt-like arrangement and the pickups in several pieces that looked like costume jewelry. Elena simply wore the outfit to the first performance I could get her a good seat for and went off afterwards to return the unit and have the recording transferred to a standard-sized replay module. She rented a replay room under her own name, though with my credit, and the next afternoon after a festive lunch we went to view the projection.

Even if you know the play you won't know my adaptation of it, so I'll remind you or tell you that the first scene features Iago and a minor character: Rodrigo in the original play and a composite character played by S'vry in the adaptation. The recording began with a scan of the audience. Elena had turned the recorder on early to make sure she got the curtain rising. The "curtain" was a projection, but not from our Spelvin: it was a fixed projection that belonged to the stage and was hand keyed by a grip: some kind of union rule. When the curtain "rose"—dissolved actually—we got our first shock.

We were expecting the highly imaginative and striking stage set for *Othello* projected by our Spelvin: what we saw was the bare stage. I turned to Elena. "Did that unit have some kind of cutoff so it didn't record other holos?" I could imagine there being use for such a device and thought we might have got one by mistake.

She shook her head. "I don't think that's even possible; anyway it recorded the curtain and that was a projection."

Before she could say more we got our next shock. S'han entered as Iago, clad only in her finely scaled epidermis: the costume projections were not recording any more than the scenery. But the greatest shock was that she was addressing her lines to the empty air: where Elena and I remembered clearly seeing S'vry standlng and speaking his lines was only empty space and silence. For a while Elena and I were too stunned to talk or turn off the projector: we watched in stupified silence as S'han spoke her lines and exited and I came on for the next scene, clad in leotards and a singlet, thank heavens, and spoke my lines. Iago is on stage in that scene too and while S'han and I were interacting the play came briefly alive. After all there was no scenery at the Globe and very little in the way of costuming.

The next scene starts with neither Othello or Iago on stage and we got only the empty stage. Elena moved to shut off the projector but I stopped her. "Wait," I said. "Desdemona is on later in this scene. We might as well know about Jocylon too." We watched in silence while I came on again and my heart contracted as I heard myself speak her cue:

"She loved me for the dangers I had pass'd
And I loved her that she did pity them
This only is the witchcraft I have used
Here comes the lady: let her witness it."

The lady did not come; the stage was blank and silent where I had seen Jocylon Dark's lovely form last night. I gestured to Elena to shut off the projector and buried my face in my hands for a few moments.

When I looked up at Elena her voice was unemotional but there was sympathy in her eyes. "One more piece of data, Edward. You were busy looking at what wasn't there: I was scanning the background for clues. I saw several of your stage attendants—grips you call them, don't you—moving around behind the scenes."

I looked up at her as she stood next to my chair. "There's a desk backstage: Gedeon Dark is almost always there, keeping an eye on things. Did you see him?"

She shook her head. "The desk, yes, but not Dark. No one but the short men with the strange eyes."

"Not conclusive," I said, "he might have been out of sight. But probably him too . . ."

Elena looked at me and I could see that she was a little shaken under that iron control. "My grandmother used to tell me stories about vampires who didn't show a reflection in mirrors . . ." she said slowly.

I shook my head. "Anything solid reflects light," I said, "and I would have sworn they were as solid as you or I. Dammit I pretend to smother Jocylon in the last scene. I wonder what would happen if I actually tried to do it. You were right about the curtain: if this recorder didn't record other projections it wouldn't have recorded the curtain. So there weren't any projections, and there isn't any Jocylon Dark or any S'vry and very likely there isn't any Gedeon Dark either."

There was a calculating look on Elena's lovely face and she said slowly, "The little men with the strange eyes . . . . ?"

I shook my head. "Maybe, but I don't think so. If they could create an illusion of Jocylon and S'vry being competent actors why couldn't they just have acted themselves? And if Gedeon Dark is an illusion too, why bother? One of the silver-eyes could have done everything he did."

Elena shrugged. "There are some strange races in the Commonwealth, Edward. There's a rather decadent race that doesn't make love to each other in person: they create an illusion for their lover to be with, and the lover does the same for them. They reproduce by artificial means. Maybe the silver-eyed men can't act in their own personalities and have to create an illusion to do it for them."

It was plausible but I wasn't convinced. "It's one possible explanation Elena, but I have the feeling it isn't the right one. I'd like to see the inside of that spelvin unit: I could see it sitting in the background. If it isn't projecting holos what the devil is it doing?"

She looked at me uneasily. "Edward, do not do anything foolish or precipitate. You know I have to flit tomorrow, my ship is locked into a schedule I can't break. I was going to ask you to let me keep a copy of this tape to remember you by, but . . . ."

I took her hand in mine. "Elena, you've done more than enough already. We've been friends as well as lovers and you've been a wonderful friend. But you have your own job and your own life. I won't do anything rash, but I think it's my job to get to the bottom of this. I feel . . . used . . . . I thought that Gedeon and Jocylon and even S'vry were friends as well as colleagues. Not I find out that they don't exist."

Elena raised a beautifully arched eyebrow and sighed. "I would resent it if you tried to protect me, I suppose, so I have no right to try to protect you. You won't be sensible enough to take this tape to the planetary authorities, will you?"

I shook my head. "No, Elena, but I'll leave it with you. If anything does happen to me do whatever you want with it." She wasn't satisfied, but she agreed. And I was right about her having her own life and her own job: when we made love for the last time that night I could feel already that her thoughts were already partly with her ship and the voyage to come.

I don't know what my performance was like that night and the next. I suppose technique carried me through, because my mind certainly wasn't on my acting. The morning after Elena left I got a message chip, personal delivery, from the starport. When I put it in the projector I saw Elena's head and shoulders; her face wore a somber expression.

"Edward," she said, "I have another piece of information. I'm leaving this planet one man short; one of the crew jumped ship. There are always a few crewmen who get sick of Q-time or form an attachment planetside and stay awhile, but all of my crew have been with me a long time and I thought I knew them, I believed none of my crew would leave me without notice, When one did I made it my business to find out why. His best friend aboard told me that he'd 'gone crazy' over a girl he met planetside. A girl named Jocylon Dark."

She paused, almost as if she could hear my startled protest. Elena went on. "Apparently he's been seeing her at the theatre after performances. If the Jocylon Dark that appears on stage is some sort of illusion so is the one he's been seeing. It may tie in, Edward, with something that's been bothering a lot of star captains: crewmen who jump ship and disappear. I secretly thought that the men had grievances that their captains didn't know about: that it couldn't happen on my crew. I was wrong."

The holo image looked into my eyes as if it could see me. "Edward, don't . . . disappear. And keep a lookout for my crewman. His name is Laris. Greyish face, short black hair with a widow's peak, scar along his jaw, big nose. Not an easy man, but a good man. Look after him if you can, but first look after yourself. I've got to go: we flit in a half hour realtime. I'll see you again Edward—I hope." The holo blinked out, I retrieved the chip and put it away carefully.

Then I began to think, something I do not do enough of normally: I usually act on instinct and later figure out why I did what I did. The quarrel with the director that had cost me my place in the Avon Shakespeare company had happened that way. This time I had better think before following my instincts, because following my instincts might be fatal.

The forms of Jocylon, S'vry and probably Gedeon Dark were illusions; psionic projections. Either real people or holographic projections would have shown up on the recorder. Psionic projections had to be projected by a mind, one with extraordinary psionic powers. Dark himself or rather whatever controlled the image of Dark, had quoted Stugiatski's Law to me: psi effects cannot be produced mechanically. So where was the illusionist? Of course, Elena could be right: the grips singly or collectively could be the illusionists. But somehow it didn't feel right.

I would stake my life it wasn't S'han. Aside from everything else, she, like myself, was the type of actor who can't get out of the theatre fast enough after a performance, and Laris had been meeting "Jocylon" after the performances. After the performances, then, was the crucial time. But the grips were often out of the theatre then, too. I had seen them on the streets and in restaurants after performances. I tried to think: had I ever seen all of them out of the theatre together? But I couldn't be sure. Except for their leader Myanzek I couldn't distinguish them very well.

Alright, Laris had only jumped ship last night, perhaps even this morning. Perhaps he would be meeting "Jocylon" tonight. And if I wasn't actor enough to go out of the theatre normally and obviously and fade back into it silently and unobtrusively, I might as well give up.

That part was, in fact, childishly easy. S'han had a little entourage of male Szilara waiting for her at the stagedoor, and was carried off by them almost immediately. I had a few people for autographs but no one persistent enough that I couldn't get rid of them without hard feelings: word had gotten around among starcrew that Elena and I were a pair, and no one quite had the nerve to try to move in the night after she left. I was dressed for the street in the somewhat flamboyant clothing we actors usually wear planetside, but there was no one to notice when I simply stepped back to my dressing room and didn't go out again. Four of the six grips had gone past me as I signed autographs: the others might have left before I did. If they were still in the theatre I saw no sign of them.

I had thought about the vantage point I wanted and decided to be up off the floor: most theatres still have some access to the upper levels of the stage and some machinery for the occasional production that uses solid scenery. I went up a ladder near my dressing room door and edged my way slowly to where I could see the stage, trying to make my mind perfectly blank. If whoever projected the illusions could read minds totally and continuously, I was a dead duck anyway. But if he or she or it merely got enough feedback to make sure the illusions were getting across I might still be alright.

When I act I sink myself totally in the character, so the illusionist probably had not picked up anything at the two performances. What I was trying to do now was to make myself purely an unresponding observer; to project no emotion, no personality. It's something you have to do onstage sometimes: if done well it can make you psychologically invisible even though you're in plain sight. I've done it in the second scene of *Hamlet*, releasing my personality with a shock effect when Hamlet speaks his first lines. I've done it occasionally offstage too, but I had no way of knowing if it would work against the illusionist.

Someone had left a working light on the stage, but aside from that the theatre was dark and seemed empty. Several hours passed slowly: locked into my "neutral observer" role I was hardly aware of the passage of time. At last the stagedoor opened quietly: either it was keyed to freeopen or whoever was coming in had his thumbprint recorded on the lock mechanism.

I strained my ears to hear the footsteps: they weren't, I thought, those of anyone in the company, actor or grip. Soft steps, but not stealthy: it could be the catlike prowl of a starcrew member in full conditioning. Was it Laris? Even when he came into sight I couldn't be sure: in the dim worklight most dark hair would look black and most fairish skin grey. Then there were swift light footfalls from the direction of the dressing rooms. Jocylon came onstage and ran to the man who had come in. As I watched him take her in his arms I was suddenly struck by how much Jocylon looked like half a dozen actresses I'd known, and how close she'd been to some subconscious idea I must have of an ideal female lead: undemanding personally, supportive on the stage, not threatening professionally. Did Laris, if that was Laris down there, even see the same face and form as I did?

There was a murmur of voices and the deeper male voice carried better. "Given up everything for you . . . no one on this damned planet but you . . . ." I could only hear a reasurring murmur from Jocylon as she led him toward the center of the stage toward the Spelvin. The end came with shocking suddenness. As they reached the Spelvin Jocylon flickered and vanished. From a sudden darkness in the side of the Spelvin a whiplike tentacle darted out and twined around the man's neck. I heard a dull crack as his neck broke: he must have died instantly. Other tentacles crept out more slowly and dragged him slowly toward the dark aperature in the spelvin. He vanished inside and the metal was whole again.

In another second I would lose my neutral observer stance, feel emotions and project them. There was only one thing to do: I willed my mind to give up its hold on consciousness: to dive deep into darkness. My body slumped on the catwalk and I knew no more.

Sometime later I awoke, aware that the stage door had opened again. Myanzek, the chief grip, came onto the stage and turned up the lights from the console in back. Then he examined the stage around the Spelvin minutely, twice stopping to cleanse the stagefloor with a handheld spraycleaner. He keyed the lights down again and walked offstage, his shoulders slumped with weariness or dejection. As he went I slipped back to the ladder and down it, counting on his footsteps to cover any faint noises I made. The stagedoor was ajar: I left it that way as I went out, hoping that no one was waiting for Myanzek outside. They were, but I was lucky: one of the female grips was at the entry to the little cul-de-sac from which the stage door opened, but she was facing the street. I faded into the shadows, waited until Myanzek emerged and joined her. When they both left, I emerged from the cul-de-sac and walked briskly to the nearest actors' pub. Holding in my personality again I walked in without being noticed and attached myself to a large, noisy group of colleagues gradually making them aware of my presence. It wasn't perfect, but I thought that no one would be completely sure when I had come in.

After I had established my presence, I drank more than I usually do, giving myself a cushion for the time when I would let myself think of what happened in the theatre. But starflitters have an instinctive distrust of planetary police, only too well founded in some cases. There is a curious sort of envy of starflitters among many planetaries, and a lust on the part of planetary governments to get their hands on any sizable amount of ecus. I could imagine myself and S'han spending the rest of our lives in planetary jails as accessories or material witnesses, while some overworked Universal Commonwealth officer tried to figure out what had happened and what legitimate claims the planetary government had on the assets of Dark's Blackouts. Rightly or wrongly, I thought it better to wait until Elena got out of Q-time and could be contacted, use her official leverage to hand the matter directly over to UC officers, on a planet where the locals could not lay claim to any jurisdiction over the crime. But all the time until we boarded the starship to flit to our next engagement, I tried to keep memories out of my mind: memories of a whiplike tentacle and the dull crack of a neck breaking, or Elena's voice saying, "Not an easy man—but a good one."

While we were waiting to seal hatches and lift far enough from the planet to flit safely the agent of Nemesis came to me, in the form of a harried steward asking passengers if they had any baggage that could be transferred to the unsealed holds: a last minute shipment of biological specimens had crowded the sealed holds to bursting, while the robots had baggage still to load. Trying desperately to not only act but think as if what I were saying was normal I told him, "You know the big holographic projector we carry? It's plastered with notices to keep it in a sealed hold, but there's no real reason for that: those machines are UC Standard and can take a vacuum hold. Have your robot put it in there, but don't mention it to the rest of the company: actors are touchy about their equipment, There won't be any explosive decompression will there?"

His face brightened as he assured me that air was valved out carefully. "If you were in there yourself you wouldn't even notice the air going until you blacked out . . . . What's the matter sir, you look kind of sick."

I fought for control. "I've had a bad week. Do you have anything that will knock me out for the whole time we're in Q-time?" He had, and was eager to do me a favor in return. He was a nice young man, though a little too trusting. Still, it was my name on the stereoads as director and principal actor: how was he to know I didn't have authority over the properties? I took the stuff he gave me as soon as I got to my cabin. Like all actors I'm more superstitious than I admit. I'd taken the chances the gods gave me: if whatever was in the Spelvin could survive a vacuum maybe it was meant to survive. I wondered what it would do to me if it found out what I had tried. In fact, I wondered as I drifted off what would have happened if I or anyone else had tried to open the Spelvin case and see what was inside. Maybe I'd done the planetary police a favor.

I didn't awake rested: you can't really rest in Q-time. My emotions, of course were frozen. It was intellectually interesting that Gedeon Dark, Jocylon Dark and S'vry had not emerged from their quarters during the flit and could not be found at disembarkation time. When Myanzek came to me after disembarkation and reported that the Spelvin was inoperative it was like finding that a mathematical problem had worked out: satisfying but not exciting.

Professional reflexes took over: the show must go on. I rented a used Spelvin. I hired local actors. With one of them I even found myself using part of the spiel that "Gedeon Dark" had given me when he hired me. We rehearsed. We began to live again. There came a day when it occurred to me to put in an open transcreen call to Elena at her destination planet, to tell her I was alright, that the rest I could only tell her in person. We matched schedules and found we could meet in two flits. I told her I was going to play out the engagements Gedeon Dark had made before I left blackouts. I promised her holos of what I was doing. No problem now; I could hire professionals to record at a regular performance.

The day my emotions came alive again, so did S'han's. She began missing S'vry and nothing her new partner could do was right. I was exhausted after that day's rehearsals, but when I found Myanzek waiting in my dressing room after everyone else had gone I was almost glad. I had been remembering Jocylon Dark all day, though I hope I was kinder to her substitute than S'han had been to S'vry's.

Myanzek looked at me somberly. "You know, do you not, what you did? I thought at first that you did not, that putting Myan in the vacuum hold was just carelessness on your part. But somehow you knew."

I nodded, almost but not quite indifferent to what he might do to me. "I was in the theatre on the night Laris was there," I told him. "I saw what happened. I saw you afterwards. Why do you call it Myan?" I asked almost at random.

He shrugged. "Myan was its name. I am Myanzek, the chief priest, I suppose you could say, of Myan. On our planet there were always those like Myan. They grow in the desert. They were small ones, once, who captured animals by making them see what they wanted to see. But they do not die. They grow. Not so much larger, as more complex. Some of our ancestors made gods of them. Some of my ancestors became their priests. When the UC came to our planet there was a revolt. The people no longer offered themselves willingly. Some were destroyed, but Myan was very old, very cunning. It found a way to leave our planet, to travel from star to star, taking a few here and there who would not be missed or easily traced. You know some of the ways, you can guess others."

He paused and looked me in the face. "This I will tell you. If you had not done what you did sooner or later Myan would have needed someone . . . . and taken the closest to hand. Like Gedeon Dark, like the others."

I interrupted. "Dark was a real man then, who was . . . eaten?" I brought out the last word harshly and Myanzek winced. But he answered readily enough.

"He and Jocylon, though she was later and not his daughter, and S'vry and so many others. Those like Myan are not creative. They need those like yourself with strong imaginations. Then they respond, but you would know if it was only your imagination. So they remember, recall, the others before."

I grinned at him mirthlessly. "Some of my ancestors would have understood that: they believed that you could absorb your enemy's spirit by eating him. If I had the courage of their convictions I'd make a vegetable stew of Myan and eat it. But I don't. Well I've killed your god. What will you do?"

He shrugged, with the weariness I had sensed the other night. "You have, I suppose, set us free. We do not know what to do with freedom any more, it has been so long. But I would like to see the Blue Desert again before I die and so would the others. Will you let us go? I can turn over the rest of the credit in the accounts to you after paying our passage; that sort of thing always had to be done by one of us, one of flesh and blood."

He was an accomplice to an unknown but certainly very large number of murders, but I had nothing but pity for this priest without a god. "Take it all but enough operating balance to get us through the rest of the tour," I said. "You can go as soon as we get replacement grips."

He inclined his head and stood up. "I will not thank you and I will not curse you, Edward Black," he said. "But I would like to know why you did it. Was it for the man you saw die—for pity?"

I tried to answer honestly. "Not really. It was because I'm an actor. I serve my profession. Myan used it as bait. That's what I couldn't stand. Somehow or other, sooner or later, I would have brought Myan down."

Myanzek bowed to me with an ironic smile and said softly, "I see that you too are a priest, Edward Black. But your god is not so easily killed." Then he walked out with a curious impressiveness. I've tried to use what I saw in him then, in roles I've played since.

There's only one thing left to tell, possibly something foolish though I don't think so myself. I contacted the local secretary of Equity and found that there was an actor's cemetary on the planet we were on. I bought a plot and had the Spelvin unit containing Myan's freeze-dried body put on it as a memorial. There are two inscriptions on the base. The first says simply:

'To the deceased members of Dark's Blackouts'

I like to think that whatever there remains of Gedeon Dark and Jocylon and S'vry and the others before them is honored and remembered by those words.

The other words on the base are for Myan: the words that Othello spoke before he began to smother Desdemona with a pillow, in order as he says not to mar her beauty but really perhaps because he dared not face her eyes as she knew what he was about to do:

'Put out the light . . . and then put out the light.'

PAY THE PIPER

I'm a tinkerer, basically. There are always a few of us around, and we probably make more difference to the way people live than the great scientists, because we tinker their discoveries into things people can use. Thomas Alva Edison was one of the best of us; he didn't discover electricity for instance, but he made the electric light with its profound influence on human life. A tinkerer likes to see principles at work doing something for people. I didn't discover the existence of quasi-space: it took several great mathematicians to do that. I didn't perform the experiments that showed that it was possible to rotate matter into Q-space and make it emerge again into ordinary space: Mboya at Kenyatta University did that. What I did do was to build a Rotator that would move a whole spaceship into Q-space and move it out again practically instantaneously, light years away. Mboya created non-Einsteinian physics, but I created faster than light space travel.

After that I could have rested on my laurels, I suppose, but a tinkerer likes to tinker. I've gotten credit for things since that I only improved; the brightwall for instance, and lifestretching. But all in all I suppose I've affected my age as much as Edison affected his; I've been told so often enough in after-dinner speeches. But from the time my wife Maybelle died until the day I saw her again it all meant less than nothing to me;

the work was a drug that kept me going through the motions of living.

It happened so suddenly, her death. I left, proud and excited, for a conference where I was getting some of the first recognition for my work on "flitting", as they were already calling faster than light travel. Maybelle was as happy and proud as I, but she had never liked conferences and meetings; she'd rather stay at home and watch the speeches on the 3V, the first one we'd been able to afford. When I returned, tired and quite a bit swell-headed, she'd gone from buoyant youth and beauty to the first stages of the completely baffling degenerative disease that killed her a few months later. After that I sleep-walked through fifteen years improving other men's work and doing nothing creative of my own, until the day I read the article that changed everything.

It wasn't even in a recognized scientific journal; too wild and crazy for that, even though its author was a well-known mathematician. It was a sort of fringe journal, semi-popular and semi-professional; I read it as I read anything then, to keep from thinking. But suddenly, I felt a thrill of interest. The point of the article was that just as from quasi-space every point of real space is theoretically accessible, so from quasi-time every point of real time is theoretically accessible. The mathematical proof the author gave was no doubt an elegant game to him but in one derivation I suddenly saw a possibility, just a possibility of a modification of an ordinary rotator which might move a ship in time or blow it away altogether. Either would end my problems.

Money hadn't been a problem for years; for all practical purposes I had an inexhaustible supply. When my own ran out all I had to do was hint at a new idea I was working on to be buried in money from eager backers. I built a one-man starship, very nearly a contradiction in terms. I modified the rotator, doing all the essential work myself. I studied and planned and waited until the day when I slipped out into space and fired the rotator.

The subjective time, Q-time as they call it, was long enough for a voyage half across the Galaxy. My first triumph came when I came out of quasi-space and saw that I was still in the Solar System. Not that I felt any thrill; the emotional anesthesia that always follows travel through Q-space and Q-time wasn't affected by the fact that I had travelled through time rather than through space. That emotional freeze was very useful as I edged my ship through the air defenses of Earth, defenses I had gone to great pains to look up in still-classified archives before beginning my trip.

It helped that at the time I had returned to the gravity effect drive was even more primitive than it was when I had begun my voyage through time. I was able to give a fairly good imitation of a meteor until I was almost at the surface of the ocean and then kill my momentum suddenly in a way that the air defense system wasn't built to take account of. Then I quickly submerged and submarined my way to the beach near the place I'd lived, avoiding some submarine defense systems which had been even harder to get infomation about than the air defenses. It's hard now to remember what an armed camp Earth was in those days; when we discovered Q-space we'd also discovered that we had competition out in the stars, and we didn't know what to expect from them.

I left the ship under water and walked ashore in a support suit. With a scuba mask and flippers I'd bought in an antique store it would pass for some new kind of wet suit, and there's plenty of snorkeling and scuba-ing along that bit of coast. Luckily it was very early in the morning, a period when people aren't nearly as suspicious of you as they are in the dark of night, as I've discovered on many "thinking walks" when I was working on a problem.

A newspaper machine near the changing rooms told me that I'd hit within the right week; not the best possible day but not the worst either. I stripped off the support suit, crammed it into a carrier bag and set off to walk to the house. Luckily I'd found a key before my voyage; ironically it was in some personal stuff of Maybelle's that I'd never had the heart to sort through after her death.

I felt nothing then of course, but I've had nightmares since where I walk into that house and open the bedroom door to find Maybelle looking as she looked when I came back from that convention and saw death in her face. I wake up in a cold sweat and remind myself that it wasn't so; that she opened her eyes and showed me a face with all the health and beauty it had possessed when I had left her for the convention. She was startled, of course and worried, wondering what had gone wrong to bring me home from the convention early, confusedly aware that I looked fifteen years older and was in some abnormal emotional state.

In a way that made it easier to get her to scramble into some clothes and drive us both down to the beach where I'd left my ship, put on the extra support suit and walk into the water with me. She almost balked at the ship; she knew that at the stage of my career I had been when I left for the convention I had no access to anything like that. But she must have seen the desperation on my face through the face plate of my suit; she made an act of faith and came aboard with me.

We crept out to sea, took off in what I hoped was a blind spot in the overlap of the defence systems and went Q just as soon as we were far enough from the planetary mass. After that, of course, her emotions were frozen too. Without elation we found ourselves at almost the very time and place from which I had begun my voyage. Without hope or fear we waited for the report of the medical team I had assembled on my estate, without any emotion we found that she was free from any detectable kind of disease.

When our emotions returned, things were harder in many ways, She always feared, I think, that whatever hidden killer had caused her death the first time around was only delayed. or suppressed by her trip through Q-time, and might leap out at her at some moment of happiness and apparent security. Without ever becoming a real Q-time addict, Maybelle became very fond of taking intersteller trips with me, seeking perhaps the surcease of emotional anesthesia as well as new experiences to distract her from her fears.

My own fears were different. From the time the doctors gave her a clear bill of health I decided that we'd escaped whatever had killed Maybelle fifteen years ago. What I was afraid of was that we had somehow distorted the fabric of time in a way that might harm us, or our planet, or perhaps even the whole Universe.

Because the past had not changed. All the records, all the memories still showed that Maybelle had died fifteen years before. To explain my "new" wife I had to enter into an elaborate deception with a cousin of Maybelle's whom she trusted implicitly. My biographers have commented, discreetly or indiscreetly, on the "curious obsession" that caused me to marry my dead wife's cousin and have her undergo plastic surgery to increase her resemblance to Maybelle. Actually, Marion did undergo plastic surgery and lives very comfortably in a tropical country with a face quite unlike Maybelle's or her own former face.

I never dared use my time-ship again, nor did I dare to destroy it. But theories of Time became an obsession with me. The view I liked best was a very pragmatic one: it starts with you yourself here and now. Past events are events that theoretically can affect you here and now, future events are events that theoretically you can affect by something you do here and now. In the old Einsteinian physics that led to the theory of the Minkowski cones. What could theoretically affect you here and now were things which could send you a signal of light speed or less: close things a short time ago or distant things a longer time back. What you could affect by doing something here and now were things that you could send a signal to at light speed or less; close things a short time from now or distant things a longer time from now. Plotted three dimensionally with one spatial dimension standing for time this led to two cone-shaped projections from you here and now; the backward cone of past events and the forward cone of future events. Of course on this theory some events were neither past or future to you here and now; no signal could pass from their location to you here and now at light speed, or less.

That bothered some people and they were glad when by using Q-space we were able to send objects "around" the fabric of realspace, so that they reached their destinations with no lapse of realtime. It was now theoretically possible to send a signal from one point to another with no elapsed time; in effect we have instantaneous signals and absolute simultaneity has been restored. Event A is simultaneous with Event B if a starship flitting from the location of A arrives at the location of B as B is occurring. Relativity theory now becomes a special case of a more general theory: light is still the limiting velocity in realspace. In fact some theorists think it's the limiting velocity, period, and hold the theory that you don't actually move through Q-space.

But the mathematicians had argued, and I had proved by my time voyage, that any event could theoretically affect or be affected by any other event; causation could run from "future" to "past" as well as from "past" to "future." The cause of my ship arriving on Earth to pick up Maybelle was a series of events that took place fifteen years later. And that meant that given my original definition of past and future, the distinction between past and future had vanished; every event was both past and future to every other event.

People have been speculating for centuries what would happen if time travel was actually invented; I'd always thought that if you could travel back in time and change the past you would either change the whole future or at least find yourself in a new future, whether your act created that future or whether you just shunted yourself onto a new "branch line" that was somehow already there. What was driving me slowly out of my mind as the years passed was that I had altered the past, had snatched my wife out of the past before she died, without seemingly affecting any future event. As I've said, all the memories, all the records still confirmed that Maybelle had never vanished and that she had died. There was even a body in her grave, though I never let Maybelle know that I had confirmed that.

Of course there was much more to our lives than our fears and questions. I was tremendously happy to have Maybelle with me again on any terms and that happiness gave my work the creative impetus it had lost for those fifteen dark years. There was money and fame and travel, all the things that most ordinary people long for, and aside from my talent for tinkering, Maybelle and I were very ordinary people. But over it all was a shadow.

I never knew how closely Maybelle had followed my obsession with Time until we went in for our third lifestretch. Our eligibility for life extension was unquestioned, of course, and most people can take a third treatment, or even a fourth. Maybelle was one of those who couldn't; her cells wouldn't regenerate a third time. Disaster came as simply as that; no time to explore alternatives, to start a new research program, no time for anything. A year at the very most, only weeks at the worst; Maybelle was living the last days of her life. I didn't even have them test me; I was not going to watch my wife die and live on afterwards a second time.

We walked home from the Life Extension Center without speaking and Maybelle made coffee, one of those little luxuries we had learned to take for granted. When at last she began to speak I realized that all of those years she had been following my struggles with the paradoxes of Time.

"You know what we have to do, don't you Frank?" she asked.

"Do?" I said dully. "There's nothing we can do."

She shook her head gently. "Oh, yes there is, Frank. You have to take me back to the time you took me from. We have to pay the piper."

I stared at her. "Take you back?" I said uncomprehendingly.

She nodded, her face serene. "The symptoms of that disease I died from; I've pored over them often enough over the years, Today the doctor told me a little bit about . . . how it will be. The symptoms are just the same. Back all those years ago I died from delayed senility. The doctors then didn't know because lifestretching hadn't been invented yet."

I tried to get my whirling thoughts in some kind of order. "But why go back . . ." I floundered.

She smiled sadly. "To pay the piper, Frank. The reason there was never a time paradox, the reason all the records said I died back then was because I did die then. You'll take me back because you did take me back."

And in the end I did. The final irony was that she was absent from home only a few hours. We didn't meet ourselves, but the car was still in the parking lot where we had left it and the engine was still warm. I watched her drive away and then walked into the ocean again in my support suit. The cycle was complete; because Maybelle would die I would someday invent time travel and travel back here to rescue her from death. Because no one can escape death in the long run we would have to return here, to pay the piper, as Maybelle had said. No contradiction, perhaps even no paradox, unless a causal circle is a paradox. Her death caused the rescue. The rescue caused her death. Everything had a cause.

For fifteen years I lived with that death, for the rest of our life together we had lived with the shadow of how we might have to pay for her rescue from death. What I had done to save my wife had led to that death and that shadow. Had we ever been out of the dark tunnel from the land of the dead?

THE CHRYSENOMIAN WAY

I looked up from my dinner to find a Szilara looming over me. She wore the bands of an official of the Universal Commonwealth at neck and throat and she was smiling broadly: for a Szilar that is an indication of extreme formality. All of those formidable looking teeth make a Szilar smile rather a disconcerting experience for those of other races, but since I have several Szilar crewmen, I'm used to it. I smiled back just as broadly, which is the correct formal response, and realizing that I was at least somewhat familiar with Szilar customs, she relaxed somewhat and the smile faded.

"Captain Elena Petros of Starship *Argo*?" she asked. The question was purely a formal one: if she was seeking me out on UC business, she had undoubtedly keyed my file and looked at holos of me. I inclined my head the few centimeters appropriate for acknowledging an obvious truth and waited for her to make the next move. "I am S'mar, the local representative," she said, no need to say of what. Her bands proclaimed her status as a UC representative. "I have business of an official nature with you," she continued. I rose to my feet and spread my hands in the appropriate welcoming gesture.

"Sit and take food, Honorable S 'mar," I said, making sure to give the initial "S" of her name the full three beats she was entitled to. S'mar sat down and looked over the table for some small item of food which she could consume to establish the appropriately cordial relation between us for doing business. Unfortunately she chose the dish of Greek olives, which were imported from Home and had cost as much as the rest of the meal together. She took a handful and putting them in her mouth, crunched them up, pits and all. She laid her hands on the table and closed both sets of eyelids: a ritual expression of the fact that having eaten my food she now put herself at my mercy. But her dark, glowing eyes were shrewd as she opened them and got down to business.

"Starship *Argo* is on the roster of vehicles available for emergency service," she said. So that was her business. I didn't think that I'd bent any UC regulations far enough to bring a local official down on me. Ordinarily I'd have a dozen plausible and quite legal excuses to get out of emergency service, but this time I wasn't sure I wanted to. My next contract for cargo had been made with a fellow Greek who was just as good at bargaining as I, perhaps even a bit better. A few unexpected extras had come up which might bring my next flit precariously close to a net loss. But emergency service would provide me with a perfect excuse to break my contract, and though you will never get rich on emergency service fees, you will never lose on them either: your costs are covered and a modest honorarium is paid on top of that.

But it would never do to seem too eager. "What is the nature of this emergency service?" I asked, as was my right.

She blinked both sets of eyelids, which meant that she was a little uneasy or embarrassed and said, "A starship damaged by a quasi-space anomaly has been located: it is necessary to retrieve its cargo." I gave no sign of reaction: some Szilar are quite as good at interpreting human reactions as I am at interpreting theirs. But I was impressed, very impressed. To plot the course of any starship flitting through Q-space in relation to real space is tremendously complex and expensive, requiring as it does access to the Prime Model of the Fabric of Space. But the mathematical analysis of the course will still only yield several hundred possible Points of Emergence. To actually locate the ship would require sending recording drones through Q-space to each POE. The cargo must be extremely valuable to justify all this effort. My next question was obvious.

"What was the cargo?" I asked.

The Szilara actually touched her teeth with one finger, a sign of extreme agitation. "The cargo consisted of a number of human infants in a state of Suspension," she said, then went on reluctantly. "The information from the recording drone indicates that they are no longer in Suspension." My mind raced. The infants had probably been sent from a planet with surplus human population to a colony planet which needed population quickly to meet some UC population deadline. That kind of trafficking is morally questionable in my opinion, although it is not illegal, perhaps because of the advantage it offers. The host planet gets rid of surplus population of a kind which is least valuable to it, persons without skills which would make them socially valuable, whose potentialities would require expenditure of resources to develop. The colony, on the other hand, acquires population consisting of persons who make minimal demands on physical resources and who are completely adaptable to their new environment, having had no previous conditioning to another environment. The practice of importing infants also enables the colonists to be completely sure that the new planet is safe for human young before starting their own families.

On the other hand, the whole point of the UC population deadlines is to ensure that the colonists make a real committment to a planet before they receive title to it: importing infants enables the colonists to hedge their own committment, pass on some of the burden to persons who have no possibility of objecting. The practice may preserve the First Right, the right of all intelligent life to live, but I doubt that it really observes the Second Right, the right of all intelligent life to respect.

In this particular case, the colonists had probably lost their game. Even if I could retrieve the infants without any problems, they had come out of Suspension and had been exposed to some environment for a time: either that of the starship itself or that of some planet if the crew had managed to land the disabled starship. That would make their adaptation to their original planet of destination more difficult and perhaps even impossible.

"How much realtime has passed since the TOE?" I asked.

The Szilara blinked again and replied, "It equates to about twelve Human Standard Years since the Time of Emergence."

I calculated quickly: thirty five "extra" days in a Standard Year over a real year at Home: a little more than thirteen Home years, then; at least some of the children would be pubescent. "How many seem to have survived?" I asked.

The Szilara gave the little yawn which indicates satisfaction. "Apparently almost all," she said. "About a thousand."

"I can't transport anything like that number," I shot back, "even in Suspension."

S'mar gave a minimum nod to indicate assent to the obvious. "It is not yet clear that you need transport any," she said. "The starship is on the surface of a planet: if the situation is viable and there are no intelligent or pre-intelligent life forms, the commissioners will entertain a petition to license the planet as a human colony: there is a quota position available."

Very likely the colony license lost by the planet which had tried to import these infants. Serves them right, I thought to myself. "You want me primarily to act as an investigator, then," I said.

The Szilara gave her longest blink so far and said, "In conjunction with another person, yes. We are asking you to transport to the site a scientist, a member of the Independent Research Cooperative."

I couldn't help a little reaction at this. The IRC, commonly called the Invisible College, is the most prestigious group of scientists in the UC. Simple membership in it is a greater honor than any official scientific award, whether planetary or Commonwealth. Membership in the Invisible College comes only by election by the total membership: the best selecting the best. Of more personal importance was the fact that the only member of the College on this planet was one of my lovers. It takes a man very sure of his own worth to enter into an emotional relationship with a woman who is a starship captain, and members of the IRC have very good reason to be sure of their own worth. In addition, Academician Donal Derry was a very warm and lovable man, if a trifle eccentric. It would be nice if the IRC member they were sending with me was Donal, even though we couldn't be lovers aboard ship. It might also explain why *Argo* had been chosen for this job.

But the Szilara's next words suggested another explanation. Blinking rapidly several times she said, "In a matter having to do with young persons I would have preferred to leave the final decision to an Egg-bearer, rather than to an Impregnator. However, my instructions require that if you disagree, Academician Derry, the IRC representative, has the deciding vote, unless you invoke privilege and appeal to the Commissions."

I concealed a grin. The Szilar are a highly matriarchal race and regard humans as patriarchal despite our claims to sexual equality. The Szilara's use of the honorific "Egg-bearer" for "female" and the somewhat derogatory "Impregnator" for "male" made her own feelings obvious: she didn't like the male having the casting vote in this situation. I wasn't worried myself: in the unlikely event that Donal and I disagreed I relied on the fact that starship captains necessarily have more forceful personalities than academicians. To appeal to the Commissioner would amount to an insult to Donal. I would do that only as a last resort.

"I will accept the service," I told her, "but in the light of many unknown factors I request danger pay for my crew as part of the expenses." By agreeing to do the service before making my request I put her at a psychological disadvantage: to haggle with me after I had put myself at her mercy by agreeing to do the job would not be civilized behavior by Szilar standards. She hardly hesitated before agreeing: UC officials are responsible about disbursing funds but for all ordinary purposes the financial resources they command are inexhaustible. Besides that, the cost of flitting anything as large as a starship is so enormous that expenses like crew compensation are negligible in comparison.

We agreed on the next morning as a time of departure, and the Szilara handed over a chip containing all the available information about the ill-fated starship. I thought of contacting Donal, but I have a great deal to do the night before any flit without the added job of scanning the information on the chip, so quickly finishing my interrupted meal I went aboard *Argo* and set pre-flit operations in motion before I inserted the chip into a projector and settled down to learn what I could from it.

The first surprise was that the missing ship was of Caphellan registry. The Caphellans are not a race widely known to the rest of the UC. They are extreme empaths and find the unregulated emotions of other races highly painful. What makes Caphellan commerce with the rest of the UC possible is the fact that travel through Q-space has the effect of freezing emotions for a period of six to ten days. Caphellan ships land and accomplish their business planetside while the emotions of the Caphellan crew are inhibited. Even so they avoid much contact with other races, since a strong emotion in someone else can apparently trigger their empathic response and unfreeze their own emotions. I have had a few conversations with Caphellan starflitters while we were both in a post-Q state, but of course I recall no emotional reaction to the Caphellans since I had none.

On reflection, this was not an untypical job for a Caphellan starship: picking up a large number of persons in Suspension and delivering them to a colony planet with a small population. It was a person-oriented job, natural for empaths, but at the same time there was built-in protection against too much exposure to the emotions of others.

I was naturally curious about the Q-space anomaly which had damaged the starship. Since the ship hadn't vanished completely it had met a snark not a boojum, but snarks are bad enough: their effect is to throw you out of Q-space and blow your Rotators. If you are within range of a habitable planet at sub-flit speeds you may survive: otherwise you do not. Mathematicians have speculated that boojums force you out of Q-space into some other realspace: what happens to you then is anyone's guess. Snarks follow no known pattern except that proverbially they never bite twice in the same place. But every starflitter has a few superstitions about how to avoid meeting a snark. The data for this ship neither confirmed nor disconfirmed my own superstitions. Like many other flitters, I incline to think that snarks are living inhabitants of Q-space and may be attracted by the unusual. A Caphellan ship full of Suspended human infants is unusual alright, but so are a lot of other combinations which have escaped the snarks: for instance, ships with a Greek woman captain and a mixed species crew.

When Donal came aboard the next morning just before departure, he gave me a warm embrace, but warned by my lack of response made it more brotherly than loverly. He was being carried on the ship's roll as Science Officer and I realized that my inhibition against sexual relationships with crew members was operating. In a few hours we would go Q and it wouldn't matter anyway. "Just my luck," chuckled Donal into my ear, "a voyage with the most beautiful woman in known space and we'll both be under emotional anesthesia." I didn't mind that comment, of course, though he exaggerated: many women are more beautiful than I, but none of them are starship captains. Nor did I mind his raised eyebrows when the ship's chaplain blessed the ship before takeoff. I am never sure how seriously I take my ancestral religion myself, especially when the priest is Neo-Orthodox, with her normally waist-length hair in a hasty bun and her ship's boots peeking from below her vestments.

Just before we entered Q-space, though, he did manage to annoy me, by referring to my Szilar crewrnen as "lizards" and my B'neh navigator as an "owl." Planetaries are planetaries, I suppose, even when they are great scientists. No starflitter refers to members of other species by comparison with lower animals of our own planet: to some species it would be a deadly insult, to others merely distasteful. I was beginning not to like Donal so much, and was almost grateful for our entry into Q-space.

On the voyage, of course, nothing happened. Some philosophers claim that the reason that travel through Q-space takes no realtime is that no real events occur there. But I argued in one of my doctoral theses that this is a sophistry. There is certainly a perceived sequence of events between entry in Q-space and emergence from it: one can walk, talk, even eat and sleep though the sleep does not refresh nor the meals nourish. To say that these events are not "real" events because they take no realtime, only Q-time, begs the question: all you are saying is that the voyage takes no realtime because it takes no realtime; the argument is circular. Just as well say, with some of the more mystical races in the UC, that during Q-time you are actually dead and that is why Q-time takes no time from everyday life.

After five standard days of Q-time we emerged into realspace, using the backkick of our rotators to send back a drone which would broadcast our safe arrival to the pickups in the system we had just left. To communicate again, we would have to get this far out from a planetary mass and fire up the Rotator to send another drone back. On the other hand our planet of origin could use the big orbiting Rotators to send messages to us by drone. We approached the surface of the planet using gravity effect engines: it was painfully slow but in the emotional anesthesia which followed our flit we could not feel impatience any more than we could feel any other emotion.

We had to land, of course: most of what our instruments could tell us from space had already been learned by the drone which had preceded us. But every kiloklik closer to the planet we approached told us a little more, since the drone had made its observations from the POE before automatically rotating back to its base station. By the time the planet showed a disc the size of a human head on straight visual, the resolving instruments were showing us pictures of a fair-sized compound of huts spreading around the grounded starship. As we got closer we got glimpses of some of the inhabitants: humans of both sexes and of every age from adolescents down to toddlers.

Landing by gravity effect on an unprepared surface can be rather messy, so I took the ship down over the horizon from the compound on a piece of ground which had few lifeforms and was relatively flat. I made no attempt to buffer the side-effects of the g-e field, so we came to rest in a bed of very fine sand created by the stresses to which we'd subjected the ground below us.

I ordered two cargo discs deployed and had one loaded with a variety of equipment which I have found useful in exploratory situations, in charge of some of my tougher and more flexible crew members. The other disc I used as a transporter for Donal, myself, and a few selected experts, for instance, the ship's psychoecologist. We gave the discs a slight positive buoyancy and skimmed toward the crippled starship, riding a meter or so off the ground.

The analysers had given the planet a .987 terranorm reading, well within the parameters for colonization. We were skimming over a grassy plain, startling an occasional bird or ruminant: the experience would be a pleasant one if your emotions were operating, and I ordered the crew on the other disc to record the journey for recreational use as well as for data purposes. The ship and compound we were heading for seemed to be in a small river valley and we grounded both discs in a grassy hollow just below the ridgeline: the contact party would walk down the hills into the compound while the support equipment group waited there.

There were fields around the compound filled with vines which seemed to bear only large yellow flowers: either the flowers themselves were useful or the vines would bear some fruit or vegetable later in the season. We soon crossed a track which seemed to lead toward the compound and this turned into a slagged road which led to a gate in the wall which surrounded the huts and the starship. The perimeter fence was sturdy, made of a combination of local material and removable elements from the ship, but the gate was wide open and there seemed to be no guard on it.

The first inhabitant of the compound to notice us was a young girl who looked pre-adolescent. Since Donal has a bushy red beard and my figure is definitely that of a mature female, she realized immediately that we were not part of her group of castaways: it took her a little longer to realize we were adult humans. She showed surprise but no fear, which told me that her environment must be a pretty peaceful one.

Hesitantly she came forward and laid her hand gently in mine for a moment. "You're real, then, not holos," she said in a high, sweet voice. She spoke one of twelve Standards, of course, English as it happened. But, like all flitters, I had autolearned all twelve Standards and once her first words keyed the reflexes, I was hardly conscious of the language she used.

Her eyes widened as she worked out the implications of our presence. "Are you from Home?" she asked.

I smiled at her. "If you go back far enough, yes, we're all from Home. I was actually born there, in fact. But more important for now, we're on a Commonwealth mission, sent to see if you need any help. Whom should we see?"

She looked thoughtful for a minute, then shook her head. "You don't seem to come under any of the regular committees. I guess we'll have to disturb Nanny," she said.

Something about the way she said it told me that "Nanny" was a title, not just a name, but my English patterns gave me no referent for the word. We still speak Greek at home and I was educated in Russian, so English is only an autolearned language for me: I know I miss nuances. Some day I plan to study English properly.

The girl led us through the compound, where we caused rather less stir than I would have expected. There seemed to be some sort of social practice against pointing or staring, and though we were undoubtedly being observed and discussed, it was done very unobtrusively. I have been in cities of ancient and formal cultures where a party of offworlders caused as little stir, but this was a raw and accidental colony of children.

From the different apparent ages of the children, they had evidently been taken out of Suspension in small batches over a long period of time. How had they been brought up and who had guided them during their growing up? I had seen only children so far, and even the oldest of them appeared pre-adolescent. Of course the eldest children might be busy running things or doing other work which kept them off the streets.

When we reached the starship, which was the hub of the compound, I saw immediately that it had made a hard landing: very likely it had been using the last few ergs of its power. Looking around at the low hills which surrounded the colony I realized that the whole little valley might be a crater: a dozen or so years would be enough to reclothe the ground with vegetation. Starships are tough, of course, but cargo ships necessarily have some rather large openings in their hulls which weaken their fabric. The port which the girl was now leading us to looked as if it might have been opened with difficulty and might not easily be closed again. Anyone who left this planet, even for the other planets of this system, would have to do so in *Argo*: this ship would never lift again, much less flit.

Inside the ship the brightwalls were still functioning and the corridors looked fairly normal, but the transport flats were either inoperative or had been removed for use planetside: we had to walk what seemed a long way before we got to the crew cabin area where presumably "Nanny" had his or her or its quarters. Eventually we reached what had probably been the captain's quarters and our guide keyed the door and said, "Visitors, Nanny, people from Home." There was no verbal reply but the door slid open. Our guide, apparently satisfied that we were now in good hands, headed back down the corridor in the direction from which we had come.

Inside the cabin there was a smell which reminded me of aromatic spices, and the temperature was noticeably higher than it had been in the corridors. From somewhere I heard the splashing sound of a fountain, and I saw colored balls chasing each other lazily near the ceiling: some kind of mobile sculpture. In the center of the room was what looked like an untidy heap of furs, but it heaved itself up and revealed itself as a Caphellan, half-lying on some kind of couch or chair.

A husky voice which sounded very old and tired said, "I perceive that a rescue party has arrived at last. Unfortunately, you have taken almost the maximum time I calculated that a rescue would take to reach us. Fortunately you arrived while one of us was still alive to watch over the children."

"I'm Captain Petros of *Argo*. Are you the last survivor of the Caphellans here?" The Caphellan did not answer directly but fixed me with all three of its eyes which were a disconcerting light blue, and began giving what amounted to a report on the disaster in that husky, tired voice, which occasionally faded almost into inaudibility.

"As you can probably tell from the appearance of the vessel, we landed badly here. Some of the crew died when the Rotators blew, others were put out of action by the . . . backlash. Those of us remaining discovered that we lacked the ability to keep the human infants in Suspension for a long period of time. It was decided to wake them over a ten-year period in groups of about a hundred per year. We Caphellans are extremely sensitive to emotions, Captain, as perhaps you know. Infants have very strong, very basic, emotions. We were constantly bombarded with those emotions over a period of years. One after another the crew members . . . overloaded. I survived this long for a rather discreditable reason: I am addicted to a substance which decreases my sensitivity to emotion. Even so I found it necessary to give the human children certain . . . conditioning . . . to control their negative emotions. Will you take them back to a human planet?"

I answered frankly. "That depends on our judgment, mine and that of Academician Derry, here. There is a possibility that this planet will become a human colony if it has no promise of indigenous intelligence. We will need to investigate before we can make a recommendation."

The Caphellan drew itself up and spoke in a slightly stronger voice which gradually faded as it went on, "That would mean other humans would come . . . . I don't know . . . . We did what we thought was best at the time . . . . Talk to the children and then we will consult . . . . I must rest again now." The thin voice faded and the creature slumped again into a furry heap.

Donal looked at me, frowning. "I thought those children were too quiet and well-behaved," he said. "What have these three-eyed monkeys done to them?"

I was glad that both he and I were emotionally neutered: if we had been feeling in a normal fashion, Donal would probably have been in a rage and I would very likely be enraged at him for his attitude to the Caphellans. "We have no evidence that any harm has been done them," I said. "Investigate before you come to conclusions, Academician." I turned to my psychoecologist. "George, what was your impression?"

He shrugged. "Too little data, Captain. If you want a preliminary guess, I'd say that Caphellan behavior patterns have been imposed on the children to some extent. Scrupulous respect for the privacy of others, which seemed to be the pattern we observed, is highly typical of an empath culture, highly atypical in the kind of culture I'd expect from young humans. But I'd like extended observation, as extended as possible. I don't completely trust psychological observations made under emotional anesthesia."

I nodded and looked at the quiescent Caphellan. "What about this entity?"

George shook his head. "I'll key what we have in the banks about Caphellans and see what I can derive from my observations of it. But any creature which consistently drugs itself to inhibit the functioning normal for its species is going to damage itself seriously in the long run. I doubt if our host here will ever return to Caphella."

I looked around the cabin, which was littered with musical instruments, readers and knickknacks, and squinted at a View which was slightly out of focus, having been designed to give an illusion of reality for the trinocular vision of a Caphellan. "A pity," I said. "The creature seems to have done its best and it must have had a bad time of it since the last of its companions died." I knew intellectually that the littered but somehow homelike cabin would haunt me when my emotion returned. “Let’s get out of here,” I said.

We made our way out of the starship to be met by a little delegation of children who looked somewhat older than any we had seen before. A short, dark-skinned boy said to me, “I am Peter, the Chairman of the Committee of the First. Nanny keyed your meeting with her into our learning terminals: most of us have seen it. What investigations do you wish to make of our community?” He looked a little ill at ease, as they all did. If “First” meant what I thought it did, these were probably the first children taken from Suspension: all of their lives they had been used to being the oldest of the humans and had probably had responsibilities for the others for some years now. Now suddenly a group of humans much older and more powerful than they had appeared: they must be having very mixed emotions.

“Thank you, Chairman,” I said gravely, “Myself and my companions here would like to observe the nomal functioning of your community, interrupting it as little as possible. A small technical party is in the hills above your compound making a preliminary survey: the rest of my crew will stay shipside for the moment. If you wish to send observers to the technical party or to the ship they will be welcome. So far as we are concerned you are Commonwealth citizens who are in possession of this planet: we are willing to recognize whatever governmental structure you have as the *de facto* authority here. If living quarters for us pose any problem for you, we can provide our own, but we prefer to live as you do and at least initially to see whatever you want to show us.”

Peter's face had lit up when I mentioned visiting the *Argo* and he said with a boyish eagerness which almost stirred my frozen emotions, "Could we really see a functioning starship? So many things on our ship are destroyed or closed off for safety reasons . . . ." He controlled himself with an effort and said more formally, "Thank you, Captain. A member of the Committee will act as host to each of you. If you would come with me, Captain Petros, I'll show you your quarters and answer any initial questions you have."

Each of my companions was given a guide of the opposite sex: evidently the Caphellans had instilled this bit of human custom in their charges or else they had picked it up themselves from their educational programs. As soon as we were out of sight of the others, Peter said hesitantly, "Captain, what the academician said about three eyed monkeys . . . ."

I stopped and looked into his eyes. "I'm sorry, Peter. Academician Derry is a very great scientist, but he hasn't had a great deal of experience with other intelligent species; he's never been far from his home planet. In his normal state, he has a kind of warmth and impulsiveness that largely robs his gaucheries of offense. Some people are rather improved by having their emotions frozen: I think in his case it's the reverse."

He looked at me wide-eyed. "Emotional anesthesia from Q-space travel! I've heard about it, of course, but I hadn't thought . . . . That's why most of you seemed so . . . . But you and the man you called George seem much more normal. I mean . . . . I'm sorry . . . ."

I remembered to smile at him as I said, "I'm afraid in our case it's only training that makes us seem to have more normal reactions. Essentially we're acting. George Stavros is a psychoecologist, an expert in the psychological makeup of human and non-human cultures. I've had similar training: as captain I have to be a generalist, know a little about all the specialties of my crew. And often the captain has to be the chief contact person with a new culture, for status reasons in some societies, or because the captain has to make judgments based on first-hand experience, as in our present mission."

Peter nodded politely but didn't look convinced, and indeed I felt much more normal than I would have expected one day out of Q-space.

The colony arrangements were about what I had expected: a mixture of sophisticated technology scavenged from the wounded starship and primitive handicrafts reflecting the colony's basic dependence on the local resources. The room I was given in a sort of dormitory building had a brightwall taken from the ship, excited by a powercell unit which was recharged by solar power. But heat was furnished by a small stove made of crude bricks. That was reasonable: heating is a wasteful use of electricity and there is always plenty of natural material to burn on a primitive terranorm planet.

The social arrangements were more surprising: everyone seemed so determinedly cheerful and helpful to each other that I had the same bemused feeling I'd had as a girl when I made a retreat at a convent. Surely it wasn't natural for human beings to be so constantly nice to each other and to their guests.

Childcare and education took a major proportion of their time, of course, since the majority of their population were so young. But as in large families in the colonies or in poor areas at Home the children at each age did what they could to help those younger than themselves. On a few occasions I saw a fretful toddler or an older child who had taken a tumble: other children seemed to cluster around the crying child, soothing it and trying to distract it. Very affecting, and if my emotions had been working normally I might have been charmed. But my emotional anesthesia helped my mind to work more clearly and I realized that this charming behavior was far from typical of ordinary children. Where were the fights, the tantrums, the ordinary childish orneriness? Perhaps Donal's crudely phrased question wasn't so off-base after all; what had the Caphellans done to these children?

It was Donal himself who discovered that, the third day of our stay in the compound. We had just come out of a little room which had been given to us as a dining and common room, and were going in different directions: I to talk to some of the Council members and he to check some devices which were relaying information from exploration drones. I had just turned to call some final instructions to him before he went out of earshot when out of a gap between two of the huts shot a boy about two or three years old running and yelling happily. He looked back over his shoulder and ran full tilt into Donal, bounced off him and ended up sitting on the ground, more jarred and startled than really hurt. The boy opened his mouth and began to howl and suddenly tears started to roll from Donal's eyes and he began to howl too. It was ludicrous but a little frightening, the small chubby boy and the big red-bearded man both weeping and howling: I was torn between laughter and alarm.

The children who had been playing tag with the boy who had bumped into Donal ran up and began soothing the crying boy. A few made tentative gestures to Donal but after a moment stared at him oddly and ignored him. As the child stopped crying, so did Donal, and after a few moments the children ran off shouting happily and Donal walked slowly over to me, amazement on his face.

"I felt that," he said, "the purest, rawest emotion I've felt since I was that age, probably. And when the kids ran off I felt their happiness, too. And now I feel embarrassed, elated. My emotions are unfrozen, Elena!"

I nodded. "Once you feel any emotion it removes the blockage. Several tactics used by starflitters to cut down the time spent in emotional freeze depend on that. But the important thing is the initial emotion." He looked into my eyes.

"Yes," he said slowly, "the children must broadcast emotion, either continuously or when the emotional intensity gets beyond a certain level. That's why they all cluster around someone who's unhappy and try to console him. They feel the unpleasant emotions themselves and want to stop their being generated. There are other clusterings, too, that have puzzled me: I think now that they must be attracted to other children who are feeling happy, to share that emotion." His eyes sparkled.

He was grinning, but still locked in my own emotional anesthesia, I replied calmly, "I agree. And you realize what the cause of this must be?"

"The Caphellans," he said softly, "this is what they did to the children, this is what Nanny was hinting at." Then with renewed excitement he said, "But this is marvelous! It's an old human dream come true: perfect empathy, the Golden Rule made concrete. They do to others as they want others to do to them because they can feel the other's joys and pains, and know the others will feel theirs. They have immediate feedback, no chance of being mistaken about what hurts others or makes them happy." His eyes suddenly grew calculating. "The Caphellans know how to induce this capacity in humans. They must have already known; the chances of it being a serendipitous discovery in this situation are negligible. They could do it to any of us! Cruelty, crime, war, they could all be abolished! How could you victimize another person when you felt that person's pain yourself? Elena, we've got to communicate with Home about this!"

Usually I put some artificial animation in my voice when I'm under emotional anesthesia, but this time I let my voice be totally cold and calm as I said, "That may well be necessary very soon, Academician. But first we need to make some further investigations. I want your best data as to the chance of intelligent or pre-intelligent life on this planet as soon as possible." As I hoped, this distracted him.

"Of course," he said, "we'll need that before the UC can make a decision. I'll get right on it, Captain." He trotted off and I called after him,

"Not a word of this to anyone!"

He stopped and grinned at me, "Yes, ma'am! But you ought to defreeze yourself. Go pinch a baby!" He went off in the direction of his equipment.

Actually, I thought, that was not a bad idea. Before carrying out the plans I had already formed, it might not be a bad idea to be functioning as a normal human being. The Persians, they say, debated every major decision twice, once when they were drunk and once when they were sober. Perhaps it would be a good idea to look at my plans again when my emotions were back. I walked through the compound, keeping my eyes open for a child alone. When I finally found a chubby little girl playing absorbedly in a mud puddle, it occurred to me that positive emotions could transfer as well as negative. Trying to remember the games my younger siblings had enjoyed at home in Crete, I began to cajole and tickle the baby. Presently she was laughing and squealing, and I soon felt a twinge, then a flood, of pure delight. I laid the child down, a little shaken. This sort of thing could easily become addictive: children's emotions were so strong and unalloyed.

I consulted my plans again and found them still good. Kissing the baby girl, I walked on toward the crippled starship. There I found my way back to the cabin occupied by Nanny and at the door I said simply, "I need to talk to you." The door slid open and I entered the aromatically scented cabin. I stood before the couch and saw the furry body heave itself up and the three pale eyes open.

"One of the children has triggered you," said the Caphellan's weary voice.

"It happened accidentally to one of my crew," I said defensively. "Then I brought it about deliberately. To reach a final decision I need more information. The man whose emotions were stimulated thinks that empathy is the solution to all human problems: cruelty, war, crime. I need to know what it's like to be an empath, from the inside. Only you can tell me."

The Caphellan's voice seemed strong as she said, "Do you know, Captain, that your emotions are very bracing? Among my people you would find yourself valued in a way you can hardly guess. What is it like to be an empath? Difficult, difficult enough to send me to drugs for refuge. If anyone is unhappy, the whole community feels it, and until someone does something about the unhappiness, we are all disturbed. But strong feelings of happiness can be almost as distracting: it's hard not to pay attention to them. And the lower level feelings all blend into a sort of emotional background: unless that background is reasonably euphoric, it is almost impossible to have good feelings: the general level drags your feelings down."

The Caphellan gave a sort of wheeze that may have been its kind of laughter. "Your man is right, Captain; Caphellans do not wage war or make slaves or cause pain to others deliberately in any of countless ways that would seem quite trivial to humans or Szilar or the other races of the Commonwealth. We do not complete—the happinesss of the winner would be overcome by the sorrow of the losers.

We do not argue: arguing causes unpleasant feelings. We do not engage in activities which involve drudgery or danger, or even boredom: too many people would share the unpleasant feelings. We have little in the way of trade or philosophy or science. Medicine we have, for it alleviates pain, art we have, of the kind that entertains, not of the kind which raises disturbing questions. We have star travel because our home planet was discovered by the Universal Commonwealth and because our peaceful cooperative society seemed ideal to people like your crewman. In Q-space we discovered what some of us longed for, the silencing of all emotions, escape from empathy. Many Caphellan starflitters flit again as soon as the emotion freeze begins to wear off."

"Why do they want to escape emotion?" I asked. "Surely after a long history of development you Caphellans must have learned to make the emotional tone of your planet a happy one; you must have learned to minimize pain and sorrow and maximize happiness in your society." Those three pale blue eyes regarded me steadily.

"Would you like to make decisions for yourself, or for your planet, on the basis of what would make everyone happy?" the Caphellan asked, "not what is best for them, not even what will make them happy in the long run, but what will avoid pain and cause happiness now. Could you be the person you are, could your race be what it is, if that was the basis on which you had to decide? Compared to other species in the Commonwealth, the Caphellans have no drive, no aspirations. And individually, we have no freedom: after a lifetime of conditioning, it is not in us to go against what others want of us."

I looked at the furry mound before me, trying to control the feeling of compassion I felt for it, trying to keep myself from imposing my emotions on it. "And yet you did something to make the human children here like you," I said. The furry figure moved restlessly.

"We had no choice; We could not let them die: the impact of their deaths would have killed us. He could not leave them in Suspension, the equipment was damaged in the landing. But when we revived them their raw emotions were driving us mad. There was no way to cure their emotional 'deafness' and for a while we despaired. Then one of us had an idea. There are techniques to help Caphellan young make their emotions known to others, to 'broadcast' more clearly and effectively. We used these techniques intensively on the human infants and the result was a society much like the Caphellan society. To use the analogy of speech, the children here do not 'hear' as well as a Caphellan but they 'speak' more 'loudly' and 'clearly'; the result for them was communication of emotions as effective as that of Caphellans on our own planet."

"We were able to live with the result but it tended to burn us out. That is why only I, with my drug-habit defense, have been able to survive. The others would have refused to use my drugs even if my supply had been great enough: the drugs are regarded as a shameful weakness by Caphellans. They would not have admitted that their own pursuit of emotional anesthesia through starflitting arose from the same motive as my use of drugs."

I wondered if there was some self-deception in that: it did not sound as if Nanny had offered the other Caphellans her drugs. But whatever my moral judgment of this creature, it was the only Caphellan I had to work with. "Whatever your motives, you have done something to these children that is going to have profound effects on others as well as on them," I said. "I want you to come with me aboard my starship, to help me bring the best result out of this that we can."

The creature gave a sort of shudder and said, "Do you know what you are offering me? Peace, peace, after all of these years of emotional overload. If I was sure that the children could do without me . . . ."

I cut in, "Sooner or later they would have had to, Nanny. Peter told me what your name means; it's an archaic word for a children's nurse. It's time for the children to grow up, Nanny, to come out of the nursery. You must pass them on to other helpers, other teachers."

The Caphellan made one last protest. "But other humans won't know how to deal with these children."

I nodded somberly. "Yes, Nanny," I said, "I've thought of that too."

A little later in realtime but after a long flit in Q-time, Nanny faced me again, strong and erect now that the emotional anesthesia of a starflit had given her emotions time to heal. "Captain, "she said, "I still do not understand your motives. Under your guidance I have filed a claim on behalf of my people for the planet on which our ship was wrecked, to be a Caphellan colony. It was you who told me of my rights as the last survivor of the crew of the starship to first land on a planet without intelligent life. It was you who helped me persuade my people to agree to send colonists. It was you who persuaded Academician Derry to support your recommendation that this should be the disposition of the planet, despite his objections. You have given the Caphellans a planet we did not particularly want and deprived your own people of it, though they want new colonies very much. Why?"

I looked at her for a moment, wondering how much to say and how much to let her and the other Caphellans discover for themselves. "First," I said slowly, "there are the children, who are now wards of Caphella. They couldn't live with ordinary humans and ordinary humans couldn't live with them. They're conditioned not to harm others, to make others happy, only because they feel the pain or pleasure of the others. Ordinary humans can't broadcast their emotions; the children you conditioned would have no motive not to harm them, no reason to please them. If ordinary humans tried to discipline or train them in any ordinary way, the children would broadcast their negative reactions: it would take very exceptional humans to stand up to that."

I looked at Nanny consideringly and let one of the cats a little way out of the bag. "Your people had better send lots of colonists and train them how to broadcast their emotions very strongly or they'll have the same problem, in another form. Ordinary Caphellan emotional controls won't work on the human children: you'll have to find new ways to interact with them." And that will change Caphellan society too, I thought to myself, in ways that couldn't be predicted. But the Caphellans too needed to grow up, to come out of their own nursery.

"What the children need," I said, and in my own mind I added the Caphellans to that, "is to learn real respect for other persons and their individuality. So far they've operated on the principles 'I won't hurt you because hurting you will hurt me' and 'I'll make you happy because that will make me happy.' They need to learn the principles 'I won't hurt you, even if hurting you doesn't hurt me' and 'I'll make you happy even if it doesn't make me happy.' That's real morality, real love of neighbor, the real Golden Rule. 'Do to others as you want to be done by,' not the Caphellan rule, 'Do to others as you will be done by.' That's why I asked you to give the planet the name I chose, the name 'Chrysenomia:' it means 'Golden Rule' in Greek."

Nanny looked at me, narrowing her three eyes. "And you expect us, the Caphellans, to teach this when you say we don't know it ourselves?" she asked.

"It's the only chance they have of learning it," I said. And perhaps your only chance, too, I added in my mind.

"Are you so sure that this is the right way for them?" Nanny asked softly: perhaps she had some inkling of my larger hope.

I shrugged. "You've told me yourself of the problems of an empathic society. Neither humans nor the Commonwealth as a whole can take that way. Respect for others even without empathy is the only other way intelligent beings have found to live together in any kind of peace. But perhaps the children can find a new way, out of their human and Caphellan heritages; feeling for others without bondage to them, rejoicing and sorrowing with others as well as respecting them. You Caphellans haven't given us a chance to learn from you: you haven't tried to learn from us. Perhaps the children can bring us together in a new way."

"Perhaps they will," said Nanny in a voice that held a hint of fear, a hint of resignation. Then she wheezed, and her voice grew stronger with a hint of unexpected humor. "Perhaps they must, Captain, after what you have done. We will need a new way—the Chrysenomian Way."

PART TWO

SOMETHING IN THE BLOOD

I always arrive at Franco's Bar just after sunset. In the summer there is still light in the sky and on the water; the lights flick on in the town and gleam from the few boats you can see far down the cliff, on the ocean that fills the ancient volcanic caldera. Classical music wells out of the hidden loudspeakers at Franco's, a little too loud but all the more compelling for that.

I sat down at my usual table, and the tall, dark, young waiter brought me my usual ouzo and *mezedes* in silence. As I took my first sip of ouzo, I saw her at the next table. The way she was sitting brought her head just in line with the stone harpy on the corner of the terrace, and my first reaction was a purely aesthetic pleasure at the juxtaposition of the soft young face of flesh and the ageless face of stone. Then I realized that the faces were alike in a deeper way. No face that young and beautiful should wear such hopeless resignation, an expression that made her seem as ageless and as alien as the harpy.

When she turned to me and spoke, the expression was gone. Had I only imagined it, was it an illusion born of my own despair? "This must be the most beautiful place in the world," she said, her voice filled with wonder. "It was beautiful in the day, but now it's magical."

"I prefer it after the sun goes down, myself," I said. I couldn't quite keep the irony out of my voice, and she gave me a puzzled look. I had better give her an explanation she could accept. "The sun is my enemy," I told her. "My skin is very sensitive to sunlight. But even aside from that, I find the sunlight on our volcanic rock and ash too harsh. In the day, Santorini seems to me too bleak, too unfriendly to humans."

She nodded with a thoughtful expression. "I see what you mean," she said. "There is something eerie and a little frightening about Santorini for all its beauty. But you said 'our rocks'; are you a native of the island?"

"I've lived here a long time," I said, "and I consider it my home, but the local people still don't really accept me as one of them. Still, I probably know more about Santorini than most of the people born here. Is there anything I can tell you about the island or its history?" It was the first move in a familiar game, a game I had played with many of the young female tourists who streamed through the island every summer, enhancing my life and making the long winter bearable because of what I had gotten from them. But very few of them were as lovely as this girl, or as charming. Had I only imagined that deep sadness in her eyes?

She laughed a little self-consciously and said, "Oh, it's absurd, you'll laugh at me, but I am curious about . . . . Well, do the local people really believe these stories about Santorini? I mean, someone on the mainland warned me about coming here; she was really serious. She said . . . well, she said that there were vampires on Santorini. Now you'll laugh."

I smiled and said lightly, "Oh, no, it's a well-known fact that we have vampires and all sorts of weird creatures. Take the man sitting down there on the lower terrace, the one with the bushy eyebrows. He's a werewolf. Only the other day he told me a sad story. He tried to save money by taking the ferry to Athens in his wolf form—he can pass for a very large German shepherd. But a steward saw him and put an iron chain around his neck before he knew what the man was up to. He spent most of the night tied up on deck with no food or water. If a softhearted English tourist hadn't let him loose, he might have been put in the dog pound in Piraeus."

She laughed. "All right, I asked for it," she said. I guess my grandmother told me too many ghost stories when I was a kid. I still half believe that stuff. You tell a pretty mean story yourself, Mr . . . ."

"Nikolas Tsouras," I told her. "Please call me Niko. And you are . . . ?"

"Ann Morris," she said, "and I am very pleased to meet you. Let me ask you a more practical question, Niko. Can you get anything to eat here? I'm getting awfully hungry; I've been sightseeing too hard to eat much."

I shook my head. "There's a cold plate on the menu," I told her, "but usually they say they're out, of it. I often just nibble at the *mezedes* all evening—the little appetizers they bring you with the ouzo. But if you're really hungry, there are several good restaurants nearby. Let me take you to one."

She looked at me for a long moment while I tried to keep the predatory gleam out of my eyes, then she nodded. "All right," she said with a strange little smile. "After all, what did I come to the Greek islands for, if I'm going to turn down an invitation like that from a tall, dark, handsome stranger with an interesting pallor? Let's go."

I took her to Zorba's for dinner; a noisy, lively place where the waiters are friendly and the food is good. Ann enjoyed the food and the wine in a way that seemed to have a curious urgency to it, as if she hadn't eaten or drunk for a long time or expected not to for a long time. But though her enthusiasm was a little frantic, it was also delightful; she seemed charmingly eager to enjoy everything—the food, the night air, the cheerfully impudent little boy who served as our busboy and wine waiter.

"I like to see kids doing something useful," she said. "At home they seem to think the world owes them perpetual entertainment. And of course in America they'd never let a kid this young work in a restaurant where they serve drinks, much less bring the wine and open it for you. By the way, the wine is delicious; I'm really sold on your Santorini wines."

This was my chance. I told her about our Santorini wine industry, about how our volcanic soil gives a special taste to the wine. Then I said casually, "I live in an old converted winery, and have a little cellar of vintage wines that were grown within a kilometer or so of my home. Perhaps you'd like to see my house sometime and taste some of the wines."

She hesitated, and I could see her getting ready to say "no"; she wasn't the sort of woman who'd normally accept an invitation like that so soon after meeting a man. Then she looked at me and gave a strangely sad little smile. "Why not?" she said. "I don't have all that much time left, and after all . . . ."

"After all, why did you come to the Greek islands," I teasingly finished her sentence for her. She laughed and rose to her feet. "Let's go," she said. I'll always remember Ann that first night saying "Let's go," to every suggestion, with that strange little note of recklessness, almost desperation in her voice.

There were no taxis to be had at that time of night, so we walked to Theotocopolous Square and took the local bus out to my village. At a stop just outside of town, Old Mavrodontes got on, and as soon as he saw me started cursing and abusing me in his high, cracked voice. "Vrikolakasl" he yelled, "Vrikolakas!" The conductor hustled him to the back of the bus, with an apologetic smile to Ann. If I had been alone, he would not have interfered between myself and old Mavrodontes. But Ann was a foreigner, and in Greece the foreigner is a guest, not to be bothered with local feuds.

"What was that all about?" Ann asked, a little shaken by the old man's vehemence.

I shrugged. "I'm not popular with some of my neighbors," I told her. "When I converted the old winery to a home, some people lost jobs, though the ones who really wanted to found work elsewhere easily enough. Some felt injured because they had to go a few kilometers to work at other wineries instead of just walking down the road. And some people would like to buy my winery and make money by putting it back into production. The wine business is booming here."

"You seem to be proud of your local wines, but you let me drink most of that bottle at dinner," she said. "Of course you might have had an ulterior motive for that," she added drily.

"I don't drink much," I said, "not much wine, at any rate." Again I couldn't keep the irony out of my voice, and she gave me a thoughtful look, but said no more. When we got to my little village, we got off the bus to the accompaniment of a last stream of abuse from Mavrodontes and walked up the little lane to my home. I unlocked the door, turned on the lights, and turned to usher Ann in.

She was looking at the little graveyard next to my house with a strange expression on her face, but when I touched her arm she smiled at me and seemed suddenly full of energy and gaiety. I put some records on my stereo, and we danced and tasted my wine and danced again. At the end of the last record, she put her arms around my neck and, kissed me lingeringly. "Is that the bedroom behind that door?" she asked softly. "Let's go."

At first her lovemaking had that same frantic quality that I had seen in her before, but after the first time she grew calmer and it was slow and sweet and good—better than it had been for me for a long, long time. At last she seemed to sleep, but when I raised myself on my elbow and looked down at her face, her eyes opened. "All right," she said, "go ahead." She leaned her head back so that her throat arched, and smiled that curious smile.

"Go ahead?" I said, pretending to be puzzled. She laughed softly.

"Niko, I told you that my grandmother filled my head with stories—not just stories, either; she *knew*. I think she was half a witch herself. From the stories my grandmother told me, you've got to be a vampire. Your face is pale, your lips are red, your teeth are sharp. You don't like the sun, and you come out only at night. You live next door to a graveyard, and the local people all act a little leery of you, except that old man. The name he called you means vampire, doesn't it? I ran across it somewhere reading about Greek legends and superstitions. Except they aren't just superstitions, are they? Go ahead, take my blood if that's what you want, what you need. I don't mind. Perhaps later I'll tell you why."

"All right, my dear," I said quietly. "But I won't mark your lovely throat. It's much better here." I bent over her thigh, found the femoral artery and entered it with one quick bite. She shuddered, and shuddered again when after drinking deep I withdrew. The wounds closed quickly—something in my saliva has that effect—but not before a few drops of blood had trickled out. She looked at them and then at me.

"That was . . . kind of kinky, but I could get to like it," she said." You really are a real . . . ."

"*Vrikolakas*," I said. "You didn't really believe it, did you? But there's something else hard to believe. You're dying, aren't you? Something in your blood is killing you slowly; I can feel it in what I drank."

Tears welled from her eyes; she made no effort to wipe them away, but lay there naked and defenseless with the tears running down her face. "Oh Niko, will my blood hurt you?" she asked brokenly. "I didn't really want that. It was like a story I was telling myself; you were a vampire, but I'd fool you because my blood was . . . bad. I didn't think that . . . ."

I shook my head; the familiar warmth was tingling in my body, and I knew that whatever was wrong in her blood did not affect the use my body made of it. There are advantages in being one of the Undead. "No poison can harm me," I told her, "Including, it seems, whatever deadly thing is in your blood. But it can harm you, my dear. Now I know why you seemed to be grasping so frantically at enjoyment. How long did the doctors give you?"

"They told me a month before I began to get really sick," she said. "And I felt that I'd never lived at all. I quit my job, sold everything I could sell, even borrowed money. I suppose that's dishonest; I'll never live to pay it back. Then I came here to the Greek Islands, the place I'd always dreamed of visiting. If I was going to have only a month, at least for that month I wanted to live. Then I met you . . ." She touched the almost healed wounds on her thigh with wonder on her face. "Will I become a vampire now?" she asked. "What's it like to be a vampire?"

"So long as I only take your blood, no, you will not become what I am," I said. "I would have to reverse the flow and give you some of mine—quite a bit, in fact. Then the parasite that makes me what I am would grow in you, and your body would adapt. What flows in my veins is not exactly blood, but it combines with blood, even diseased blood like yours. The mixture is very powerful. My body heals itself from almost any wound, casts off every disease. And so long as I get new blood periodically, I will never die. There are disadvantages, of course; my skin has no melanin at all, and I could get a severe sunburn from being out in the sun only a short time. But I'm sensitive to cold and damp, too. That's why I live in this climate."

"And during the day . . ." she began, then hesitated.

I laughed, "Lie down in my grave?"

I said. "Well, in a way. Even a tiny bit of light or noise can bother me when I try to sleep, and I have a little sleeping room fixed up in a family crypt in the graveyard next door. It has to look like a real crypt in case anyone ever gets in there, but it's very snug and comfortable. Want to see it?"

"Let's go," she said a little shakily, and began to dress. I started to help her, and that caused some delay, but eventually we were dressed again and walked out of the house into the little graveyard. Somebody had been taking out their hostility to me on the tomb that covered the crypt—Mavrodontes or one of the others. The little ornamental chain that made a sort of fence around the top of the tomb had been wrenched from its supports and lay in a heap on the top of the tomb, and someone had battered the little frame that is supposed to hold a picture of the person most recently buried in the crypt. I used to put a mirror in the frame so that anyone looking to see the face of the dead would see their own face. But no one liked my little joke, and the mirror was always broken. I no longer replaced the mirror, but they still battered the frame.

Ann looked at the tomb and bit her lip. "Do the local people hate you so much?" she asked in a small voice. "Do you . . . ?"

I shook my head. "No, I leave the locals strictly alone," I said. "There are always young tourist girls who can spare some blood and think the whole experience is a rather kinky thrill. Half of them don't even realize what's happening, or what I am. Most of the local people know about us, though some pretend not to. Some are quite decent to me. I'll have to ask Father Athanasius to preach another sermon about the wickedness of desecrating graves—even mine."

Ann was hurt by what I had said about the tourist girls—there was no way she couldn't be. But she said nothing about that, only asked in a steady voice, "You said the local people know about 'us'—are there others . . . like you . . . here?"

I shrugged. "Not so many now as there once were, and some of them have grown very strange over the long years. There are those of them who take no food and drink at all, except blood. If you do that, your body changes in some ways I don't find pleasant. I try to keep at least some hold on humanity. The girls are as much for that as for the blood. But whether you believe this or not, Ann, you are much different from the others for me—very different."

"I believe you, Niko," Ann said quietly. "We have something in common, you and I. We both have something in our blood that's—different. Mine won't let me live, but yours won't let you die. I thought my problem was as bad as could be, but I'm not sure yours isn't worse."

In all the years, she was the only one who had come close to understanding, and my voice was not quite under control as I said, "The loneliness is the worst. I don't dare to love anyone. If they are not what I am, they will go and die and my loneliness would be worse than before. And I could never bear to make anyone else what I am, as some of the others have done. How could they help but hate me when they realized what I had condemned them to?"

Ann looked at me for a long time in silence. Then she said in an oddly expressionless voice, "Show me where you sleep during the day." The little moment of closeness was over; perhaps it never really existed. Her problem gave her some insight into mine, but not enough. To be condemned to death is easier than to be condemned to life.

I led her to the little slab near the tomb that gave access to the crypt. The slab carved with a skull and a motto in Greek. "Vanity of vanity, all is vanity," I translated for her. "Plenty of people believe that now, but they don't dare remind themselves of it. This slab was made by people who still believed in an afterlife; they didn't mind being reminded of their mortality. It's a different kind of reminder for me; I could die, but I'd have to choose to. I've never had the courage, even when things seemed worst. As Hamlet says, 'For in that sleep of death what dreams may come . . . Must give us pause.' But perhaps someday I'll lose something that I can't bear living with the loss of, and I'll make the choice to die . . . Sorry, it's chilly out here. Will you step into my grave?"

She gave a shaky little laugh as I lifted the slab and capped my quotation with another from *Hamlet*:

"Indeed, that is out o' the air." A wave of desolation swept through me as we descended the narrow steps. I had more in common with Ann than with any other woman I had ever talked with, laughed with, loved with. But she had only a month before the sickness drained her of life. I was at last facing a loss I couldn't live with.

My little crypt is ancient and has some paintings on the wall; strange, wild-eyed saints with golden halos. I had restored them little by little over the years. So long as I am shut away from the sunlight, I can be active for much of the day. Perhaps I am shortening my extended life span by doing so. Surely the coma-like state we normally enter during the day accounts for some of our longevity—it is more like suspended animation than sleep.

Ann was exclaiming over the wall paintings when we heard a noise from above us. Someone was battering on the door of my house and shouting. It might have been wiser to pull the slab down and lock it, let whoever it was take out their rage on my practically impregnable door, but this interruption of my precious time with Ann put me into a red rage, and without thinking I ran up the stairs with her at my heels.

What we saw when we emerged was like a scene from an old, bad movie. Hammering on my door was a wild-eyed young man, obviously an American. Standing beside him with a flaring torch in his hand was Mavrodontes with a wicked grin on his face. When he saw us emerge, he pointed his finger at us and shouted melodramatically, "There is the vampire and his victim!"

"Fool," I spat at Mavrodontes in Greek. "This time you have gone too far! Have you forgotten that the house you live in is mine and on my land? Always before I have thought of your wife and daughter and left you in the house, despite your mischief-making. But now I will give your wife a choice. Either you behave yourself or the whole family must leave the house. How do you think she will choose, Mavrodontes? She is as tired of your antics as I am!"

The old man's jaw dropped and the torch almost fell from his hand. He was as lazy as he was mischievous, and his drinking was paid for by what his wife and daughter earned. Their home was important to them, and he knew very well that if I threatened them with the loss of it, he would get no peace—and no more drinking money—if he made any more trouble. He took a step backward, and I knew that at the first opportunity he would slip away, abandoning his American ally.

As soon as I stopped speaking, Ann stepped forward and blazed out at the young American. "What the hell are you doing here, Harry? Before I left, I told you I never wanted to see you again! Did you follow me to this island?"

The young man flushed but looked stubborn. "What did you expect me to do when I found you'd sold everything, including some stuff of mine, and told everyone you weren't coming back? Your doctor wouldn't tell me anything, but I know you flew off the handle right after you went in for that checkup. All right, maybe I gave you something; you know I play around sometimes. But I always come back to you, don't I? Damn it, Ann, I need you!"

Ann's voice when she replied was full of honeyed malice. "You need me, do you, Harry? Well you're going to have to do without me. Do you know what I got from you, Harry? AIDS, that's what. You just have to show what a big swinger you are, ready to try anything once. Well, you tried "anything" once too often, Harry. The doctor told me I had only a few months to live!"

Harry's face was paler than mine in the light of the torch, and his voice was barely under control. "Oh my God," he whimpered. "If I gave it to you, I must have it myself. I've got to get to a doctor, to a hospital . . . ." He turned and stumbled toward the road, where I could see a car parked, probably one of the rental cars from the town. Mavrodontes called a curse after him, seeing his last hope of making trouble for me vanishing. Perhaps the old man had even hoped that he could egg on the young American to kill me; I saw that in his other hand he actually had a sharpened stake!

"On your way, old fool," I snapped. "And as for that stake, you can take it and . . . ." But I had pushed him too far; he was both drunker and crazier than I had thought. He threw the stake like a javelin, right at my face. At that distance he could hardly miss; I felt a blinding pain in my head, and blackness descended on me. The last sounds I heard were Ann's scream and the fleeing footsteps of Mavrodontes.

I awoke in the crypt with an aching head, feeling strangely weak. Ann was sitting on the floor beside my coffin, leaning on the wall behind her. Her eyes were closed, and there was an odd-looking tangle of stuff on the floor beside her; I recognized some old tubing left over from when the winery had been in operation which she must have found in my storage closet.

When I tried to move, a pain shot through my head and I gave a little involuntary groan. Ann's eyes opened, and she smiled at me. "Your head probably feels terrible, but that stake didn't hit you square on, and the gash it made on the side of your head was half closed when I started to bandage it—I've never seen anybody heal so quickly."

She took a deep breath and went on. "If you feel weak, Niko, it's because you've lost blood while you were unconscious. I transfused about a pint of your blood into myself, and probably wasted almost another pint with my makeshift apparatus. I'm sorry, but I didn't think I could persuade you to do it yourself, your way. You said you'd never make another person like yourself because they'd hate you for it. Well, you didn't do it to me. I did it to myself."

I was already feeling a little better, and I raised myself on my elbow to peer into her face in the dim light of the fluorescent camp lantern that lit the crypt. "But why, Ann?" I cried, "why did you do it?"

She smiled at me. "Because I love you, you idiot. I won't say that it wasn't partly fear of dying, fear of the kind of sickness I'd have to go through before dying, but it was mostly because I wanted to be with you so you won't be so terribly lonely anymore . . . ." A thought struck her, and she looked at me with panic in her eyes. "Niko, will it work? Have I wasted your blood for nothing when you were already wounded?"

I sighed, "My darling fool, if you took a pint of my blood, the parasite should be well established in your body," I said. "And there's no reversing what you've done. Give me your hand. A little blood from your finger will tell me if the change is complete yet,"

It was; the "blood" might as well have been my own, and had as little sustenance for me. "My dear," I said gently, "you've accomplished what you wanted to. I hope you'll never regret it. But now both of us will need blood. I can last for a while on what I took from you last night, and the conversion of your own blood will last you for a long time. But eventually both of us must . . . drink."

She smoothed the bandage on my head with gentle fingers and smiled. "I have plans about that, Niko," she said. "No more tourist girls for you, my lad. I'm a registered nurse—that's why I know how to do the transfusion—and if there's one thing I know about, it's blood. That's why getting AIDS myself from Harry was such a tragic irony. What you and I are going to do is open a blood bank."

I stared at her, speechless, and she laughed at me. "Sounds crazy, doesn't it? Two vampires running a blood bank. But it will work—if you could tell I had AIDS from one drink of my blood, I bet you can detect other things wrong with blood that we get from paid donors. Hepatitis is a real headache, because people aren't always aware they have it. You can screen the blood, and we can take any "bad" blood for our own use. Brokering blood can be a profitable business anyway, if it's efficiently run. I'll bet we can make a living at it as well as supplying our own needs. There's always a market for a reliable source of blood—and who knows more about blood than a vampire?"

It was utter madness—but it worked. It took time and a great deal of money to get established. For a while we thought we would have to sell the winery building. We had to take a Greek doctor into partnership to satisfy government regulations, but that gave us valuable contacts in the medical community, and Dr. Elias is too well armored with scientific prejudices to ever realize what we are and what we do with the blood that we screen out.

We have to be in Athens much more than we like, for Samorini of course is too small to support a blood service on the scale we need. With factor-twenty sunscreen and extra strong photogray sunglasses, we can stand brief exposure to the sun, and we usually take the overnight ferry to and from Piraeus. Our blood clinic in Athens is an old warehouse with no windows, lit by fluorescent lights. When the sun goes down, we enjoy the late leisurely Greek restaurant meals and the nightlife of the city.

But Santorini is still our home. We spend as much time here as we can. Ann has softheartedly bribed Mavrodontes into behaving himself with a "caretaker's" job where he does a minimum of work and earns enough for a maximum of drinking. Perhaps the old fool will drink himself to death soon, but I doubt it—he's too tough. Ann's ex-lover, Harry, was not tough at all—we found out that he had committed suicide when it was confirmed that he did have AIDS.

So we live untroubled by old enemies and have even made a few friends. Ann has hopes for a research program that may someday turn our curse into a blessing. We already can synthesize the substance in my saliva that heals bite wounds, and we use it at the blood bank. Perhaps we will tire of our life, perhaps we will even tire of each other, but I do not think so. There are deep bonds between us. My blood saved Ann from death; her companionship rescued me from loneliness and despair. We do no harm and perhaps a little good now.

For old times' sake, whenever we are on Santorini, we go for an evening drink at Franco's Bar. We always arrive after sunset.

GORGONISSA

Gorgonissa is a small island, so small that the ferry does not dock there, but stands by offshore while small boats take passengers and cargo from the ferry to the harbor. There were not many of us going ashore, but I waited for the second trip rather than be squashed in the first boat with the returning islanders, their bundles and their small animals. There were three lambs and two young goats in the first boat, bawling piteously and getting underfoot. There was one man in the boat who looked English or American, along with a white-bearded priest who except for his black robe might have posed for a picture of Santa Claus.

The second boat held mainly cargo along with myself and two elderly English ladies of the kind you find traveling in pairs in the most unlikely comers of the world. I wondered idly what they wanted on the little speck of an island in the Aegean, what they would find to do for the week until the next boat. What would I do, for that matter, if my half-brother was no longer on the island or if I finished my business with him quickly? But both were unlikely; according to the purser, he had come on this boat, the only one to serve the island, and had not left on it. As for finishing my business quickly, nothing involving Jerry had ever been quick or easy, and I didn't suppose that was likely to change now.

When we got to shore the boatman demanded an amount that seemed unreasonably large to me. I understand Modern Greek fairly well, but I refuse to wrap my tongue around its barbarous distortions of the pronunciation and accent of classical Greek. At any rate it is sometimes convenient to pretend not to understand. I held out about half the amount he had requested and he took it with a shrug. One of the elderly Englishwomen gave him about the same amount.

I opened my mouth to protest but thought better of it. I would have been quite willing to pay the whole price of the boat if it had been a fair price, though I would have expected thanks and at least an offer to pay their share. As it was, I had paid as much for my seat as they had for their two, and this irked me unreasonably. I nodded distantly to the two women and set off for the hotel with my bag.

There was only one tiny hotel in the town, fourth class, but reasonably clean. The two Englishwomen did not appear; they were probably renting rooms in the village. That pleased me, for I was still a little annoyed with them, but it pleased me less that Jerry was not registered at the hotel. It would make it that much harder to find him.

The bored young girl at the desk told me in her school-learned English that there was hot water, so I took a shower immediately; hot water in even the best Greek hotels tends to come and go erratically. It was siesta time, what the Greeks call "mesimeri" and I knew everything would be closed, so I lay down on my hard narrow bed for a nap; I might be up late looking for Jerry in whatever bars the little port town had.

When I awoke it was still light but the air was cool. The sun had set behind the high hills at the center of the island so that the whole town was in the cooling shadow of the hills, but the sky was still blue. In fact, with the breeze from the sea it was almost too cool. I put on a jacket and set out in search of dinner and information. One of the little tavernas on the edge of the harbor had a large sign saying that English was spoken; I might get both food and news of Jerry here, with luck.

I ordered a beer, a salad, and the shish-kebabs the Greeks call souvlaki and let myself be drawn into conversation with the gray-haired man named Nick who owned the place. He had worked for most of his life in Chicago to earn the money to buy this little restaurant-bar in his native village, and he spoke English with a Midwest twang. In fact, his Greek seemed a little rusty when he gave an occasional order to a waiter or bus boy.

"I prob'ly shouldn't have come back," he confided in me as he sat at my table drinking a beer that would probably go on my bill though I hadn't offered it to him. "You forget what a dead-alive hole your hometown was; you only remember the good parts. I thought at least I'd get all the tourists who speak English here, but people who get this far off the beaten track usually talk some Greek and half the time they go to the little local places and I never see them."

This was too good an opportunity to miss and he might as well earn that beer. "I stopped here because the purser on the ship told me that a relative of mine is on the island," I told him. "I wonder if you've run into him. His name is Jerry Doolan; a big red-haired man."

Nick grinned. "Oh yeah, got the map of Ireland on his face, like they say. He was in here a couple times for a beer but he's a case of what I was talking about; he talked Greek pretty good and he liked to spend his time in those little dives down the end of the harbor drinking ouzo. You don't look much like him, for a relative."

I hope not; I like to think my features are aristocratic and Jerry's are pure peasant. "He's the son of my step-mother," I said shortly. "I usually call him my half-brother to save explanations. I'd like to get hold of him; do you know where I could find him?"

Nick questioned his waiters in Greek, but their replies seemed to me sullen and evasive. Nick turned back to me with a frown. "They don't know and don't want to know," he said in a puzzled voice. "He must've got the people here mad at him. Prob'ly over a girl, that's usually what causes trouble in these little places. That's about all I can think of 'cause when he first came here he was pretty popular—always having a drink and a laugh with the fishermen."

There was nothing much more to be got out of Nick; I finished my dinner and moved on before I found myself buying him more beer and listening to more of his reminiscences of what seemed to me to have been a very dull life in Chicago. I wasn't sure which at end of the harbor the "little dives" were located, but the harbor had only two ends; the town made a little crescent around the small bay which was the town's reason for existing.

I went to the wrong end first, of course; there was nothing at that end but small houses, children running and playing, and women gossiping on the doorsteps. It was getting dark when I got to the right end of town and I followed the sound of recorded bouzouki music into a little bar filled with men who could have been fishermen. There was no red head in the crowd and few that weren't white or grizzled; I supposed the younger men left the island in search of opportunity.

Still, I had to start somewhere. I sat at a little table and ordered a whiskey, settling for a brandy when they didn't have whiskey. The whiskey they usually had would have been terrible, but the order established me as a rich foreigner and I could let Greek curiosity go to work.

They let me finish my first brandy in dignified silence, but my second brandy came unordered. Then came the questions asked by a rabbity little bespectacled man whose English was very good. He relayed my answers in Greek to the other men who had pushed up their chairs to make a sort of circle around me. One Greek tradition that has survived from the time of Homer is giving hospitality and expecting a good story in return; Odysseus got the same treatment at the court of the Phaecian king. The questions nowadays are rather more personal than the ones Homer records: Are you married? Do you have children? What is your job? How much do you earn?

This inquisition usually annoys me, but this time it served my purpose; eventually I was asked why I came to Gorgonissa, and I replied that I was searching for my "brother," Jerome Doolan. I had decided to say "brother" rather than "half-brother"; family is important to Greeks and if I called Jerry my brother it would give my inquiries into his whereabouts more authority.

As soon as I spoke Jerry's name, even before the rabbity man translated my question, I felt the mood change in the room. Everyone had been staring at me as if they had never seen a foreigner before; now they looked away and began to murmur among themselves. There were no more questions and I had to ask my interlocutor directly if he knew where Jerry was. He shook his head. "He is no longer on the island, sir," he said. "He has gone away with a . . . local person."

Wondering if Jerry's proclivities had at last got the better of his rigid Catholic upbringing, I asked whether his companion had been a young man. That might account for the odd reception I had been getting to my questions about Jerry: rural Greeks have none of the Classical Greek tolerance for homosexuality. But the rabbity man's surprise seemed genuine. "Oh no, not a man," he said. "Your brother went with the lady."

That was an odd way to put it: Greek uses "the" far more than English, but this man's English had been fluent and correct up to now, a little pedantic, if anything. And it did not sound like a slip back into Greek idiom; there was a special tone in his voice as he said "the lady." You could write down what he had said as "He went with The Lady" to convey the impression his words gave. Who was this "local person" who was referred to with such respect?

"Perhaps he'll return soon," I said. "Where did he stay in the town?" The man hesitated, then said, "He had a room with Kyra Sylvia, down the street. But I believe that 'he will not—that he was not planning to return."

I nodded with pretended indifference and asked *him* a few questions, about the island and how the islanders made their livings. He answered courteously, but soon made an excuse to leave my table. I finished my brandy, nodded to the bartender and went out without offering to pay; my money would be refused but I was in no mood to give thanks for their hospitality.

I thought I might have to wait until the morning to check out the place Jerry had stayed, but there was a light in the window of what had to be the house, and I knocked on the door. A black-clad crone answered the door and looked at me inquiringly. "Are you the Kyra Sylvia who rents rooms?" I asked.

"Room, yes, good room for the tourist; you look." She thrust a big old-fashioned key at me and pointed to some outside stairs near the door. I hesitated, but the way she bellowed the words, she was probably deaf; I might learn more from looking at the room than from questioning her.

I went up the stairs and opened the massive wooden door, and switched on the one light which hung from the ceiling, wondering idly where the electric power came from on Gorgonissa. The room was bare but clean with a narrow bed that was even harder than the one at the hotel. I stood on the bed to get at the high cupboard above it. Even in some fairly good Greek hotels if you go off for a few days, they are likely to tidy your luggage into a closet and rent your room while you're gone; the more honest places don't charge you for the room if they rent it, but some places just pocket the extra room rental and say nothing to you.

For once I was glad of this practice; it meant that if Jerry had gone off intending to come back his luggage might have been stuck away to await his return. I was right; when I wrestled the warped cupboard door open, his bag, his shaving kit, and a jacket I recognized were right at the front of the cupboard. But there was a surprising amount of other luggage here, too; some of it old and dusty, but some of it surprisingly new and expensive.

I opened one case which wasn't Jerry's; it was some sort of salesman's sample case by the look of it. Then I searched Jerry's things thoroughly; what I was looking for was not there and there was no indication of what he was up to, except an old book on the Greek Islands, with a place marked by a used ferry ticket. I opened the book and the reason for Jerry's visit to the island was immediately apparent. The crude line drawing in the book might have been a copy of the golden plaque we had found on our dig on the Turkish coast. But the legend below it said "Rock carving in a cave in the White Cliff, near Chora on Gorgonissa Island."

Just then the door opened and the black-clad woman came in, her dark wrinkled face more curious than alarmed at seeing me apparently looting the luggage of the absent guest. I decided to take the offensive. "Jerry Doolan is my brother," I said, pointing to the luggage. "Where is he? What have you done with him?" She opened her mouth to speak, then caught sight of the book in my hand, opened to the drawing. She began to laugh, a wheezy cackle.

"Ask her," she said in Greek. "Ask that one." Then she began to laugh again so hard she started to cough. I could get nothing else out of her and finally flung out of the room in a temper leaving the bed strewn with Jerry's luggage and the old woman cackling and coughing. Serve her right if she choked, I thought viciously. I was halfway back to the hotel before I realized that I had left the book in the room. Might there be more information in it? But I didn't want to argue with the old woman that night, so I continued on to the hotel and fell into bed. In the morning, the hotel seemed deserted. I walked over to Nick's place and got some breakfast. The waiters seemed to look at me strangely, but Nick was as friendly and garrulous as ever. I asked him about a guide book or map of the island, but all he had was a crude map intended as a handout for tourists, with advertising for several businesses on the other side. It was enough, though. "White Cliff" was marked on it, a little down the coast from a landing marked "Mules' Path to Xora." It must be the place, and I might find either Jerry or some trace of him there. "I'd like to rent a small boat," I told Nick. "Preferably without a boatman."

He shook his head. "Guys around here won't rent their boats," he said. "Can't blame 'em, the boats are their living. I got an old tub I inherited from an uncle that died. But I already rented it to some English people. Hey, maybe they'll take you along. They're just rowing up the coast to climb up to Chora. Prob'ly haven't left yet."

"That would suit me fine," I said. "Thank you, I'll go see if I can find them." Following Nick's directions, I got to the dock just in time to catch the English party pushing off in a shabby old-fashioned rowboat. The two English ladies from the boat nodded at me rather coldly. But the man at the oars gave me a friendly grin.

"By all means," he said. "I could use a spot of help with the rowing. I suspect this tub weighs a ton. I'm Tony Carradyne: you probably know Miss Briggs and Miss Thwaite from the ferry trip over; you all traveled first class. I find it much livelier in third class, with the Greeks. D'you know some old ladies were doing a village dance on the lower deck to music from a transistor radio? And some of the kids were playing at being Odysseus and others were playing video games in the lounge. "That's what I love about Greece: ever old and ever new." He chuckled, his eyes alight with enthusiasm.

"Are you the Anthony Carradyne who writes the travel books?" I asked. "Used to be an academic, didn't you? I'm James Deveraux of the Archeological Institute; we met once long ago, I believe."

He nodded. "Fraid I don't remember, but we might very well have. Yes, I retired here after my wife died and eke out my pension with travel books and mystery stories. Gives me an excuse to wander about Greece. Are you on that Institute dig on the Turkish coast?"

"Yes, I'm taking a bit of a break while they get down to the interesting levels," I said. I wanted a little break from Turkey, but I'm afraid I don't share your enthusiasm for modern Greeks. They're a bit of a mongrel race, really; they've intermarried with their conquerors and neighbors."

"That's just as true of the Classical period Greeks," said Carradyne argumentatively. And the language has survived though it's changed and grown. Language and culture are what make a people, not just genes. Heaven knows that we English are a mongrel race, but . . . ."

I shrugged. "It's just the culture that *hasn't* survived," I said. "Modern Greeks are a superstitious, church-ridden lot. Not much Classical rationality around in Greece today." I was content to argue with him while he pulled the heavy oars, taking me where I wanted to go.

Carradyne laughed. "Like a good many classicists you concentrate on the Apollo side of classical Greece and forget Dionysus," he said. "Plenty of what we'd call superstition in ancient Greece. Pan in the woods, nymphs in the fountains, mermaids in the sea . . . ."

We bickered amicably as Carradyne rowed down the coast, and I never did take my turn at the oars, which suited me well enough. He had been a professor of philosophy or literature or some such subject, not a scientist, but he knew a great deal of classical archaeology for a layman; you had to be careful of generalizations or loose statements arguing with him.

When we reached the landing place I had seen on the map, Carradyne and the women hiked up the trail to look at icons in a church in the village. I have little interest in Byzantine church art and invented an interest in possible ruins on the shoreline to excuse not going with them.

I had spotted a much lighter and more modern boat pulled up on the shore, a sort of reinforced rubber dinghy and as soon as they were out of sight, I borrowed this and set off in the direction of the White Cliff.

The trouble was that there was not one but many white cliffs, all of them riddled with shallow caves. It took me hours to investigate them all and I began to envy Carradyne and the women who had planned to have lunch in the village after seeing the icons. Finally, however, I did see some stones that might have been the remains of a small temple; some still on shore and some visible below the boat in the clear water. There was one nicely carved column base, with traces of the lead-covered centering plug still in it, so that I wished I could get on shore for a closer look.

Next to the ruins was a deeper cave, and I paddled cautiously into it, watching out for sharp rocks that might hole my boat and leave me stranded. Then I looked up and there, carved on the wall near the entrance to the cave was the same figure I had seen on the golden plaque we had found in Turkey, the plaque Jerry had stolen. In the damp cavern the fish scales on the lower part of the figure seemed to have a silvery gleam. On this larger scale figure you could see that it definitely was a sort of veil which covered the face, in curious contrast to the bare breasts below.

"Do you like her?" came a voice from behind me. I whirled around. almost capsizing the boat, and for a moment I thought there was a statue in a niche on the opposite wall. Then I realized that it was a young woman in an elegantly simple, light-green dress, which suited the darker green of her eyes and the dull gold of her hair. She was on some sort of walkway on that side of the cave, which I had missed because it blended so well into the rock.

"I find it extremely interesting," I said when I could find my voice. "I'm an archeologist and I've never heard of anything like this in this part of the Aegean. Why isn't it famous?"

She shrugged her shoulders with delicate grace. "She has been in the past, perhaps she will be again," she said. "But the island people tend to be secretive about her; perhaps they don't want her to be a tourist attraction."

"Tourists be damned. It ought to be studied properly for the sake of science," I said. "Does it have a name, a local name, that is?"

She smiled enigmatically. "The local people call her many things," she said. "One name for her is 'Potnia tis Thallasas'." She added something in a curious sing-song intonation; it sounded like Homeric Greek but the accent was so strange I could only catch a few words. Not a modern Greek accent certainly, and not the way a classicist would pronounce the words I could catch, but it sounded somehow right.

"I couldn't get all of that," I said, "Potinia tis Thallasas" would be 'Lady of the Sea,' would it not? But 'Potnia' is a Mycenean word. Surely people here don't speak Mycenean Greek; that's even older than Homeric Greek."

She shrugged. "On the islands old words are remembered," she said, "even the Kaphtui name, 'P'dare Mia', they use sometimes. You may call me 'Mia' if you like, it's one of my names."

The first part of this seemed nonsense to me, and the name 'Mia' had associations of film-making and Beautiful People. She must be some rich girl vacationing on the island, perhaps even from a yacht moored somewhere nearby. If Jerry wanted to sell the plaque, she or the people with her might be the kind of people who would buy. She might even be the mysterious "lady" Jerry was said to have gone off with. I had to learn more about her. "Are you staying somewhere nearby, Mia?" I asked, putting as much charm in my voice as I could. I'm not unsuccessful with women, though I don't like them much.

The charm seemed to work; she smiled and said, "Come and see." Unfortunately just at that moment I heard the sound of oars outside the cave and voices calling my name. The woman's eyes narrowed in calculation for a moment, then she said softly, "I will see you in the port tonight, at the ouzeria they call 'Gorgona'. Keep the boat you are in until then; we may need it. Now I must go." She walked further into the cave on the walkway, vanishing into the shadows.

I wished I could investigate where she had gone but it was urgent to prevent whoever was looking for me from finding the carving on the wall. I rowed swiftly out into the sunlight and around the next headland I saw Carradyne standing up in the boat we had come in and scanning the shoreline.

"Where on earth did you get the rubber dinghy?" he asked, but swept on without waiting for an answer. "The two ladies caught a minivan which passes for a local bus, back to the port town. I think we bored them with our argument on the way here. I was having a leisurely ouzo with the priest from the church with the icons when I happened to mention that I'd left you exploring the shore. He got most agitated and insisted that I come down and 'rescue' you; I'm not sure from what. Even gave me a holy relic to preserve me, bless him." He pulled a small jeweled' cross with a sort of box at the center from his shirt, petted it affectionately and put it away again.

"A rather wealthy-looking young woman gave me permission to use the dinghy; I think she may be off a yacht or be vacationing at a villa near here,"I told him. I'm supposed to return it to her in town tonight; do you think we can pull it behind the boat? I'll give you a hand rowing back." I was that eager to get him away from the cave.

In the end, he did more than his share in rowing back, too; whatever his faults, Carradyne was not mean. He asked no questions when I asked to be dropped off in the rubber boat a little before we reached the town. I pulled the boat up in a little cove around a headland from the end of town where the bars were, and as I hiked back to the hotel I discreetly spotted the little ouzo bar called the Gorgona down a side-street near the end of town. The faded sign over the door had a picture on it that might have been intended for the rock carving in the cave, but no one who had not seen the carving would have recognized it. I was lucky enough to arrive at the hotel at hot water time; I showered and rested a while before going to Nick's for dinner. There I found Carradyne arguing with Nick about the Chicago Cubs and I couldn't avoid joining him for dinner. When he caught me looking at my watch, he chuckled. "Don't worry, Deveraux, I won't horn in on your rendezvous," he said. "I have one myself; I have to meet Father Photis at the church to return the cross and look at some old church records."

Relieved of that worry, I became more amiable, and we argued cheerfully enough through dinner and a drink afterwards. Carradyne had a good deal of out of the way information and a ready wit, and I found him amusing. However, it was not so amusing when he brought up the subject of Jerry when we were having our final drinks.

I understand you've been looking for Jerry Doolan," he said casually. I know Jerry a little from digs he'd done in Greece, and I share your concern. He's a good archaeologist and a good man. The locals say he's gone off with a woman."

My temper got the better of me. "That's a crock," I said bitterly. "Jerry's a faggot, and besides, he's a thief."

Carradyne's voice was quiet as he replied, "I'm probably more likely than you are to think that homosexuality is a sin. But it's not my business to condemn Jerry for it. Why do you think it's yours? And what did he steal?"

"He stole a gold plaque from our dig in Turkey," I said bitterly. "The Turkish authorities know it exists; if we don't get it back, it will reflect on the Institute."

"And on you, because you're his half-brother," said Carradyne softly. "You're thinking more of your reputation than of Jerry, I think, Deveraux. Perhaps about the other thing, too. Well, I ought not to judge you either. But I think I'd rather be Jerry than be you." With that he left some money on the table and walked out.

I shrugged. The man was a fool. Reputation is important in itself and important for other things, the big rewards. I wasn't going to let Jerry get in the way of my plans. If he had sold (or given—he was that foolish) the plaque to the girl I was to meet tonight, no doubt I could get it from her one way or another. Some ways might be more distasteful than others, but I'd do it. I'd settle the mess in Turkey, then come back and "rediscover" the veiled figure in the stone carving. It ought to be good for a monograph, even a bit of publicity in the popular press. Every little bit helps. As for Jerry . . . . But first the girl.

It was lucky I had located the Gorgona by day or I would never have found it by night. There were as many women here as men, which is very unusual in Greece. The women weren't prostitutes either; they were mostly middle-aged or older women with an air of authority about them. Their men seemed rather subdued.

The music was live; wailing laments and occasional satirical songs from a middle-aged woman who reminded me a little of Mia. There was one guitarist; a thin young man whose burning eyes never left the singer. There was only ouzo or brandy to drink; I nursed one brandy for a while, then drained it and ordered another.

Toward midnight, everyone in the place stood up; I imitated them, thinking it was some local custom. I looked around and saw Mia standing by my table; she sat down when everyone else did. Whatever the odd little ceremony had been, it was over; there was a quiet hum of conversation around us.

Mia looked at me, her green eyes enigmatic. "You are looking for Jerry," she said.

I decided to try shock tactics. "And a gold plaque he stole," I said.

She shrugged. "Perhaps the plaque stole him," she said obscurely. "Perhaps it wanted to come home."

I felt a sudden thrill. "Did it come from here?" I asked. "Are there more here?"

She smiled. "Perhaps. Do you know what it is?"

"A decoration from a cult statue," I said confidently. "Like the ones you can see at Delphi, that were on the ivory statue of Apollo. They made a sort of stole, like a priest's stole. This one had holes at top and bottom, as those do. Perhaps the cult statue here was some sea-god. The Delphi plaques have gryphons and other fabulous monsters, this one has . . . ."

"Not fabulous," she said, "and not a god. As for the other, perhaps."

I was tired of the riddling talk. "Do you know where it is?" I asked. "Where Jerry is? Will you show me?"

"Oh yes," she said with a smile, "come and see". That was what she had said before we were interrupted at the cave, but this time there was no interruption. She led the way out of the cafe. As we went out, everyone stood up again; the same strange ritual again.

She seemed to know where I had hidden the boat and led me straight to it; I supposed she had spotted it coming into town. The sea was calm, the boat light; we had an easy row to the cave. She pointed around the next headland and I went past the cave and into a little bay beyond it. I expected a yacht, or a villa on the shore; there was nothing. "Is this a trick?" I cried, my voice harsh. "There's nothing here. Where's Jerry?""

"Look below," she said, with a strange little laugh in her voice. I looked down into the clear, moonlit water. The hair of the floating figure did not look red in the moonlight and the face was puffy, but I knew it was Jerry. He seemed to be caught by his feet in the seaweed on the bottom so that he reached up from the floor of the sea like some obscene flower swaying in the water. Beyond him was another body with darker hair but the face—oh, God, the fish had been at the face . . . .

Deep in the water was a shifting green-gold glow. "There is my bed," she whispered. "The gold is there. Come and see." I looked in the water beside the boat and she was there, her breasts bare, her powerful fishtail flicking occasionally to keep her in place. There was a veil on her face, but it seemed to be melting away . . . .

Then I heard oars and the heavy rowboat came around the headland; it must have been hidden in the cave. Carradyne was rowing and a white-bearded priest in black robes stood easily in the prow like some strange figurehead. He had some sort of candle-lantern in his hand, richly decorated, like a sanctuary light. Gravely he addressed the creature in the water. "First the salesman from Athens, then the red-haired man, now this one. You grow greedy, girl! You know the promise you made; no more than one man for each moon of the year, or you lose your right to take any . . . ."

The creature from the sea gave a bitter laugh. "When have I ever had even a half of that since you priests came to spread guilt and fear, to threaten the young men with hell-fire if they came to me? In the old days they were proud to be my consorts, to live with me till I tired of them."

The priest's voice was steady as he said, "And were their mothers and wives also proud to have you steal their men at your whim, and let them drown when they angered you? How many in all the centuries have pleased you for more than a little time? Do you think this one will?"

She laughed again. "This one is safe from me, priest. You don't need to threaten me with the bones of the terrible old man who bound us here. I brought this one here to frighten him; his body is young, but inside he is old and withered. A good thing for me; had he been more to my taste he might have tempted me. The second one left me hungry—oh so hungry; he was not for women. I do not know if I can bear it until another comes I can take."

Carradyne's voice came then, seemingly confident, but with a little tremor in it. "How about me then, mistress? I'm old outside but young inside. And by all that's holy, what a way to go!"

The creature in the sea looked at him, and there was a green fire in her eyes. Her tongue-tip touched her upper lip delicately. "Yes," she said softly, "you have much life in you."

The "priest's voice broke in deep and soft. "Sin is sin, my son, even if you do it to save others. You may not do evil that good may come."

Carradyne laughed, and the tremor seemed to be gone from his voice.

"What sin, Father, fornication? Why, marry us then and I'll go down to my marriage bed down below there. Then the young men won't have to leave Gorgonissa when they become men and come back only when their hair is gray."

"But she is not . . ." the priest began.

Carradyne cut in, "Who knows what she is, Father? But you said yourself that Saint Photis baptized all of them. He must have thought they had a soul to save. Get out the book you brought, Father, but turn to the wedding ceremony."

I have never seen a Greek Orthodox wedding before or since, so I have no idea what they left out, but it didn't take long. There was some sort of business with crowns, which appeared suddenly floating on the waves. They looked ancient and even in my dazed condition, I longed for a clearer look at them. The "servant of God Anthony" took the "servant of God Mia" to wife for better or worse, for richer, for poorer. At least I think these were the words; if not, something like them. Then the priest gave a blessing and Carradyne clasped my hand and then slipped out of the boat. The two of them sank beneath the waves and vanished, and I looked at the priest in horror.

"But it's suicide . . ." I said incoherently. "What does the other matter, all that . . . But he'll die under there . . . How can you . . . ."

The old priest shook his head. "They do not all die, if the stories are true," he said quietly. "Not those who go down willingly to her. And even the others not at once. When they awake and know where they are, they panic and die, if she has left them, if she is displeased. Perhaps she will not leave this one. And if he does die, he did it for the people of this island. 'Greater love hath no man . . . .' Perhaps he would be a martyr. Or perhaps you are right and it was suicide. I must pray about it. But now, we must go home." And he took the oars in his hands.

When we got to the dock, he laid his hand on my shoulder and smiled. "I have prayed and I think this was for the good, my son. Do not fear. After all, you were best man at the strangest wedding you will ever see. And sometimes the best man is asked to be godfather, later on."

It meant nothing to me; I went ashore and walked away from the sea until I could no longer see the water. I stayed inland until the ferry came and stayed in an inside cabin until we got to Piraeus. I flew from Athens to Istanbul, and went directly to the dig by car and tried to bury myself in work. When Jerry's body washed ashore in Turkey with the golden plaque in his pocket, the Turkish authorities made a fuss, but their threats meant nothing to me. Eventually they went away, grumbling.

That was last year. Today, two things came in the mail. One was the plaque, finally released by the Turkish authorities because their experts had decided that it must be a modern fake. Such a figure, they said, is never found on really ancient work: the "gorgona" or mermaid, is a modern Greek superstition. They were wrong, but the decision meant that I was free to do whatever I wanted to with the plaque. The other thing that came in that mail was a letter from Father Photis from Gorgonissa; the Island of the Gorgona. I am invited to a christening there. I think I know of a present for the baby. I wonder if they will have a gift for me?

OTHERS' EYES

I first discovered the fantastic truth about my nephew Bobby when he was about four months old. I had been out of the country when he was born: I do quite a bit of traveling in the business—or profession, if you like—that I'm in. I'm a consulting transportation engineer: If you want to move people or material from Place A to Place B, I'll tell you how to do it with the greatest cost-effectiveness and then hand you over to the specialists to implement my solution. Most, though not all of the problems I deal with come up in out of the way places, so I travel a lot. I missed my brother Bob's courtship and wedding as well as Bobby getting born, and I was sorry to miss both, but for rather different reasons.

Bob had married a girl—I'd call her a hippie, but I suppose that word is out of date now—who was "into" all the pseudo-scientific and antiscientific things that are floating around in our confused culture. She believed in astrology, of course, and talked to her plants, for openers, and went on from there to believe in "out-of-body experiences" and probably reincarnation, except she was a little dubious as to whether she could reconcile that with Christianity. She belonged to some kind of Christian sect, and of course she was ultra-liberal politically and an ecology nut. Because I started out as a highway engineer and do some work for DOD, she was just as suspicious of me as I was of her.

Still, she seemed to make Bob happy, and though I've been looking after Bob ever since our folks died when I was still in my teens, I try not to run his life for him. So Diane and I had arrived at a sort of truce: she knew Bob respected me and depended on me and she couldn't change that, and I knew that a mere brother couldn't and shouldn't come between man and wife. I was genuinely pleased when I heard that a child was on the way. When I decided that I liked roving better than being tied down in all aspects of my life, I had a vasectomy—one of the old, nonreversible kind—so even if some woman catches me in a weak moment and marries me, I won't produce any young Paul Winterfields. So Robert Winterfield, young Bobby, is as close to a son as I'm ever likely to get.

Bob talked about the baby all the way from the airport where he had picked me up, and I was really anxious to see him. Diane delayed me a little with small talk and a cup of tea sweetened with honey—coffee and sugar are both against some part of her patchwork belief system—but eventually I got to see my nephew. I was a little surprised that there was a fairly bright light over his crib, which Diane said they left on until she and Bob went to bed, in order to make it easier to check and make sure the baby was all right. Then she said something I discounted at the time, because it sounded so completely ridiculous.

"Actually, to get him to go to sleep I usually have to shut my own eyes for a while," she said. She went on with some Diane-type explanation of how the baby was "attuned to her" or something like that. I thought it was just a good excuse for putting her feet up and taking a little rest after she'd settled the baby. But Bob startled me by saying that he had to do the same thing when he occasionally put the kid to bed.

Bobby was a cute little thing: even though I know intellectually that the cuteness of young animals is a survival trait that's been developed by natural selection, I'm a sucker for a kid or a puppy or a kitten. Hell, I've even seen young crocodiles in some of the jungles I've been in that were cute in a raffish sort of way. I congratulated Bob on a fine-looking kid and I suppose the unfamiliar voice woke the baby up. I got my first shock when he opened his eyes. It wasn't just that they didn't focus on things. I knew very little then about when babies begin to really see things. His eyes just looked wrong, somehow, dead, nonfunctional. I began to have a sick, cold, feeling that there was something wrong with my fine, young nephew.

But just then he started to fuss, and Diane picked up one of those pacifier things they let babies suck on and asked in a soothing voice whether Bobby wanted his "pa." The kid reached right for it and took it out of her hand; he had to be able to see it to do that. But I still didn't like the look of those eyes. Diane shooed Bob and I out then, so she could put the baby back to sleep, and it gave me a funny feeling to see her rocking him in a rocking chair by the crib, her own eyes shut and the baby's eyes open and staring.

Bob took me up to my room—really mine, because wherever Bob and Diane moved, they rented a place with an extra room for me, which I used as a base whenever I was in the States. I payed them a good rent for it, and the result was that they had a nicer place than they could afford otherwise and had a paying guest who was hardly ever there. It was worth it to me; not only were the books and personal mementos I couldn't carry on my trips safe and well cared for, I also had a sense that there was someplace I could call home, though I lived most of my life in fancy hotel rooms and primitive construction camps.

I unlocked a cupboard and gave Bob and myself a drink of good Scotch as I unpacked. His drinks with me are probably the only hard liquor Bob gets, which is just as well since Robert Winterfield the first, our old man, was a bit of a lush, and I don't want to see Bob go the same way. I tried to think of a tactful way of putting it, but I'm not much for tact; so after Bob and I had chatted a little about my last trip, I came out with it: "Bob, my nephew seems to be a fine healthy little kid, but his eyes look kind of funny. Has a doctor looked at them?"

I knew the chances were that a doctor hadn't even seen the kid. Bob's letters had told me child was delivered by a midwife at home, and I knew from frustrating conversations with Diane that she was against most of modem-practice. I suppose that if there was a common thread in Diane's various enthusiasms, it was being 'natural:': natural food, natural childbirth, "natural" medicine. So far as I could figure out that meant that you could let a doctor set a broken leg or something like that, but x-rays, "chemical" medicines, and so on were out.

Bob confirmed my suspicions: Bobby had been given checkups by the midwife, mainly weighing, checking reflexes and that kind of thing, and had gone to the Public Health clinic for the usual shots—Bob had convinced Diane that innoculation merely stimulated the body's defenses and so was "natural." But no M.D. had given him a real going over. Bob had noticed the peculiarity of Bobby's eyes of course and had been worried by that, and by other things.

"He's just beginning to be able to express his wants of course," Bob said, "but all the time he's awake he seems to want someone paying attention to him. You can't just be in the same room with him; you have to look at him or at least look at something he's interested in looking at. Do that and he's a perfectly good baby. He'll play with his toys or look at television with you or look out the window with you at the birds or whatever. But if you look away from him and try to read a book or something, he complains. If he wakes up in his room he can't seem to amuse himself with toys or playing with his fingers like some babies; he wants Di or me to come and be with him. But it's not his eyes, or at least I don't think so: I've tried to test him and he sees as well as I do."

I think I was beginning even then to have some suspicion of the truth, but I bided my time and let Diane get used to having me around. Bob was at work during the day, of course, and pretty soon there came a time when Diane wanted to go out and I was around the house. She asked me diffidently if I'd mind watching Bobby for a while, and concealing my eagerness, I said that I would. As soon as she was gone I went to work. I spotted various props to use and had some of them assembled in my room. I grabbed Bobby and a few of his favorite toys and took him up there. The tests I wanted to make were pretty clear in my mind, though some occurred to me as I went along.

All the details of those tests, and many I made afterwards, are written down in my records: I'll just give you some idea of how I went to work. For example, I took a bright-colored ball that Bobby was fond of and a goodsized plate of thin steel I'd dug up from some forgotten project. I held the steel plate right in front of Bobby's eyes and held the ball out to him; he took it from my hand unerringly. I held the plate between Bobby and me, with the ball on his side so I couldn't see the ball but I could see Bobby. I moved the ball around: he didn't have the slightest idea where it was, though I could tell since I could feel where my hand was. As soon as I brought the ball into my own field of vision, Bobby knew where it was.

There were lots of other tests, eliminating various unlikely hypotheses; in the years that followed I thought of a lot more unlikely hypotheses and eliminated them. But by the time my first series of tests were over, I was sure I had the right explanation: I'm just as sure now, though I can no longer test the theory. Bobby couldn't see a damn thing with his own strange-looking eyes. But he could see whatever I was looking at just as well—just exactly as well—as I could. Presumably he did the same thing with Bob and Diane. Whether he could do it with those who weren't blood relatives, we'd have to test. But basically Bobby couldn't see with his own eyes, and he could see with others' eyes.

I suppose you'd have to call it telepathy, but he didn't read my thoughts as such; when I knew by touch or sound where the ball was, this didn't get over to him; only when I saw it did he know. So far as you can tell with a baby that age, he didn't sense my thoughts or emotions. It was as if he spliced into the nervous system somewhere between the eyes and the brain. That's all he could do: see through my eyes, but he could do it. And of course it was scientifically impossible.

Luckily, I'm not a scientist, I'm an engineer. If I'm sure something works, I don't give a damn, basically, why it works. Also I've been reading science fiction since I was a kid: one of the best presents my dad ever gave me (one of the only presents come to that) was a copy of an old *Amazing Stories* he'd found on a streetcar. Tommy Cross in *Slan!*, Kimball Kinneson, the Grey Lensman, could read minds, see through others' eyes, why not Bobby? I hadn't expected to ever see something like that, but I hadn't expected to ever see men walking around on the Moon in my lifetime: But what I could see and test I could believe. Bobby read minds. Or eyes. Or, more likely; the part of the mind that received messages from the eyes.

I didn't say anything to Bob or Diane then, though I gave Bobby further tests as often as I got the chance. A consequence of this that I hadn't foreseen was that Bobby, who seemed to enjoy the tests, became very fond of me. Diane grew friendlier toward me as a result, and I knew that when I decided what was best to do I'd now have a better chance of persuading her as well as Bob. But I wasn't sure myself what was best to do.

Still, when I went off for a short trip to Canada, I was pretty sure that I ought to tell some responsible scientists about Bobby. I was pretty sure that J.B. Rhine was dead, but I believed that there was still some kind of research institute on parapsychology at Duke. I was toying with the idea of getting an introduction to somebody there through some of my academic contacts and sizing up the people involved in the research: I didn't want to let just anyone loose on Bobby.

The trip was to Alberta, Canada, in connection with the on-again, off-again development of the Athabascan oil sands. It was on at the moment, but the oil companies were afraid the conservation nuts would stop it again, and they didn't want to put a lot of money into access roads. So the question was how do you move a lot of very heavy stuff over rough terrain without building roads? The hovercraft equipment movers I came up with as a solution to that problem were never used in Alberta, as it turned out, but I've used them in other places since.

But the trip landed me in a small town in northern Alberta with nothing to do one evening but watch television and no channel but the Canadian Broadcasting System. It happened that evening that there was a special about the Dionne quintuplets, how they were exploited, how the publicity ruined their lives and the lives of their parents. It was a powerful program, and the next day in Edmonton I bought the book it was based on, by a Canadian writer named Pierre Burton. The book finished the job the program had started. Five ordinary kids had been ground up by a great machine of government and business and show business, just because all five were born at one time. If anybody, no matter how well-intentioned, outside the family, got to know about Bobby's powers, the same thing would happen to him and to Bob and Diane.

Even aside from anything else, there was the national security angle. Think what a spy a grown-up Bobby would make: able to see through the eyes of anybody on the other side. There was no way any government that knew what he could do was going to let him grow up in any normal way. I'm a patriotic man, even a bit of a Cold Warrior. I don't trust the Russians or Chinese, and I think we ran out on our obligations in Southeast Asia. But I don't like spies, theirs or ours, I never have. I thought the American Way of Life could survive without Bobby as Superspy.

So it had to be secrecy. Nobody except Bob, Diane and I could know anything about Bobby's powers. I wasn't even all that hot about telling Diane, but I knew that there was no way to avoid it. As it happened, Diane was easier to convince than Bob was. She believed in enough crazy things already, and a blind baby who saw telepathically through other people's eyes fit in with some of her other odd beliefs, like out-of-body experiences.

Actually, I thought, it probably went the other way: if people who were clinically dead but later revived were really able to see their own bodies from above and recount events that went on in the operating room while they seemed to be unconscious, it was very likely due to something like Bobby's wild talent. After doing some reading in parapsychology, I was willing to concede that many people may have latent "psi powers" which came out under crisis conditions.

Bobby's crisis condition was being born blind and needing desperately to see.

Bob didn't want to believe in Bobby's telepathy because he didn't want to believe that the boy was blind: I suppose every father wants to deny that anything is wrong with *his* kid. But when I eventually convinced him he saw the point of keeping it a secret: he could see what would happen to Bobby if the secret got out. The three of us kicked it around, but we couldn't see any way the kid could have a normal life without someone getting to know about his powers. How can you play hide and seek, for example, if you can see what the other kids see but can't see your own surroundings unless they do? How can you take a test in school if you can see other people's papers but not your own? There were just too many ways Bobby would be bound to give himself away if they tried to bring him up in an ordinary environment.

To my surprise it was Diane who came up with a workable solution. She knew of a little farming commune whose members put a high value on family togetherness and on privacy. They educated their own kids at home; using correspondence course material designed for kids in isolated places. They'd fought a legal battle with the school system to win the right to do it. The kids spent a lot of time with their parents, helping out with chores and learning to take their place in the community. And even if they did find out about Bobby, or at least guessed there was something odd about him, Diane thought that they wouldn't press or probe, or tell outsiders what they saw or guessed.

I wasn't so sure about that, and I didn't like the fact that the group was some kind of religious sect, but aside from asking Bob and Diane to live like hermits, it was the only solution I could see to keeping Bobby's secret and at the same time giving him some kind of fairly normal life. Bob would have to become a part-time farmer, but he could use his training as an accountant too. The group was an offshoot of the Amish or Mennonites or one of those groups: irrational about some things but with a certain amount of hard Germanic good sense. They didn't use tractors or chemical sprays but they made their farming pay and they had no objections to double-entry bookkeeping. If fact, Bob wound up spending more time with government forms than he did with a hoe or a horse-drawn plow.

I was getting to be fairly wealthy from my consulting business and had no one to spend it on but myself. I helped Bob and Diane over the transition and helped them buy into the commune, which was run a little like a condominium; each family owned their own home, subject to certain agreements, and a share in the farm enterprise. It was a sound business arrangement: my lawyer and my taxman assured me of that. My story for them, and for anyone else I had to explain things to, was that my hippie sister-in-law had talked my brother into a back-to-the-land movement and I was helping him get it out of his system. As time went on, mutual friends stopped asking when Bob would get over his craze: these days we're used to people doing funny things with their lives.

For Bobby it worked out well. Most of the day he spent with his mother, but as he got older he went out to work on the farm with his father. At the pace of non-mechanized farm life one person can act as the eyes of another. But of course someone always had to be looking where he needed to look: Bob or Diane had to "watch" for him while he dressed and washed himself or ate. They discovered fairly early on that he could see through anyone's eyes, only one person at the time though, and that person had to be fairly close to him at least to start.

The trigger for his "transferred sight," as I came to call it privately, was for someone to look at him. The sight of his own face or body in some way locked him into that person's eyes until the person went too far away or shut their own eyes. When Bob wanted to take over "watching" for him from Diane, she would shut her own eyes and Bob would look at Bobby. He never seemed to have much trouble adjusting to the new viewpoint, which surprised me until I thought of how easily we accept sudden changes of point of view in the movies or on 3V. And Bobby, of course, had never learned to coordinate his point of viewing with his physical position.

On the farm with plenty of animals around they soon learned that Bobby could see through the eyes of animals too, and after that they got him a dog of his own. That solved some problems, because with Ranger at his heels Bobby could move around the farm without other people to see for him. But even the best trained dog won't always look where you want him to look, and a dog doesn't look at things the way a person does. After Bobby got old enough we had some interesting conversations about things like that: I suppose I know things about the way animals see that experimental psychologists would give their eyeteeth to know.

I don't know if they're still arguing about whether animals see colors: according to Bobby they do, but they don't pay any attention to them. And even after Bobby learned to read he could never read anything through the eyes of an animal: their eyes don't focus on letters, don't attend to them. So Bobby, just with Ranger for company, couldn't really cope with all the things that a kid his age should have been able to cope with. But having Ranger as an alternate "watcher," even an inadequate one, took some strain off Bob and Diane.

It was a strain, no question about it. If Bobby had just been blind, he could have adjusted to it, learned to move cautiously, to read Braille, all the tricks a visually handicapped person learns to survive in the world. But Bobby would be "seeing" as well as anyone else one minute, and then his "watcher" would look away, glance down at a book, or shut his eyes, and suddenly Bobby was visually disoriented. It was hard enough for Bob and Diane to remember that: it always took me a while to get used to it again on my visits. If he was depending on the eyes of a person who wasn't deliberately "watching" for him, Bobby could be suddenly struck with what amounted to intermittent blindness. If you're running down a road or chopping wood and your "eyes" look away suddenly, you can hurt yourself badly.

Bobby learned to "coast past" transitions like this, after a fashion, but there was a limit to what he could do. Try going about your normal activities, shutting your eyes at irregular intervals and keeping them shut for even, say, thirty seconds. Sometimes it wouldn't make a bit of difference, other times it could be disastrous. In a city with traffic, with modem machinery all around, Bobby probably wouldn't have lived to grow up. Even on the farm, even with Bob and Diane "watching" for him, Bobby had some accidents and some close calls. But he did grow up.

I visited him whenever I could, even though it was less convenient at first; making my headquarters in the States on the farm rather than in a city. Actually, I had to rent space in a nearby town and install, first, communications equipment and, then, computers; the people in the commune didn't want that kind of equipment on their land, and I couldn't function without it. So when I was in the States I spent my working day at my office in the town, and lived at the farm.

I tried not to break any of their rules because I thought sometime we might depend on their good will. I even tried once in a while to give them advice on making their operation more efficient. Sometimes my solutions were too technological for them, but gradually I learned to work within the limit they set for themselves; after all, an engineer is always working the limits of the possible, whether the possibilities are natural or artificial (budgetary for instance). I came to value my visits to the farm as a change of pace from the increasingly technological society outside, though I was never convinced they weren't crazy to throw away what technology could do for them. After a few tentative attempts the people in the commune knew better than to talk religion to me. So they restrained from preaching to me and I restrained myself from trying to talk sense to them.

It was too good to last, or course, and there's' a bitter kind of satisfaction in the thought that it was my own actions that brought it all to an end, not betrayal from the commune or probing from the outside. I was always trying to keep Bobby, and Bob for that matter, from being too shut in by the peculiarities of the group they lived in. I got a fairly expensive 3V for my office, for instance, when a chance remark made me realize that the last television Bob had seen was the old flat kind and Bobby had never seen any kind of broadcast entertainment. (Of course by then movies were all being broadcast from Burbank or New York).

I could never get them to go with me to the city and perhaps it was just as well; even aside from Bobby, Bob and Diane would have had quite an adjustment to make after sixteen years on the farm; street ads hadn't been controlled yet. But anything "natural" was still "good" to Diane, and eventually I discovered she'd always wanted to see the Grand Canyon. I worked on her quietly and finally she agreed to a family vacation on the North Rim, which had been kept pretty primitive. She didn't like the ATV I rented for the trip, a hovercamper with lots of gadgets, but I convinced her it would let us keep our contacts with the outside world to a minimum. She had the last laugh though: she dug up some old nylon camping tents from someone in the commune, and when we got to the North Rim I found I had to park the ATV in a storage area and help carry the tents and other primitive "camping equipment" to a campground some distance away.

I wasn't doing so well introducing Bobby and Bob to the delights of civilization, which had been one object of the trip, but at least I had got them off the farm for a while, which was part of my plan. Now that Bobby was old enough to conceal his gifts, I had no intention of leaving him buried in the Middle Ages, which was what life at the farm amounted to. I relaxed and enjoyed Diane's cooking, which was always good, helped "watch" for Bobby and took family hikes along the rim of the Canyon. It was on one of these hikes that the beginning of the end came.

The South Rim is pretty well patrolled and civilized now, but on the North Rim there are still little trails going down the wall of the canyon for a way: almost all of them peter out after a while, but people still go down them, and the Park Service doesn't have enough people to stop them or close off all the trails. We knew better than to try them, especially with Bobby in tow, but one evening when we were hiking past a trail head, we heard a feeble call for help and a rattle of loose stones. I was just grumbling about the necessity of going and getting help for the idiot when I saw Bob stripping off his day pack and preparing to go down the trail.

"He might not last until we get help, Paul," Bob said with a determination he rarely showed, at least to me. "I'll be careful, but I've got to go see the situation he's in." I started arguing, but he was already down the trail. I started after him but the trail narrowed and I was fool enough to look down. I clung to the wall; sick and dizzy. Acrophobia is one weakness I've never been able to overcome, and somehow it makes it more humiliating that it's a weakness I share with Diane; she can't stand heights any better than I can. She couldn't control her own fear well enough to come and help me or bring Bobby to help me, I had to wait until Bob came back up the trail from his reconnaissance, face his sympathy and submit to having him help me up the trail.

I sat down on the ground, still sick and dizzy, and somehow before I knew it Bob had taken over. He sent Diane for help but he told us that the ledge was crumbling and the man had to at least be dragged back onto the firmer part of the trail and it would need two men to do it. "It's our Christian duty," he told Bobby, matter-of-factly, and even with everything else happening it made me feel sicker to realize how deeply the values of the farm community had sunk into them.

I forced myself to speak. "It's his own damn fault," I said. "You don't owe him a damn thing, Stay here until . . . ." It was too late, they were gone down the trail. I got to my feet and then decided that was a bad idea: I crawled as close as I dared to the trailhead. I kept telling myself there was no danger, I had to control myself, but you can't argue with your gut. Just before it happened, I was worrying more about whether Bobby would lose respect for me than I was about the actual danger. Surely Bob wouldn't put Bobby at any real risk for a total stranger, Bobby with his unique powers.

Then there was a horrible sliding and grinding sound. My heart stopped and then started racing and I even got a few feet down the trail before my weakness immobilized me again. "Bobby," I yelled.

"Bobby, are you all right" I breathed again as his voice came from not too far away.

"I'm here, Uncle Paul. The ledge gave way. I think the man is dead. I grabbed Dad and he didn't go over, but he hit his head. I'm here with him and I'm not sure how safe the ledge is where we are. I don't dare move." He paused and I could hear him draw a breath and try to steady his voice. "Uncle Paul, there's nobody to watch for me. I can't see." The disaster we'd avoided for sixteen years came as simply as that.

"All right, Bobby," I said, trying to keep my voice confident. "I'm going to go along the edge and try to look down on you from above. If I can't do that I'll come down that path if I have to crawl on my belly. I probably won't be able to help you much, but I can watch for you." From his voice, Bobby wasn't much reassured. "There's an overhang above us, Uncle Paul: Dad looked up when we were coming out here. And there's one very narrow place right round the bend from you: the only way to get around it is to hug the rock and move your feet one at a time." He didn't need to say it: I just couldn't make myself negotiate a place like that.

I refused to accept that. There was still the noise of a rock falling now and then, and I didn't dare wait for help. "All right, I'll have to come that way, Bobby. Hold on." His voice came back, quick and alarmed. "No, Uncle Paul, nobody without a good head for heights could get around that narrow piece. Wait for a minute and don't talk, please." The silence lengthened out, punctuated by an occasional falling rock.

"What are you doing?" I called at last. Bobby had the grace to sound a little embarrassed. "Praying,

Uncle Paul." I almost lost my temper and shouted at him. While I was still fighting for control, his voice came again, calm now and under control. "Don't worry, Uncle Paul. Nothing can happen that . . . oh . . . it's so beautiful . . . ." His voice had changed completely on the last words, and I wondered if he'd cracked under the strain. Or maybe . . . my heart bounded . . . maybe someone had him under observation, perhaps with field glasses. Could Bobby's talent bridge a distance like that? "Bobby, can you see?" I shouted.

His voice still had that strange, enthralled note that had made me doubt his sanity. "Yes, Uncle Paul, I can see really . . . wonderfully. Wait a minute while I get Dad back from the edge. Then I'll be up," There were dragging sounds and then light, confident steps. Bobby came into my view: he was smiling but his face was pale, his freckles standing out like print on a page. Once more I suffered the humiliation of being led up the path like a child. When Bobby faced me on the main trail and said simply, "My prayers were answered," something snapped inside me. I swear I just meant to slap his face to snap him out of whatever state he was in, but somehow my hand became a fist. He fell at my feet and I gathered him in my arms, "Bobby, I'm sorry, I'm sorry," I said, but he was unconscious. I was still there cradling him in my arms when the blessed sound of machinery came up the path and a Park Service vehicle screeched to a halt beside me.

The Park Service has some pretty sophisticated equipment for emergencies now: they got Bob up in two shakes and the body of the fool who started it all up in not much longer; then they coptered us all over to the new hospital on the South Rim. Bobby and Bob were whisked off for examination, and Diane and I were stuck in a waiting room. Later they came for Diane and I was left to pace alone.

I was getting madder and madder: the one thing that distinguishes M.D.s from other technicians is their highhanded attitude toward their clients. I was about to sally out of the waiting room and tear the place apart until they gave me some information, when finally a man in a sickly green disposable surgeon's outfit came into the room. Incongruously, he had on hiking boots, covered by transparent booties.

"Mr. Paul Winterfield?" he asked brusquely. "Your sister-in-law thought I'd better fill you in on what's happening. Your nephew is a very fortunate young man." I gaped at him. "Bobby? But he wasn't . . . didn't . . . ." He gave me a professional sort of smile. "No reason for you to know, but I'm an eye man: one of the best in the Bay Area, if I say so myself. Your nephew was born blind, wasn't he? Bad condition too, nothing we could have done about it, even as late as last year. But the pericorneal transplant is almost a standard procedure now: I've done dozens. And the man your brother and nephew tried to save had an organ donor's card. PoetIc justice. The operation's all done in fact. Your brother's fine too; just a crack on the head. But your nephew, as I said, is a lucky boy—me being here on vacation, the staff here knowing me, the body definitely dead but fresh as a daisy. Couldn't have worked out better."

I stopped gaping and thanked him profusely, letting him know tactfully that his fees would be taken care of promptly and in full. You could tell he hadn't worried about that, though: the really good people in any line always care more about the job than the pay. Since they wouldn't let me see either Bobby or Bob, I checked into a motel near the hospital, but I got very little sleep that night. I was trying to figure out what I'd say to Bobby when I saw him again.

I saw Bob before I saw Bobby, and he was a little annoyed because I'd forgotten about Diane the night before, we were too excited about Bobby's operation to talk about much else. I camped in the waiting room then, and by bugging the nurses politely got in to see Bobby as soon as they were allowing visitors. I meant to start out with apologies for hitting him, but I was too surprised at the sight of him. Some memory of old movies had led me to expect to find him swathed in bandages, with a grand unwrapping still some time away: I'd forgotten modern quick-heal medicine. For the first time since I'd first seen him as a baby, Bobby's eyes were alive and functional. He looked at me and saw me with his own eyes.

He grinned a little shyly and said, "Yeah, I can see, Uncle Paul." Then he looked around the room: he hadn't quite got the hang of doing it by moving his eyes yet, and he moved his whole head in a way that looked a little unnatural. He spoke again in a lower voice. "I can see with my own eyes. And that's all." He didn't need to say any more; I had been half afraid of this. His strange talent had been called forth by his blindness; now that he could see with his own eyes, it had gone, along with the need that had brought it out. But I wondered whether the trauma of being hit by someone he'd always trusted had anything to do with it.

"Bobby when did you . . . lose it?" I asked cautiously. "Were you unconscious until after the operation, or . . . ."

He shook his head. "Oh, no, I wasn't out long, Uncle Paul. I heard Dr. Morrow discussing what he wanted to do with Mom, and I told her I wanted him to try. But I haven't been able to see . . . the old way . . . since I came off the path. When I was talking to you just before I fell or passed out or whatever it was, I was already blind again."

He either didn't know, then, or had suppressed the knowledge that I had hit him. Like a coward, I didn't tell him. Instead I asked, 'What happened on the path? Was there an animal, or someone observing you from a distance, or what? How did you see?" His face got the same spaced-out look as it had just before I had hit him, as he said, "Oh, no, Uncle Paul. Not an animal, and not a person—a human person, that is. You know I told you that you can tell lot about a person by the way he looks, like Pete Jones and the way he looked at girls? Whatever came when I prayed . . . well, it was looking over my shoulder, looking just where I needed to see. And the way things looked! Everything was beautiful, everything looked important and valuable, even the pebbles and the thorns on the cactus. Uncle Paul . . ." his voice dropped, "I think it must have been an angel."

I didn't take that very well. In fact, it was my day for not taking things well. Eventually the nurse came in and told me I was disturbing the patient and I had to leave. All right, maybe I was shouting a little. And it wasn't too smart, maybe, to storm off to Bob and ask him when they were leaving that cockeyed commune, now that Bobby's eyes were OK. I didn't like it when he told me that they were at home there and had no intention of leaving: soon I was asked to leave another room.

I guess in my annoyance at their muddle-headedness I said some pretty cutting things. Telepathy I'll buy, but when someone starts talking about angels, when a man who's been reasonably educated starts quoting the Bible at you, well, I just lose my patience. Whether or not we can explain how it's propagated, telepathy is a physical event. But when you start bringing in nonmaterial beings and talking about God, you're clear outside reasonable argument, so far as I'm concerned.

I suppose eventually we'll all cool down and I can pick up my relationship with my brother and nephew on some basis. But at the time it seemed wisest to check in with the office and turn an urgent request into an emergency that required me to go off on another trip. Some people might have thought it funny that it was Diane I could say goodbye to, but aside from surface politeness we'd never kidded each other: we were enemies fighting for what I guess she'd call the souls of Bobby and Bob.

"I'm sorry you quarreled with them," she said. Hell, she could afford to be generous: for now at least she'd won. "They always had hopes that you'd come around, but I didn't think you would. They're both still fond of you Paul, and we all appreciate all you've done for us. Maybe you'd have become less interested in Bobby anyway, now that he's not a problem anymore. You're really more interested in problems than in people, Paul."

She was right in a way, of course, though the slant she put on it was wrong: I am a problem man, not a people man. But I had gotten more than a fascinating problem in Bobby. He was still the closest thing to a son I'd ever have; that's why it hurt so much when he rejected my values. And there had been something, I don't know, an openness to new possibilities in the years Bobby had been in my life, that kept things from getting stale. Who knows what his "angel" had really been? An alien in an invisible space vehicle? A very earthly mosquito whose sensory input had been strange enough to cause the curious effect Bobby had reported? We'd never know.

And I'd never know, either, what I'd seemed to almost touch in my association with Bobby—what it's really like to see through others' eyes.

THE GREY WOLF'S TALE

"Nu, what's a poor wolf to do? Trying to make a living on the steppes of Rus is a hard job. The prey is scarce and wily and keeping body and soul together gets harder and harder as you get older. (All that grey in my pelt is more the result of age than of my species.) So if Baba Yaga offers you a steady job how can you refuse? The job looked easy. There's a crossroads where three paths branch off from one path. There are signs that say "Take this path and both you and your horse will die," "Take this path and your horse will live but you will die," and "Take this path and your horse will die but you will live."

What does that mean? How many knights or heroes are going to take the path where he and his horse will die? And how many are so fond of their horses that they'll choose the path where the horses live and they die? I'll tell you: nikevo—no one. So all you have to do is guard the path where the horse will die and the rider will live. Then, after lulling the rider into a false sense of security, you leap out of the bushes and kill the horse.

Supposedly, you have to keep an eye on the other paths but it's a waste of time: everyone will choose the path that sacrifices the horse. If no one comes for a while, Baba Yaga will give you some meat to get by on. I don't ask what the meat is, but knowing Baba Yaga's habits, believe me, I don't want to know.

On the other hand, if someone comes down the third path, the horse is all yours. Look, there's good eating on a horse.

So one day I was lurking near the path and this kid came up riding a horse. From one look at him I could tell that he was the youngest of three brothers. Being the youngest of three brothers is not always easy, but in matters of magic it does give you the advantage.

He dithered about a little, but eventually he took the path that meant death for his horse and a meal for me. I always like it when they hesitate to take that trail: it shows a little respect for their horse and maybe for animals in general. Not always—one knight who was really fond of his horse got me with his spear as I ran away after killing his horse, and it took me a while to recover.

Well, this one was easy. I darted in, slashed at the horse's throat, and was ready to run for the bushes if the kid showed any signs of resistance. But instead of attacking me, the kid knelt down by the body of the horse and started to cry. Look, I'm not all that hardhearted; I think humans are almost as sensitive as wolves. After all some humans can change into wolves, but did you ever hear of a werehorse?

"Look, kid," I said to him, "it's nothing personal. It's my job to kill horses on this trail." He gazed up at me tearfully. "I'm Prince Ivan," he said. "I have to find the Firebird. I thought I was so clever not letting myself fall asleep in my father's garden. He wanted to know who was stealing all the best fruit from his trees. I almost caught the Firebird then; I caught a feather from his tail. But as soon as my father saw the feather, he wanted the Firebird itself. So he sent my two brothers off for it—the very ones who went to sleep on watch in the garden. I had to beg and plead before he'd let me go after the Firebird. Now without a horse how can I get across the thrice-nine kingdoms to get to the thrice-ten kingdom where the Firebird lives?"

I gave a sigh. "Look, kid, stop your crying," I said. "I'll carry you to the kingdom where the Firebird nests. All you have to do is follow my directions and you'll soon be on your way back to your father with the Firebird." If I'd only known how much trouble the kid was going to be for me, I would never have made the offer.

Well, he stopped crying and mounted on my back. Frankly, I don't understand "thrice-nine lands" and "thrice-ten lands." Maybe it means leagues or virsts or whatever measure they use. If some place is 27 leagues from your own country's borders it's far away, but not too far away; while if it's over 30 leagues away it's really far away by their standards. But anyway, I know where the Firebird nests; so long as you're reasonably sensitive to magic, you know where a being like the One True Phoenix lives.

So presently we arrived at the place where the Firebird nests: it was at the palace of the Tsar Afron. I know that the Tsar would be just as glad to get rid of the Firebird. A Phoenix is very hard on any fruit trees nearby, as well as requiring constant praise: none of the Magical Animals is as vain as a Phoenix. "Now look, kid," I said to him. "You'll find the Firebird in one of the trees in the Tsar's garden. There's a golden cage nearby, but *don't touch the cage!* The Firebird will come with you if you keep praising it and keep on describing the fruit in your father's garden. Frankly, the bird is greedy as well as vain and all you have to do is convince him that he ought to come with you voluntarily. As soon as you try to put him in the cage, he'll give the alarm."

So the kid went off; but did he listen to me? No, he got worried that the bird would fly off and put the Firebird in the cage. So when he finally came back to me, not only did he not have the Firebird, but he had promised the Tsar Afron that he would steal the horse with the golden mane from Tsar Kusman. Actually, the Tsar told him that if he had come and asked him nicely, he would have given him the bird. And the kid just couldn't give up because the Tsar promised to spread it around that Prince Ivan was a thief, and had been caught trying to steal from the Tsar Afron. That was pretty good thinking on the part of the Tsar, since no nobleman, much less a prince, wants to have that kind of talk going on about him.

I'm not sure that Tsar Afron would have done it, even if Ivan hadn't gotten the horse for him, but it was enough to send the kid into the depths of depression. "All right, kid," I said. "I'll help you one more time. I know the meadow where the horse with the golden mane grazes. It's not far from here; climb on and I'll take you there." When we got near the place where the horse with the golden mane grazed, I looked the kid straight in the eye. "Now listen up, kid," I said. "There's a golden bridle hanging on a tree near the horse. *Don't touch the bridle!* If you try to put the bridle on the horse, it will give the alarm to Tsar Kusman, whose meadow this is. If, on the other hand, you keep praising its beautiful golden mane, and keep describing how the horse will be admired if he comes with you to your father's kingdom, it will carry you without any bridle. All you have to do is tell him where to go. All right, go and convince the horse."

Nu, so you know what happened already, right? The kid got worried that the horse would run away and tried to put the bridle on the horse. So when he came back it was the same story as Tsar Afron; if he didn't bring back the fair Yelena for the Tsar Kusman to marry, he'd spread the news that Ivan was a thief. If, on the other hand, Ivan brought the fair Yelena back, the Tsar Kusman would give him the horse, which he could trade for the Firebird, and his mission would be a success.

"Look, kid," I said. "I'm through giving advice. I'll take you to the kingdom where the fair Yelena's father is Tsar. Once I take you there you're on your own! I don't owe you anything and I'll take no further interest in what happens to you. Is it a deal?"

The kid agreed and I took him to Tsar Dalmat's palace. "She's someplace in the garden," I said and walked away from him, not looking back. Of course I only went to the next bit of cover; I wanted to know what happened just as much as you do. And what do you know? Within half a candle's length he was back with the fair Yelena! I hadn't even told him not to tie her up with the golden rope which was hanging nearby; he hadn't even noticed it. So catch me giving advice again. Maybe if I hadn't mentioned the golden cage or the golden bridle, he wouldn't have noticed them! Or maybe he was just contrary?

Now the fair Yelena was quite a woman. As soon as I poked my nose out of the thicket I was hiding in to look at them, she carne over to pet and praise me. "Grey Wolf, Grey Wolf," she said, "Ivan and I owe you so much! I know you said you wouldn't do anything more for Ivan, but for my sake would you carry us both to Tsar Kusman's kingdom?"

Look, with that kind of line a beautiful woman can do anything with me. I carried them back to Tsar Kusman's kingdom and, believe me, the fair Yelena was no lightweight. She was a real Russian beauty, but she was tall and had dancer's muscles. When we got there, the fair Yelena began crying. Believe me, that woman knew how to cry without spoiling a bit of her beauty. "Grey Wolf, Grey Wolf," she said, "I don't want to marry an old man like the Tsar Kusman. Can't we get the horse with the golden mane without trading me for it?"

I told her exactly what I had told Ivan, but she *listened!* She was off, telling Ivan to take it easy after his great exertions and within half a candle's length she was back, riding the horse with the golden mane. She was praising it and telling it what a wonderful horse it was, but I wasn't jealous because I felt that the fair Yelena really meant what she said. She praised me for my strength and cunning, and she praised the horse for its strength and dexterity, as well as its wonderful golden mane.

She put Ivan on the horse with the golden mane and rode me to the Tsar Afron's palace. "Grey Wolf, Grey Wolf," she said, "how can we give our new friend, the horse with the golden mane, to a blackmailer like Tsar Afron? Is there any way we can get the Firebird without giving up the horse?" I told her the same thing that I had told Ivan, but *she listened!* Within half a candle's length she was back with the bird on her shoulder, praising him for his beauty and cleverness. She asked me to carry her until we reached the triple crossroads while Ivan rode the horse and of course I agreed.

At the crossroads, she looked at Ivan. "Are you prepared to marry me and take care of me?" she asked.

"Well," said Ivan, "I like you very much, fair Yelena, but the fact is, I'm Princess Maria, disguised as a boy, and I really can't marry you and take care of you."

The fair Yelena grinned. "You think that's news to me?" she said. "Go on, take the Firebird to your father and tell him never to underestimate his daughter. But if you encounter your brothers, don't trust them. They'd gladly steal the Firebird from you and claim the credit."

Ivan—that is, Princess Maria tossed her head and said, "As if I couldn't always run rings around both of them. But what if the Tsars Afron and Kusman spread the story that I'm a thief?"

"Don't worry," said the fair Yelena. "In the first place, there isn't any 'Prince Ivan'; that was just a name you used. And if word gets back to them that a young princess stole their Firebird and horse they'll be ashamed to complain because you fooled them so completely."

"All right," said Princess Maria. "But what will you do, fair Yelena?"

"Don't worry about me," said the fair Yelena. "The wolf and I will work something out." When Princess Maria had gone off carrying the Firebird, the fair Yelena turned to me and asked, "Are you a werewolf?"

"Well, yes," I said "but I haven't Changed for a long time. It's easier for a wolf to make a living on the steppes than a man."

"May I see your human form?" she asked.

I Changed and looked at her. "As you can see," I said, "I'm not as young as I used to be."

She kissed me and said, "If you're a real princess you can always tell the real hero of the tale."

BY THE DRAGON'S CAVE

One bright day in the morning of the world, a wise man came to a dragon's cave. The cave was in a remote part of the kingdom, for the dragon was old and weary, and she had carried her treasure to a place where no one came in the ordinary way. At first the dragon had hidden herself and her treasure deep in the cavern, but after many years she found that the cold of the cavern got into her bones. She had been undisturbed for so long that at last she thought it safe to drag her treasure out into the little valley at the mouth of the cave. There she lay drowsing on her heap of treasure, warming herself in the sun by day. As the sun went down she breathed out a hot fog that filled the little valley and kept the warmth in. A few small, careless creatures wandered into the fog at first and died, but soon even the birds learned not to fly into the valley, and the dragon had been undisturbed for centuries.

This day the dragon woke from a fitful doze knowing that there was a living creature in her valley but not guessing at first that it was anything more than some unwary beast. She searched the valley lazily with barely open eyes, until she saw with a shock of surprise the man in the gray cloak standing on the one patch of green grass in the arid valley. Was it only chance that he stood in *that* place?

The dragon opened her mouth and asked the question, the only question she had for any creature who came to her hiding place: "Have you come to kill me?" She knew that any man or creature in man's form who had the wit to find her valley and the courage to enter it would be a threat to her, and her courage had begun to leave her long ago when she had decided to hide herself from the world.

"I am a follower of Wisdom," said the man in gray. "I do not kill; neither am I killed." The dragon took heart from his first words, and a little cold cruelty, born of her earlier fear, stirred in her heart. She sniffed the air, trying to remember the smell of magic, and when she found no scent of enchantments, she grew bolder.

"A man who does not kill may have no choice whether he is killed," she said in a soft, cruel voice, and let a little wisp of flame escape her lips. "I smell no magic about you to protect you from harm," she taunted, and let the flame grow a little.

"One protection I have," said the man. "And it is this: Whoever kills me will die as I die. Since I threaten no one, there has never been anyone who would give their own life to kill me." The dragon did not want to believe him. But in her heart she did, and she was suddenly afraid. Men were fragile things, she remembered, and in a moment's rage or carelessness she might take his life and lose her own.

"What do you want, then?" she said sullenly, letting her flame die away.

"In your hoard," said the man in gray, "is a book with a golden cover, though I care nothing for the cover. It has many pages, richly illuminated but I care nothing for those pages, only for the last page in the book. I have come to read that page, and if you let me read it and go in peace, you will live here undisturbed for as long as you have been here already."

It would have cost the dragon nothing to let him read the page, but the greed that makes a dragon what it is stirred in her heart. "What's mine is mine," she said. "Why should I let you take anything of mine, even a useless piece of knowledge? There is no other copy of that book in the world."

"There is one other copy," said the follower of Wisdom, "and I suffered many things to read it. But that copy has its last page missing, and that is why I am here. I am only a seeker of Wisdom, but I am not foolish enough to ask a dragon to give me something for nothing. I will pay you for my look at that page."

Greed grew stronger in the dragon, and she planned in her mind to take the man's price and give him nothing in return. If she could not take his life, she would take whatever she could. "What could you offer me?" she scoffed, hoping to make him boast and tell her what he had to offer and reveal a hint as to how she might seize it.

"The only thing I have to offer is knowledge," said the man in gray. "But it is knowledge you need for your own safety." The dragon believed him, and fear struggled with greed in her heart, but she was still determined to cheat him.

"What can you know that concerns me?" she scoffed, still hoping to tempt him to boast and give away information.

"I know a great deal," said the man quietly, "for a man of my sort does not venture to a dragon's cave without learning all he can. I know, among other things, what you have buried under the ground where I stand. It is a holy and powerful thing; and you do well to keep it away from yourself. I am surprised that you can sleep with it so close, though it would be worse if you had it in a cave with you."

The dragon had almost forgotten how much she feared and hated that object: perhaps it had been it and not the cold that had driven her to pile her treasure in the open air and bury the thing where she could see the place where she had buried it. Still, she would not part with the thing, and she would not give this man what he wanted. But she pretended to give in.

"Well, give me this knowledge you say I need, and I will promise to let you read my page," she said.

The man in gray nodded gravely and spoke in a voice that was almost a chant, as if he were saying words of lore: "This day three will come to the dragon's cave: one wise, one brave, one without guile. One seeks for knowledge, one for joy, one seeks the dragon's life. Three must die, or one, or none at all; every one who breaks faith must die."

The dragon, like all dragons, loved riddles and was wise in their lore. She knew that it was not safe to take anything for granted in a riddle of this kind, not even that the man before her was the wise one, the one who sought knowledge. After all, he had disclaimed wisdom, and it had taken bravery for him to come here . . . .

"I wish to look at the page now," said the man in gray, interrupting her musing.

She laughed an evil little laugh, making small flames dance in the air. "Why, I think that you must be the one without guile," she sneered, "to make so careless a bargain with one of the Fireborn. I promised that you could read the page, fool, but not when you could read it. Come again in a hundred years, and we will speak of it again."

The man in gray showed neither anger nor disappointment. He smiled grimly and said, "I think I will see you again before that. But for now I will go and let you receive your other visitors. Call when you want me. My name is Aranar." And with that he turned and walked away. His gray cloak made him hard to see against the gray rock; in a moment the dragon had lost sight of him. She dismissed him from her mind and went back to pondering the riddle.

One of her visitors sought her life. It must be the one who was called brave, for neither the wise nor the guileless would want to kill her. A hero, then, bent on dragon slaying, and she was in no state to fight a hero. Surprise was a good weapon for an old dragon; it was folly to lie out in the open where her enemy could spy out her weaknesses. But could she bear to go down into the cave out of sight of her treasure? A fog would hide her, but it would hide her enemy, too . . . . And so the dragon pondered.

The next one to come to the dragon's cave was a soldier named Karl. He had been a captain in the wars and served in the ranks, too, when times were bad for captains. He had won many victories but never found his fortune, and he had come to the dragon's cave following a slender thread of rumor and legend. He would like very well to have a dragon's treasure, but he knew that to get a dragon's treasure you must kill the dragon. So be it; he was weary of killing men, but he had never killed a dragon and would like to see if he could. And if there were a dragon at all here, it would be an old, old dragon.

As he came near the cave, his excitement rose, for there were signs here and there in the countryside that a great flying beast occasionally made forays hereabouts for food. Karl left his saddle horse and packhorse in a small, dry cave with as much fodder as he could cut with the back of his sword, pulled on his armor, slung his shield, and went very softly forward, keeping a good lookout around him.

When he came to the valley and the cave, it was about noon and he was sweating heavily, but he was going at a steady, even pace, like the old soldier he was, covering the ground, ready for battle. When he caught the glint of gold in the valley, he moved even more slowly and quietly, and stood a long time in the shadow of a rock, looking down at the valley. There was no sign of any living creature, but a great pile of gold and jewels was almost a living thing itself, glinting and gleaming in the sun.

At last Karl moved down into the valley, taking a route he hoped was out of sight from the interior of the cave, though he kept a good eye on the mouth of the cave and listened for the slightest sound. At last he stood by the entrance to the cave, listening and wondering. He half-feared, half-hoped that the dragon was in the valley, hiding in the shape of a rock or even a piece of the treasure. If that was the dragon's plan, Karl might be taken by surprise, but if he could catch the creature beginning to change back to dragon shape, he could kill it before the change was complete.

One thing he did not want to do was go into that cave looking for the dragon: finding it there in the dark would be bad, and coming out of the cave to find the dragon waiting would be worse. On Karl's side was the fact that leaving the treasure unguarded for long would be sheer agony for the dragon. Perhaps if he pretended to make off with a piece of treasure . . . . At that moment he heard a sound from the cave, but it was not the sound of a large creature. Gaining size takes time even for a dragon—perhaps the creature had overreached itself with some trick. Karl went into a fighting crouch, sword poised and shield well up.

The sound was—footsteps, human footsteps! Out of the cave staggered a red-haired girl, gaunt and not too clean, in the draggled remains of a green gown that matched her green eyes, which were blinking now at the light of the sun. She shrank back when she saw Karl's armored figure. "Have you come to kill me?" she babbled in a voice that seemed rusty from disuse. "It doesn't matter; I'll starve to death soon. I can't make myself eat much of the burnt animals the creature gives me. And I'd rather die by a human sword than be . . . eaten." She gave a little sob and staggered back against the wall of the cave.

Karl kept his guard up but spoke softly. "Why, Lady, if you are what you seem, I mean you no harm in the world. How did you come to this place?"

The girl shuddered. "I was riding my palfrey; a long way from here, I think, but I don't know where 'here' is. The winged thing came from the sky; my horse threw me and bolted. The thing caught it and . . . ate it. I thought it would eat me, too, but it caught me up in its claws and brought me here. It feeds me and . . . watches me. I think . . . I think I'm its pet." She burst into tears.

Karl lowered his sword but kept a wary eye about him. "Where is the creature?" he asked, watching her closely.

She shook her head. "Hunting, I suppose; it flew away awhile ago. It's usually gone a long time, but I never dare try to escape; the county is so bare, and I can't stand to think of the creature swooping down on me again . . . ." Her brilliant green eyes lit up suddenly, and she was almost beautiful despite the dirt. "Could you get me away?" she pleaded. "I'd do anything, anything at all if you would. And if you could get me home, Father would reward you no matter who you are or what you'd done . . . ."

Karl sighed. "Lady. I took knight's vows once, long ago. I can't refuse you, though it may be the death of both of us. All we can do is flee straight for the nearest cover and lie hidden till night. In the dark we may get to my horses, and that will give us more speed. But if the creature tracks us, speed will be little help."

The girl straightened and tried for some degree of dignity with an effort that was visible. "I thank you, Sir Knight," she said. "One favor only I ask of you. If the creature comes on us from the sky and there is no hope, lend me your dagger."

"Why, Lady, let us pray it does not come to that," said Karl. "We must be gone as quick as we can. Go before, Lady, and I will follow:'

They passed the pile of gold and jewels without a glance; neither was thinking of treasure then. They climbed the walls of the valley and set out for the low hills, which promised some cover. The hills seemed near, but after a weary walk they seemed no nearer. Then the girl gave a gasp and pointed to the sky. Some winged creature high in the sky was coming toward them.

Karl drew his sword again and looked around, his face grim. "Lie down by those rocks, Lady," he said, "and keep still. The creature will use its fire, no doubt, so I will go some way from you. It is not the best place to fight, Lady, but do not despair."

She looked him in the eye and said quietly, "I do not, Sir Knight, but I pray you, lend me that dagger. I will not use it unless there is no hope."

He sighed. "There's a grace dagger in my belt at the back," he said gruffly. "How you use it is between yourself and God. But do not use it too quickly; you may win free even if I do not." As she fumbled for the dagger, his eyes searched the sky, watching the flying thing draw nearer. As he gazed, his sword dropped and he started to turn. "Why, Lady, we feared too soon. That is only a bird. The dragon . . . ."

"The dragon is here," she said in a voice that no longer sounded quite human. Karl felt a sharp pain in his side as his own dagger found the chink in his armor. Then there was a roaring in his eyes, and blackness swooped on him like the dragon he had expected from the sky.

"One," said the dragon, still in her human form. Then she closed her eyes and put her hands at her sides. She took a deep breath, but suddenly her eyes opened again. There was someone else in her valley, someone touching her treasure; she could feel it.

No time, for the change, and this form might still be useful. She begun to run at an easy lope back toward the valley, leaving Karl's body sprawled on the ground, bright blood soaking into the ground. Time enough later to return and feast.

When the dragon in her human form got back to her valley, she stood in the same place that Karl had stood, shaded by the rock so that she was hard to see from below. At first she thought that the creature scurrying among the treasure was only an animal, but presently she saw that it was a small, ragged boy, skinny but agile. She would have changed shape then and killed him, but she remembered the riddle told her by Aranar. "Three must die, or one, or none at all." Too late for none at all, and if two died, then a third one must. Not Aranar, for if she killed Aranar, she would die, too—and that would make four. But if she killed the boy, then she might die in some unexpected way, and the riddle would be fulfilled. So she must get rid of the boy without killing him, and that might be easier in her human form. She walked slowly down the slopes of the valley, ready to give chase if the boy ran.

But he was oblivious to her approach for some reason. He was crouched over a piece of the treasure, and she heard little bells chiming, golden bells. She reached back in her long dragon's memory and recalled what the thing was: a marvelous golden toy she had taken from a king's palace in her days of youth and strength. Tiny figures danced and golden bells chimed after you wound it up with a little jeweled key. Like everything else in her hoard, it was unique;

she had never bothered with coins or bars of gold or common jewels.

"Boy," she said. The child cringed and almost ran, but he could not bear to leave the toy, which was the most beautiful thing he had ever seen. When he saw it was a woman approaching, not much larger than he and without weapons, he relaxed a little. In his short life he had met a few women who were kind, and even if they were not, they did not usually hit as hard as men.

"Have you come to kill me?" the dragon asked, because she had always asked that question since she came here, but as she said it, she realized the question was absurd. This was no hero but some beggar brat strayed from one of the caravans that had come near her cave a few times in the centuries she had hidden there.

The boy grew cocky at this sign of weakness and straightened up, the golden toy in his hands. "No," he said, laughing. "I was running away because my master said that I would die if I stole one more time, and this time I think he meant it."

"Then why did you steal?" asked the dragon. The boy's shrug confirmed her fears. His upbringing had made a thief of him; he slept where and when he could, ate whatever he could get, stole whatever he could steal. If she let him leave this valley, he would come back to steal, no matter what promises he made, come back when he was older and more clever and more dangerous. She did not know what she could do with him, but the first thing was to get hold of him.

She reached out her hand, but she had forgotten that Karl's blood was still on it. The boy twisted away and ran, frightened by the blood and what he could see in her eyes. In her human form she could probably not catch up with him, and if she took time to change her form, he might hide in some cranny where he would be hard to find. And he had the toy, part of *her* hoard.

Rage took her, and in her rage she grabbed for the nearest weapon, a jeweled spear that some temple guard had carried in ceremonies, before she looted the temple. She threw the spear, and it flew straight and true, hitting the boy full in the back. The gold-chased blade pierced his heart and came out of his chest until it was stopped by the jewels on the haft. The boy was dead before he hit the ground.

The dragon stood staring at him for a long time trying to think. But something about that small, twisted form disturbed her thoughts and gave her strange feelings. She decided that the human body she wore was the reason for the feelings, and she made the change back to dragon form, turning her back on the boy's body because it distracted her.

She lay brooding for a while on her treasure. Presently she would get the toy and the spear and restore them to their places in the hoard, but not yet. The sun was on its way down, and there had been only two deaths. How could she make sure that the third death was not hers? There was no one she could kill but Aranar, and if she killed him, she would die. She believed that even more strongly after what had happened so far. But wait! If she died, too, four would die, and the riddle would be a lie. The wise man would have broken faith, and everyone who broke faith must die. But if she killed him without letting him read the page, she would be forsworn . . . . Her thoughts went round and round.

At last she called out softly, "Aranar." The man in gray appeared on the edge of the valley, as if he had been waiting for her call, and came down slowly to stand by the boy's body. He looked down at it, his face compassionate.

"Read your page," the dragon said harshly, and turned away from him. When she looked back after a while, she saw that he had removed the spear and straightened the boy's body. Now he was reading intently, the great golden book propped on other pieces of treasure, for it was too heavy to hold. At last he looked up. "So that is how it ends," he murmured to himself. Then he looked into the dragon's eyes and said quietly, "If you let me go in peace, you can still live. The knight is not dead."

The dragon shook her massive head. "No," she said. Even if the knight was not dead when she left him, he would soon have bled to death. The wise man was trying to trick her, to escape with his life and the knowledge he had taken from her hoard. Either everything he had said was a lie, or only one more could die here today. If she killed him quickly, she would be safe; she had to be safe.

He opened his mouth to speak again, but she opened hers, too, and her flame burst forth. His body flared and began to char, but as he burned she felt herself burning with the same fire. Her wings beating furiously, she hurled herself into the sky, trying to escape. But there was no escape; the outer fire met her inner fire, and she exploded in the air, raining flaming pieces on the valley she had ruled. And so the dragon died.

Karl the soldier saw her die, from the place on the plain where she had stabbed him, the place where the man in gray had found him and bound up his wound. As the sun was setting, he made his painful way to the valley and looked at the treasure and the bodies. After he had rested, he would have to give the boy and the man in gray some kind of burial, he thought.

The treasure was his to do with as he wished, but he did not feel that he had earned it, and he still did not know if he could kill a dragon. In the end he took only a small box he found, which held a red-gold feather that he thought he had heard of in an old tale once. The golden toy he buried with the boy, and the golden book he buried with the man in gray. The other treasures he left; in the wars he had seen men killed for treasures or tortured to tell where they had found the treasure, and every piece of the dragon's hoard was treasure enough to start any number of new wars; Karl had seen enough of war, so he left the treasure and went on to seek new adventures.

When the seekers of Wisdom tell this story, they ask three questions. Who was wise? Who was without guile? Who broke the faith? But you must find the answers for yourself.

FIREBIRD

One cold winter day in the morning of the world, a knight named Karl rode into a city. He had been a captain in the wars, but for many years now he had been wandering the world seeing what he could see. He had wandered far from his home and this land of Rus was one of the fairest he had seen, though it was a difficult land to get to know. He did not know the name of the city he was entering, though from the evidence of new building he thought that one of its names was probably Novogorad—the New City. There were many places with that as part of their name, for the people of Rus were prospering and expanding, building new cities where none had been before.

He was not sure of his welcome though by and large he had been treated well in Rus. A lone man in armor is not always welcome in peaceful cities like this one seemed to be. So he was not surprised when the city guards told him to halt and give an account of himself. But the first question surprised him: "Are you a Bogotyr?" He thought a little and said,

"Sirs, in your language a Bogotyr means a knight of God. I have taken the knight's oath and I try to serve God, as best I can. But the word also means 'hero,' and I do not claim to be a hero."

The next question surprised him even more: "Have you had to do with a dragon who died?" they asked. He replied without hesitation,

"Sirs, that is curiously phrased. I do not claim to be a dragon slayer, and yet I did have dealings with a dragon, and the dragon died, though not by any action of mine. So in a very curious way I can answer 'yes' to that question."

Their third question left him completely astonished: "Do you bear a feather of the Bird of Fire?" He replied steadily,

"Sirs, I bear on my breast a wonderful feather which I brought away from that same encounter with the dragon. That it is from a Bird of Fire, I cannot say, but if any feather be worthy of such a bird, it is the feather I bear. And yet I would swear that no man, neither living nor dead, would know what I took from the dragon's cave."

Then the captain of the guards said, "Sir, by your answers I am strictly bound to bear you to our Tsaretsa. But by my oath I may not admit any armed man to her presence. Will you render to me your sword and spear, so that I may keep both my oaths?" Karl looked at him and thought that he was an honest man—if you could not trust this man, whom could you trust? and he answered him:

"Sir, many men have tried to get my sword and spear from me, and none have succeeded. But at your request I will give you my sword and spear, and my shield also, for without sword and spear what good is a shield? Because I want you to take me to your Tsaretsa, so that I may resolve this riddle: how come that your questions answer so curiously to my state?"

They led him through the city, and it was a good city, not so much beautiful as filled with strength and enthusiasm, so that even the buildings, half or hastily constructed, gave a feeling of gladness. They led him up to the high house at the summit of the town, and here he saw men of knightly bearing and women who looked intelligent as well as beautiful. Karl thought that this was a goodly town and a goodly court and a man could do worse than end his days here.

Then they led him into the Tsaretsa, and he thought no more of the town or the court or of ending his days in peacefulness. She was beautiful, he supposed, though in some ways less beautiful than some of the ladies in her court. Her face in repose was sad, and only when she turned to some of the people around her and talked and laughed with them did she appear more beautiful than any of the other ladies. Then she was the center of attention, and every man in the room was aware of her. Yet when she sat quietly, her face looking as if she were thinking on some sorrow, she almost seemed to disappear among the crowded court.

But it was then that Karl liked most to look at her; he felt that in this mood she was more truly herself than when she was charming the court. He had a while to look at her because there were other visitors to greet, and a message about him had to be passed from one person to the other until it reached the circle around her.

So he stood and watched her, very content to do so. He felt as if he would never want to go out of sight of her, and yet at the same time that he would like to go out and do great deeds for her and come back and lay them at her feet. More than anything, he wanted to take that look of sadness from her face by removing whatever sorrow troubled her. To do that, he felt, would be worth dying for.

Finally a message was passed from the guards who had brought him in, to one of the men who surrounded the Tsaretsa: an old man with a lively, intelligent air. The man bent over to speak to the queen. She nodded and the old man gave a sign to the guards to bring Karl forward. He stood before the Tsaretsa, and felt that this was where he belonged. Wherever he went from this time forward, it would be at her will and in her service.

"Lord Bogotyr," said the Tsaretsa, "you have answered the questions which one of the wise told me to put to any who came to our town in arms and armor, and you have answered them in a way which gives me some hope that you are the one he foretold. I do not doubt your word, but would you show me the feather which you were asked about?"

Karl reached into his chest armor and took the little box he had taken from the Dragon's cave. He handed it to her and she opened the box and looked within. He could see, and wondered if others saw, the light which flooded out of the box when she opened it, bringing out the red glints in her dark hair.

She closed the box and handed it back to him. "Thank you, my lord, for showing it to me. It gives me even greater hope that you are the one who was foretold. They say that touching this feather shows you the truth behind every illusion, and that is what you need to carry out my task. As well, it commands all the birds of the air," she said. "I have need of your help in a certain matter . . . ."

He spoke before she could go on. "Yes," he said, "I will help you in any way I can."

She looked at him gravely, "You don't know what I'm going to ask you, or what it may cost you to help me," she said.

"Nevertheless, I will help you in any way I can, and the cost does not concern me," Karl said.

She looked at him for a long time then she smiled. For Karl that smile was more than adequate compensation for anything he might do, even laying down his life. "Thank you, my lord," she said. "May I know your name?" Karl told her his name and she said, "Thank you, Karl. My husband is or was—for I do not know whether he is dead or alive—a nephew of a powerful witch, and among us all such witches are named Baba Yaga. My husband is gone, and I rule here alone. But my daughter, my only child, has gone too, and I think that my husband left her with his aunt, Baba Yaga. Will you find Baba Yaga and see if she has my daughter, Karl?"

"Yes, my lady," said Karl. "I will find Baba Yaga, and if she has your daughter I will bring her back to you."

The Tsaretsa looked at him and said, "That is more than I asked of you, Karl."

He bowed to her and said, "Nevertheless, I will do it, or die."

A deed is a long time doing, but it is short in the telling: it took more than one day for Karl to prepare himself and his horse and find the direction in which to look for the country of Baba Yaga, the Tsaretsa's mother-in-law. But whether it took a short time or a long time, at last he was ready, and he went to say farewell to the Tsaretsa.

"You have not asked me how I will reward you if you bring me back my daughter," the Tsaretsa said.

Karl looked at her and shook his head, "There is no need to speak of rewards to me, my Lady. I will gladly serve you without any reward. Only, if I please you in this, let me continue to serve you."

The Tsaretsa smiled, "That is easy to grant," she said.

Karl went out from her and rode many days on the strength of that smile. At last he came to a way where the road he had been taking divided into three parts. There were signs at each road, written in letters he had learned to read in his travels in Rus. On the first road the sign said, "If you take this road, you and your horse will die." On the second road it said, "If you take this road, your horse will live and you will die." And on the third road the sign said, "If you take this road, you will live and your horse will die."

Karl groaned aloud, for his horse had served him faithfully in many adventures, and he would have given almost anything to save his horse. But he had no choice. If he retraced his steps his horse would not die, but his quest would not be accomplished and he could not bear to think of the face of the Tsaretsa if he returned without accomplishing his quest, or if days and weeks and months and years went by, and she heard nothing of his quest.

"My good horse," he said. "Each of us has to die, and some of us die for others, while some of us die for no reason we can see. Will you take the right-hand path, my noble steed?" The horse looked at the signs as if he could read them, then he bowed his head for a moment and took the right-hand path, without any guidance from the reins. They rode a long time or a short time, who can say, and then a grey wolf carne from the bushes at the side of the trail, and killed the horse with a single slash of his fangs.

Karl jumped from his dying horse and faced the wolf with spear and shield, but the wolf turned and ran and Karl was left with the dead horse. "My good horse," said Karl, "I cannot stop to bury your body now, but I will corne back to do you whatever honor I can." And hanging his saddle bags from his spear, Karl trudged off down the road.

After a long time to Karl, though perhaps it was shorter than it seemed, he reached a village. It seemed peaceful enough, but there was something secretive about it, and the men who passed Karl as he walked down the only street of the village did not look him in the eyes, though he had the feeling that they looked round at him once he had passed them. He came to an inn and went in. The innkeeper looked at him but did not speak.

"My horse has been killed," said Karl, "do you know where I might get another?"

The man hesitated and said slowly, "This is a bad country for horses. The only horses near here belong to the Lady at the castle."

Karl asked him "Do you think that the Lady might sell me a horse?"

The landlord looked at him and said, "She might trade you for a horse. She sometimes has need of a man such as you."

Karl wondered what the man meant by "a man such as you." An armored man? A man who lacked something he needed to carry on his concerns? "How do I find this iady?" he said.

"Follow the road," the innkeeper said, "It only leads to Her land."

Karl nodded. This village had the air of one which waited at the gates of something powerful and was afraid to talk about it. He wondered if he said the words "Baba Yaga" how the innkeeper might react. Karl walked down the road, carrying his saddle bags on his spear. He had not taken any rest or refreshment at the inn; it did not seem a place to take rest or refreshment.

When he caught a glimpse of a grey form out of the corner of his eye, he shook the saddle bags off his spear, and cast it at the wolf. A cry came from the wolf, and it ran off, carrying Karl's spear in its side. The person who it had seemed to be chasing was a young child, barefoot and tousle headed, very small, but not at all afraid.

"You chased the grey wolf away," the child said.

"It looked like the wolf who killed my horse," said Karl. "Was it a friend of yours?"

The child shook its head. "Not a friend, but not quite an enemy," it said. "More like . . . one who guards me. Or perhaps keeps me prisoner. Sometimes it's hard to tell."

Karl nodded. "Sometimes it is hard to tell," he said. "Much may depend on the reason why someone keeps you safe: whether it is for your sake or not."

"I don't think that it was for my sake," said the child. "Are you going up to the castle? I'll come with you for a way."

They walked companionably along the road. The child offered to carry Karl's saddle bags, but feeling the weight of the saddle bags and looking at the small form in front of him, Karl gruffly refused. "My name is Karl," he told the child.

After walking a little the child said, "They call me Ivanushka." A certain idea began to grow in Karl's mind, but he reminded himself that he really needed a horse to get back—a good horse to outrun pursuit if it should come to that. And the Lady at the castle had horses, and perhaps men to ride them. And also the same impulse in his nature that had sent him to see the dragon told him that he had never seen a Baba Yaga, and would like to see what happened if he did.

Presently they carne in sight of the castle, and the child said, "There's Her place," and lifting a hand in farewell went off down a side road. Karl thought that the child would find him again more easily than he could find the child, knowing the ways of this place as Karl did not.

At the outer gate of the castle, Karl knocked on the door with a mailed fist. Presently servants came and let him in, leading him without a word into the great room of the castle, where the Lady awaited him. The Lady was beautiful beyond the dreams of men, but Karl looked at her unmoved. If he had not seen the Tsaretsa, he might have fallen to that beauty and he might not have. But as it was, his heart was armored. Also he had a shrewd suspicion that the beautiful face he saw was not the way this woman really looked.

Under pretense of bowing to the Lady, Karl put his hand into the armor at his breast and put his little finger into the box with the Firebird's feather. A piercing pain came from his finger, but as he straightened up he saw the Lady as she really was. Her hair was grey, and although her face had beauty, it was a terrible beauty, enough to make any mortal man run away, if he did not stay transfixed by that beauty.

"Lady," said Karl, "I am a knight without a horse. I am told that you have many horses. Would you grant me one as a favor?"

The Lady looked at him, perhaps displeased by his bluntness, and his disregard for her apparent beauty. "And what favor will you do me?" she said, and Karl thought that her voice was her true voice, deep and yet very feminine, the voice of an older woman than she appeared to be.

"Why, Lady," he said, "whatever I can do without breaking the oaths I have already made. For you know that a knight is his honor and a knight without honor is no knight."

She looked at him, and he tried to make his face go a little slack and foolish, as if he were bedazzled by her beauty.

She said, as if to herself, "And yet a knight without honor may be what I need. Let us see if you can keep those oaths." Then speaking directly to him she said, "There is a herd of horses in the meadow outside my castle. They have a tendency to stray away. Choose one of them and ride him. If you can keep the rest from straying away for three days, the horse will be yours, and you may ask me one other boon."

Karl nodded his head. He thought that this being, whatever it really was, would keep her promise, but that she was very sure she would never have to keep it, so certain was she that he would fail. Well, time would tell about that. He accepted her hospitality and lay down to sleep that night in a chamber which was grand and yet comfortable: he remembered humbler, but much more comfortable, accommodations at the Tsaretsa's house.

In the morning he saw a great herd of magnificent horses let loose from the stables and he followed them into the pasture, telling the servants that he would choose his horse after watching them for a while. The horses competed among themselves, running races with each other, both stallions and mares except for one horse which cropped quietly at the turf and paid no attention to the races. Karl walked up to the horse and put a saddle on it and mounted it. Before he could put the horse to the test he saw the child Ivanushka watching him from under a tree nearby. "Why did you choose that horse?" Ivanushka said.

"A horse who does not race with the other horses may simply lack the spirit to compete," said Karl. "But this horse looked as if he were a seasoned warrior watching the recruits practice war. I may be wrong, but I think that he did not race because he knew that the others could not compete with him."

Ivanushka laughed. "You're right," the child said. "This one is the King of the horses. Try him."

Karl touched the horse with his heels and immediately the horse exploded into action, galloping past the leaders of the race as if they were standing still. Karl pulled on the reins and the King horse ran so fast that he circled the rest of the herd and gradually forced them into a compact mass with the King horse ready to dash out and run down any horse who departed from that mass. Karl circled around and came to where Ivanushka stood, the horse poised to go if any of the other horses wandered too far.

"Very good," said Ivanushka. "But if you keep them in a group like that they won't get their exercise. But if you let them graze and run races sooner or later they'll slip away from you. No one is stealing the horses really. *She's* trained them to slip away and hide, so that anyone trying to keep the horses from disappearing will fail. Then after the person trying to herd the horses gives up, She sends out a magical call to bring them back."

"By 'She' you mean the Lady of the castle," said Karl.

Ivanushka shrugged. "That's one of her names," the child said. "I just call her Aunt."

Karl nodded. "Yes," he said, "Aunt Baba Yaga."

Ivanushka looked at him. "Perhaps," the child said. "And if so, what of it?"

Karl nodded. "Nothing—for now," he said. "Later we will talk more of this. Where do the horses hide when they slip away?"

Ivanushka grinned. "Usually in the woods near the hornets' nests."

"If someone disturbed the hornets' nests, they might come back to the meadow faster than they went," said Karl with an air of innocence.

"But who would do that?" said Ivanushka with an equal air of innocence. "After all, they might get stung."

Karl nodded. "Unless they were very clever."

Ivanushka nodded and Karl thought he didn't need to say any more. The child would help him, he thought: the casual mention of the hornets' nests showed that. If he was mistaken about that, he might be mistaken about other things.

It was a long day, and Karl didn't have to pretend to be weary in the afternoon. He did pretend to fall asleep, and watched from slitted eyes that looked closed from a distance as the horses slipped off, until only Karl and the King of the horses were left in the meadow. Then he waited, the tension growing as the rest of the afternoon slipped by. Just as Karl was about to give up he heard noises in the woods. A group of large heavy creatures was plunging through the woods, and as they came closer, he could hear the buzzing of the hornets. Then one after the other the herd of horses came out of the woods and into the meadow.

As they came out Karl and the King of the horses herded them into a group and herded the group in the direction of the stables. By the time they got to the stables the hornets had mostly given up their pursuit of the horses, and, except for an occasional shying movement when one of the remaining hornets came up close to them, the horses were mostly calmed down. Karl swung down off the King horse, led him to the place in the stable that was plainly for the best of the horses, and cleaned and groomed the King horse himself. Then he headed toward the castle.

As he came into the gates he reached his hand into his armor and thrust his ring finger into the box with the Firebird's feather. A new sharp pain in that finger was added to the old throbbing pain in his little finger, and Karl saw the castle as it really was: a great box of a house, without doors or windows, kept off the ground by a series of legs that might have been the legs of a monstrous chicken. There were some rough outbuildings around the house, and he was glad to see that the places he had eaten and slept were outside the house of Baba Yaga. He thought that if one went into that house it would be a very hard job to get out.

He cast a glance at the castle servants, and thought that they were not as human as they appeared on the outside: certain movements and the look in their eyes made him wonder if they were the result of some of Baba Yaga's enchantments. Presently they brought him some food, and he ate, and slept until the next morning.

In the morning the King horse greeted him with a whinny, and seemed as eager as Karl himself to get out to the meadow. About the middle of the morning Ivanushka appeared and Karl said, "Where do you think the horses will hide today?"

Ivanushka grinned and said, "They'll go down to the lake. She's given them a spell so that they'll look like waves on the shore. She wasn't pleased that the hornets drove them back to you, but she's not entirely sure that it wasn't an accident."

Karl looked at Ivanushka and said softly, "I wonder what might drive the horses out of the water, as the hornets drove them out of the woods?"

Ivanushka said casually, "There are snapping fish in the water. If someone throws raw meat into the water, they go into a frenzy, and they'd attack the horses, despite the enchantment. They can smell them."

Karl nodded. Later that afternoon he pretended to sleep, and when the horses slipped away, he rode into the woods and set traps for some of the woodland creatures. There had never been trapping in those woods so the creatures were unwary and soon the traps were full. Karl killed the creatures which had not been killed by the traps and cut the meat into rough chunks with his sword. Then, mounting the King horse, he rode along the shore, throwing the meat into the water. Then he waited.

Presently the waves dashed on the shore, even though there was no wind. Eventually the horses had to come so far from the shore that the enchantment would no longer work, and they could be seen as horses, even though they still had a foamy look about them. Karl used the King horse to round them up and drive them back to the stables.

This time the King horse had to nip at some of the stallions to make them come into the herd, and even threaten to kick a few. Karl drove them into the stable, groomed the King horse, ate and went to sleep. But his heart was heavy, for he knew the witch would be suspicious, and the last day would be many times as difficult as the first two.

In the morning he drove the horses out into the pasture and the King horse was as nervous as he was, but they were both eager for the last day. This time Ivanushka was there already when they arrived and said to Karl, "She knows that you know. This time she has given the horses an enchantment so they can fly. They will gather at the topmost branches of the trees in the wood, and you can do nothing to get them down."

Karl smiled at Ivanushka gravely and said, "Don't despair. Will every horse have the power to fly?"

Ivanushka stared at him. "Yes, even your horse. So you can get to them, but I do not think that even the King horse can force them to come down, but if he does the enchantment ends, because if a horse gets a foot on the ground, the enchantment ends."

"I'll have to think about this," said Karl, and this time Ivanushka did not go away, but sat on the ground beside Karl's horse, looking at him anxiously. Finally Karl pretended to go to sleep, and watched behind slitted eyes as each of the horses jumped up into the air and floated like a cloud up near the tops of the trees. From the ground, at any rate, each of the horses looked cloudy, so that if you tried to look directly at them they looked like a cloud, and only looking out of the corner of your eye could you see that the cloud was a horse. It was a very good enchantment and Karl sat on his horse and admired it for a while.

Then he raised his hand and urged his horse upward. With a mighty spring the King horse leapt into the sky and soared far above the other horses. Karl took the box from his chest armor, and took off the lid, so that the shining feather within cast its light all above and around. From all parts of the sky birds began flying toward that light. When some of the birds had almost reached him, Karl urged his horse down among the cloudy horses, dodging in and out among them. The birds pursued him, bumping into the cloudy horses and sometimes using their beaks if the horses did not get out of the way. The horses began to panic, and headed for the familiar ground, each losing its ability to fly once it had touched a hoof to the ground.

When all of the horse herd had landed except his own, Karl closed the box and put it away. His whole hand ached from holding the box aloft, and this was added to the pain from his two fingers. Karl used the King horse, who was still flying in the air, to drive the herd of horses to the stables. Then he let the King horse descend almost to the ground, dismounted with a leap, and said to the King horse, "Wait here until I come back." The King horse flew a little bit more up into the air, so the stable hands could not get hold of him, and then waited, floating in the air.

"Take me to your mistress," he told the servants, and they led him into the house. Waiting there was Ivanushka, who gave him a grin. "Lady," said Karl, "I have herded your horses for three days, and I have not lost a one. I claim the horse I rode and the boon you promised me."

"You are the first man to herd my horses," said the Lady of the castle, "and the stake which was sharpened for your head will have to go empty. You have claimed a good horse: what boon do you want besides?"

Karl looked at her and then at Ivanushka. "I would like to take your grandniece back to her mother," he said.

The Lady of the castle changed her appearance and he saw a bony-legged figure sitting in a pestle with a mortar in one hand and a broom in the other, but he knew this was just as much an illusion as the fair figure he had seen on his arrival.

"Do you dare to ask this of me?" the figure asked.

"Yes, Lady, I dare to ask," said Karl. Ivanushka turned toward him and said, "I would never have helped you if I knew you wanted to take me away. I like living in the village. I don't want to go back to the court."

Karl said gently, "I would not like to make you do anything you don't want to do, my friend. But your mother misses you very much."

Ivanushka looked at him and said, "Why can't she come and live in the village with me?"

"She has responsibilities, my friend," said Karl. "She cannot always please herself, but if you will come back with me, I will ask her to give you as much freedom as she can. She wants your happiness, as do I. Do you remember your mother?"

Ivanushka looked at Baba Yaga and said, "It is very difficult to think of her."

Karl said gently, "She misses you very much."

Ivanushka was silent for a while, seeming to be thinking and remembering, then she turned to Baba Yaga and said, "I want to go with him."

Baba Yaga scowled at her and said, "All right, but if I can catch you after giving you the start of an hour, you must stay with me for seven years, and if I can catch him he will have to serve me for seven years."

Ivanushka nodded and said, "Done," and her voice for a moment was very much like the voice of her great-aunt. "Let's go," she said to Karl and they walked out of Baba Yaga's house together.

They walked to where Karl had left the King horse, and Karl tossed Ivanushka into the saddle and said, "Run for your mother's palace with only your weight. This horse will outdistance my pursuit. I'll try to lead anyone who follows you astray, and I may well escape."

Ivanushka looked at him and said, "I remember now I am the Princess Maria, and I command you Karl to mount this horse of yours and come with me. We will either win back together or serve my aunt for seven years together."

"My lady," said Karl and leaped into the saddle behind her, for there was no time for debate, and perhaps—a very faint perhaps—they might escape together.

They rode off through the air, covering all the ground that Karl had trudged with the saddle bags over his spear, and were almost back to where Karl had lost his horse before Princess Maria said, "I think the hour is up, she'll catch us easily in the air: we need to descend to the ground and conceal ourselves." Karl urged the King horse downward, and as its hoof touched the ground, it lost its ability to fly. They were at the place where the wolf had killed Karl's old horse, and his horse lay on the ground there, stark and stiff.

"Put your horse in the bog yonder," said Princess Maria, "and leave me with the King horse." Karl stripped the saddle and other accouterments from his old horse, and dragged it to the bog.

"Do me this one last service, friend," said Karl, and cast his horse into the bog. When he returned he found the King horse lying on the ground, and Princess Maria had painted it with paints she had taken from her pocket, so that it had the markings of his old horse, and it looked as if its throat had been torn out.

"Lay here quietly," said Princess Maria, "if you wish to escape my aunt's service."

The horse whinnied and then lay still. "Now we must conceal ourselves," said Princess Maria, and Karl took her to the stream that ran through the swamp, and they entered the water. Karl cut reeds and when they heard a whistling sound in the sky they ducked under the water and breathed through the reeds. Overhead there passed a figure, and when Karl dared to come up from the water he saw off in the distance a figure in a pestle, with a mortar held before it and a broom held behind skidding across the sky.

"She made an agreement with my father that she would not enter the kingdom that he and my mother ruled," said Princess Maria. "So she'll patrol the border for a long time, thinking that we've come some unexpected way."

Karl nodded. "So it's worth the chance of heading straight for the border from here," he said. "She'll think that if we were on a direct course she'd have seen us by now."

They mounted the horse and rode for a long way. It was already getting dark when they came to a small cabin at the edge of a wood. "Stop here," said Princess Maria. She slid down from the horse and said to the cabin, "Stand with your door to the woods." The cabin heaved itself up on legs like a chicken and faced the woods, then it crouched down again and looked like an ordinary house. "We can sleep here, and no one will bother us," said Princess Maria. "In fact, no one will even see us: when the cabin has its door to the woods it and those who live in it are invisible to all others."

Karl wondered if a magical house like this might be known to Baba Yaga, and perhaps with her powers she might even overcome the enchantment and find them within, but he swallowed his doubts, and said to Princess Maria," As you say, Princess."

He led the King horse into the door and it trotted quietly into a corner, where he took off its saddle and groomed it as best he could.

"There is food for the horse and some simple food for us in the cupboards there," Princess Maria said.

Karl opened the cupboard, and found a bucket of oats for the horse and some dried meat and hard cheese. There was a big bottle of wine, and when he turned away from the cupboard he saw that Princess Maria had found a bucket and a jug and brought water in, perhaps from a nearby well. There were pottery plates and cups in the cupboard, and they ate at a table in the center of the room. The bucket of water Princess Maria gave to the horse, along with some of the oats that Karl had found.

Maria poured herself a glass of water with a little wine in it, and Karl watered his wine: he wanted to have his wits about him. After dinner they made a fire in the fireplace and sat there, talking quietly.

Presently Princess Maria lay down on the bed which was in the room, and Karl wrapped himself in his cloak, and lay across the threshold of the door, sleeping a little and watching a lot. In the morning, Princess Maria took some of the oats which they had not given to the horse, and made an oat gruel, which they had with water for breakfast.

"The problem, my lady," said Karl to the Princess, "is how to get across the border into your mother's kingdom without being caught by your aunt."

Princess Maria nodded. "She'll be looking for three of us," she said. "So I think that the first thing to do is to send the King horse across the border, as far from here as possible." She turned to the King horse and said, "Meet us in the water meadow." The horse whinnied, touched Karl with his nose, and then bowed to the princess, his front foot stretched out and his head touching the ground. Then he left the cabin, and for a while they could hear his galloping hooves.

Princess Maria said, "He didn't come under the threat to have to serve her for seven years if she catches him, but I think that on his own without having to worry about a rider, he can probably slip across the border. But now the question is how do you and I cross the border?"

Karl said, "Lady, if you would cross alone, while I create a diversion . . . ."

She shook her head. "That is what she expects, and she will be on the lookout for it. The only way for us both to get across is for you to cross over while I create a diversion. You must trust me in this, Karl. Take off your armor and lay it on the ground with your sword and shield. I will give you a belt that you must put on, and you must cross the border in the form that belt gives you."

Karl was moved to protest, but he had trusted her so far, and he was not about to not trust her now, simply because he was older and more war-wise than she was. He stripped off his armor, while she went behind a screen, and then he handed his armor over the screen. When she passed him a belt, he hesitated to put it on, but then a masked figure came out from behind the screen, wearing his armor. Perhaps the figure was a little smaller than his own, but it was much larger than he would have thought. Perhaps she had changed her own shape beneath that armor.

At a nod from the armored figure he put on the belt, and at once he felt his shape shift, until he had the form of a great hawk.

"Fly to my mother," a voice came from somewhere in the room and, hardly knowing what he did, the hawk which had been Karl leapt up into the air and flew straight for the border. The armored figure came out of the cabin and headed for the border on the ground, running so fast that it kept pace with him. As they neared the border, the hawk which had been Karl saw the figure of Baba Yaga, flying in the air in her pestle, and coming toward him.

Then the Baba Yaga saw the figure on the ground, and after a moment's hesitation veered off from Karl and headed towards the figure on the ground. As Baba Yaga approached it, the armored figure seemed to explode, scattering Karl's armor far and wide. At the same time the hawk which had been Karl crossed the border, his heart aching with a sorrow which his animal form could hardly contain. But he could not help himself, he flew straight for the Tsaretsa's house, as if he were bound to this action.

When the hawk which had been Karl came to the Tsaretsa's house, he flew straight into a room which was evidently a private room of the Tsaretsa. As he landed he felt the belt which he had been wearing slip off his waist. At once he regained his human form, and when he saw the Tsaretsa regarding him without fear he began to say "Lady, I have failed you." But before all the words could come out of his mouth, the belt hit the floor, and there standing as she had stood in the meadow was the child he had called Ivanushka. What had come out of his throat was, "Lady, I have . . ." and the Tsaretsa nodded calmly.

"Yes, Karl, you have succeeded," she said. "How are you, Marushka?"

The child went and embraced her mother, and as they clung together Karl saw for the first time that the one he had called "Ivanushka" was not only a child, but a beautiful young girl.

Princess Maria turned toward him, her arm still about her mother, and said quietly, "I was in the belt, Karl, and the figure in armor was only an illusion. Thank you for trusting me."

The Tsaretsa stretched out her hands and said to Karl, "Give me your hands."

When Karl stretched out his hand the Tsaretsa saw the scars on his hands and said, "You have suffered to bring about what I wanted, Karl."

Karl nodded his head, "Lady," he said, "whatever it takes to do your will, I will do. Will you take me into your service?"

The Tsaretsa looked at him for a long time and said softly, "It might be better for you if I did not."

"Lady," said Karl, "this is what I want for whatever service I have done for you. But I have done little. Your daughter, once reminded of you, could have saved herself."

Princess Maria regarded him and said quietly, "I played a part, Karl, but yours were the actions which started it all. You do not offer to serve me, Karl, but if my mother refuses your service, I would be glad if you would serve me."

The Tsaretsa smiled and said, "Oh no, my daughter, this one is vowed to my service. Because I love you, you may command my knight Karl, but he serves you for my sake."

Karl smiled at Princess Maria and said, "You are always my friend, Princess, but your mother is right. First I am vowed to her service. But any service which I cannot do for her sake, I will do for the sake of friendship."

The Tsaretsa nodded. "You will have knights of your own, Marushka, but this one is mine. And your friend, too, do not regard that too lightly."

Princess Maria grinned a grin which reminded Karl of the first time he had met her. "Treat him well, Mother," she said, "Or I may steal him from you. Karl, you have a horse to meet in the water meadow, and then you will want to see the court armorer to replace the armor I used. We may need you again soon, and I want you to be prepared. While you do that, I need to talk to my mother, the Tsaretsa Eikaterina."

Karl saluted both of them and went out to find the King horse and to get new armor. He thought that the service of those two would have its challenges and its dangers, but that there was nothing that he would rather do. And whatever happened in the future, he was sure he would never be bored.

THE DRAGON'S DAUGHTER

Once there was a kingdom ruled by the Tsaretsa Eikaterina, and a Knight named Karl served the Tsaretsa. He was not a knight of Rus, but had come into the kingdom on his wanderings, after having been a captain in the wars. He had done the Tsaretsa good service in that he had rescued her daughter from the witch Baba Yaga, but the only reward Karl wanted was to continue to serve the Tsaretsa. He was a faithful knight and was a good friend of the Princess Maria whom he had brought back from Baba Yaga's house.

The kingdom was a peaceful one and the knights in the service of the Tsaretsa had little to do, so when Karl was summoned to the Tsaretsa's presence, he hoped that she had some task for him, which would enable him to show his devotion to her. When he saluted her, the Tsaretsa looked at him for a long time and then said quietly, "I have a hard task for you, Karl."

He bowed and said, "The harder the better."

She looked at him and said, "Perhaps it is harder in a different way than you think, though it will involve many dangers. As you know, Baba Yaga was Princess Maria's great-aunt. Her nephew was my husband. As I told you when I sent you after Masha, he left me, taking our daughter, and left her with his aunt, Baba Yaga. I do not know whether he is alive or dead, but now I need to know. If he is alive I need to know if he has any message for me. Only that: I do not wish him brought back to me as you brought back Masha."

"You are right, my lady, it is a hard task, but I will do it for you," said Karl.

She looked at him steadily and said, "If he is dead, my counsellors tell me I need to marry again, to one of the princes of Rus. They say my people would not accept any foreigner, or anyone not of princely blood as my spouse. And I have a responsibility to my people."

Karl said to her, "Yes, my lady, a hard task. But I will do it for you."

She smiled at him, "Yes, Karl, I am sure that you will. Come and see me before you go."

When he left the Tsaretsa's room, he found Princess Maria waiting for him. "Follow me," she said. She led him to one of the upper rooms of the castle, where she had a little nest full of books and toys. "Sit," she said, and Karl sat cross-legged on the floor, while she perched on the only couch in the room, looking at him seriously. He saw things he had given her in the contents of the room, and he was moved. "My mother is sending you after my father," she said.

"As you say, Princess," said Karl.

She looked at him thoughtfully for a long time, then she said, "Will you take my advice, Karl?"

He smiled and said, "I will certainly take your advice, as long as it does not interfere with my vows, I don't think we would have got back from Baba Yaga's house if I had not trusted you, my friend."

She nodded and said, "Probably you would not have," and her voice reminded him for a moment of the voice of her great-aunt, Baba Yaga. "First," she said, "I think my father is alive. He is one of the people we call in this country 'dragons' which means that although he is usually in human form, he can take the form of a dragon. Such men are very hard to kill, but it is not impossible to kill them, especially if they encounter a hero when they are in their dragon form. So the first piece of advice I give you is to kill no dragons."

"Lady, that is a hard piece of advice to take," said Karl, "but I will promise you not to kill any dragons unless there is no other way to keep my vows."

She nodded, "That is enough, but make sure that you tell any dragons you meet that you have made that promise."

She hesitated and then said, "I know my mother's counsellors have been urging her to marry one of the Princes of Rus. If she does, and if she has sons then I will not rule this land after her. I don't want my mother to ever die, Karl, but if she does, I think I would make a better ruler of this land than any son of a prince of Rus. My mother will not marry unless she knows that my father is dead. So my second piece of advice is not to assume that my father is dead unless you are as sure of his death as you are sure of your devotion to my mother."

"That is a very high degree of certainty, my friend," said Karl, "and it may well make my task more difficult. But I will promise it to you, and it is not as hard as my other promise."

Princess Maria looked at him and said, "Thank you, Karl. My third piece of advice to you is not to take the King horse, which you won from my aunt Baba Yaga. Remember what happened to your horse on the way to find me. The King horse may be needed on another quest, but I do not think you will need him on this one."

Karl nodded, "That requires no promise," he said, "I will simply arrange for another horse, but you must look after him while I'm gone."

Princess Maria smiled. "Oh, I'll do that," she said.

On the morning when he left the court of the Tsaretsa, Karl went to say his farewell. The Tsaretsa said to him, "I hear that you have been making promises to my daughter. I want you to make a promise to me, Karl. Come back to me, I need you as my knight and as my friend."

Karl hesitated and then said, "I promised Princess Maria to kill no dragons so long as it did not interfere with my other vows. This promise you ask of me would change that oath; I could kill a dragon if not killing it would prevent me from coming back to you."

"That is my intent, Karl," the Tsaretsa said, "and my daughter too, is anxious for you to come back to us. Will you swear to do as I say?"

Karl sighed, "I will swear, my lady," he said "and God grant that I am not in a situation where my oaths conflict. For a knight who is foresworn is no knight."

The Tsaretsa smiled, "I believe that if you think carefully you will find that your oaths will not conflict, Karl. Whether you will be gone a short time or a long time no one knows, but I am sure that I will see you again."

Karl bowed, "That is as God wills," he said, "but that I will see you again and serve you again is my dearest wish." And he went out and on his quest.

Karl retraced the path that had taken him to Baba Yaga's house when he rescued Princess Maria. But a little before the crossroads he dismounted from his horse and sent it back to the Tsaretsa's palace under the escort of a groom who had come with him so far. Then he walked to the crossroads, where the signs said, "Go this way and you and your horse will die." "Go this way and your horse will live and you will die." "Go this way and your horse will die and you will live."

Sitting at the entrance to the third path was a great grey wolf, who was sitting on his haunches with what may have been a grin on his face. "Well, maybe I have robbed you of your prey this time, grey wolf," said Karl. The wolf stood up and looked at Karl. "Shall I ride you to your mistress' kingdom?" said Karl. "Well, perhaps I will." He mounted the great grey wolf and clung to him frantically while the great wolf ran along the path. Before he knew it, he was at Baba Yaga's house, this time not looking like a castle, but like a great dark house without doors or windows, mounted on legs like those of a monstrous chicken.

"Turn your face to me and your back to the woods," said Karl, remembering what Princess Maria had said to the house on his escape from Baba Yaga. He slipped down off the wolf's back and watched as the house turned around on its chicken legs, and Baba Yaga came to a door which appeared in the house. Baba Yaga looked as he had seen her one time before, with grey hair, but with a terrible beauty on her face.

"For your grandniece's sake, I ask your hospitality," said Karl."

Baba Yaga laughed a laugh to chill one's blood, but she said, "You may come in and you may go out Karl, and I will do you no harm, for my grandniece's sake. And for her sake I will grant you a boon. Come in and partake of my hospitality."

Karl went into the house and there Baba Yaga's servants took him to a bath where he washed himself and put on his best clothing, and then he went in to Baba Yaga's palace and partook of her hospitality; a great feast which was served to them by invisible servants. At the end of the feast Baba Yaga said, "You have not saved your horse, Karl. The groom killed it, and went back and reported that you were both killed by a grey wolf."

"I don't think that the Tsaretsa or your grandniece will believe him," said Karl.

"I am sure that my grandniece won't believe him," said Baba Yaga, "What my son's wife believes is not so clear to my eyes. What boon do you ask of me?"

Karl bowed. "Lady, if anyone knows where your nephew, who is married to the Tsaretsa Eikaterina is, I think you must. Will you tell me where to find him and how to deal with him?"

Baba Yaga laughed a laugh to chill one's bones. "That is two boons, Karl. Do you want to know where he is, or how to deal with him?"

Karl smiled a little sadly. "Where he is Lady, for if I cannot find him, I cannot deal with him," he said.

Baba Yaga nodded. "I will give you a token which will lead you to him, Karl. As for how to deal with him, I will give you one hint: deal with him honestly."

"I have heard and partly know from my own experience that the dragon-folk are great deceivers," said Karl.

"They are," said Baba Yaga, "and they expect their enemies to be the same. So by dealing with them as honestly as you can you throw off their calculations."

Karl said quietly, "I would not call myself an enemy of your nephew."

Baba Yaga gave him a bitter smile, "But perhaps he considers you an enemy. By returning my grandniece to her mother you spoiled some of his plans. My nephew does not like his plans spoiled."

"My concern is what the Tsaretsa Eikaterina wants," said Karl, "and if your nephew's plans fit in with her desires, there is no reason for us to be enemies."

Baba Yaga laughed, "If his plans fit in with her desires, there would be no reason for them to have parted, or for my nephew to steal my grandniece from her mother."

Karl nodded, "As you say, Lady. But from what you say your nephew is alive, and knowing that is part of what I needed to find out."

"He is alive now, but he may not be much longer," said Baba Yaga grimly, "He has made many enemies, whether or not you consider yourself one of them, and they are pressing him very hard."

Karl smiled, "Then perhaps he needs an ally."

Baba Yaga looked at him thoughtfully, "Yes, it could go that way," she said, "My nephew has many names, but one of them is Zvie Gorowich: the dragon of the Mountains. To reach him you will need to climb many mountains and a horse will not be of much use to you. But I will give you a token which will lead you to him."

She reached into a basket by her side and took out a little ball of scarlet yarn. "Throw this on the ground and it will lead you to my nephew. If you need to rest, pick up the yarn and make it into a ball again and put it in your pouch, then cast it down again when you are ready to go on."

Karl bowed. "Thank you for this boon, Lady," he said, "I bear you no ill will, and if after my quest is accomplished I can do you some service, without breaking any of my oaths, then call on me."

Then he cast the ball of yarn on the ground: it unrolled and began moving along the ground like a snake. Because of its scarlet color, it was easy to follow, and the end of it toward Karl was always within reach of his arm, so when he grew weary of following it, he could reach out and pick up the yarn, roll it into a ball and take his rest with it in his pouch.

A deed is long in the doing and short in the telling: following the scarlet yarn, Karl travelled many a weary mile, wondering if he could follow the path that the yarn took, but always finding that he could, though it led him up some perilous slopes, and once or twice he fell, while the yarn waited for him to pick himself up and follow it. He soon ran out of the supplies he had brought with him in his pack, and had to stop and roll up the yarn in a ball while he hunted for food, or looked for good water to fill his water bottle. Usually, though not always, he found a cave or a thicket to hide him while he slept.

After a long time or a short time, he came to a little valley hidden in the peaks near the top of the range he had been climbing. This valley reminded him of the valley where he had encountered the dragon a long time ago, and he walked carefully, looking around him for a cave, where the dragon might hide. Presently he saw a figure coming toward him, a young man, not armed, but having the air of a noble or prince of Rus. When they came within speaking distance the young man said, "Welcome, brave knight, have you come here of your own will or by compulsion?"

Karl bowed and said, "I am a knight of the Tsaretsa Eikaterina, and I am here to fulfill certain oaths I have made."

The man looked at him and said, "Perhaps one of your oaths is to slay a dragon?"

Karl shook his head. "No, lord," he said, "In fact one of my oaths is to slay no dragon unless slaying a dragon is the only way to fulfill my other oaths."

"And may I know what your other oaths are?" said the man.

"One oath I made," said Karl, "was to return and serve the Tsaretsa."

The man smiled, "That is perhaps more easily sworn to than accomplished. But I see that you could slay a dragon if the dragon tried to kill you or imprison you to keep you from going back to serve the Tsaretsa. Whoever made you swear that oath did not want you to be defenseless against the dragon-folk, as the first promise might have made you. What other oaths did you swear?"

"My other oaths have to do with my mission, which is to find out if the Tsaretsa's husband is alive, and ask him for a message for her," said Karl, "May I know, lord, to whom I am speaking?"

The man smiled bitterly and said, "You may call me Prince Ivan. As for the Tsaretsa's husband, so far as I know he is alive, but he may not be much longer. He has made many enemies."

"Are you one of those enemies?" asked Karl.

The man who had called himself Prince Ivan said, with the same bitter smile, "I would like to be his friend, but sometimes I think that I am his worst enemy. What about you, sir Knight, are you one of his enemies?"

Karl shook his head, "It is not for me to call myself his friend or his enemy. So long as he does no harm to the Tsaretsa, I will give him proper honor. If, on the other hand he does anything against her, I am bound to defend her."

"Yes," said the man called Ivan, "I sometimes think that Katushka has as many friends and defenders as her husband has enemies. Well, perhaps we know a little better where we stand, sir knight. I don't think we have a quarrel at the moment. Will you come to my hunting lodge for some refreshment?"

Karl bowed, "Gladly, Prince." As the man who had named himself Prince Ivan turned away to lead the way, Karl saw that the yarn which had led him to this place had crawled up the back of the man called Ivan and was resting along his spine.

So that answered one question thought Karl. If the token given him by Baba Yaga was to be trusted, this man was the Tsaretsa's husband. But could the token be trusted? After all the Tsaretsa's husband was Baba Yaga's nephew, wouldn't she try to protect him? And the yarn might be laying on the man's back as a way of indicating that if he stuck to this man, then he would lead him to the husband. Remembering his second promise to Princess Maria, Karl thought that he was not as sure as he needed to be that this was the man he sought.

Prince Ivan led him to a small hut on the edge of a wood, and Karl wondered if one spoke the proper words whether the hut would arise on chicken legs and turn around. He was given wine and cheese and some dried meat, and it was good to sit down inside a hut and rest. "Lord Prince," said Karl after his meal, "You say that you would like to be the friend of the Tsaretsa's husband, and I see nothing in my oaths to make him my enemy. Perhaps he could use some allies in his present troubles."

The man called Ivan smiled, a more genuine smile this time and said, "Perhaps he could. What is your name, Knight?"

"My name is Karl, Lord Prince, and I would not like to have to report back to the Tsaretsa that I found her husband in difficulties and did nothing to help him," said Karl.

"Perhaps she would like that report, they did not part as friends," said the prince. "No more lords or princes, Karl, call me Ivan. Shall we be allies for awhile against the enemies of the Tsaretsa's husband? Give me your hand."

As Karl took his hand Prince Ivan shuddered and almost fell. "The enemies we spoke of are attacking the husband of the Tsaretsa and his friends," he said, "Will you go on the path I will show you, and see if you can do something about this attack?"

Karl nodded. "I will, Prince Ivan," he said. The prince showed him a well-marked trail leading out of the valley and Karl walked along it, holding on to the handle of his sword, ready to draw it.

At a turn in the path Karl was faced with a three headed dragon who spoke with a human voice, "What have we here, a, dragon slayer?" it said.

Karl kept his sword up, but spoke as courteously as he could, "No," he said, "I have sworn to kill no dragons unless it would prevent me from keeping my other oaths. The dragon stretched out its middle head and Karl saw on the back of this head a scarlet line going down its spine. He was sure that this was the scarlet yarn he had seen on Prince Ivan's back. So this was another form of Prince Ivan, but Baba Yaga's token still marked it for him.

"If you do not come to slay dragons, then I have no quarrel with you," said the dragon. "Pass me." Karl sheathed his sword and went past the dragon on the path. To go past the dragon without turning was almost the hardest thing Karl had ever done, but the dragon did not attack him, and Karl went down the path unscathed.

After a long time or a short time, Karl made another turn in the path and saw an old woman, crouching over a kind of doll on the road. She was holding long pins in her hand, and was poking at the doll with the pins. As she struck the doll with the pins, the doll writhed like a living thing. "Lady, what do you do?" said Karl.

The old woman looked at him and said, "What concern is it of yours?"

"Lady," said Karl, "I think I recognize what you are doing: that doll has hair or fingernails from a man you wish to torment, when you poke with your pins the man suffers as if you had poked the pins into the part of the body that you poke the pins into on the doll. It seems to me to be a cowardly way of attacking someone without meeting him face to face."

The woman looked at Karl and said without expression, "How do you know that the man does not deserve what I am doing to him?"

Karl looked back at her and said, "Who made you his judge, Lady? Or is the man injuring you himself and you are doing what you do in self-defense?"

She shook her head, "I am doing what I am doing at the behest of another. He has something of mine which I need, and by what I am doing I am earning it back."

Karl thought a little and said, "Did this other get what you need by stealing it from you, or tricking it from you? And if so, how can you trust the promise that you will earn it back this way?

The old woman looked at him with grudging respect, "He tricked it out of me, and you are right: I do not entirely trust his promises. Well, Sir Knight I will make you a bargain. I will stop what I am doing for three days. If you will bring me back what I have lost, I will destroy the doll in a way which will do no harm to the victim. If you do not bring me what I need, I must pursue this course until the victim is dead, because it is the only way I know of to get my broomstick back."

"How will I know the man who has taken it from you, and since this is a matter of magic, how will I recognize your broomstick?" asked Karl, "I know that in such matters, what you seek is often concealed under some other form."

The old woman considered, and then said reluctantly. "There are two things I can tell you: the man's name is Peter the Thief, and he will be a tall man. The second is that the broomstick will look not unlike a broomstick: it has enough magic that you could make it look like a staff or crook, but not like a ball or a thimble or a cup. That perhaps is not enough. My broomsticks name is Grimalkin, and if you drop that name into your conversation, the broomstick will give some sign."

"Lady, I will try to bring your broomstick back to you, and if I fail, I suppose your victim is no worse off then if I had not met you. But if I succeed will you grant me one boon?" said Karl.

The old woman nodded, "When you return with my broomstick, I will grant you any boon that is within my power." Karl bowed to her and went along the path, since there was no other way to go.

After a long time or a short time, Karl met a man coming along the road. He was a short man, coming only to Karl's shoulder, and he did not carry anything which even remotely looked like a stick. Karl said to him, "Hail, stranger, I am looking for a man named Peter the Thief. Do you know where I could find him?"

The man said, "It would be better if you did not find him, because Peter the Thief steals from whomever he encounters. I have just lost something I value greatly to him."

Karl said, "Perhaps if you tell me what it is, I may be able to get it back for you. I am already trying to get back a broomstick for a lady I met on the way."

The man looked at Karl and said, "What Peter the Thief has stolen from me is a dog, and if you can get it back for me I will grant you any boon within my power."

Karl said, "In these matters it is not always easy to recognize what has been stolen. Is there any way that I can recognize this dog?"

The man said, "The dog's name is Farsight, and if you speak his name he will give you some sign that he is there."

"Farewell for a while," said Karl, "and I hope to return and give you your dog and claim that boon." And he went along the road until he encountered a child sitting by the side of the road, weeping. "What is the matter, little one?" asked Karl.

"A man has stolen my wonderful toy," said the child.

"I will try to get it back for you," said Karl, but he may conceal it: how will I know if it is your toy?"

The child said, "If you say the words 'Go toy, go,' then it will come to life: If you bring it back to me, I'll let you play with it."

"Thank you," said Karl gravely, "I hope that I can get it back for you." He went along the road until he encountered a family: a tall man, and a tall woman with a puzzled look on her face, pulling a cart behind her with a group of noisy children in it. The man had a staff in his hand.

"Hail, stranger," said the man. "My name is Sadko, and I am a trader. I support my family here by trading. Here are some wonderful jewels: what do you have to trade for them?"

Karl put on a foolish expression and said, "Well, I don't know much about trading. Those are certainly wonderful jewels, though." And indeed they were, or appeared to be: jewels that sparkled and shone, and almost filled the cupped hands of the man who had called himself Sadko. "All I have," said Karl, "is a casket with a feather in it: the feather shines like fire, but what other use it has, who knows?"

"Well, I might trade you some of the jewels for it," said the tall man.

Karl laughed and looked as foolish as he could, "What use have I for such pretty things? No, my shining feather is more beautiful than those gems. My soldier friend, old Grimalkin, used to say that a soldier needs nothing but his sword and armor." As Karl said the word 'Grimalkin' the tall man's staff seemed to twist in his hand and he almost fell.

He caught himself and said, "Well, let me have a look at it, and perhaps I can find something to trade you for it."

Karl laughed and said with a cunning expression, "Oh, I won't give you a free look at it: you must pay me to see my feather: many people have said that it's well worth paying for. Give me that staff you're leaning on: it doesn't seem to be doing you much good."

The tall man said haughtily, "Why should I pay you to look at your merchandise?"

Karl laughed, "I have no thought of trading: you were the one with that idea. If you don't want to pay me for a sight of my feather, I'll go on my way, and you go on yours."

The tall man looked at Karl and hesitated, "Well then, I'll give you the staff for a look at your feather, but I've started by giving you something, so you must next give me something.

Karl stretched out his hand for the staff, and tucked it under his arm. Then he took out the casket from his chest armor and opened it, so that the Firebird's feather shone out brightly, casting a light on the surroundings which made them look different: the tall man looked more clever and less ordinary, and the woman and the cart with the children in it looked insubstantial, as if their real form was concealed under their apparent guise.

Karl put back the lid on the box and said, "Well, that seems to me to be a fair trade: you've seen my wonderful feather, and I have this old staff of yours, which might come in handy. So far as I'm concerned, I'm ready to go on my way. As another comrade of mine, old Farsight, used to say, there's no use staying once a good piece of business is done, because you might lose on the next exchange."

"No, stay a while," said the tall man, "after all, you must give me something now, as we said. Just let me have your feather in my hands for a moment."

Karl laughed, "That's what you said, not what I said. To hold the feather in your hands you must let the woman with you come with me, if she wants to."

When Karl had said the word 'Farsight,' the woman looked at him and her hands came up like a dog sitting up and she made a sound that was almost a bark. Now she dropped the handles of the cart and came to Karl, ranging herself behind him. The tall man's face grew dark, but he said, "Well, she may go with you if she wants, but let me hold the feather in my hands." Karl smiled, and opening the casket, spilled the feather into the tall man's hands.

The man started a complex motion of his hands, but as the feather touched his flesh he cried out and dropped it. As swift as thought, Karl scooped up the feather and sealed the casket with its lid. "Well you have held the feather and little good it has done you," said Karl, who had the scars of holding that bright feather on his hands. It would take a man inured to pain, like a knight or one of the Wise, to hold that feather in his hands, and Karl had counted on that.

The man's face was dark with anger, and Karl knew that by some sleight of hand this man, who must be Peter the Thief, had hoped to cheat him of his feather. "You didn't give me a fair chance," Peter the Thief cried.

Karl reflected to himself that there is no man who cries out so much at injustice as a man who will not give justice to others. "You held the feather in your hands," said Karl, "and if you could not keep it, that is your problem."

Peter the Thief begged and threatened, but Karl would not budge: if he wanted anything more out of Karl, he must trade him for it. "What do you think I am," said Karl, "some sort of plaything for your amusement, so you can say 'go toy, go' and I will do what you want? No, I am a man going about his business: you were the one who wanted to trade." As Karl said 'go toy, go' the children in the cart linked hands and began dancing in a circle, going faster and faster so that they were hard to follow, and almost became a blur of movement.

"Stop," said Peter the Thief and the children stopped dancing. "Alright, what do you want to trade for the box you have the feather in, so that I can take a proper look at it?"

Karl grinned, "I will not *give* it to you, but I will loan it to you for a minute in trade for your cart of children." Peter the Thief saw that Karl would not yield, and at last he gave in, and gave Karl the cart with the children for a look at the feather in its box.

Karl took the feather in its box from his chest armor, took off the top of the box and laid it in Peter the Thief's hands, but Karl kept the lid of the box in his own hands. "There," he said, "You may look at the feather now without being burned."

Peter the Thief blew on the feather, and it seemed to blow away. "Quick," he said, "follow the feather before it gets away." But Karl did not follow the feather that seemed to be blowing away. Instead he grabbed Peter's pouch, out of which a golden light was streaming.

"Oh, I think I have found my feather," Karl said. He took the box with the feather out of the pouch, put the lid on it, and put it away in his chest armor. Then he weighed the pouch in his hand, "Perhaps I should keep this, for the trick you tried to play on me," he said.

"No," said Peter, his face grey as ashes.

"Well," said Karl, "I am sure that whatever this pouch contains was probably stolen from someone, but if you will take the pouch and go, to trouble me no more, I will give it back to you."

"Yes, I must have it back," said Peter the Thief, "give it to me and I will go and trouble you no more."

Karl tossed him the pouch, and Peter ran off into the woods. Karl looked around him and now that the illusions cast by Peter the Thief were gone, he saw that he had an old broomstick under his arm, a small dog laying behind him, and a small box laying beside the dog.

Karl stowed the box in his pack, whistled to the dog and said, "Come Farsight," and used the broom as a staff on his way back along the path he had come. As he strode along he noticed that when the broom hit the ground all traces of his passage were obliterated, whether it were footprints in the wet dirt of the path, or more subtle signs in his passage through trees and shrubs. Karl realized that even though he was a skilled tracker, he would not be able to follow anyone who carried that broom.

After a long while or a short while he came to the place he had met the child, and there the child was, looking at an anthill and observing the comings and goings of the ants. "I have your toy," said Karl.

"Thank you," said the child, "But I'm busy right now, you can play with my toy one time and then it will return to me."

Karl said, "Thank you," and went on his way.

Presently he came to the short man, and Farsight barked and wagged his tail. "Here is your dog," said Karl.

"He's a good dog," said the short man, "and he can detect dangers a long way off. Keep him with you for awhile, and after he warns you of a danger, he will come back to me."

"Thank you," said Karl and he went on his way.

Next he came to the woman with the doll. "Here is your broom," said Karl.

"Alright," said the woman taking a little packet from the doll, and letting the contents blow to the wind. Then she squeezed the doll until it lost any human shape, and cast it away from her into the rocks. "Now I will give you your boon," she said. "I was only one of those people who were set to torment and kill the man whose life you have saved from my arts. If you wish this man to be safe you must find the other two. All of us met on the top of the high hill yonder. My broom put behind you will wipe out traces so no one will be able to follow you, but if you sweep it in front of you, it will reveal the traces of the passage of those other two, no matter how they tried to conceal them. Keep the broom until you have found what you seek: after it is no more use to you it will return to me."

"Thank you," said Karl and climbed to the top of the hill she had indicated. He began to sweep with the broom, and presently he found the tracks of two people traveling together. By using the broom at every choice of roads, and keeping along the track when there was no choice, he was able to make better progress than if he had kept sweeping all along the track.

Presently the track went up a very high hill which dominated all the hills thereabout and Karl thought that no one would climb such a hill only to climb down it, so he thought that the people he sought were most likely still on the top of the hill. He climbed up the hill, occasionally stopping to sweep the path for traces of the people he sought. When he got to the top of the hill he cautiously peered over it.

What he saw was a group of children, chasing after a fox. The fox was twisting and turning, but there were enough children so that no matter how the fox ran, there were always enough children to keep him from getting away. The children were enjoying themselves, but the fox looked exhausted, and was going slower and slower as he tried to escape.

Karl took the marvelous toy from his pack, and tossed it in among the children. "Go toy, go!" he cried. The children looked at the toy, as it began to revolve, and forgot about the fox. The toy revolved like a top giving out marvelous colors, and presently all the children were dancing around it. The fox had collapsed in a thicket, and Karl gently crept up on it, and concealed it under his cloak. "Peace, little fox," Karl said, "Why were all the children pursuing you?" The fox coughed up a duck which it had gobbled up, and then slunk off, occasionally stopping to lick his bruises.

Karl looked at the duck in his hands and as he was looking at it he saw the dog, Farsight, pointing to a thicket of bushes nearby. Karl thrust the duck in his cloak, took the broom in one hand and his sword in the other. He swept the ground with the broom and saw the tracks he had been following, and he aimed with his sword for the thicket where the tracks led. "Wait, we're coming out!" cried a voice. From out of the thicket two men appeared, dressed in the skins of animals. "We're hunters we are," said one of them, "Why do you interfere with our hunting?" asked the other.

"It depends on what you are hunting," said Karl, "I was told that two men were seeking the life of a man I know." The two men looked sullen.

"How do you know he doesn't deserve to be hunted?" said one, "We were offered a great reward if we could bring about his death," said the other.

"Who made you a judge of whether he should live or die?" Karl said. "Who made you hunters of men? And as for your reward, can you trust the man who promised it to you?"

"I told you we couldn't trust him," said the one man to the other. "We're hunters," said the other man stalwartly, "Once we have the sparrow out of the duck's craw, and the needle out of the sparrow's craw, we can hold on to the needle, and not break it until we have the reward Peter promised."

Karl shook his head, "I have met Peter," he said, "and I think that he would cheat you if he could."

"We'll be the judges of that," said one man. "Give us the duck or we'll kill you," said the other. They drew long knives and advanced on Karl. He knew that if he tried to keep the duck from them, he would be hindered in his fighting, so he threw the duck into the air and defended himself with his sword. The two men were cunning, and good fighters, but they were no match for a trained knight, and soon Karl had them on the ground, groaning from wounds he had given them with his sword. When he had defeated them and had no more to fear from them, he drew out the box with the Firebird's feather from his chest armor, and opened it.

Immediately birds from all quarters began to flock to him, and presently he saw the duck flying toward him. But the duck was attacked by some falcons, and when they were almost upon him, the duck coughed out a sparrow who flew so low and so swiftly that the falcons could not touch it. Karl directed the light from the feather on the sparrow and it came to him and settled on his arm. Karl put the sparrow inside his cloak, and then shut the box, so that all of the birds which had been flocking around him flew away, no longer attracted by the Firebird's feather.

Karl was about to go on his way, when out of the same thicket that the hunters had come from, a great scaly tentacle came out and wrapped around him. He saw out of the corner of his eye the dog Farsight, which he now realized had kept pointing toward the thicket during his exchange with the hunters. The dog gave him a reproachful look and trotted off back to his master.

Karl waved the broom in front of him, and he saw that hidden in the thicket was a great seven headed dragon. One of the heads was wrapped around him, and the others were snapping around him. The dragon gave a squeeze of the head that was wrapped around Karl, and Karl dropped the broom, which flew off in the air in the direction of the old woman who had the doll.

"First, I will have your sparrow, then the box with your Firebird's feather, and last of all I will have your life," said the dragon. But as the dragon squeezed Karl with the head wrapped around him, an axe flew from a thicket nearby and cut the head off the dragon's body. Six heads still menaced Karl, but a hooded figure on a horse began to harass the dragon, running from side to side so that the dragon was always snapping at a place where the horse had just been. Karl pulled his hand with the sword out of the coils of the dragon. With one stroke he cut off three heads of the dragon, with a second he cut off the remaining three heads.

As Karl stepped out of the coils of the dying dragon he looked at the hooded figure on the horse. "The horse looks familiar," he said, "and I rather think I know who is riding it."

Princess Maria unwrapped the hood from her face and said, "When you used the broom to wipe out your steps on the way here you made it very hard to follow you. No one but my great aunt or me could have done it."

"Thank you, Princess Maria," said Karl.

"You are welcome," she said smiling, "Would you give me the sparrow?"

Karl handed it to her and she gave it a sharp pat on the back. It coughed up a pin-shaped object, which she pinned to her tunic. Then she tossed the bird into the air, and it flew away. "Now we have to see my father," she said. She and Karl took the path to the valley, the King horse following behind them.

When they came to the valley, the man who had called himself Prince Ivan was waiting for them. "Well, Ivanushka," he said to Princess Maria, "You found me." Princess Maria shook her head. "No, my friend Karl found you: I just followed him on the horse he left me to take care of. He got rid of your enemies, too, I only helped a little at the end. Now he wants a message for my mother and then we can go home."

"Do you want to go home?" Prince Ivan asked.

Princess Maria nodded, "My mother needs me now, more than you do. The days we played at being

Prince Ivan and Ivanushka were good times, but I need to grow up now. How about you: do you want to come home?"

Her father shook his head and turned to Karl. "Tell my wife," he said, "that I wish her well, but the things we disagreed about we still disagree about: if I went back to her, we would not stay together. And thank her for sending you to me: I know what you did for me was for her sake."

"That is true," said Karl, "and also for the sake of my friend Princess Maria." The Princess Maria nodded.

"Well then, they may reward you, though perhaps not in the way you would like best," said Ivan.

Karl said, "All I want from them is to serve the Tsaretsa, and to be Princess Maria's friend." The Princess smiled.

"If that is all you want, I am sure you will get it." He turned to Princess Maria. "Goodbye then Ivanushka, or Masha, if you prefer. Come and see me again. And take care of your friend Karl."

"Oh, I will," said Princess Maria, though she did not say which of the two things she would do. "Come on Karl," she said. "We have to stop at my aunt's house, and then we'll go home."

Karl smiled. "Yes, Princess," he said, and he was well content.

Made in the USA
Middletown, DE
17 September 2022